IN HIS HANDS

Praises
Iva Choice—In His Hands

"Congratulations! Your manuscript, In His Hands, has received an "AWARD OF EXCELLENCE" in the Deep River Books Writers Contest . . . we congratulate you for your fine work. You are to be applauded for such a fine achievement as a new writer."
—Bill Carmichael, CEO and Publisher, Deep River Books

"This book has the potential to transform lives! Choice captivates her audience using her personal story, spiritual insight, and practical steps for healing. Grounded in a deep abiding faith in Jesus Christ, the author courageously gives voice to the victim as only a victim can."
—Denise Goertzen, Director of Case Management at Mount Hope Sanctuary, a long-term transitional home for women and their children.

"This story of one woman's battle to escape the fear and torment of an abusive marriage is an inspiration for other women also trapped in abusive marriages. Through her trust in God and his power to help her, she is able to navigate the long and difficult journey to safety and restoration."
—Katherine Grimsley, MD, Psychiatrist, Wichita, KS.

"Julia is abused, distraught, down and out, but never gives up hope or losses faith in God. The angels and Demonics come alive and leap off the pages as their characters develop and give new insight to the spiritual realm and how angels are constantly battling on our behalf. This book delivers a wealth of knowledge about the cycle of abuse, warning signs, and precautionary steps to be taken."
—John Lester Barnes II, Domestic Violence Emergency Shelter (D.O.V.E.S) Advocate of Morehead, KY, Social Work Professional

"In His Hands reminds me that no matter the circumstance or how dark it feels, the HOPE is with me and will forever hold me."
—Susan Spencer, mother of three, small business owner

IN HIS HANDS
the unseen battles of domestic violence

IVA CHOICE

EDITED BY: CHRISTIAN LOZUKE/
MICHELLE ANAYA/W.M.

iUniverse, Inc.
Bloomington

In His Hands
The Unseen Battles of Domestic Violence

iUniverse books may be ordered through booksellers or by contacting:

iUniverse
1663 Liberty Drive
Bloomington, IN 47403
www.iuniverse.com
1-800-Authors (1-800-288-4677)

ISBN: 978-1-4620-6515-8 (sc)
ISBN: 978-1-4620-6516-5 (ebk)

Printed in the United States of America

iUniverse rev. date: 08/08/2012

In His Hands

Table of Contents

Chapter One: The Confrontation.. 1

Chapter Two: Getting Help.. 10

Chapter Three: Working It Out 28

Chapter Four: His Side vs. Her Side... 45

Chapter Five: Reality Sets In.. 61

Chapter Six: Taking Action.. 74

Chapter Seven: The Battle... 90

Chapter Eight: The Decision... 110

Chapter Nine: The Divorce... 128

Chapter Ten: Desperation 145

Chapter Eleven: Letting Go 167

Chapter Twelve: New Beginnings... 178

Chapter Thirteen: Healing Begins 232

IN HIS HANDS
the unseen battles of domestic violence
Excellence
Iva
Choice

To Michelle

❦

Thank you for your prayers, support, time and love!
Thank you for all the nights you stayed up editing!
Thank you for making this "dream" a reality.
"was was is gone"

To Chrissi & Ray Ray

❦

God bless you for all you have gone through!
May your "gifts" serve Him all your days.
I am proud of you!
I love you!

The Making of "In His Hands"
Preface and Acknowledgments

Due to the prodding of my twin sister, Michelle, I will reveal to you the awe in which God created this book. It was all done by people willing to share their gifts to help the abused, victimized, and helpless.

> "And the King shall answer and say unto them, Verily I say unto you, Inasmuch as ye have done it unto one of the least of these my brethren, ye have done it unto me."
> Matthew 25:40 KJV

Since I was young, I have had a story in me that came in a lengthy series of dreams, which I shared with my roommate, my twin sister. She urged me to write it down and so in my eighth grade year I began to write. Through the years it developed into a wonderful trilogy, which now our children love to read over and over. Thus, an idea to get it published was born.

In my search regarding the proper channels towards our goal, I came across a first time author's writing contest by Deep River Books. My trilogy did not fit the requirements so I dismissed it, but the Holy Spirit did not. Constantly He reminded me of the contest and my mind began to work it over. Could I revamp the trilogy? No. Then what? As I continued my search, I read advice to write about what I know, write about something I am passionate about. I knew exactly what He wanted me to write. With a sigh, I called my twin and told her about the contest. Then I asked her, "Do you think I could write a novel in three weeks?"

Her answer was simple and confirming, "Yes, I do."

From then on, I was a writing addict. I kept my focus on my goals and I wrote from my experiences and my heart. At the end of each day, I would send what I had to my sister and she would edit, between work and kids and her other obligations, bless her heart! We developed a color coded system to keep the confusion down and forged ahead, chapter by chapter, until it was finished. With only a day to spare, we read over the compilation, I formatted it to specifications and sent off a fiction novel we felt was full of action, wisdom, affirmation and how we imagine colorful characters that influence our world. Whew!

I have to admit-my twin could attest-we were quite embarrassed by what we had sent to a national writing contest when we finally got some rest and looked at it with fresh eyes. I remember saying to her, "If the spelling errors don't get us knocked out then it'll be the grammar. If they are kind enough to overlook the grammar, it'll be the inconsistency. If they can overlook that it'll be a miracle!" We laughed and she encouraged me that we did our best by following through with what the Holy Spirit nudged us to do and that alone was worth the time and effort.

I cannot express to you the shock I was in when I received notice that we had made it to the finals! If that was not a miracle enough, I then received a certificate of excellence for making it to the top seven! We knew then that God had a plan for this book. After much prayer, and no funds, we decided to rely on Him and work towards getting it published. Remarkably, in my search for a professional editor, Mr. Christian Lozuke, a man I only met through his website, followed the nudging of the Holy Spirit and offered his services for free! Furthermore, God brought more people forward to offer their opinions and expertise, not wanting praise or compensation. My, how God provides! Still, I needed money for the publishing fee. I made a website and offered pre-orders. By faith, I not only believe that this fee will be taken care of but that a larger goal of helping families of domestic violence across the nation will be met! God can do greater things than we can imagine!

Now, here I am, after writing and re-reading about my pain, suffering and healing over and over again, I see God making good come from it all. I see how many people have given to me and my girls to make this book a vessel of confirmation, love, understanding, and support to be available for others that need it. When I wrote this, my prayer was on these goals: Let the abused know *You* are with them, Lord! Let their loved ones be empowered to understand and help without hurting them more! Teach the readers empathy and wisdom as they are motivated to get involved according to *Your* leading and the gifts *You* have given! More than anything let this book point to how great *Your* love is for ALL!

> "Let us not become weary of doing good, for at the proper time we will reap a harvest if we do not give up."
> Galations 6:9 NIV

IvaChoice.net

"Lord, I will fast for him! I will pray for him every day for as long as I can. I will stand in the gap for him. Help me, Lord! Help me be a ministry to him. Help me to bring the kinder self of him to the surface! I beg You, Lord. I beg You . . ."

Chapter One

The Confrontation

Julia Anderson stood on the subfloor in her half remodeled kitchen with a paper printout of their June phone bill in her hand. She looked around seeing how the reused oak cabinets could add beauty to the space, how the plywood countertops would be replaced with granite and how the light fixture would replace a hanging bulb. Her brown eyes focused beyond the space to other parts visible from where she stood. There was so much work yet to be done! What started out to be a basement shower replacement spread through the house, like a cancer, moving to nearly every wall and leaving behind a skeleton covered in dust with electrical wires protruding everywhere.

It was ironic how vulnerable she felt, much like the exposed wires around her. She seemed stripped of what she had been a year earlier when she won the 2007 Kansas Association of Broadcast (KAB) Award for best commercial. Numbly she sat down letting the paper slide over the grime of the substitute counter, past her opened Bible. She had run out of time. Tomorrow she would be picking the girls up from camp. All week she had prepared to confront her husband, through prayer and fasting. Now the time had come. One number on the paper caught her notice. She had wanted to trust him, but trust was dwindling like their motivation to complete anything in the house. Her eyes drifted.

When she saw the phone bill at three hundred dollars, her heart had dropped. It was another bill they certainly could not afford. After looking over the charges on the Internet account, she found that one number had received a lot of attention, especially in texts. She sighed knowing their plan did not include this feature. Jacob's reaction the other day was certainly a surprise. He said he did not know the number and just shrugged it off, when normally he would immediately call back any number he did not recognize. He was obsessed with knowing things about people, even the makes and models of their vehicles. Rethinking her position, as was her custom, she decided to be patient and pray.

Day after day the phone number would not leave her mind. She tried to convince herself that it was business. After all, opening a scuba shop in the middle of Kansas required a lot of time and money. Not able to afford any full time staff, Jacob ran the store and did all the instructing. He often did not get home until late and spent many hours on the phone.

She wanted him to tell her the truth. He knew to whom the number belonged. However, every time she brought it up, Jacob denied knowing who it was, claiming to be too busy to look it up. She did not want to have to investigate it on her own. But that is exactly what she ended up doing for the Spirit would not let her rest.

Everything inside her did not want to dial that number. She struggled to even look up the records again. The web page came up and the number stood off the screen. Whoever it was, he was not too busy to visit with that person daily for long periods of time. Her fingers tingled as she pressed the number pad on her cell phone. A message immediately broke the silence, a woman's voice with an accent. Julia hung up knowing exactly who it was: Elma.

It is weird how, in hindsight, events can tumble forward as stark clues just because of a bit of knowledge. As if a gentle wind were sweeping through her home clearing the air, Julia's mind began to recall bits of stories Jacob had shared that, at the time, were easily dismissed. Elma, originally from Turkey, had been taking scuba lessons from Jacob. They found they had something in common. Elma's husband had the same mental illness, Bi-polar, that Jacob's ex-wife had. It struck Julia as odd that Jacob helped Elma find an apartment as a ministry, riding in the same car together. He had always told her he would never ride in a car alone with a woman that was not his wife.

Julia's mind diverted, recalling how angry Jacob had gotten when she rode with her boss to a meeting. By carpooling, she was trying to cut spending since they were so far in debt. But Jacob was so upset he broke the car's keyless entry on her key chain.

Her anxiety spiked. How would he react to her confrontation? She prayed he would not choke her again. She thought of setting out the counselor's number but remembered the woman had retired. Her eyes went to the Bible again seeking a verse of strength. She read Isaiah 41:13 (NIV), "For I am the Lord your God who takes hold of your right hand and says to you, do not fear; I will help you." The concern did not leave her.

The hum of the garage door interrupted her thoughts. Julia took a deep breath, lacing her callused fingers. He would be stepping in through the garage door any minute, even though he could not pull the SUV in because the construction material blocked the way. Laying a hand on her Bible, she quickly prayed for strength, acutely aware of her unshapely, chipped nails. The garage door to the house opened with a series of squeaks and slammed shut as Jacob headed for the only other chair, and her attention was brought back to task.

Since her normal welcome was lacking, he slouched his large frame into the chair and asked, "No dinner?" He laid a hand on the plywood bar, drumming his fingers.

"I can make some rice." Julia managed a smile while disciplining some strands of her auburn hair to stay behind an undecorated pierced ear.

He scoffed; cocking his head of freshly trimmed hair, and looked at the Bible and then to the print out, knowing something was up. "What's this about?"

She noticed the slight gesture of his large hand. Julia had trained her body over the past year to appear relaxed. She knew the slightest aggression would have consequences. Gently she answered, "I was looking over our finances and praying."

"Praying, huh?" He narrowed his light blue eyes.

Experience had taught her to get to the point or divert fast. "I found out who the number belonged to," Julia pointed to it on the paper.

He nodded slightly and then shrugged before getting up to get a drink of water.

"It is Elma's number." She sat back trying not to look at him.

"Oh, that makes sense. She's been calling lately for her scuba card." He sat back down, turning to look out the dining room bay window, although it was black outside.

"There are hundreds of minutes for her number, Jacob." Julia kept her eyes down.

"What's this?" He picked up the print out. "You're keeping tabs on all my calls?" he sneered.

"No. I was looking into the phone bill. There are a lot of texts and our phone plan doesn't cover that. It's over a dollar for each one." She knew her voice was pitched too high and had too much of an edge, but she could not help it.

He sat back again with another shrug. "Change the plan. People want to send me pictures and texts."

"At midnight?" it slipped out before she could catch it.

He slammed the paper down. "I don't make people's schedules, Jules."

"Tell me what is going on, Jacob. God won't let my spirit rest. I know something isn't right here." She raised her eyes to his, growing too bold.

He smiled. "Finally," he laughed, "you are human after all. I'm glad you found out. I enjoy talking to Elma, not you. I'm surprised *you* haven't found someone else."

Julia's blood seemed to drain away as he filled her ears with his rebellion, although no one would have noticed as white as she was without a tan. She managed to speak, "You and God are my 'someone'."

"Then go to your god," he spat, leaning forward.

"He's your God, too." She decided to leave it there. She did not want another rough experience. At least she confronted him and now she would allow God to work. She needed to think.

Getting up slowly, she closed the Bible and walked around him, feeling smaller than five foot seven, through the dining room to the side room containing the computer and spare bed. She heard him yelling that if he got the chance he would @$#? Elma every way he could. She never had anyone talk to her like this. Not knowing what to do, tears brimming on the edge of her lower lids, she fought for control. *This is not how it is supposed to be.*

Suddenly she was knocked from her feet, immediately feeling the impact of the matted carpet. Looking up she saw the spinning wheel of the old exercise bicycle, so close she could not focus it into clarity. Her sight went, instead, to the piercing blue eyes of her husband for only an instant, before he mashed the paper printout into her face. Without a conscious decision, she heard herself screaming out over and over.

"Don't make accusations you can't back up, Julia!" Jacob snarled.

One last push and he stepped back watching her. Julia shook as the papers drifted off, her mouth still feeling the pressure. He looked so big from the ground, his chest growing from his exertion. Timidly, she sat up to test his mood noticing only then that she had urinated all over herself. He stomped out muttering how she was a @$#? psycho. Still shaking, she moved to sit in the computer chair, not even resituating her tussled ponytail, thinking the worst was over and counting her blessings.

Her mind knew she should call 911. She also knew they depended on him financially. If anything happened to him the business would fail. All her sacrifices would be for nothing and the debts would still need to be paid. She knew this would only be for a moment and then he would return to the man she loved. Calling the cops would make things worse for them all. It would not take long in their small town for everyone to know and he would not be able to hold his head up in public. The church would not allow him to be in ministry, which she knew he would want to do as soon as the business did not ask so much of his time. No, she could not make the call, but she had to do something or it would continue since they could no longer afford the counseling. Her hands moved to the computer. Her in-laws had agreed to hold Jacob accountable. She could only think to e-mail them that another outburst had occurred. In the middle of typing, she felt a burst of hot breath over her shoulder.

"What are you writing?" Jacob questioned, having come back into the room.

She tried not to sniffle as she held her head up, trying to gain control over the shaking as she typed. Any answer would cause an escalation at this point so it was best to keep quiet.

With crushing blows, he pounded the keyboard, her hands, and the desk with his fists while cursing and calling her explicit names.

She yanked back and fell out of the chair, the dampness of her pants disgustingly clinging to her as she tried to get back up. Her mind was blank as her eyes took in information. Holding her throbbing left hand, she stepped back watching him resituate his diamond wedding ring and then delete the message for help. She found herself stepping towards the door, which usually caused him to be more aggressive. Still she had to try. Out of heavenly mercy, she made it out the door, through the dining room and back to the kitchen.

The phone sat on the edge of the wood counter as if ready for her. She eyed it knowing she should make the call. She was scared. Her hand now felt hot and her thumb painful. She looked to the spare room door. She looked to her left hand, the thumb swelling twice its size. She looked back to the phone, now appearing even closer than before. It was time. She reached out and dialed. She heard it ring. She heard it ring again. Then a familiar man's voice answered. She opened her mouth, inhaling. However, before she could say anything, her head smashed into the phone. She fell to the floor dropping the receiver.

"Who are you calling?" Jacob questioned and hung up the phone. "Who the @$#? are you calling?" He looked down on her with twisted rage, sucking air through his nostrils.

Julia curled up on the floor under the wood counter and cried out loud like she had never allowed herself to do since she could remember. Cradling her left hand, thumb abnormally large, she sat in her own urine and sobbed uncontrollably.

After an immeasurable amount of time, Jacob dared to speak in a low tone. He had moved into remorse. "Can this be fixed?" He was calm now and sitting by the living room. It amazed her how quickly he could flip moods.

"Evidently not." She sniffled and began to cry again.

Time passed and Julia was emotionally exhausted. She was not going to make that call again or any other call, for Jacob sat steadfastly on watch. He just sat there resting his arms on his knees wrinkling his pressed pants. When she felt strong enough, she stood and timidly went to the bathroom to shower. She was relieved to hear him go to their room in the basement.

Camael, the lead angel, ruffled his feathers calling his angel team to gather around him in the hall between the bathroom door and the stairway. It had been a rough battle with the Demonics, unseen by Jacob and Julia, and now it was time to regroup before the next attack. This marriage was definitely in crisis! If his team was going to save it, they were going to need to persuade Jacob back to the Father and Julia was going to need much healing. As Julia's guardian angel, Camael felt personally responsible for her.

Hearing the muffled sobs mixed with the sound of falling water from within the bathroom, he glanced down the stairs leery of the demons lurking in the dark. He then shifted his sights to his team. Only five of seven were able to make it in time, which was unacceptable, especially since they had a week to prepare!

Sophia, an ancient angel of great wisdom and a master of disguise, had done an impressive job over the past week speaking wisdom to Julia and nurturing her. Although quiet in nature, Sophia is steadfast and can be rather unrelenting at times. Unfortunately, even with undaunted persistence, she always returned from the husband looking worn and saddened that she was unable to reach him. Nevertheless, Camael was glad to have her on the team. She skillfully proved her abilities when she carefully presented Julia with the computer already logged on to her hotmail account and then moved the phone to a perfect position without alerting the Demonics. Camael could not have been prouder of her today. He nodded his praise and she pointed to Heaven.

Camael, however, had taken the brunt of the battle against Aboddon, the great warrior under Baal, since his other teammates were absent. Aboddon took advantage and attacked with such force that Camael was not able to help Julia when she went into the spare room. Although both wings were broken, another angel was able to pull Julia down before she landed on the exercise bike. He bravely shielded her and did not flinch even when evil hairy Uzza drew his sword. Camael had to abandon his fight with Aboddon to tackle Uzza, giving the biggest angel on his team enough time to lift Julia to her feet. If it had not been for the skills of his team, Julia would not have made it through alive since Uzza was determined to make good on his promise to end her life.

Camael slowly shook his head as he looked over his battered team. The bathroom door began to glow and they all grinned knowingly. The healing angel touched him and he closed his eyes, soaking in the wonder of God's great medicine. She touched all their wounds healing them instantly. Then she glanced at the bathroom door and stepped through unimpeded. The door darkened and she returned frowning. The water stopped. The light went out.

Camael did not need to sound the alert since the five angels already had their swords drawn and their restored wings up. The basement light went on revealing the Demonics. Aboddon stood strong at the bottom of the stairs with his chest exposed to display his scars from previous battles, his long sword held outward like a gate holding back fuming Uzza. Just the looks of him made Camael shutter. It was no coincidence that two of his teammates were not present, for Aboddon was a great strategist. It was going to be a long night.

Julia stepped out of the bathroom still holding her hand, towel wrapped around her body and another around her wet hair. She stared down the stairs for a moment and then leaned back against the wall. Everyone watched her except Sophia, who jumped into action and comforted her, whispering into her ear. Julia closed her eyes tight, pressing tears from the corners. Softly, Sophia began to glow. Then the healing angel, too, brightened ever so slightly as she touched Julia's shoulder. Julia straightened, taking a deep breath as she walked into the kitchen towards the phone. Everyone held their breath, waiting to see if she would call for help. As she contemplated, they waited. A noise of something breaking downstairs jolted her back away from the phone. She sighed and whispered the word, Forgive. With a nod, Camael turned his focus to the Demonic's leader, Aboddon, watching carefully as his teammates urged Julia to the safety of the spare room for the night.

Aboddon slashed his sword down through the air and Uzza rushed forward. Before clashing swords with the mighty warrior, Camael spotted the harassing demon dashing to the husband again. In the hall they battled for the rest of the night.

I began my healing with trying to forgive because I did not want to be a bitter and angry person. It seemed I was hearing "forgive" a lot but did not truly understand what it really meant. So, as I looked up words as part of my search for peace, I gained a better foundation to obtaining it.

Definitions to Ponder

Domestic violence is a pattern of behavior used to establish power and control over another person through fear and intimidation and often including the threat of violence or the use of violence. Domestic violence may be physical, sexual, emotional or financial. ("Wichita Salon's of Hope Program." *City of Wichita—Domestic Violence*. 13 March 2011. City of Wichita. 13 March 2011. http://www.wichita.gov/CityOffices/Police/Investigations/Sex+Crimes/Domestic+Violence/)

Forgiveness is when we strive against all thoughts of revenge (Romans 12:19); when we will not do our enemies mischief (1 Thessalonians 5:15), but wish well to them (Luke 6:28), grieve at their calamities (Proverbs 24:17), pray for them (Matthew 5:44), seek reconciliation with them (Romans 12:18), and show ourselves ready on all occasions to relieve them (Exodus 23:4). (Thomas Watson, Body of Divinity, p. 581)

NOTICE
Forgiveness is NOT:

- NOT the absence of anger at sin.
- NOT the absence of serious consequences for sin.
- NOT the granting of trust if it was broken. Trust is earned by a proven life change.
- NOT based on feeling good about what was bad—we don't wait until we feel forgiving—we choose to forgive for our good.

Therefore, it is a choice of ceasing to feel resentment, indignation or anger against another person for an offense or ceasing to demand punishment or restitution. It does not mean to minimize or condone the offense, forget it or to remove any consequences. Rather it is letting go of the pain and hurt for ones own sake, validating self worth.

Remorse is when we may admit the wrongness of what was done, but does not necessarily imply any kind of change in heart attitude or lifestyle.

Repentance involves a change in the way we think and act. It results in a change in lifestyle. God requires this change in us (Acts 17:30). He also makes this change possible (Romans 2:4).

"O God, I am so weak! I know there are few that can understand what I am going through. Even as the hurt tingles in my body, I must comply, forgive, and submit according to my vow. I am completely aghast of what he says to me. My GOD! It hurts my soul! How do I live with such fear? How do I continue to love him knowing I must be the most stupid of women to continue with this behavior! How does it stop? When?"

Chapter Two

Getting Help

Before the natural light of day shone through the antique French doors of the spare room, Julia awoke with a start to see a shadowy figure by the dining room table watching her. Last night's event was as vivid as if it happened moments ago. Her right hand immediately went to her left thumb as she sat up to limit the pain from the change in position. She recognized her husband's form and a ping of fear flushed over her. Not saying a word, she waited to see if he was still remorseful or back to the irrational stage. Her elbow brushed a hard surface and she glanced down to see her Bible. Sticking out of the cover was a bookmark with a verse on it she knew well, "And we know that in all things God works for the good of those who love Him, who have been called according to His purpose." (Romans 8:28 NIV)

Still silhouetted by the increasing light outside, her husband muttered to himself audibly and turned to leave, shoving a chair from his way. Some of the words made it to her ears and they conveyed his feelings clearly. The cycle had changed and he knew it. Normally after a fight, he would come and apologize. He would reason with her rationalizing why things happened the way they did. He would explain how she needed to change to help him overcome his struggles with his past. Only then could there be peace between them. They would recommit to each other. Sometimes he would refuse to talk about what happened and insist that they immediately put it behind them.

"Forgive and forget," was his motto, which did not apply to his past hurts.

It always baffled her how he could just push things into the past for a fresh start without ever addressing them. Once, he slapped her and within seconds held her in his arms telling her he was madly in love with her. It almost sickened her to kiss him while still feeling the tingling of his blow on her cheek. If she even said a word that was close to what had happened, he would tell her how she needed to learn to forgive, to understand his past, and let go of things or it would ruin their love. She even went as far as to talk to her mother-in-law about it and got the same reasoning. No matter how recent the event, if it is forgiven, it should be left alone. They would quote 1 Corinthians 13:4-7 (ESV), "Love is patient and kind; love does not envy or boast; it is not arrogant or rude. It does not insist on its own way; it is not irritable or resentful; it does not rejoice at wrongdoing, but rejoices with the truth. Love bears all things, believes all things, hopes all things, and endures all things." As a Christian woman, she could not argue with that.

Julia sank down to her pillow. Why did she stay then? Julia knew she had become one of those reality talk show guests. She now understood how love kept her tied to her abuser. She really did love Jacob, at least the Jacob she first met. She almost smiled remembering the man she dated. That Jacob is gentle, sensitive, fun and congenial. His charisma made the most mundane chores interesting and even adventurous. He believed he could reach the stars and gave one hundred percent toward the goal. He is liked by everyone, including her children. He did things with the girls and even went out of his way for them, going above and beyond.

Still, no one is perfect, she knew that. Her smiled faded in the growing light from outside. Everyone has problems. She figured they had issues to deal with like any couple, especially being a blended family. However, over time, as his rage grew in intensity, it was hard for Julia to even see him as her Jacob. She could even see that her girls were becoming more distant with him, though they never witnessed his outbursts. She lightly placed a protective hand over her throbbing thumb, wrapped with a washcloth, damp from the melted ice.

She recalled how he came gently on his knees, pleading for forgiveness after using some harsh words during an argument. "I'm so sorry, Julia; I don't know why I treated you that way. I am so ashamed! I never ever want to yell at you again. You deserve so much better. I know, Jules, that I don't deserve you," Jacob's chin quivered as he tried to hold back tears, sitting at her feet. She saw his sincerity and opened her heart in sympathy. They embraced as he swore to never be like his grandfather again. He clung to her begging for her to help him. "Please, Jules, help me to not be like him. I know," he looked her in the eyes; "I know I will conquer my past with your help. I can't do it without you." Rocking to comfort him, Julia assured him. "Please, Jules, I'll do anything . . . I will spend our last dime on counseling if you want!" She believed that with God's help they could overcome anything. She made up her mind to avoid certain triggers that caused him to hurt her. Their love grew and life with him was wonderful again.

Julia's heart now grew lethargic as she remembered all the fun they had together, as a family, bonding. She could see how her heart deceived her mind. Her inner voice told her he was no monster. No, Jacob was a wonderful man who longed to be the Godly Christian he was meant to be. She told herself that a Christian wife does not leave her husband over a few occasional incidents that spiraled out of control. She stubbornly held to the hope that her husband would indeed be freed from his past. "As long as he is looking to the Lord, there is hope," she always reassured herself.

Closing her eyes tight, she chastised herself for being so gullible. Where had all that trust and appeasement gotten her? She tried to turn to her side and felt the sharp sting of pain travel from her lower back down her left leg. Quickly she settled to her original position and the pain went away. Pain means stop and see what is wrong, she recollected from Adrian Roger's sermon on resolving problems. Julia could see that unsettled confrontations cannot be cured with an apology alone. Without change in action, the words did little to protect her from another episode. It was a painful cycle of the problem leading to an act of aggression and then a remorseful apology to normalcy, only to wait for the same problem to rise again. She should have stopped it when it was just words, but he was a great salesman and she allowed it to continue. Now, she had grown wise

of this tactic. Now she knew what real truth was. Words + actions/
(over) time = truth.

For a moment, Julia thought of going to the emergency room to
have her thumb and the pain in her back looked at, but then reality
set in. It had been over a year since they had health insurance and, as
their debts grew, she knew she could not afford to go. Feeling sore
all over, she lay there knowing she had time before she needed to
get the kids from camp. For now, she needed consoling. She needed
God. She wanted to pour out her hurt to Him, but was emotionally
spent. Looking to the Bible again, she opted not to read. So, for the
next three hours, she fell into her habit of thinking over what had
happened and reprimanded herself for overreacting. She thought
about how she might have contributed and what she could change
in herself. It takes two to fight, right? They were in this together and
she should be more supportive. That is what marriage is about! Still,
Elma should not be part of the picture.

The angels plopped down on the chairs around the dining room
table exhausted. For hours they had fought the Demonics, protecting
Julia while she slept. Although they managed to keep her safe, they
could not boast of a victory. Camael looked over his team and saw
that this had been a grueling battle. Without support, they had lost
ground, little by little, through the night.

Aboddon almost smiled when he had pushed them back against
the spare room's threshold. The hostile spirit had coaxed the husband
back upstairs and Camael was forced to send Sophia to rally support.
Thankfully it was dawn and one of the prayer warriors from the
church was an early riser. Without that, they may not have been able
to keep Aboddon from overcoming them. He offered thanks to his
Creator as they all recuperated in the morning sunlight.

The flapping of wings in the distance brought back Camael's
attention. He looked up to see Ariel rushing to him. Unable to stand,
he shifted forward. Her wings dipped and she hung her head in
shame, her dark long hair draping down over her shoulders. However,
Camael was not disheartened. He knew that young Ariel would have
come if she had not been detained. What he needed now was for

Ariel to help the team regain their strength with her gift of passion, rallying the Sealed for prayer.

"I . . . I tried to get here," Ariel's strong voice whimpered.

Camael assured her, "I know. Tell me what happened."

Ariel timidly looked to him and explained, "I was at the church, getting ready to aggressively campaign for our battle at the ladies Bible study, when the Demonics just walked right through the doors!" The other angels sat up astonished. Ariel turned to the rest of the team wide eyed. "I have never seen Demonics in a church building before. They surrounded me so fast I could not go anywhere. I tried to speak, but they screeched so loud I could not be heard." She knelt before Camael. "I spoke the Word and they obeyed, but not without harming those near them. The other guardians joined me and we drew our swords to engage in battle until now."

Camael nodded. "I was concerned for you and Chayyliel." He sighed and laid his hand on her shoulder. "This was a good offense from Aboddon. I have underestimated him. For that I am sorry."

"No, Camael, I let the team down!" Ariel cried.

He sat back. "I am the leader and I am to blame. But now, Ariel, we need you. We are weak and need support. Go quickly," he ordered.

Ariel stood with a twinkle in her eye. "Those I fought with through the night are already building support. You see," she pointed to the now glowing healing angel, Suriel.

Before long they were all glowing and feeling refreshed. In their renewed strength, Camael was ready to clear the house. Members of the team pointed to Heaven and then to their heart before going to position. Talented with the horn, Zazriel trumpeted their intention and the angels swooped through the house chasing demons from corner to corner. Camael, however, went straight to the basement.

Aboddon was certainly taken by surprise, having assumed he had possession of the entire house. Camael came in strong, slashing his sword with precision maiming a demon on his way to the leader. Aboddon was quick to draw his sword and defend his life. However, seeing the retreat of his kind, he reluctantly stepped back. Knowing the laws well, Camael tried to get one more strike in before Aboddon bowed, but was not quick enough. He was forced to halt and so allow Aboddon an honorable forfeit.

The husband, with the clinging spirit of hostility, stormed past Camael and stomped up the crude stairs, a packed bag in hand. The guardian listened a moment longer for the door to slam shut. Before checking on Julia, he took a look around. Shaking his head, he made his way through the broken pieces of tiles and scattered tools in the basement. Even in the bedroom, there were items broken and strewn about the floor and surfaces. The husband must be a tortured soul to do this kind of damage to his own home and wife.

Ariel entered, also taking in the sight. "How could a Sealed do this? I do not understand," she questioned.

Camael remembered asking the same thing when he first came to work among the humans. Ariel was inexperienced to be sure, but she was an angel of assertive passion and moved people like he had never seen before. For that, he was happy to have her. "The saddest people are the ones that are sealed but have turned their hearts from the one that sealed them . . . for the Lord disciplines the ones He loves, who belong to Him."

"How can the Sealed turn their heart from such love?" Ariel picked up a devotional book from the floor and flipped through the pages.

"It is called free will. People are special and experience enormous amounts of pain and suffering due to their sinful nature. Concentrate on the outcome and you will find your job full of blessings. Remember, every knee will bow and every tongue will confess in the end that Jesus is Lord. Amen." Camael instructed.

"I shall try," Ariel smiled back quickly placed the book on the bed.

Just then Julia stepped into the room, joined by the other angels. They watched as Julia tip-toed around the room to gather some clothes to change into, each wishing they could have the permission to clean up the space for her. Then she hesitated by the bed, interested in the devotional book. Camael gritted his teeth. He should have reprimanded Ariel for disturbing it but now it was too late. Julia tilted her head and lightly ran her fingers over the open pages.

The damage was done. Camael caught Ariel's attention and shook his head. Camael prayed that God would have mercy and not raise Julia's hope that her husband had made a choice to turn to God, when in fact he had not.

15

Driving over an hour to Kansas Bible Camp outside of Hutchinson gave Julia time to rehearse how she was going to explain Jacob's absence to the kids. Luckily her daughters were only a year difference in age making it more like raising twins. The oldest, Shannon, was quiet and content; whereas, Brailey was loud and free spirited. Somehow, Shannon kept Brailey grounded and Brailey pushed Shannon to try things she would not otherwise have dared. It was a nice balance. Being athletic, they both played most of the sports offered at their small town middle school. On the flip side, they were blessed with higher than average intellect, so they participated in advanced classes and Scholars Bowl as well. Their schedule was very full and kept them busy.

Julia wondered how they would take the bad news. They had been through so much already having lost their father in an airplane accident when they were young. At the time of the divorce, they were not old enough to understand it and dealing with his death had overshadowed their split. For them, it had always been just the three of them up until a few years ago when she met Jacob.

They took to him so easily that she felt it was a sign. She was sure God had placed them all together to be a family. When Jacob began to change, she protected them from learning about his outbursts. For the most part, they did not see that side of him. He was a good man; he just needed to address the issues he had with his grandfather during his growing years. After seeing the devotional book open on the bed, she could not help but think there was still hope for their marriage.

She prayed for strength as she pulled into the drive that circled in front of the main building of the camp. Groups of kids were running everywhere saying their last good-byes. She carefully rolled to the grassy field they used for parking and looked for her twin sister's Caravan, which they called a Var, because it was like a van and a car put together.

Jan's son, Jared, joked that they could not call it a Can. "Who wants to say 'I'll race you to the Can'?" he laughed. He was a jovial boy the same age as Shannon so he attended camp as well. It warmed Julia's heart to know their kids were getting the same wonderful Bible experience Julia and her sisters had gotten when they were young campers. She parked and called Jan on her cell phone as she carefully got out of the car.

Although she enjoyed seeing her daughters' smiling faces and hearing their stories, in the back of her mind the events of last night dampened everything. Jan, a nurse, immediately noticed her thumb and wanted to examine it, but Julia was successful in diverting her attention to the kids' artwork. An hour later, she managed to get the girls packed and ready to head home.

They were cheerfully singing some of the camp songs so she put off the inevitable news. Ever since she got married, the car had become a great place for her to spend time with the girls. Jacob always liked to drive his red Expedition, so when she drove the car it was usually just with the girls. It was a great time for sing-a-longs, sharing how God was working in their lives, or solving problems. She loved that.

Both girls were pretty tired by the time they reached home and ended up falling asleep while unpacking their bags. Julia stood in the hall so she could look into each bedroom, one to the left and the other to the right. They were peaceful. She wished she could be at such peace.

The phone rang, causing her to jump. Quickly she dashed to answer it.

"Hi," Jacob's voice vibrated through the earpiece.

"Hello," she answered hesitantly.

"I'm staying at a hotel for a while." He paused. "Maybe later we could talk."

"Yes," she could feel her throat tighten.

"Did you get the girls ok?" He sounded his sincere self.

"Yes. They had a great time." She held back her usual chatter.

"Okay, well, I have to go. Call you tonight?"

"Okay," she agreed.

"Love you, Jules." He hung up.

Julia sat down with the phone still in hand. Things were definitely different. She eyed the phone, made a decision and punched in the numbers. "Hello, Tina? This is Julia. What are you doing for lunch tomorrow?"

⁓⚜⁓

Julia called the girls when dinner was ready. The rice was good with ground beef mixed in, seasoned perfectly. It did not take much for them to get full these days. The girls told more camp stories, revived from their nap. So, now was as good a time as any to speak with them about Jacob.

"Girls, I need to talk to you about something important," she began.

"Is it about Jacob?" Brailey's blue eyes rarely missed details. After she was born, one eye turned bluer than the other. So, Julia told her she was special and could see things others overlooked. The girl had a muscularly lean body of a gymnast and the spunky spirit of a brunette Pippi Longstocking. Julia considered her the free-spirit of their little family.

"Yes, it is about Jacob." She drew a deep breath and tried a different approach. "Remember when we talked about things you cannot control?"

Now Shannon, built like a swimmer with a quiet determination within, spoke up, loving the challenge to answer. "There are things that are not our fault, which we cannot control."

"That's right. This is one of those times. Jacob is moving out for a while," Julia paused and then added, "He needs some time alone with God."

"What happened?" Brailey demanded, wiggling her thin frame forward so her chair would fall back onto all four legs.

Julia watched both the girls' body language as she explained briefly, "He . . . has made some bad decisions."

Shannon leaned on toned arms, her bleached locks swinging forward, and almost whispered, "Is that why our fridge and pantry are empty all the time?"

Julia nodded unable to say anything, not expecting the conversation to turn that direction. "Money is tight because we started a business. It is difficult, I know . . ."

Shannon interrupted quietly, "Mom, look at our house. It isn't just the food."

"How are we going to fix all this?" Brailey began to get overwhelmed, tilting her chair back again, balancing on two legs.

"Brailey." Julia motioned for her to set the chair down. "Don't worry, girls." she took their hands. "God *always* takes care of those who belong to Him." She smiled and believed it with all her heart. "He is going to take care of us. We have been without before. Do you remember, when you were younger, all the fun we had making tents all over the apartment? And we had picnics in our clubhouse under the stairs! Remember that? We didn't have any money then, but we had fun and all that we needed, too." They started to giggle at the memories. "You see, I am not worried. I told you about Jacob so we can pray for him. He needs our help."

"Let's pray now." Brailey took her sister's hand joining them all together.

"That's a great idea." Julia's heart filled. It was a joy to see her daughters so strong in light of a crisis. How could God refuse a child's prayer? They bowed their heads and she prayed out loud.

"Has he done this before?" Tina questioned, looking concerned as she opened the cooler to pull out her lunch. Tina was an athletic woman with thick wavy hair that seemed to do whatever it wanted and her style in fashion tended to have the same flare.

Sitting under the trees at an old picnic table, Julia was glad they decided to meet at the town park for a Saturday lunch. It was certainly more private than the café. "Nothing like this." Julia took a bite of her peanut butter and jelly sandwich and set it on her recycled plastic grocery sack.

"But he has been physical with you," Tina wanted to be clear. She tapped her spoon on the edge of a fruit dish.

"Well, yes. But we went directly to a Christian counselor, who said I triggered something from Jacob's past in the way I handled the conflict. After a couple of sessions alone with him, she said he would not do it again. She felt confident that they had dealt with what triggered the negative action," Julia tried her best to explain and maintain Jacob's confidence as well.

"Did he ever do it again?" her friend asked nonchalantly, picking through the fruit then waving to some kids that passed by on their bikes.

"Last night was different," Julia diverted the question, watching her friend scrutinize her answer. "Usually he loses his temper and does little things. You know, like break something . . ."

"Or push you down and break your thumb?" Tina sat forward putting her spoon down on a cloth napkin. "Why didn't you call the police, Julia?"

She shook her head. "I tried to call for help but he wouldn't let me. Look, I called you because I knew you would understand. I remember your testimony you gave during Sunday school about your abusive ex-husband."

"Oh, Julia, my ex never got physical with me. He called me names and whatnot but never laid his hands on me. Where are your girls now?" She changed the subject while opening a pudding cup.

"They are at the pool," Julia motioned over her shoulder to the city pool next to the park. "What should I do? I don't want another divorce, Tina! I still love him. I love the man who isn't angry. He really is gentle and considerate most of the time. He is a good man. It's just when his temper flares it changes him into . . . into . . . Mr. Hyde." She tried to explain. She knew how she sounded. She recalled all the times she watched pitiful women on talk shows say they loved their abusive husbands and she, along with the crowd, would sigh in disgust.

She did not understand then. How could she? Now, she knew. The talk show host would ask, "Why do you stay with him?" And the pitiful women would answer, "Because I love him." She loved Jacob. Not the Jacob that was out of control, of course. That Jacob was not her husband. Most of the time, Jacob was the wonderful man she fell in love with. He just needed her to be patient as he worked on this issue. If she could be careful not to trigger his anger, he could work on it. He loved her and desperately wanted to change. He really was a good man. She wanted to explain all this but she could see Tina could not understand. How could she without experiencing it?

Julia appealed to a different perspective. "Twice divorced? How do you think the church and the community will see that? I can't call the police. We're running a new business and financially . . . all I could think to do was call you for advice." She threw her hands into the air and almost lost her bag. Julia was disappointed by misunderstanding the woman's testimony

Tina sighed and gave it some thought. "I think you should call Pastor Elden. I know he's temporary, just filling in until we find a permanent pastor, but he's a good man," Laughter from the pool interrupted her advice.

"Okay. I'll call him. I'm just afraid that if this gets out . . ." Julia left it hanging.

"Believe me, the pastor will be discrete." Tina reached out her hand. "Come on, let's pray." They bowed their heads and her friend prayed such a prayer that tears trickled down both their faces.

All day long, Sophia had been with Julia's sister, Jan. She arrived before Jan awoke and was granted the opportunity by her guardian to whisper to her dreams. Sophia loved such peaceful moments because they are the most powerfully influenced. Sophia spoke directly to Jan's heart. She needed her help.

Jan was a very busy woman in spite of reducing her hours at work to part time. She was in many ministries and yet always kept her children first. Sophia liked Jan very much. As if they were linked, Jan opened herself to Sophia and they, together, prayed throughout the day in spurts for Julia. Towards the middle of the day, her guardian, Faith, began to push toward action. Although this was not Camael's order, Sophia allowed Faith's intervention.

Shortly after three, Jan called her mother and found that she, too, had been very concerned for Julia. They decided to meet at the church to pray. When the two women met, Sophia smiled and greeted Ariel, who had come in with the mother and her guardian. The women prayed a long time until the secretary, coming in to finish a bit of work, interrupted them. Although this frustrated Ariel, Sophia and the guardians stood back, allowing the intrusion to give the women rest. Experience would teach Ariel soon enough that rest is a wonderful tool towards lasting prayer support. "Fast heat gets it done in a hurry, but slow heat cooks it all the way through," the seasoned angel whispered to the young one.

As the women visited on their way to their vehicles, Faith asked Jan if she would like to go shopping for groceries. "You could help your mother prepare for the youth that are coming to stay during the coming weekend's conference," Faith whispered as she turned and winked at Sophia, who clasped Ariel's hand in excitement.

"Why are groceries exciting?" Ariel questioned her elder.

"Food has a way with people," Sophia explained softly. "It is more than substance. It brings people together." She nodded her appreciation to the other guardians before leaving.

Julia was true to her word and scheduled a meeting with the interim pastor following Sunday service. She dropped the girls off at home and headed back to church. On her way, she thought over what had transpired the night before when Jacob called again. She thought he would apologize, but he did not. He chatted as if all was well between them. She could not believe she was going along with it while her heart was torn in two, her swollen thumb throbbed, and her tailbone was so bruised she could not sit straight. With all this, he was telling of how a scuba student's bikini malfunctioned. Julia decided to end the small talk and test the waters. She asked if he had paid the bills and he assured her he had, with disgust in his tone, which caused a lull in the conversation. She then tried to address the marital problem so he ended the call. Frustrated, she found herself surfing the web for help. She came across a web site called DailyStrength. com. It was free to join and she soon was engaged in reading public posts under the subject of abusive relationships. Late into the night, she read and found she could relate to most everything posted. She also added a short description of what she was going through before heading to bed, wanting to reach out to someone who understood.

She remembered the flicker of hope she felt that night and smiled while pulling into the church parking lot where there was only one car left. The aged pastor greeted her pleasantly. So nervous about sharing the intimacies of her marriage to a stranger, she began to tremble. Still, she was determined and pressed herself to share. He listened and nodded as she explained her past three years with Jacob in summary, not only sharing the outbursts but the good times too. When she finished, she watched him purse his lips in thought.

"So, what do you want to do?" Pastor Elden asked, running his fingers through his thinning gray hair.

She sat dumbfounded. "I . . . want our marriage to be a good Christian marriage."

"Then it sounds like you will need to go to counseling," he casually deduced.

"We did. But . . . now we have a financial problem. Jacob left me with no money. We found twelve dollars and eighty-six cents in change around the house, but that barely got us a box of rice, milk and crackers." She looked to her lap and silence pressed her to refocus on the marriage. "Look, I came to you because you are our pastor. I read last night from multiple web sites that we should not go to counseling together until the abuser gets some anger management. He doesn't know how to handle certain feelings. Will you go and talk to him?" she pleaded.

He sat back a moment. "I like Jacob." His eyes earnest, "I will talk with him. Until then, you take care of those great girls of yours." He stood and reached out to shake her hand.

Numbly, Julia offered her good hand and then made her way to the car. It was a strange meeting. She did not feel at peace about their conversation and he did not console her, advise her, or even pray with her. In a way, he seemed very detached and unconcerned. Still, it was in God's hands and she was taking steps to save their marriage, quietly. This would soon be in the past and their dignity would be intact. She still had hope of having a healthy and loving marriage.

Moments after she got home, she heard a car in the driveway. It was her mom and sister! They came to the door hauling groceries and asked if they could store some items in the fridge during their visit. At times, they would make a trip to Wichita to buy groceries from Sam's Warehouse in bulk. Since it was close to their little town, they would come by for a visit. Brailey and Shannon helped haul in boxes and bags while giggling and talking with their cousins, Jared and Mary. It was always a fun time between them since they were all so close in age, Mary the youngest by two years.

Julia helped put things in the fridge and freezer, pleased that she had the space for them. Soon she realized that food was going into the pantry as well. She stepped back and watched as her family filled her kitchen with food. There was a soft glow in the room with an air of kindness. Mixed feelings began to wash over her. She was embarrassed. She was overjoyed. She was grateful. Jan gave her a side hug and the kids all went to the back yard to climb Wilson Grove, the lone tree that stood by their dilapidated, empty, underground pool.

"Well, isn't this a nice day?" Julia's mom came and gave her a hug.

"It's a very nice day. What brought this on?" Julia pointed to the groceries.

"Oh, we went to Sam's and thought we'd pick some things up for you." Jan replied and waved to the kids through the kitchen window.

"You know me, Jules, I tried all the samples. Then I thought your girls might like to try them, too." Her mom went to the window as well. "Look at those kids, all four of them in that little tree. What did they name it?" She turned to Julia.

"Wilson Grove," she answered still unsure how to react to their generosity. She could not help but wonder if they knew just how desperate her situation was.

"They're entering into their teens and still climbing trees," Jan added shaking her short stylish hair.

The visit was short but a nice reprieve from what she had been experiencing. They took a few of the freezer and fridge items for the hour drive home but left almost everything they had brought in. Not once did they ask about Jacob. Nor did they mention the construction or her attire. They were cheerful and sweet. Above all, Julia had managed to keep her thumb out of view and mask her pain. It was a nice time and the food was an immediate answer to prayer! Who says God does not answer quickly?

Now, Julia and her girls were sitting on the subfloor in front of the refrigerator and pantry with the doors wide open for viewing.

"It's beauuutiful!" Brailey exclaimed, snuggling up to Julia.

"I don't remember ever having so much food before," Shannon added in awe, pulling her toned legs in close.

"God is certainly good." Julia stared.

Camael and the six other angels sat on the floor around the family with glowing smiles, causing the kitchen to be brighter than it had ever been before. The support felt good and ministry made his job easier. Empty tummies make for grumpy humans and grumpy humans make poor decisions. This act of kindness not only brought a blessing to this household, blessings to those who ministered, but blessings to the spirit world as well. Only God could bring so much goodness from groceries.

His smile broadened and he sang, "Praise God for His kindness! Nothing good comes without His touch!" the others joined in and Zazriel's baritone voice soared, overpowering them all.

Camael and the others had to chuckle for they knew how much Zazriel loved music! He was an angel whose music directed the hearts of both worlds. In spite of his large frame and muscular build, he was like a teddy bear, tender and sympathetic. His loyalty to Shannon no one could match. Absolutely nothing was going to get near his Sealed without his permission. Since birth, she was treated like a delicate vessel. Camael watched Zazriel with Shannon on many occasions in awe of how he could blow a demon away while gracefully dancing around his precious loved one, singing a soft lullaby to boot!

He had good reason for being so protective of her, for she possessed the extraordinary gift of a tender heart. Shannon is sanctified for something rare, tenderness with great empathy. She has the ability to feel what another person feels, to hurt with the same degree, and to celebrate with the same amount of delight. Those with tender hearts can be broken too easily. It can be a painful gift, but a joyful one as well. Yes, it was God's great design to have Zazriel be her guardian.

All people possess gifts that God planted in them before they were born in order to edify the church. Some gifts are in abundance because so many are in need of it. He looked to Brailey who was gifted with a caring heart. People need someone to care about them and their struggles. It is a wonderful gift that nurtures the Sealed to maintain their faith, gifts, and ministries.

Camael watched Brailey's guardian, Sablo, rubbing the girl's back. He was tall and cheerful with playful golden curls and light blue eyes, one darker than the other. It was clear that Sablo loved Brailey. Before she was even born, Sablo would not leave Julia's belly. He could not wait to see her. He sang to her and played with her, pushing on Julia's belly until Camael stopped him. When she entered the world, Sablo put honey on her lips and her tongue licked and licked for almost an hour, not at all interested in feeding. Camael had to laugh at the memory. Sablo's attention was caught and he laughed too, not knowing why. Soon, Brailey was giggling. Laughter is contagious.

Rolling on the floor, Brailey tickled her sister, who in turn tried to hide behind her mother. The angels found themselves all entangled in a tickle war and laughed until their sides hurt. The whole house glowed from the joy.

I cannot really recall when "control" became so important in my relationship with my abuser. It seemed that there were times I thought something rough was done in a joking manner that eventually became apparent it was not. I do remember when a very powerful shift occurred during what seemed to be a mild disagreement where he busted a hole in a wall. My shock brought him back to his senses and I thought that it was more of an accident than anything. Then, when we attended the theatre with my parents and in-laws he purposely pushed me. I knew he was upset with me and I immediately addressed that action. Thinking it would never happen again, I said nothing and we joined the performance again. I did not have a clear understanding that these consistent actions and reactions were paving the way to escalate harmful abuse that would remain concealed for the sake of the marriage and to protect our reputations.

Power and Control

Domestic Violence is a learned behavior. Often an abuser learns during childhood that violence can be used to gain power and control. An abuser may feel entitled to control and the fear of losing it may prompt them to more excessive attempts to physically and emotionally dominate their partner.

After the first incident of violence a victim will often react with disbelief, shame and embarrassment and will believe it is an isolated incident. The victim will try to keep it a secret, hoping that it will not happen again; sometimes convinced it was some fluke, high drama moment that got out of hand. As the incidents become more frequent and severe, the victim will lose his/her sense of control and will begin to fear for his/her safety as well as the safety of those he/she cares about. The victim becomes numb and learns to control his/her reactions to the abuse. The victim may or may not seek help. After years of domestic violence the victim will feel powerless, worthless, shame, and is less likely to be able to break the cycle.

"Lord, I love him! I pray for him that he would come to You. God, You can do anything! You are the Almighty! Help us, Lord! Show me where I can change. Teach me the way to be better. How can I make our marriage a testimony? Give me a sign . . ."

Chapter Three

Working It Out

The phone was ringing. Julia slowly awoke barely comprehending where the ringing was coming from. Since the confrontation, she had taken to sleeping in the spare room and was still getting used to it. Making her way to the kitchen to answer the phone, she glanced at the clock that declared it to be six o'clock in the morning. The conversation with a man from her church was short. He was letting her know that he did not advise Jacob to divorce her as the rumors were indicating. Great! Now the whole town would know, but *what* would they know. She put the phone down. He had said he did not advise *Jacob* to divorce *her* . . .

Thus, she started her day. She spent some time in prayer and looked up the responses to her post from DailyStrength.com. They were all supportive and one explained that through the site she could get professional Christian counseling as well as join a group that met online each week for accountability free of charge. This website gave graduating psychology students experience and was monitored by a licensed counselor. Since it was free, she signed up for it. God managed to answer this need she had not even uttered in prayer.

While listening to a sermon online from Chip Ingram about marriage, she checked to make sure Jacob had paid the bills and searched for graphic design jobs where she could put her degree to use. For almost ten years she had worked for television stations doing on air graphics for news and animations for commercials. However, the economy was changing and stations began to consolidate, moving her job to Oklahoma, feeding the graphics digitally to Kansas. Although she missed television, she did enjoy doing all the graphics for their scuba business. She even learned some web design and it saved them a lot of money in marketing costs.

Unfortunately for her, the business and accounts were in Jacob's name. She had no claim to any of it and no access to any profit it produced. Jacob had the keys and controlled the money. He never did like to discuss anything that had to do with finances. In fact, most of their arguments stemmed from money management, ending in some sort of physical altercation. Still, he expected her to pay the home bills creating the need each month to ask for the money, which she dreaded. Drawing on her savings and any other resource that was available to her, she had depleted her money supply and was now broke. Her only recourse at present was to find a job, and fast.

During breakfast she talked with the girls about the possibility of others in the community knowing of the separation, and made a plan on how they should address possible questions. After their father passed, she had followed a children's program that helped families cope with loss. Suggested games trained their minds to follow paths of constructive coping skills. It brought them closer as a family and was a tremendous help in many different facets of their lives. The girls were happy and well adjusted, seeming quite resilient when facing problems of their own. She was confident that they would deal with this situation in the same way. After all, they were used to being just the three of them.

Late that morning, after the girls had gone to basketball day camp, she got another call. This one was different than any she had ever gotten. It was a woman demanding payment on their credit card bill. Although Julia tried to explain it was a business card and that she would look into it, the woman was in no mood for politeness. Not able to come to a reasonable resolution, they ended the call at odds. Before she could start the laundry, she got another similar call. This time it was for their personal credit card bill. When a third call came from another business, she knew there was a bigger problem. How much debt did they really have?

With only one load of laundry underway, the phone rang again. Tempted to answer abruptly, she took a deep breath and tried to stay calm. It was Pastor Elden.

"I visited with Jacob today at his scuba shop. It is really a neat shop with the walls all painted like a sun setting over the ocean. Jacob praised you for that addition," he politely shared. "We did have time to talk and I really think you should move on for both your sakes," the pastor was simple and direct.

Julia let her mind catch up. His advice completely took her by surprise. "Divorce?" she managed.

"Yes," he stated flatly.

"But," her mind was swimming, "I thought divorce was the last option."

"In this case, the two of you cannot get along and so you should hand him a certificate of divorce like God did to Israel." He justified his reasoning.

"I don't want a divorce," she blurted. "Did you talk to him about counseling or anger management? He needs help, pastor. Divorce will not help him. He will go on to hurt someone else." Tears were coming to her eyes.

"He seems to have a good head on his shoulders and from my visit all I can conclude is that the two of you just cannot get along," the pastor rationalized.

"I try to get along, I truly do," she tried to convince him. "You don't understand. Jacob is a wonderful man, but his past causes him to . . . He needs help. We need to get him counseling. Do you think the church would help with the cost of counseling? I found a place that has a good program for anger management . . ."

"Julia," he interrupted, "Jacob is a good man. He says the physical part of your fight was an accident. He didn't mean to hurt you. You know, it takes two to fight and *both* of you have things to work on." The pastor was not listening.

"I promise you, Pastor Elden, it does not take two to fight. Sometimes it just takes a bully and a victim. Of course, he did not *mean* to hurt me but he *did*," she felt an inner strength help her stand up for the truth. A truth she was only beginning to understand.

"Well, as a pastor with many years of experience counseling couples, it is usually a matter of pride. Perhaps you should look inside of yourself and see where *you* can improve. We all have things we need to work on. My advice to you is to move on, look at your pride issue, and concentrate on those lovely girls of yours." Pastor Elden was finished.

They said a polite good-bye and Julia sat down from the blow. Pride? She did not even realize she had any pride left. Looking around her unfinished house, she happened to catch a reflection of herself. She looked worn out. Her clothes were torn, stained, and too big. They were not even her clothes. They were an old pair of Jacob's pants and the shirt was a hand-me-down from her sister. She had come a long way from the suits she used to wear to the office. Her hand went to her hair. She could not remember the last time she had a haircut. She had sacrificed everything to make Jacob's dream come true. Pride? She shook her head feeling anger building.

The phone rang. Like a reflex, she answered it, "Hello."

"So you sent the pastor?" Jacob's voice was on edge.

"I went to him for help," she fell into her routine, "for me. We are members of the church and the pastor is the Shepherd. He can't tell anyone. It's all confidential."

"You should have asked me first," his voice rose in volume.

"I'm sorry," she succumbed but did not want to. She wanted something real to come out of this. "We need help, Jacob. You need help."

"He said we should just get a divorce," his voice softened.

"I don't want that. I want the man I married," she confessed.

"I don't want that either." She heard him sigh. "Okay, let's go to counseling."

"Thank you, Jacob." She felt her chest relax. "First, will you go to an anger management counselor? I found a good one that will meet with you whenever you want. Don't worry about the cost. It will be paid for." She spoke with faith that God would surely provide.

There was a pause. Then he spoke with resignation, "Fine. I'll go when I have time."

"Great! I'll e-mail you and the pastor the information," she promised.

They ended the call recommitting their love for each other. He even said he had not called Elma and would not again because he wanted to focus on their marriage. Her heart soared with hope. "My Jacob is back," she whispered to herself. Praising God for His wonderful mercies, she felt a new vigor to her day. Yes, it started out rough, but God can bring a blessing in the midst of any situation! The phone rang again and she answered rather cheerfully. When the conversation was over, she sat the phone in its cradle. Her former cheer vanished and was replaced with renewed anger.

Suddenly, she jumped up and ran to the garage. Dashing to the back of the car, she brushed her finger over the sticker on the tag. She squatted by the trunk staring at the numbers. It had expired. Jacob never paid for her tag and the lady on the phone informed her that their check bounced again so her car and life insurance were two months past due. Since February, she unknowingly had been driving illegally. Thank the Lord she had never been stopped. She sighed. They would have to walk to everything in their little town. Still, she would need a car soon. Then a thought raced across her mind. Since when did she have life insurance?

She felt betrayed. She was even rationing the toilet paper to save on money! Why would he put money towards life insurance when they could not even afford groceries? Going to the computer, she decided to check if any other bill payments bounced. Every account showed payment so she was thankful for that. Then she felt a nudge to check the phone records. Part of her wanted to believe his word that he would not call Elma again. She felt like she was stalking him. But her curiosity pushed her to justify the search. It was so easy to do. With one click, she would know if he was being honest with her.

The website brought up all the calls for the past month. Her eyes scanned the days she had not checked since the confrontation. There it was; the same number. It lasted twenty-two minutes during business hours. Hurt surrounded her already sensitive heart. Her eyes welled but she did not allow tears to release. Instead she clicked the button that showed the texts. She saw that they texted each other yesterday just before midnight. Scooting her chair back, she put her head into her hands. She let out a groan from her aching heart, fingers curling through her hair. Moving to her knees, she bowed her face to the floor and prayed mournfully.

Camael held Julia as she rocked back and forth, curled into a ball on the floor. He could feel her heart ache and prayed with all his might that God would ease her pain. This marriage was not going in a good direction. Chayyliel, the largest of their team, had reported that Jacob was resisting all their help just as he had his own guardian. If he did not turn to God soon, the Father would order a retreat letting him reap the consequences of his choices. For now, his orders were to protect Julia and the girls, who would be home any minute. He needed to get Julia under control.

"Julia, the girls are coming soon," he warned. "You need to clean up and be ready for them. Stay strong. You can do this. God is with you."

The encouragement worked. She quieted her emotions while getting herself to the bathroom. After washing her face, she stared into the mirror. Slowly she shook her head and tears welled up again.

Camael pointed to the cabinet, "Look at that hair, girl. You need to brush your hair." He diverted her attention like a pro.

Julia bent down and brought the brush up. She got the job done and her appearance began to shape up. Straightening her clothes, she stepped into the hall. He watched her just stand there, arms dangling by her sides.

He snapped his fingers and she jerked as if coming out of a trance. The garage door opened and she quickly ran her fingers through her hair taking deep breaths. The girls barged in already involved in conversation about what had happened at basketball camp. Sablo was in great shape keeping up with Brailey and Zazriel was like a line backer bringing up the tail.

Julia welcomed them and Camael took this opportunity to have a team meeting. They huddled by the front door. "Did you have any trouble?" Camael sensed something from the children's attitudes.

"Boy did we!" Zazriel nodded, folding his enormous arms of muscle.

Sablo pitched in, "Julia doesn't even know half of the people that are talking about her."

Camael would normally be patient, but seeing how the husband was not on a good path and the church was in transition, he knew the Demonics had strong footholds. They could strike at any time and probably with sufficient force to make sure the family split. The Demonic love destruction and the division here had plenty of pressure and pain to ensure an evil victory. "More has happened so I need the information," Camael prodded.

"Right," Zazriel focused. "The coach tried to bully the girls, but with one hit I had the bully demon off the coach's back and so stuck in the ground it took the entire practice for him to get loose." He did not even crack a smile.

Sablo, on the other hand, was laughing out right. "You should have seen that poor sucker! I mean it was a sight!" His blond curls bounced.

"Some of the other kids had anti-guardians," Zazriel kept the information flowing. "One in particular informed everyone that Shannon's mother isn't as holy as she's cracked up to be. I almost knocked down her demon, too. None of the other guardians wanted to get involved; therefore, I sang a little jig to keep troublemakers busy. Those Irish songs sure can get things jumpin! Did you know that the term jig actually derived from the French?" he smirked as Camael raised a brow. "Sablo here is the master of irritation," Zazriel whacked him on the back sending him forward, "Anyway, anytime that demon or the anti-guardians even thought about starting rumors I gave 'em a look of warning to sick Sablo here on 'em," Zazriel winked. "One time, Sablo gave a demon an illusive itch that lasted an entire day causing it to go mad!"

Sablo added, "A verse from the Word pressed on my tongue and I shouted it. 'Have nothing to do with the fruitless deeds of darkness, but rather *expose* them!'" His arm was in the air reenacting what he had done. "Ephesians 5:11 seemed bold at the time," he sniggered. "That shut them up."

Camael patted him on the back. "God's Word is powerful. Good job, Sablo. They will target the girls, but we must not allow it. If Julia does not fall, then they will target the children." He pressed down on their shoulders. "That will be your burden to bear."

Having used the night to pray, Julia felt recovered enough to address a boundary with Jacob. It was the Fourth of July and fireworks were popping all over the nation while her life was being destroyed. She went to the porch to watch the girls set off smoke bombs, saved from last year, as she dialed Jacob's number. Trying to sound positive, she greeted him, "Happy Fourth, Jacob!"

"You, too," he responded dryly.

She tried a different route. "I sent you the information for the counselor. Did you get it?" The girls were giggling at some boys down the road slamming snappers.

"Yeah." He sounded like he was in his SUV and a little distracted.

"Good. I thought you would e-mail me back so I would know you got it but . . ."

"Did I need to?" he remained short.

"No, its fine." she answered quickly.

"Look, I'll take care of it. I have to go," he tried to cut the conversation short.

"Um, Jacob, I think since we are working things out you should not talk to Elma." She needed to address the continued calls.

"I'm going to do my business, Jules," he asserted.

She would stick to her boundary as directed by her new internet counselor. "I'm not saying you can't do business. I'm just saying, with Elma, you can communicate with her indirectly. You have dealt with other students through one of the advanced divers. Why can't you do that with her? I stopped talking to several of my male friends because you did not want me talking to them. You can do the same thing for me with this woman."

"I never asked you to stop talking to anyone," he claimed.

"What?" Julia was dumbfounded. A whistling sound filled the air and ended with a loud pop.

"Whatever. Can't talk to you anymore," he muttered and hung up.

Wind whipped around the house and the trees waved as if in a frenzy to welcome the approaching fall season. Chayyliel approached with vigor. His massive torn wings fanned out to bring him to an abrupt stop mid-air and then closed allowing him to drop right in front of Camael, his strong legs, cut and bruised, taking the impact easily. Chayyliel's chest expanded to twice Camael's width, spraying light from cuts and abrasions. He was like a GI-Joe replica with the pride to match.

Julia stepped out onto the small back deck taking care her bare feet did not slide on the splintered wood. She looked to the sky, her arms folded close to her body. Camael and Chayyliel stood still, waiting for her next move before talking. She drifted past them to the hot sidewalk around her dilapidated pool and stood looking over the back fence where a field allowed a view of the horizon.

Looking over Chayyliel's battle scars, Camael called for Suriel's healing gift and then took the opportunity to find out what had detained his strongest teammate. "It is nice to see you, Chayyliel. I have been worried about you, even asking the Archangel after you." Although Camael was considered rather tall, Chayyliel was an army angel and thus stood two feet above him.

Chayyliel smirked. "You worry too much, Boss. You can't blame a guy for being late when he's fighting a legion of Demonics, can you?" he curled his bottom lip in.

Camael shook his head. "A legion? I would not doubt that." He looked at the large muscles God had empowered him with and the size of his frame all marked with signs of a great battle. Yes, he could possibly fight an entire legion of Demonics."

"I kid you not, Boss!" he declared, putting his enormous hands on his hips. "There was no way Aboddon was going to allow me to make the battle here. They caught me before I made it to Earth and I fought the legion all the way to the edge of this lil town. I disintegrated half of 'em." he shook his crew cut head with a snort, "Truth be told, the other half survived only because I wanted to get here as soon as possible."

Camael wiped his forehead, thinking over what this meant to his strategy against Aboddon. Clearly they knew that Chayyliel was their champion. The real question for Camael was why they were meeting such resistance with this couple. Why was Aboddon interested in this family?

Chayyliel nudged Camael as he pointed toward Julia sitting on the hot cement looking back at the house. Both could see the pain in her eyes. Camael turned back to the battle-torn angel before him. "Praise the Lord you were able to overcome. I am sorry you had to fight so many without our help. I have a feeling we are going to really need you."

"No worries, Boss," Chayyliel said with a shrug. "I was concerned about that gal over there. But, if you don't mind a bit of advice, better rethink how we do things for the next strike, eh?" he grinned.

Camael was glad Chayyliel was made for battle. His name actually meant "army" and he certainly was an army all wrapped up in one being. "I welcome whatever advice you have." Seeing the healer he waved for Suriel to tend to the battered angel.

"Well," Chayyliel swayed forward a tad, feeling God's medicine through Suriel's touch, "you could try to make me less important and strengthen the gifts of the others on your team. Seen that done. Put the army on standby if you get my meaning. Makes for a great comeback when things get tough and the demons' pea brains think I'm not active."

Camael thought it through. Chayyliel was on the team because he was significant in battle. However, as long as he was around, Aboddon was going to make efforts to keep him ineffective. Yes, it could work. This was a chess game and Camael was gifted in discernment. "Done. I will make you an informant."

Chayyliel raised a brow, "Really?" He laughed out loud, which consisted of maybe two to three huffs. "Well, that's a first. I think I'll like the change."

A week had passed and Julia found everything to be difficult. Since she was left handed, she wanted to reach for things with her left hand. Then the pain in her thumb would remind her that it was not a good idea. Turning on the floor lamp required some extra strength since the knob would stick. Folding anything meant draping the material over something. Opening a jar meant the use of her legs to hold it, which triggered the pain in her back. Even washing her hair had to be a one handed affair.

Then there was the pride issue the pastor seemed to think she should address. Listening to sermon after sermon about pride and marriage began to confirm what her Daily Strength community and counselor were saying. She was not the problem. This whole time, she had accepted or shared the blame. Jacob was going to have to take responsibility for his own actions this time.

She went to church on Sunday and Wednesday night. She walked the girls to swim team practice every morning and evening. She sent out resumes via e-mail, unable to afford postage. She worked hard on the ministries she had already committed to, from teaching girls purity class to painting sets for vacation Bible school.

However, each day she felt more alone, praying for some sign that God was with her or someone cared about what she was going through. But no one called or visited. Everyone was too busy with schedules and responsibilities. It was her own fault for allowing Jacob to distance her from nurturing other relationships. Taking her counselor's advice, she called five of the strongest Christian women she knew and invited them to join a team that would pray for her and her specific needs. They all accepted and she felt at least someone would be checking in on her.

Financially, she still had nothing. Jacob had promised to put some money into her account and take care of the debt collectors calling. Much like his many other promises, the collectors continued to call and her account remained empty. She then discovered Jacob had gone on a trip to Colorado with some of his friends, closing the shop for the week. The big jerk!

This information built anger deep inside her. How can he go on vacation and enjoy himself while she and her girls sacrificed and lived on charity? What kind of man leaves his family with nothing? Does he not feel guilty or responsible? She was struggling and he seemed to be living without a care in the world. Julia wondered how he could afford it. She was constantly looking for ways to reduce her budget and, unfortunately, it cost more to remove Internet and cell phone service than to keep them, due to contracts. The economy was so bad she would still owe if she tried to sell the house, especially in its present condition. She doubted she could even sell it and her morals could not let it foreclose. She was stuck and he was in Colorado! When checking phone records again, she found he also enjoyed visiting with Elma through text from eleven at night to one in the morning. The anger plugged her tears ducts and hardened her heart.

Finally, something happened. She got an e-mail that asked her to come in for an interview. It was weird how one spark of hope could fill her heart. She was so excited, she ran around the house yelling praises to God and the girls joined her. It did not have to be a fabulous job, just something that paid enough to get them by. This job, she figured, would get them barely by.

True to the pattern of recent events in her life, she got a call from her ministry partner for the girls' purity class. Ruth was gracious about her purpose but in the end insisted that Julia withdraw from the ministry due to her separation from her husband. Although they both agreed to take some time and pray about it, Julia already knew where Ruth's heart stood. She would withdraw for Ruth's sake. Steeped with resignation, her soul was warmed as the Bible verse Matthew 5:9 (ESV) "Blessed are the peacemakers, for they shall be called sons of God" whispered through her spirit.

By the next night, Julia had heard from several other women that she should step back from all ministry and concentrate on her family. All Julia's life she had been taught that when in crises she should apply herself to the Lord in prayer, devotion, accountability, and *ministry*. Helping others often helps the one in crisis see beyond their problem. They also learn they can be blessed in any trial or tribulation. Evidently, this was not the viewpoint of her church. Thus, the next Wednesday night when she went to teach her class, she was given a chaperone, Donna, since a replacement teacher could not be found. Donna would be considered, by appearance, an average country girl, with her long light-brown hair most often pulled back into a pony-tail, though she had to be in her forties already. Fashion was belt buckle jeans with a button down plaid shirt, boots, and no make-up. Still, everyone in town knew her for her kind spirit and her boys had a reputation of being top gentleman, helping anyone they came across.

Remarkably, Julia remained diligent to her upbringing. She would stand her ground and persevere, aiming towards the goal of reconciling with her selfish husband and becoming a testimony of staying true to their vows to the Lord. Someday, when they were old, they would look at this time and see how God delivered Jacob from his past and made them a wonderful testimony. This goal motivated all her actions. She prayed for him, sometimes for hours at a time. Fasting from entertainment, since they did not eat much to fast food, became a weekly sacrifice to grow closer to her Lord. She worked at becoming healthy mentally and spiritually since in James 5:16 (NLT) it says, "The prayer of a righteous man is powerful and effective."

Dumbing down her resume, Julia drove illegally to her interview praying for forgiveness. It was definitely an interview set up by the angels for not once did they ask to see her resume much less her portfolio. It was not as glamorous or creative as her previous jobs. However, it was a good family-run manufacturing company with the appearance of cleanliness and professionalism that gave her a sense of security. She would be working on a computer setting up and printing fire evacuation signs for hotel rooms. Although she never read any of these signs when she stayed at a hotel, she was aware that it was the law to have them in each room. So, it looked like stable work that would not cause too much of a problem for her hurt thumb. They said they would let her know their decision in a couple of days.

When returning home, she could see Jacob's empty red Expedition in the driveway. Everything she had been thinking vanished and now she had that same sinking feeling she got when she did something without talking to him first. Immediately she started working on how to explain getting a job. Then, she realized what she was doing and stopped herself. No explanation was necessary. He abandoned her with nothing, therefore giving up the right to have a say in her decisions. With trepidation, she rolled her car next to his and with anxiety she slid out of the car. Her thoughts raced to find a new way of thinking as she entered through the garage only to find him on the phone in the kitchen. There were pixie red carnations wrapped in clear plastic lying on the plywood bar. He quickly hung up and handed over the flowers, hugging her.

"I'm sorry, Jules," he whispered and held her tighter.

"When did you get back?" she lightly placed her hands on his back.

"Yesterday." He pulled back a bit. "I went to think things over. It was the best thing I could have done. I really needed it. All I could think about was you and how I've messed everything up. I need you in my life, Jules." He looked her in the eyes the way he had when they first fell in love. He held her tenderly as he had when they were dating. She remembered the man she fell in love with.

"Wow." She took the flowers and smelled them while cautioning herself not to trust too quickly as she had done many times before. Julia was learning a great deal from her online counseling website. The materials she had to read before each session were more than an explanation of why she and her girls had been living the way they had, appeasing their abuser at every whim. They were an education on what a normal healthy relationship should be like, what behaviors and responses are acceptable and which are not. She wondered if Jacob was just trying to regain his status quo in the cycle of his abusive behavior. Clearly she was not the only one on his mind during his trip, according to the phone company.

She looked away. "Thank you for the flowers." She smiled. "Thank you for coming, too. It means a lot."

He took her hand and looked at her thumb, lightly stroking the base. The nail had turned black and the base had bubbled up with inflammation. "Does it still hurt?" She nodded and he kissed it. "I'm so sorry, Jules." Tears welled up in his eyes but did not fall.

"I think it's broken." She wondered if he would insist she go to a doctor.

"I want to come home," he let go of her hand and hugged her again.

"I want you home, too." She closed her eyes wondering if all her prayers were finally showing results. "As soon as you see the anger management counselor, write a letter to both our parents explaining what happened, and stop corresponding with Elma, you can come home and we can be a family again."

He pulled away. "You want me to do what?"

Julia went to the table, pulled out a paper from her notebook and handed it to him. "I've been going through domestic violence counseling. This is a list of things that have to happen before you can come home. There will be more to do before we share a room again, but we can be a family." She watched his reaction cautiously.

"Domestic violence counseling? Like you can afford that! This is stupid," he scoffed. "I'm not doing some list to come home."

"I need counseling just like you and it's free. You can do it, too," she still needed to keep on track, "About the list, it's my security. Love would naturally do these things. There has to be accountability. There has to be something that motivates a true change." She was standing her ground as advised by her counselor, though shaking internally. She prayed he would not become angry.

"My word should be enough, Jules, and I say I've changed. There's no *domestic violence* here. You had an accident." He put up his hand, "Still, I said I would go to the counselor because you insist and it's paid for, but this letter thing I'm not going to do!" He wadded up the paper and threw it down the hall.

She watched it tumble to some stacked boards. Although it was a paper, he was beginning the action to throw and destroy. As minute as it may seem to her, she was supposed to treat it with caution and label it for what it was. She stepped back. "I e-mailed the list to you in case you change your mind."

He came to her and touched her face, lightly kissing her lips. "No boundaries, Jules. Let our love bring us together." He kissed her ear and then down her neck.

Lightly she guided his face to look at her. "We have tried that before. Now it is time to try something different. I need something that has been proven to make a change."

"Don't you want me?" he kissed her again and tugged at her skirt. "You look so beautiful, the way I remember you when we were dating."

"Yes," she confessed, yearning for the affection. "But I don't like to share." She wiggled away from him and sat by the bar to distance herself from the temptation.

"Elma?" he laughed. "You have that all wrong from the beginning. She's just a friend I could talk to." He sat too. "You don't want me to talk to her, fine. I won't talk to her anymore."

"Wonderful!" Julia saw progress. Smiling, she handed him his cell phone from the bar where he laid it. "Call her and tell her."

"I will." He did not take the phone.

She put the phone before him and sat back. "Maybe you should call her when you can talk more privately." She tilted her head as she challenged him. She knew it was too bold and held her breath as she waited for his reaction.

He sighed and rolled his eyes. Picking up the phone, he dialed the number without looking it up. Julia did not dare roll her eyes. He left a message saying that he was going to work on his marriage and needed to end correspondence with her. Julia had little confidence but was slightly impressed that he did it at all. *If* he did it. For all she knew, he dialed someone else. Nevertheless, it felt like a small victory.

After a few more kisses in hopes of gaining sex, he did promise to do the things on the list and rejoin the family. He kissed her one more time before going through the garage and hopping into his

SUV. She watched him drive all the way down the block before returning to the kitchen to put the flowers into some water. It was a step in the right direction. It was hope. Of course, the coming days would be the true test. Words + actions/(over) time = truth, she reminded herself as she picked up the wadded up paper in the hall.

The phone rang. She answered. The man on the other end explained that he would have liked to offer the job but that the girl who was leaving had decided to stay after all. Perhaps God had closed that door since Jacob had opened his.

This cycle did become apparent to me as it began to cycle faster and the abuse become not just verbal but physical towards me. The happy times were so wonderful, full of laughing and family time. It is true that I lived for these moments. Everyone lives for these moments. However, they become shorter and the uncomfortable times become longer. I explain it like a pressure cooker. Everyone experiences heated water at times and it takes a while to bring the water to a boil. However, when the pressure builds enough to be released; my abuser would be instantly great again and in his mind, how he released that pressure no longer needed to be addressed. Then the pressure would build again, sooner this time around, and the release more intense. Eventually, either the heat needs to be turned down or the pot will be ruined.

Cycle of Violence

Tension Building: The abuser begins building towards a violent outburst. Demands and intimidation increase in frequency and efforts to calm and reason with the abuser fail.

Acute Explosion: The abuser uses physical force, verbal abuse or even sexual abuse, to hurt and/or intimidate. Abusers can be creative and determined to maintain control. Threats range from physical threats to child custody issues and are usually accompanied by an assault on the victims self esteem (i.e. you can't pay the bills, you're worthless/helpless). Abusers cultivate fear in their victims. Dependence is key to their sense of control as well.

Honeymoon: The abuser begs forgiveness or promises to never do it again. Normally this will include concessions to the victim such as going to church, attending support groups, or showering the victims with declarations of love. The abuser will claim he or she was out of control, for any number of reasons.

The victim wants to believe that the person will change. The Honeymoon phase is very persuasive that change is occurring and the main reason why people stay in abusive relationships. This phase is pleasant and rewarding and can last for quite a while. This is what the victim lives for. This is what the victim holds out for. This phase is where the victim bonds with the abuser and sympathizes, vowing to help the abuser to overcome issues.

After the Honeymoon stage, the process starts over. This cycle progressively increases in intensity and frequency as the abuser builds momentum and the need to outdo his last performance. The victim becomes desensitized to the outbursts, so the abuser must increase the intensity to get the shock from the victim.

"I pray, with all my might, to appeal to You, the Almighty. I know all things are in Your control. I beg, Lord, for Your love and peace in this situation that I can do what You call me to do. Tell me, my Savior, tell me plain and I will do it. Change my heart from hurt to Your will! Above all, let me not doubt Your will in this. Let my words and actions be those of Your teaching and not my anger or hurt or brokenness! Let my daughters see it as strength to learn from. Praise You in my pain! Praise Your ways, O God!"

Chapter Four

His Side vs. Her Side

On Camael's orders, Chayyliel went as an informant to the scuba shop in Wichita to see how Jacob was fairing. Most everyone was in good spirits thinking the marriage could be salvaged. Camael, however, was wary since he had seen the hostile demon clinging to the husband like a leech from the beginning of their relationship. If Chayyliel had seen his Sealed gravitate to that, he would have tossed that demon into Hades in spite of the rules. This thinking kept him from being a guardian angel. A righteous temper is good for his business, fueling the power he needs for combat, but not for guardianship.

He walked into the scuba shop like a weight lifting gold medal Olympian. The Demonics took notice. Chayyliel looked each one in the eye as he surveyed the store. There was a sealed teenage boy sitting behind a glass display case visiting with a man in his thirties. The boy's guardian sat by the front window looking more interested in the cars passing by. The older man had a huge demon of lust and another of greed propped against him, weighing him down.

Chayyliel went over to hear a bit of the conversation, demons moving out of his way. He looked directly into the boy's eyes and saw goodness in them. He then turned his attention to their words. They were discussing the one he sought.

"He jumped the fence and ran from the guy? What a wuss!" the customer snickered leaning on the glass case.

"Yeah, Jacob was totally talking tough, man, and then BAM, he was like runnin' and yellin' to call the police. Like, right after he told the drunk guy he was an officer," the boy laughed while handing the receipt. "But hey, the police totally arrested the drunk and treated Jacob like one of their own, man. That was rad."

"Peter, how do you work for this guy?" the man looked over his shoulder.

"He's cool most of the time, yo. Plus, he keeps givin me things towards my dive gear. Sometimes I get to go on dives free of charge. Just have to lug stuff, ya know," he rolled back on his bar chair.

"That *is* pretty sweet. What sort of gear did you get?" he became curious.

"Check this out," Peter pulled out a gun and Chayyliel snapped up straight at the sight of it. The demons jeered. "He gave me this Glock instead of two weeks wages, yo!"

"Man! What did your parents say?" the man took the gun and looked it over.

"Dude, I didn't tell 'em," he laughed and took it back.

"Jacob's payin' you in firearms now! He's gotta be sufferin'," he said shaking his head. "He doesn't listen to anybody . . . not even his wife," he scoffed.

Chayyliel shook his head and decided to go through Jacob's desk to see where Jacob was staying. Before he left the conversation, Peter added something important that caught his attention.

"He's got nothin' good to say bout her, man, but he's protectin' himself, yo. I've seen his other Glock and it is *sweet*. It has a laser sight and, get this, a silencer." Peter shared.

Chayyliel put his face right in front of the boy and asked, "Where is Jacob?"

Peter cocked his head and stated. "You know where Jacob's stayin', dude.'"

The man answered, "Of course, I do. He's stayin' at the police guy's house, Adam. Got the place to himself, man, cause Adam stays with his woman."

"If you knew, then why'd you ask me?" Peter asked confused.

Chayyliel did not stay to hear how they would work out his interference. As he headed out, he stopped by the guardian and gestured to the boy.

"He stopped listening to me four years ago," the guardian explained and looked back to the window.

"Whom are you working for? Him?" Chayyliel pointed to the boy. "Or Him?" he pointed up.

The guardian angel slowly got up. "You are right. Thank you for reminding me." He went towards the boy as Chayyliel headed out to find Adam's residence.

Just before he took off, a red SUV pulled up into the parking lot. It zipped around the store and slid to a stop in the back, the tires let out a sharp squeal. Then a burst of fuel to the engine sent the SUV backwards only to be stopped short with its tailgate right in front of the shop's back door. Chayyliel watched Jacob jump from the driver seat, leaving the door open, and stomp into the shop with the demon of hostility hot on his heals. The back door banged open and Jacob carried out a crate of files and tossed them into the truck without care.

Peeking into the SUV, Chayyliel saw a number of strong demons quite at home. They all sat up when they saw him near their territory. He narrowed his eyes, threatening that they should be careful of him. One jumped onto the driver's seat and put its face inches from Chayyliel's. He put his hand on his sword. The demon snapped its head to the side, watching, its eyes darting from the sword to Chayyliel's eyes, deciding.

Jacob continued to toss stuff into the SUV. The back was beginning to look like a tossed salad of paper, construction tools and scuba gear. Ignoring the small aggressive demon looking him over, Chayyliel poked his head in further to look at some of the mail on the console. The demon struck, but Chayyliel caught its arm and sent it flying to the back with the rest of the junk. One envelope had an address for the west side of Wichita. Another was from the judicial courts. He was being sued . . . again. The last was a small handwritten note signed "Elma"

The demon was back and hissing, so angry its eyes looked to be on fire, feeding off of Jacob's apparent anger. Chayyliel pulled back out of the SUV, taking in a breath of fresh air. With a powerful pull of his wings, he took off into the air, slamming the door in the angry demon's face. Camael will not like to hear what he witnessed. The hope from yesterday's words and restoration of their marriage was far from the healing stages. More than that, the news of the gun was disturbing.

⁂

Daily, Julia watched for the letter Jacob promised to write. She knew he would send it via e-mail since he was not good with handwriting. It was certainly slow coming. He did call at times to visit about nothing, which irritated her to no end. When she brought up the letter to their parents, he would either need to go or say he was working on it. Meanwhile, other mail increased. She was now receiving letters from companies regarding their delinquent accounts. Due to the constant calls from debt collectors, Julia instructed the girls not to answer the phone anymore and she did the same when the caller ID showed a non-local number. It was a sad way to live.

Then it happened. Her counselor had prepared her for the time that the renewed commitment would be tested. She received their phone bill that had risen to six hundred dollars. Not understanding the bill since her online account showed payment, she called them immediately to find out that bounced checks are not reflected on web accounts. Not only had the bill not been paid, but now there were penalties for returned checks. She went to the account and sure enough, it still indicated that it had been paid. It also illuminated that her husband was continuing to call Elma!

Julia shook her head in wonder of how stupid she had been. He just could not give that woman up. In anger, she called him; glad the girls were at volleyball day camp. When he answered, she did not even bother to greet him. "You are still calling her?" She did not even check her tone.

"What?" he gave her his challenging tone. "You're still checking on me? Is that trust?"

"Are you even worthy of trust, Jacob?" she spat. "Trust is *earned* and I have been freely giving it to your undeserving soul!"

"Don't talk to me that way." He hung up.

She sat down knowing that he would call back. The phone rang. She did not answer. It stopped and then rang again. She answered, "You hang up on me again and I won't answer." Her anger was expanding in her chest. "Now cut it off with Elma or else."

"Or else what, Jules?" he yelled.

"Or I will call her myself. It isn't like I don't have her number!" she yelled back.

"You call her and I'll knock your block off. I'll haul you're @*# to court you #@$? %&*#! You'll wish you had never lived!" He yelled louder.

Julia calmed herself. This was not going to solve anything. This is what he thought of her. This was his love for her. "I see. She means that much to you? This woman is worth taking your wife to court and threatening her life? Elma will never love you like I have. Clearly I have loved you beyond what is healthy." This time Julia hung up.

The phone rang many times over but she had gotten use to not answering calls. Since the answer machine was full he called her cell phone, but she did not even listen to those messages. She knew he would have more of the same demeaning words. Instead, she went for a brisk walk, pressing her thumb from time to time to remind herself of the pain he caused her. That is not love, she stated over and over.

When the girls got home, she had to pretend that nothing was wrong. She was used to pretending. Pulling out the paints and scrap paper, they had fun painting abstracts. With walls unfinished and no flooring, they could be as wild as they wanted and Julia was the first to enjoy such freedom. Brailey had no problem holding back, but Shannon stuck to her controlled nature.

Late that night, depressed and hurt, Julia began an e-mail explaining the decline of her marriage and sent it out to Jacob and both their parents. The Daily Strength group she belonged to encouraged her to stay strong and to erase the messages her husband had left. However, still holding onto a shred of hope, she entered in her code and listened to the messages. There were only three. The first one was full of anger and cursing. The second was half of an apology and then justification. The third was a surprise. He was angry again and threatened her life making it clear that he could leave her children motherless. She immediately deleted them, never wanting to hear them again, and went to the floor wailing her fear to the Lord.

It was evident the marriage was dissolving and Camael's caution paid off. The orders from the Father were clear: let Jacob go his own way. Saddened by this loss, they mourned with the family as Camael worked over new strategies to protect the innocent from the coming sufferings of Jacob's consequences.

The entire team of angels stood in a circle around Jacob, their swords gleaming and looking sharper than ever, as he went through his things in the garage. The demon of hostility sat in the SUV, unable to come within the circle. Jacob remained calm and as long as he did, there would be no trouble from the team. They could not stop him from taking things from the garage, but they would protect Julia and her daughters should he choose to act on his rising anger!

A clattering noise awoke Julia from her restless sleep. Shaking, she rushed to the side door and quietly made sure it was locked. Then she checked the front window to see the red Expedition outside. Julia knew if she were explaining this to someone they would ask why she did not call the police the minute she heard the noise. The question alone would tell her they had never lived with someone like Jacob.

Calling the police could insure her death. Jacob was always telling her if he wanted someone dead he would not bat an eye. With his military experience and knowing he owned a gun, she believed him. Once, he came into the bathroom while she was sitting on the toilet and stated he could kill her, making her vanish while leaving her children to wonder what happened to her. Then he calmly left. On his message yesterday he said if he wanted to he could knock down her door and no one would get to her in time. He had enough experience diving for search and rescue teams to make him very believable. There was no doubt in her mind that he could hide a body so no one could ever find it. The combination of his lovable personality, skilled sales abilities, and police connections made him exactly what he bragged himself to be, unknowingly dangerous.

So, Julia knew that police could escalate the situation. From her experience, calm and rational reactions were more effective in subduing him. She opted for what worked. She stood by the door listening to him rummage though things in the garage, occasionally going to the window to see him throw tools into the back of the SUV. In the back of her mind, she formulated plans on how to protect her girls should he switch personalities.

When he was loaded up, he drove away. It took a while before the anxiety inside her dissipated. She stepped out into the garage to survey the damage. Things were tossed into piles on and around materials for the house. From what she could see, he only took the scuba stuff and most of the electric tools. Maybe he was not thinking of moving out and giving up on the marriage. Maybe he just needed to get some things for the shop. Hope still lingered.

She went inside and checked e-mails. This had become her outlet. Julia had not realized how few friends she had since Jacob had come into her life. Upon reflection as an exercise in group therapy online, she could not count one person that she spent time with other than her daughters and her husband. Even her family had become distant and visits were few. In fact, she hardly heard from her other two sisters. She had no appointments with salons, doctors, or dentists. That cost money. The only time she really saw anyone was at school events, which required little interaction, or church, which she mainly spent with the younger generations teaching.

So, now, her world was revolving around Internet connections since they seemed to understand her and her present lifestyle. In time, of course, church would return to what it used to be as people overlooked her issues. And with a job, comes a whole new set of people to interact with. The holidays will come and family will re-establish relationships and create new memories to bond them. Yes, in time she would fan out her social sphere, but for now, this was a nice comfort zone.

She was actually surprised by the emails she received from family regarding her marriage. Although none were from Jacob, she got one from her mother-in-law, sister-in-law, and her own mother. Little did she know the impact these e-mails were going to have on her. Julia was quite unprepared for what her in-laws had to say.

Dear Julia,

My silence has been based on the hope you and Jacob could reconcile. Unfortunately it seems not to be. I'm very sad and my heart is broken that the problems you both have could not be resolved. I do know, however, Jacob had no other woman. The woman you are referring to is a student and they became just friends. I'm sorry you think Jacob would be so shallow as to take his marriage vows of fidelity so lightly. Yes, he has shortcomings in his life like we all do. But your statement that he is not willing to work on them is truly false. He has been seeing a counselor about anger management and trying to find a way to save his marriage, but he cannot do it alone.

Counseling is a partnership done together to find out the root of both people's contribution to the problems. However, when one thinks they are not part of the problem, then it cannot be solved. No matter what you are feeling on this matter, I'm right and you're wrong. I'm sorry if I upset you about this but I talked to our pastor and he said in his 60 years of counseling he has never found any person to be sinless in marital problems. That even though one thinks they are, there is underlying triggers that they can pull to start the ball rolling.

I have heard both sides and have told Jacob of my disapproval and heartbreak of the situation. Julia, I want to also say that I feel you want your marriage to work but each time Jacob fell short of this measure stick you set up for him to live by, growing your disappointment. No one can live to such a high standard. I hope that there will be no bashing of my son. No matter what anyone thinks, he is a good man and a Christian.

I also want you to know that dad and I still love you and the girls and our door is always open to you. The problems you and Jacob have are yours and should not hinder our relationship. But it will totally be up to you.

There will be no distancing on our part. Please give the
girls our reassurance of love and will be hoping to see
them and you in the near future.
Love, mom and dad

Julia sat back before reading the e-mail from her sister-in-law,
Cheryl. How could her mother-in-law be so ignorant after all she had
shared about what Jacob had done to her! Not once did she address
the abuse in her e-mail. Julia recalled a time in their kitchen when
Jacob's mother said if any man were to lay his hand on her daughter,
they would drive all the way from Colorado and immediately take her
away. She said this after Julia shared how Jacob had taken a hose from
the shower and sprayed Julia down in anger, cursing and calling her
names because she had expressed how lonely she was on a dive trip
to Puerto Rico. It did seem like a small thing when she shared it, but
it was the anger that made it so cruel. She turned her eyes to Cheryl's
response.

Julia and girls,
It saddens me very much to hear of this. The issues
that you & Jacob have are yours personally and no one
else's. I am restraining my opinions on this matter, because
it is not my business and I don't want to hurt anyone's
feelings on either end.
Jacob is first and foremost my brother and I will
always support his decisions whether or not I agree with
them. We have all made mistakes in the past and try to
work through them. However, I feel that sometimes
the mistakes and the hurt that we endure during our
relationships set a boundary of trust and cause us to bring
the problems into the next relationship. Neither you nor
Jacob is innocent in keeping the past in the past. But we
learn to accept and move on with each other. We have to
decide to open our hearts and our minds and decide to
trust the one that you love.
I honestly can tell you that I fully know in my
heart that my brother has not cheated on you. Yes, he
has talked to a student that has become a friend and a

friend only. I do want you to know that I understand the insecurity that you have on this, but know this; Jacob has been very committed to being true to you, no matter what the problems you two may have. He loves you very much.

Julia, I want you to know that I am not upset, mad or angry with either of you for this marriage dissolving, because it is what it is. I do hope that in time, you will know I love you no matter what and that we love the girls very much. You need to know that you are always welcome in our home. If you ever need us to watch the girls, we would love to. Please keep the communications open so that we can see the girls, they have been hurt enough.

Take care and my prayers are with all of you!

Love, your sis

Anger shot through Julia's veins. The nerve of them! Can nothing go her way? Jacob had clearly misled them. He had yet to see a counselor and Elma was more than just a friend. Furthermore, that pastor, with all his 60 years of counseling—mostly spent on compiling sermons and visiting the sick in hospitals—probably never took a psychology class in his life or dealt with the irrational behavior of an abuser. Are pastors really equipped to counsel with such ignorance? Should they at least take a moment to research such cases with the Internet so easily at hand? With that thought, everyone should research abuse so as not to respond in ignorance when dealing with a victim.

She had just learned from several reliable online documents that most abusers are like pressure cookers, building up pressure until they need to blow off enough steam to cope. They find a person that becomes their release and thus are able to function in society, for the most part. In the mean time, the victim is forever trying to appease the abuser and unknowingly feeding them with enough shock to release the pressure. This is why Jacob could instantly flip and kiss her, pushing the event into the past although it happened only seconds prior. If she could learn this in 10 minutes on the Internet, why can't others? If only they would, then she would not have to be victimized again by ignorance. To be abused and then blamed by those who should be supporting you is beyond cruel. It is a no win situation.

Still, as a Christian in crisis, she should devote this to prayer, allowing God to open her eyes should her pain be deceiving her perspective. She knew she needed to forgive the ignorance of others as well. She, too, is still ignorant about abuse and learning every day. There was a time when she thought all these experiences were her fault so she did not want to turn one hundred and eighty degrees the other way thinking nothing was her fault. Sincerely, Julia searched for pride within and tried to investigate anything that might move her to a healthy spirit. She knelt and prayed until she heard the girls stirring in their rooms.

Gathering herself up, she dried her eyes and put on the façade of starting out a new day, fresh from worries and pains. She had to be a mom now. She did not have the luxury of falling apart or taking a week off to think. But if her in-laws thought she was going to keep a relationship with people who support abuse and allow her children to spend time with them, they have another thing coming!

The phone rang and the familiar voice of her mother caught her off guard.

Tina got into her van to leave. Quickly pulling her list from her purse, she took a moment to make sure she had given the church treasurer everything she intended. With all she was involved in, it was a wonder she even kept her list in order. Crossing that errand off, she stuffed the paper back into her purse. As she turned the key, she happened to glance at the house next door, Julia Anderson's house.

Tina paused. It had been a while since they spoke in the park. Everything looked dark and quiet over there. She wondered how Julia and her girls were doing. The thought crossed her mind to drive over and check on her. As she pulled out of the drive, she contemplated the visit but was interrupted by something she forgot to put on her list. By the time she had her van on the street, the list in her purse took over and she opted to do it tomorrow. She made a mental note to add that to her list.

⤙✦⤚

If pride was really a problem within Julia, it was about to be crushed into a million pieces and overtaken by humility. Her account showed no available balance and Jacob was failing to come to her aid. She could only assume, from the many calls to her home and the increasing mail, he could not pay his bills much less help her. The mortgage was about due and with everything that was pressing down on her, the last thing she needed right now was to be evicted. She absolutely refused to do what Jacob's sister, Kate, along with so many in this economy did and simply walk away from their homes to let others pay the price of their mortgages.

Entering the church on a weekday felt dark and cold, but the light in the office was a warm beacon. She had been serving at this church for over seven years now, always in ministry, always active, even as a single mother working to make ends meet. Today she came, hat in hand, pride dissolved, to ask for financial help.

The pastor was not in his office so she looked around only to find him in the kitchen. He was polite and asked her about the kids. She answered and was about to go into her purpose when he started telling her how his wife had an appointment with the doctor today. She listened with genuine concern and offered encouragement. She felt awkward changing the subject. By the time she managed to bring up her house payment, she was so flustered it did not come out the way she hoped.

"What do you plan on doing?" he questioned her.

"Well, I'm trying to get a job but it is slow going," she tried to sound positive.

"What will you do if you cannot make your payments?" he finished wiping his hands on a bright white napkin.

Julia felt confident that she would find the right job. Nevertheless, she had not thought past that. Off the top of her head she popped a plan. "We will probably move to low income housing and I will have to go on assistance. But," she leaned on the counter, "I have never had to go on assistance and God always takes care of those who belong to Him. That is why I am here. The Word says that the church . . ."

"Excuse me, Julia," he smiled sweetly and glanced at his watch, "I have to interrupt you and be on my way. I cannot be late for my wife's doctor's appointment." He touched her arm, "Let me know how the job hunt goes and love those girls of yours." With that said, he left her alone standing in the kitchen. Stunned. Confused. Silence engulfed her as she just stood in the abandoned church building. Time passed but she was frozen in emotional devastation.

"God?" finally breaking free, Julia looked to the ceiling, "what happened?" She felt a little silly talking out loud, but no one was there so she just let it out. She knew the pastor had interrupted her on purpose probably knowing where she was headed. She had a purpose in coming to him and she was going to express it in spite of his apparent rejection. "Your Word says in First John 3:17, 'if anyone has material possessions and sees his brother in need but has no pity on him, how can the love of God be in him?' You say not to love with only words but with actions as well . . ." It might have only been two or three sentences, but she went ahead and asked for the loan anyway. "My mortgage is $1,200, Lord. You own cattle on a thousand hills, can you spare one for me, please?" Then she slinked out the back and headed home in the rain, her heart angry and resentful.

Drenched from the walk home, Julia did not even bother drying off before dialing Jacob's number. She had made up her mind. Humbling herself before the pastor did not feel as low as begging Jacob for the money, but she had no choice. She was not going to loose the house because she did not try. She had sacrificed a great deal but integrity would not be one. Humiliated, she pleaded for money as politely as possible. He seemed to enjoy it although he pretended to sympathize with her. Other than advising her to get off her fat @%$ and get a job, he had nothing else to offer.

"Well, how is the scuba shop doing?" she almost whined.

"The business?" he chuckled. "The business *is* me, Jules. You don't have any claim to the business now."

"What do you mean? It was my savings that financed the shop, not to mention the twenty thousand my dad invested." She took a deep breath to calm down. "What happened to 'the shop would be nothing without you, Jules'?" she recalled vividly.

"You're into change. So I changed," he sugared it with sarcasm. "Be careful what you wish for. You might just get it."

"I wanted change so we could make the marriage work. What you are doing is illegal," she clarified.

"Really? Because I'm the one doing all the work," he raised his voice, "Just remember who you are dealing with before you push me, Jules. I've got all my tracks covered," he turned sinister.

Julia thought for a moment and made a decision. "You weren't the only one working on that shop and if divorce is where we are headed, I would be entitled to half. But you are right, the shop is you. We started it because it was *your* dream. Don't feel threatened, Jacob. The shop is yours." With that said she hung up and decided to put her trust in the Lord. She had done it before when the girls' dad left her and God was true to His Word. Rejected again, there was nothing more to do than go take a shower and see what she could make for supper.

When she came to the kitchen she was met with singing and the smell of cooked food. Brailey had become an expert at seasoning ground beef and Shannon had finished the rice. Julia smiled by the surprise and had to hug them both. Laughing as they recounted her surprised expression, they settled down on the couch to watch *Pride and Prejudice* while they ate. It was one of their traditions to watch a movie every Friday night.

An hour into the show, the doorbell rang. The girls' faces brightened with surprise to see their grandma and grandpa step in. The grandparents hugged and laughed as they made their way to see what each girl wanted to show them from their art to ribbons won at swim meets. When the children ran out of things to show or perform, they began to settle down to get ready for bed.

Julia did her bedtime routine for each girl after they did their devotions. She asked them about their day and then quizzed them over their Bible study. Sometimes they had questions and she would either look it up or explain the best she could. The last part of the routine was everyone's favorite. Julia lightly stroked their hair or back as she sang the song they had made up many years ago about going to sleep. As she finished, she went to the door and told them that she loved them no matter what they said or did, she would always, always love them.

Her parents had waited patiently for her to sing them to sleep, so she knew they had come for a reason. Her dad shifted forward indicating for her to sit before he spoke. "Your mother shared with me the e-mail you sent and we are both sad but very proud of you." He patted her hand, which was his way of showing his care. "We want to help you but we don't know what you will accept. How are you doing financially?" he asked.

Julia kept her feelings in check, but inside there was a raging storm of emotions. "Not good, Dad." She looked to her hands. "It seems Jacob is in a lot of trouble with debt. I keep getting these calls," she shared.

"How much debt?" her mother leaned back knowingly.

"Um, maybe twenty thousand? I honestly don't know," she answered. "I don't answer most of the phone calls. Jacob insisted on taking care of our finances alone."

"You need to answer the calls, Julia," her dad instructed, unaffected by the news. "It is important to lenders to feel you are not running away from your obligation."

"Most of them are not lenders, they are collectors." She noted her mother's glance to her father. "I didn't know. Jacob always insisted on getting the mail and answering the phone. I've never been in debt before."

"It's okay. What you need to do is answer the calls and open all the letters, compiling what is owed in your name. Make another list for what Jacob owes. When you have everything, let's get together and make a plan to take care of your credit." He patted her knee and stood. "I know you are going through a rough time, Julia. We are here for you and will help you, if you let us." Then he hugged her and her mother joined them.

"Thank you, Daddy. Thank you, Mom, so much." She held on tight.

> *My safety did not seem to be much of a concern for me until my abuser's temper had escalated to threats along with action. He usually said things he "didn't mean" throughout our time together; so when the threats began, I did not take them very seriously. However, that changed when he made the threat and then followed through. I took great care after that about exit plans and even had a packed bag in the car, never knowing when he would follow through on a threat. If I noticed him becoming agitated, I would position myself near a door. He did catch on to this tactic and even if I looked at an exit it could cause an intensified situation. Therefore, strategizing became a constant mental exercise for me.*

Safety Planning

Safety Planning is the process of evaluating the risks and benefits of different options and identifying ways to reduce risk. Those in an abusive relationship probably know more about planning for safety and assessing risks than most realize. Being in a relationship with an abusive partner, and surviving, requires considerable skill and resourcefulness. Any time a victim does or says something as a way to protect themselves and their children; they are assessing risk and enacting a safety plan.

Safety During an Explosive Incident

- Go to an area that has an exit: If possible stay in a part of the house you can get out of quickly. Not a bathroom (near hard surfaces), kitchen (knives), or near weapons.
- Go to a room with a phone: Call 911, a friend or a neighbor, if possible. Inform them if there are weapons in the home.
- Know an escape route: Practice how to get out of your home safely.
- Have a packed bag ready: Keep it hidden in a handy place in order to leave quickly, or leave the bag elsewhere (a friend's house).
- Devise a code word or signal: Tell the children or neighbors so you can communicate to them that you need the police.
- Know where you're going: Plan where you will go if you have to leave home.
- Trust your judgment: Consider anything that you feel will keep you safe and give you time to figure out what to do next. Sometimes it is best to flee and sometimes it is best to placate the abuser.

Remember advanced planning can prevent serious injury or even death.

"Lord, I want to complain even though I know I should not. I know You are in charge, but I don't think I can take much more! My plate is full, yet it is empty. I know I am griping but I need a job, I need money! Lord, the food was wonderful and I can't thank You enough . . . Still, what is left is difficult to make without milk, eggs, or butter. I am sorry to be asking for more when I should be so thankful. You say you care for even the lilies of the fields and I believe You. . . ."

Chapter Five

Reality Sets In

A shriek filled the house. Julia jumped up and followed the crying to the stairs. Brailey sat holding her foot, tears drenching her face, and her mouth wide open. Julia knew what had happened. This was not the first time. She grabbed a towel and tweezers and joined her daughter. The splinter came out after fishing for a few minutes. Brailey had calmed considerably and was now holding in the hurt. Although Julia had done extensive cleaning, the rough floors and stairs were still not surfaces without fault. She just could not get her girls to always wear their shoes and this periodic experience was not going to inspire the use of shoes inside the house either.

Her cell phone rang and she dashed to find it. Checking the number first, she answered while gathering her lists of debt and a pen. As the man spoke, she frantically searched for another scrap of paper. Giving up, she wrote the information on her hand ending the call with an excited smile.

"Girls," she yelled in delight. Shannon came running in with Brailey hobbling behind. "I have a job!" she announced. "I have a job!" she said it again. They all came together hugging and jumping, saying it over and over again.

Brailey pulled back to ask, "Where?"

"Well," Julia's smile remained, "the place is called Sign & Tech Graphics. I will be making signs that go into businesses and hotels."

Shannon tilted her head a little. "I thought you didn't get that job."

"It turns out the girl changed her mind again and resigned. They want me to start tomorrow." She giggled. "I say we celebrate and make the brownie mix grandma gave us. We've been saving it for a special moment such as this." The girls squealed and Brailey was the first to the half empty pantry, in spite of her sore foot.

The brownies tasted as good as they smelled. The three of them sat in the bay window of the dinning room, their backs to the glass, and savored every bite. Shannon mentioned a couple of times that it would have been a tad better with ice cream. They all agreed but were more than enjoying the special dessert with grateful hearts. Shannon hummed the tune to "Give Thanks" and the others hummed along, Brailey stressing yummy hums.

Then a knock on the door caused them all to stop. They were not used to anyone coming over. The last time someone came during the day, a woman delivered a subpoena for Jacob. Julia had never been served before so when she looked at the paper and saw that it was for Jacob, she tried to hand it back knowing he would want to deal with it himself. Oddly, the woman would not take it, laughing at her on the way back to the idling car.

Now, she was leery of more bad news. After peeking out the front window, she rushed to the door and opened it with a smile. It was an older woman from church she considered a pillar of faith and a friend. At first, Julia considered Betsy and her husband too high society to want to socialize with the likes of her. They were well known for their businesses, social and political influence, and large house just outside of town. Unexpectedly, the elegant woman was one of the first to welcome her. She had a warm smile and a genuine sincerity about her expressions, in spite of her rich wardrobe, which drew Julia. Over the years, she enjoyed many occasions visiting with them about their strong faith and ministries. Julia humbly welcomed her in, but Betsy insisted on staying on the windy porch in her pressed navy business suit, promising her matter would not take long.

"I'm one of the deaconesses of our church, Julia, and we wanted to give you this gift." Betsy handed her a card, her manicured nails brightly gleaming.

Curious, Julia opened it and unfolded a check for a thousand dollars along with a gift card to their local grocery store. Julia's mouth opened, but she could not force any response.

"What is it, mom?" Shannon looked around her shoulder. Her exclamation brought Brailey over to look.

"If you need anything, Julia, you come to me. Okay?" she touched her arm tenderly. "We love you." Betsy smiled perfectly. "I have to get back to work, but I wanted to get this to you before the first of the month," she nodded her meaning for the house bill.

"Thank you." Julia nodded back. "I can't tell you what this means to us."

She watched the older woman return to her car, not a blond hair out of place before closing the door. She looked to the amount. Although it would not cover the full amount of the mortgage, it was close! As if in a trance, she went to her room and knelt by the bed to thank the Lord, leaving the check in Shannon's hands. Soon the girls joined her in silent prayer, all with tears of joy.

Camael smiled as he watched the soft glow emanate from Julia's chest and grow in intensity as the tears flowed freely down her cheeks. He was filled with wonder. Communion between the Father and a human's soul was a mystery to him and nothing short of a miracle. The light suddenly burst throughout the house as the two girls joined their mother at the bedside. He could hear the angels singing praises from the throne room of the Almighty and knew deep within that three souls had inspired such worship.

> "Praise God, from Whom all blessings flow;
> Praise Him, all creatures here below;
> Praise Him above, ye heavenly host;
> Praise Father, Son, and Holy Ghost."

Chayyliel pumped his massive wings shooting through the sky faster than a jet. When he reached the little town, he spread his wings and held them strong catching the air like a parachute, stopping him almost instantly. Tucking his wings and arms close to his body, he dove like an arrow towards the house on the south edge of town with the white porch railing.

Camael looked up in time to see Chayyliel open his wings to their full extent just in time to land. He was out of breath and had an expression of importance. Quickly, Camael moved him to the front door, not wanting their alarm to influence the household. The house, full of joy and prayer, filled Chayyliel and he revived at once.

"Jacob lost his temper and attacked Peter at the scuba shop," Chayyliel reported.

Camael sighed, knowing this would catapult Jacob farther from the Father's help. The truth is, the Sealed can come to the Father at any time and in an instant possibly change an outcome or consequences but it must be of their own choosing. Julia would still have him back and Jacob could gain a better appreciation for what he originally had, making his life even better and more open for testimony than before. The choice, of course, would have to be Jacob's.

"What did you do?" Camael knew Chayyliel was an angel of action and zeal. He even fought along side of the Archangel, Michael! Needless to say, he was not going to allow some out-of-control bully to damage a young Sealed!

"I body slammed him to the ground, that spineless . . ." Chayyliel's eyes squinted, feeling his righteous anger again.

"I see. How bad is the damage?" the leader questioned.

"I didn't kill him, of course," Chayyliel smirked. "I just gave him a spasm he won't forget, Boss."

Camael relaxed. "You have a lot of muscle, Chayyliel, but I'm thankful you have a lot more control." He laughed and then quieted. "Now, we do not have a lot of time to prepare Julia. I will need Sophia and you to play defense, keeping that hostile spirit off Jacob."

Chayyliel was disappointed in his role, but understood. He was more of an offensive player, but defense can be just as important. Keeping peace was the main goal for this mission and he would do the very best he could for the sake of the family. The husband was not worthy, but Julia and the girls were. He was disappointed in Jacob. When he looked into the man's eyes, he saw that he could have become great. God could have used the man in so many wonderful ways. But, this human was weak-minded and loved his aggression and people's reaction to his intimidation. One hour with Chayyliel and he could teach the man a thing or two about how to use such power!

⚜

Gathering her list and a pen, Julia prepared to answer another phone call, but this time it was from the scuba shop. She put the pen down and took a deep breath.

"How is Jacob?" the voice on the other end was the young teen boy Jacob had hired to help him at the shop just before they separated. She did not know Peter well, but from what she learned when she went along on a scuba trip to Table Rock Lake, he was a Christian boy that was passionate about diving. "Don't you know?" Peter pushed for an answer.

"Know what?" Julia was confused.

"Um . . ." he hesitated, "Well, I guess you should know. He went to the emergency room, yo."

"What? When?" Her mind raced needing more information.

"'Bout an hour ago?" he guessed. "Look, I didn't mean to do anything to him."

"What do you mean?" she tried to put her shoes on with one hand.

"Yo, he was mad before I got there," he justified.

"Tell me what happened, Peter," she ordered him.

"He told me to come in late since he couldn't afford my hours, but, man, when I got there he was spastic cause he said he was counting on me to open the shop." He stopped to say something to someone else and then continued, "He like came at me and pushed me against the wall, yo. Meaning no disrespect, ma'am, but I had to act, ya know?"

"What did you do?" she dropped a shoe, hoping Jacob did not cause the boy harm.

"Dude, I pushed him back. Like, he fell and started to get up but couldn't. He called an ambulance and they came and got him." Peter said something again to someone at his end. "I didn't mean to hurt the old guy, but he did come after me, ya know."

65

Julia hardly thought thirty-seven was that old, but to a boy of fifteen she could see how he would think that. "Are you okay?"

"Yeah," he sounded like it was nothing. "I mean, Jacob's a strong man, yo, but like, I'm tough. Let me know if you find out he's ok. Peace, out." He hung up.

Julia quickly dialed Jacob and got voicemail. Putting on the last shoe, she dialed again and then a third time. Finally, he answered. "Jacob, I just heard. Are you okay? Where are you?"

"I'm fine. I'm getting ready to leave the ER," he answered flatly.

"Maybe I should come and get you. Stay there, I'm almost out the door," she grabbed her purse.

"Forget it, I can drive," he cut her off.

"But Jacob, you probably shouldn't." Julia stood by the car with her keys.

"I have to stop by the pharmacy anyway. I'm still lightheaded and have to take some pills for my paralysis thing," he shared like it was a chore.

"Jacob, this doesn't sound like you should be driving at all. Please, let me come and . . ."

"No," he cut her off again.

She thought for a moment. "Well, at least let me know where you are going so if anything happens . . ."

"I'm going home," he stated.

"Home? The hotel?" she questioned.

"No, I got a place a while back," he moaned afterwards. "I have to go, my head is killing me and talking on the phone isn't helping."

"Jacob, at least give me your address . . ."

"I don't think so." He hung up on her.

Julia stood by the car with her keys in hand and only then realized she had put on her daughter's shoes. Pulling them off, she stretched her toes and headed back into the house feeling like the worst wife in the world. Sitting on her bed, she glanced at a paper taped to the wall. It was full of verses and sayings from the many sermons she had been listening to. Three words caught her eye. He *is* able!

The truth will always come out, a promise from the Word. She wanted to be a good wife, wanted to be there for her husband, and wanted to comfort him. Just as Jesus came to this world to save us from our sins, it is ultimately up to each person to choose to accept

His gift. Julia slouched and held her sore thumb as a reminder. It was Jacob's decision. She had done nothing to be treated this way. All she ever wanted to be was a good wife to him. She had done all that he asked of her and yet it was never good enough. Now, it is not enough to beat her, call her names, spread rumors and lies to his family and pastor, but now he has to make sure she has no opportunity to be there for him. She looked at her thumb, still unable to move it. Her love was more than selfless right now.

God is able. He is able to protect Jacob. He is able to bring Jacob back to Him. He is able to do anything. She knew that everything bends to God's will. No person or thing can thwart His plans. If she truly believed this, then she knew He was big enough to care for Jacob as well. In His hands she placed her worry and concern. Although Jacob did not want her, he could not push away his Creator. Some would say that God is not in control of these things, but Julia knew that even a parent allows a child to go through difficult times for the sake of raising the child to be a better and more equipped person.

Sophia was tired but thankful. Julia had such an open spirit that Sophia's influence went a long way. Gifted in wisdom, Sophia had spent many months now teaching Julia strength, courage, and truth. Jacob's lies had clouded her thinking so much that Julia's love would not allow her to see the truth until now. Pouring over any resource available, Julia had listened, read, and researched anything Sophia put before her. That was a blessing. If only Jacob would be as willing!

However, unlike her twin sister, Julia could be quite stubborn. Sophia was constantly trying to dance around this side of Julia. Clearly she was going to do whatever she could to keep her marriage, in spite of her mental, spiritual, and physical welfare. The poor woman had been through so much already with her first husband, a man of deceit. Now, even after many warnings, her heart attached to a man of hostility. Getting her to let go was going to take a hard blow, which Sophia wished would not have to take place. Julia needed to learn to live in God's love rather than holding onto what she believed to be God's expectation of her.

Perhaps the goodness of God would allow Julia to see clearly before it got to a point of confrontation. Perhaps she would not need a major event to force her to take the necessary steps for healing. Sophia lowered her head to look Julia in the eye. She could see the will was there, but unrealistic expectations clouded the way. What Julia needed right now was a good night's sleep. She began to hum a sweet tune of God's never ending love.

⁓⁂⁓

August eighteenth, Julia had gotten up early to prepare for her first day at work. It had been two years since she had to answer to someone and at least seven years since she was not in charge of her own department. She hoped she would do well and fit in. On the twenty-minute drive into the city, she left a message for the girls to accomplish some goals in their day while she was gone. Then she enjoyed a sermon on BOTT Radio, happy that Pastor Adrian Rogers was on during her commute. She loved his witticisms.

Making sure she parked in the back lot where her car tag would not be easily visible, she walked around the large building to enter the front doors. Promising to put her personal life on the back burner, she raised her head and confidently went to the reception's desk where a cute petite Asian woman sat typing intensely on her computer keyboard. Reading her nameplate, Julia introduced herself and asked to see the manager. After a phone call, the receptionist asked her to wait and Julia thanked her using her name.

Kiri was sweet and very personable, annunciating her words distinctly for clear communication, causing Julia to like her immediately. The receptionist explained that a newly promoted man, named Lloyd, would be out for her shortly. Julia took the opportunity to make plans to have lunch with Kiri if their lunch hour was at the same time. Since this was a manufacturing plant, different areas had different shifts.

Lloyd was a tall man with a big mustache, which made her think of an old time Texas rancher. He wore a belt buckle with a horse on it and Levi jeans, but his boots were more of the hiking variety. He welcomed her with a broad smile and firm handshake, and she quickly congratulated him on his promotion, glancing at Kiri. He laughed and said if he had a tail he would be wagging it. He then turned to give Julia a tour of the plant.

She would be working in a large room with plotters just off the entry. Beyond that, there were three large rooms for sales teams. Had they gone left from the entry, they would have gone to an office area, where she went to fill out paperwork. All the manufacturing happened at the back of the building. Upstairs, there was a conference room with storage. She did not fear getting lost with such a simple layout.

Her Supervisor was a thin man who managed digital prints and looked like the "Where's Waldo" character. He spoke in a soft monotone voice using vocabulary that most people would envy, which gave the impression of a high intellect. However, his openness on politics and religion cautioned her not to express any opinions. He did not lose time in getting her started, but she spent most of her day getting reoriented to the advanced programs. Still, she did not feel overwhelmed and would catch on quickly enough.

Lunch break came slowly. However, when it did, she gave the girls a call to find out how their swim practice went and if the chores were getting done. She did not usually leave them alone all day, but she had little choice, and they were old enough to be responsible. The summer break was almost over and soon they would be back in school. For now at least the neighbor, who did not attend her church, said she would check in on them.

Julia really did not learn much from Kiri about the company but did get an overview of some of the people. Although she did not eat anything, she enjoyed visiting during her lunchtime. Kiri had a husband and a baby boy, looking as though she had not been pregnant a day in her life. They were thinking about going to Las Vegas for the holidays since their families lived overseas. This seemed to be the biggest concern on Kiri's mind. Julia looked to the band-aid covering her blackened thumbnail. If only that was *her* problem.

The rest of her day ticked on. Everything was timed out. She had two breaks and a half hour lunch. Since the Waldo character, Ned, had to drive an hour to work from Peabody, the company moved his hours to start at eight in the morning and end at four thirty in the afternoon. Because of this considerate adjustment, everyone under him also needed to work the same hours so the workflow would be congruent, which suited Julia just fine. She would love getting home when the girls arrived from school, once school started.

For a first day, Julia felt like things went well. In five days she would have her first paycheck. From then on she would be paid every two weeks. Julia smiled at the thought. In sixty days she would have health insurance and could find out what the real damage was on her thumb. Maybe she would have her tailbone looked at as well. It has caused her pain since Jacob pushed her over some paint cans awhile back.

She found herself recalling the event. He had said something about her father and she mirrored his sarcasm as their marriage counselor had advised. In a flash he pushed her and she fell over some paint cans and hit her head on a corner post. As she had regained consciousness, she realized Jacob was pulling her across the basement cement floor to their bed. Her head screamed for attention pounding with pain. It felt as though her brains were spilling out of her head. Julia wailed for him to help her but Jacob kept assuring her that she was fine. After resting half the day, her headache subsided and only then did she notice her tailbone had also been injured. From then on, she forewent the counselor's advice and resolved to be more careful.

She shook her head of the memory as she started the car. The radio automatically tuned into the sermon already underway. The preacher stressed the importance of obeying the Word of God. It was through obedience that the Word bursts to life and opens communication with God! Not only would the Word become alive, but also a thirst to know more would ensue.

She wondered why it was not like that for Jacob as she glanced in the rear view mirror to see a Mexican woman standing in the parking lot looking at her. The woman nodded at her. Julia thought it strange until she recalled Bluetooth technology. It was likely the woman was not nodding to her but just visiting on her headset. Julia pulled out of the parking lot. She would stay to side streets, keeping in mind her expired tags.

As she snaked through the dilapidated downtown neighborhood, she caught a glimpse of a red SUV. The preacher on the radio continued his plea for obedience, but her mind had shifted to the SUV that now followed her. She made a turn. It followed. Her heart quickened and she decided to take a different street than originally planned. It continued to follow. Eyeing a busy gas station, she opted against stopping in fear of her expired tag. Finally, heading out of Wichita, the SUV slowed down and turned away. Julia sighed, shaking her head at her paranoia.

⌘

"Jacob was pretty upset," Chayyliel shared. "I stayed with him until he turned away from following her." He flexed his wing muscles.

"Any trouble with the Demonics?" Camael asked, half expecting the answer.

"Nope," Chayyliel smiled. "There's a wee one that thinks it's a lava bomb, but to me, it's just an icicle" He flexed again and chuckled.

"Omias." Camael knew the rascal of a demon well from battles past. "Just be careful when he shifts," Camael warned, for demons that can change their appearance were dangerous indeed.

"He?" Chayyliel laughed harder. "I thought it was a little girl." Then he sobered. "All joking aside, I will keep a better eye on him. Thanks for the warning." Chayyliel never took warnings for granted. "The other two are going to be the problem. Azza is a formidable opponent of mine. He has grown strong and acts as a bodyguard for Aboddon at times. The other one I do not know, but it's big."

Camael did not like what he was hearing. He looked at Julia as she tried to decide what to make for supper, the pantry growing bare again. He was glad that she questioned whether Jacob had been following her, needing her to be careful. Something was definitely brewing. They may be loosing the marriage, but the Demonics were going to have to strike him down if they were going to harm Julia and her daughters!

"No signs of Aboddon?" he questioned. Chayyliel shook his head. "We better get our prayer support in place," Camael pointed to Ariel. "Sophia, is there anything we can do with the pastor?"

Sophia pointed to the phone as it rang. They all listened as the pastor greeted Julia and then shared that his wife's doctor visit went well. Julia twitched a light smile as her voice portrayed thankfulness. Then the pastor concluded the call. Julia held the phone for a moment and then slammed it into the cradle.

"I think the pastor is successfully distracted," she surmised from his lack of interest in shepherding.

"Yes," Camael's mind worked. "You better go through Sherry and Betsy as well as Donna, the Wednesday night assistant. They have been good church friends."

"What about Tina and Ruth?" Ariel asked.

"Tina is wrapped up in other ministries and we best stay clear of Ruth for now since her mind is set." He watched Ariel take off and then directed his attention back to Sophia. "New paths of thought have to be in place since we cannot salvage the marriage. Julia cannot fall down," he emphasized and Sophia nodded her understanding. "Sablo, you and Zazriel, be alert for the children's sake."

Sablo added seriously, "Brailey gets scared quickly and panics. She will need a plan and a song." He looked to Zazriel, gifted in music.

Camael stopped as a thought crossed his mind. "I know what we can do. Julia is the strongest when she is instructing her kids. Let us channel our work in that direction. We will press the need to make a plan for the girls; thus, working in our plan." He smirked.

As for my children, almost 100% of the abuse was out of their presence so I did not worry for their safety on the onset. Over time, as the abuse got worse, I did start to implement escape drills that I blamed on possible fires or break-ins. I had clothes for them in my bag in the car and code words if there was a need to put a drill into effect. Naturally, after my abuser left, I took great care about their safety and explained to them what abuse was and why we needed to have these plans. I believe it gave them a sense of security to have the plan and helped them not fear for me.

Safety Planning For Children

Domestic violence is when grownups in your family hit, kick, push, or throw things at someone else in your family. When the fighting starts:

Stay away from the fight!
• Stay out of the room where the fighting is
• Stay out of small rooms where you might get trapped, like a closet or a bathroom
• Stay out of the kitchen and garage, where it is easy to get hurt during a fight

Get Help!
• Go to a safe place, like a neighbor's or friend's house
• Teachers, police officers, doctors, nurses, friends, and neighbors are all people who you can go to for help
• Call 911 from a room away from the fighting

Things to Think About
• Which doors, windows, or stairs is the safest way to get out of your house during a fight?
• Which grown up could you talk to about getting help?

Remember: It's not your fault!
• It's okay to love both of your parents, even if one parent is hurting the other
• But it's not okay for that parent to hurt you, your parent, or anyone else

You won't get in trouble if you call the police. If a parent is hurting someone, the police will get them the help they need to change their behavior. Remember, police are here to help. They are not here to get people in trouble. You can call or tell someone at any time, even when everything is okay again.

"Praise Your name, Lord! Praise You! Thank You for Your kindness and hope. I started my job and at a rate that I need to make the bills. You turn life in a moment's time according to Your will and I praise You for Your kindness and mercy! Lord, I still need Your help with Jacob though! I am at the end of my hope for the good in Jacob to come back. I am weak and my girls need me to be strong. We need Your protection. Help me to see You working here. Heal me. Heal our house. Heal my thumb. I know it is a small thing, but who could have known how important a thumb is?"

Chapter Six

Taking Action

Shannon and Brailey sat on separate couches as Julia sat in the chair that had been her grandmother's. It represented the strength her grandmother had in God, so Julia often sat in it during times of consideration. This was one of those times. It was time for their monthly family meeting. Family members took turns to discuss what they wished to change in the household. Shannon was so easygoing that she rarely had anything to share. Brailey, however, used the time as a social event and often bunny trailed to her many experiences. So most often, it was Julia that would maintain the focus for the meetings.

"You girls are really wonderful. Thank you for helping around the house and getting your chores done. I know there have been a lot of changes and I want to make sure you know I see your efforts." They smiled and she knew they needed the praise. "Now, I would like to go over safety protocols . . ."

"What is protocol?" Brailey interrupted.

"Brailey, we must work on not interrupting," Julia eyed her. "Protocols are plans with boundaries. Now, one example of a protocol would be a plan if a stranger tried to pick you up from school. Our plan, or protocol, is that they must use the code word so you know it is okay to go with them."

"Yeah. That would be for a big town like Wichita. We live in a small town now, so we know everyone," Shannon stated factually.

"Well, even if you know them and they don't usually pick you up, they would still need to use the code word," Julia explained.

"What if it is Aunt Jan?" Shannon tested.

"Okay, Aunt Jan is the exception," Julia winked. "What if it is Jacob?" she tested back, raising her brows.

Brailey jumped in, "He's an exception, too."

Shannon corrected, "No, he has to have the code now."

Julia looked at both of the girls. "Does he need the code or not?" she asked. They thought for a moment and decided Shannon was right. "Then we must change to a new code word he doesn't know."

Brailey wrinkled her nose. "How about something we wear or a fashion name?"

"I know," Shannon smiled, "How about that dog's name that lived across the alley at our old apartment. Remember? His name was Bo Bo."

"Yeah," Brailey agreed.

"Bo Bo it is!" Julia declared. "Now, I know this may never happen, but it is a good idea to have a safety plan, like the fire drill at school." She took a deep breath and continued. "I think we need a plan to get out of our house if something bad happens."

"Like if Jacob tries to come in the house and hurt us?" Shannon's smile was gone.

Julia looked at Brailey and saw her nodding unafraid of the subject. "Well, yes, or anyone that might want to come in to steal or cause harm." Julia tried to pull the focus away from Jacob.

"What should our protocol be?" Shannon questioned.

"I've given it some thought, girls. If someone were to try to break in, I want you to go out the back door in Shannon's room and through the gate on that side of the house. Then, go into the neighbor's gate and knock on their back sliding door," Julia shared.

"I don't like them," Brailey complained.

"Me neither. They don't wave or smile or anything," Shannon agreed. "Can't we go to the other neighbor who checks on us?"

"I know how you feel," Julia tried to find an explanation. "But they are the easiest to reach and they go to our church. They will help you."

"They never say anything to us at church, either," whined Brailey.

"Well, they're old. Maybe they just don't like kids," Shannon leveled her ice blue eyes at Julia causing her to rethink the plan.

After a moment, she made up her mind. "I think it would be best. It is an easy and concealed route to help. Many people do not know what we are going through. The same could be said of our neighbors. They are part of our church family and we should trust in that," Julia sat back. "Plus, you won't care about all of that when you are trying to get help."

"What about you?" Shannon asked tilting her head in concern.

"I will join you, so don't worry. You take care of each other. Remember, God takes care of His sheep, even the little ones." Julia giggled and went to tickle them.

"Stop, I want to talk about whoever did not put a new roll of toilet paper in the bathroom today," Brailey wiggled away from her tickling fingers and eyeballed her sister.

Julia finished her third day of work and was ready to get home to her girls. She was about to flip on the car radio when her cell phone vibrated. Taking out a tablet and pen, she prepared to add to her lists.

"You $#@%," the man screamed on the other end.

Julia hung up. She sat for a moment stunned and then looked to her phone vibrating again. Her father wanted her to answer all the calls, but she sure did not want to take this one. Mustering up her courage, she flipped open the phone and held it to her ear.

"Don't you hang up on me, Jules!" Jacob yelled.

"Jacob, I didn't recognize you at this number," she appeased as he yelled again. "Calm down and tell me what's wrong," she spoke quietly to mask her quivering voice.

"You $@#% cut off my phone, that's what's wrong!" There was a moment of silence and the sound of a motor running in the background. "I do business with my cell phone, Jules!" He cursed and continued, "Now, how are you helping the situation by doing that kind of $%@#? I'm stuck diving at a sand pit with no service . . ." He cursed and called her names that caused her to shrink back as if he was in the car with her.

"Jacob," Julia took a steady breath and looked at herself in the rear view mirror, "I am a Christian woman and you are a Christian man. Please do not use that language with me anymore." She tried to sound strong while setting her latest boundary. She hated that he used those words when he got angry. How could a man call his wife or anyone for that matter such things? It scared her and made her fear what he was capable of doing.

When they were first married, he started cursing during his tantrums. She remembered how shocked she was to hear those words come out of his mouth. After a while, he did it to provoke her. Once, she decided to show him how it sounded coming from a Christian mouth. Although he was driving, he reached over and choked her. She honestly thought he was going to snap her neck and she was going to die right there on the highway going to her mother's birthday party! Well, no more. She was not going to allow that kind of evil in their conversations anymore!

"#$@% words are not the problem right now, Jules!" he yelled again, "I had to drive to the nearest #$%@ town just to finish a business call. Do you know how that makes me look?"

"I guess you should have paid the bill," she stated, feeling strangely strong. "We now owe six hundred dollars."

"You #%$@! Then how is it your phone is still working, huh?" he screamed.

"I asked you not to use those words with me. Although I did nothing to your service, I will call the company, but for now, I think our conversation is over," she ended the call, as her counselor had instructed, feeling successful and scared at the same time.

The phone vibrated several more times before he gave up. She could imagine him damaging the payphone he was using. A memory popped into her mind of Jacob being so upset with someone on the cell phone that he tossed it right out the window onto the street! It was an expensive cell phone crushed in traffic because of his temper. Then he had to go through the hassle of getting another one. She shook her head at his immature behavior.

On the way home, she decided to listen to the messages he had left. Each one got worse, but the last flipped a switch in her. He threatened her life for the last time! Tears began to fall and she knew she could not live with this anymore. At home she washed her face to regroup. She was getting used to putting on a mask. Today was Wednesday and she would have to teach her young girls group at church. She must get a grip of her emotions. Before she left, she checked the cell records for the last time. Elma's number dominated his calls. The Coward!

Walking into the church, she smiled and hugged a few people as she made her way to where her class met. Thank goodness they always had an evening meal together first, giving her time to calm down. The meal was more than a reprieve it was a lifesaver, for she knew her girls would have a good, filling meal on Wednesday nights.

The pastor intercepted her and greeted her with his usual insincerity. She asked after his wife and he talked a bit about getting good news. He even thanked her for her prayers and again, asked nothing about her situation or welfare. *Heartless*, she thought and continued on to the classroom.

Noticing her quick exit from the pastor, Betsy quietly called her into another room making Julia feel as if someone in this church really cared. Tears streaming down Julia's face, she let out her pent up feelings and fears. Betsy wore a beautiful face of concern as she listened to the events leading to the last phone call. Julia was careful not to overwhelm her friend with the details, grateful for someone to care, hoping she would remain a true friend.

Betsy tried to relate, "All marriages go through rough times. Bob got angry once with me and pushed me into the flower bed."

Julia stared at her seeing that Betsy did not quite understand her situation. Today she had had enough and did not feel like being patient with ignorance. For once, she was going to go into the details. She was going to tell her story so this elegant woman truly understood. Blast his reputation! "Betsy, a push is one thing, but you have to understand, this is reoccurring and escalating. What started out as name calling and cursing has moved past breaking things and physically hurting me to threatening my life! Has Bob cussed at you and called you terrible names? Has Bob choked you? Has Bob threatened to kill you?" Julia burst into tears again and the woman placed a kind hand on her back in silence.

After prayer, Betsy ushered Julia to the pastor's office insisting she give the pastor another try. With her reassurance, along with her distinguished husband, Betsy was confident they could come up with a plan to help her. Julia felt like a complaining, pitiful woman when she finished retelling her story. Her emotions were riled, but she managed to keep most of it under control, reluctant to give him that much of a display. Heaven forbid she show how she truly felt inside lest he change the subject.

She would not want to be like the woman one Wednesday night that cried in the middle of the fellowship hall between the meal line and the drink table with not a soul caring for her pain. Julia had finally wrapped her arms around the woman guiding her to a place where they could pray. When it happened again the next Wednesday, Betsy joined her for prayer with the woman. Julia asked some women about the pitiful soul and they laughed claiming she cries all the time. Julia's heart sank for the woman and others that might be hurting among them. No way was she going to cry where they could laugh at her!

Like the other times, the pastor asked questions of the future. Finally, Julia did the unthinkable and asked him a question. "Why don't you ask Jacob these questions? Why is it that I am held accountable and he is not? Are we not both members of this church?" she straightened. "How are you going to shepherd him?"

He leaned back and pursed his lips, putting his fingertips together. Then he shrugged. "What power of accountability do I have over your husband?"

"What does the Word say? Go and talk to him. Take the Elders of the church as instructed in the Bible," she seemed to school him. "I am the victim trying to cope. Why am I educating you on what you should be doing?" Betsy lightly patted her knee to calm her.

"Julia," Betsy's husband carefully addressed her in his baritone deacon voice, "We have no authority over Jacob. We could go and talk with him but I doubt it would make a difference." Bob looked to her with genuine sincerity. However, in her hurt she did not appreciate how these men were taking no responsibility for their positions over the flock. Love is an action, a sacrifice. He had taught it in his own sermon! Without trying, they were guaranteed no reaction.

"We can only deal with the ones who are willing," the pastor answered.

Julia almost scoffed out loud. Her head swam in doctrinal training. She grew up in the church and had seen members under loving discipline. In time, those individuals were thriving again and their family was in joyful reconciliation. The pastor would work with the member that was prone to harmful decisions and if that did not work, then he would bring the Elders to help. However, this church would rather not address the issue than enjoy the blessing of becoming part of a member's testimony! What they seemed to be saying to her is that Jacob was not worth the sacrifice, nor the effort, or perhaps their own discomfort. Her heart was hard and in her anger she did not detect any kindness.

She almost chuckled shaking her head. "Fine. Help me then." She raised her eyes to the pastor behind the large desk, her emotions turning numb. "What should I do, Pastor Elden? I have spent a great deal of energy working on my pride." She raised her brows. "I am under your instruction. Please! I will do whatever you ask." Her voice was humble and she meant what she said with resigned obedience. She only hoped that he would not put her into the danger of couples counseling without Jacob first going through anger management.

The pastor shook his head. "The question is: what do *you* want to do?"

Julia looked at the faces in the office blankly. Was this some sort of 'Twilight Zone' episode? She was the one coming to *them* for guidance.

With grace, Betsy leaned forward to speak, "If I may, I think the first thing to do is to report Jacob's threat to the authorities. He then would be held accountable *by the law* to get help." She turned to Julia and took her hand, feeling so soft and warm. "Bob and I will go with you. When would you like to go?"

Bob answered, "Let's go now." He picked up his leather Bible and stood.

Julia nodded and followed, then hesitated, noting the pastor gathering his Bible and a notebook. "Are you coming with us?" She felt she might have misjudged the man.

"No. I have to teach a Bible class and am already running a little late." With that said he patted her back and left. He offered no prayer or parting words.

Julia watched him go as Betsy and Bob guided her out of the office and outdoors. Since it was a small town, they only had to cross the main road to reach the police station. Pushing her feelings about the pastor's indifference to the back of her mind, skepticism that the police would do anything replaced it. She felt unsure and yet knew this was overdue. Looking at her black nail, now being held together by a bit of skin and tape, she sat slowly to one side to avoid the pain in her tailbone.

The officer had his notebook and pen ready to hear her complaint. Now intimidated, she could feel herself falling into the mindset of overplayed drama. Was she over-reacting? Through her recent education in group therapy, she was aware of how victims begin to fall into emotional pitfalls. She remembered hearing that victims start to justify the abuser's actions and see their faults in how they reacted. They convince themselves that if they had done something differently, they could have avoided heightening the drama and things would not have gotten out of control. Oftentimes that is when the abuser comes and apologizes, creating a whirlpool of justifying the experience together. Not this time.

Julia now knew that no matter what her response had been, no one should harm her or threaten her life. She did not cause him to lose control and she certainly could not avoid it. Unless trained, no one would naturally handle abusive behavior in a productive way. Abusive behavior requires actions that are abnormal, against ones normal behavior and logic. This is the reason most victims of abuse learn to submit and appease. In doing the natural thing, she had spurred the abuser to increase the behavior to obtain the satisfaction of released emotions. This information freed her. She had decided to no longer be a victim. She was taking actions for true change.

She shared the threatening voicemail left on her cell phone. The officer put down his notepad and shook his head explaining that Jacob said he "felt like coming over and bashing in her head" not that he was going to do it. Julia stared at him for a moment and then raised her hand. "Does this look like he 'felt' like breaking my thumb?"

The officer leaned forward to look at it. "Looks like an old injury. When did this happen?"

"Just before Friday the thirteenth, June twelfth." she answered.

He sat back again. "Why didn't you call us when it happened?"

"He wouldn't let me," she looked down to her thumb pushing the nail back into place. She remembered him watching over the phone.

"There was a point in which you could have called. I doubt he just sat and watched over you," he eyed her.

Julia looked away. He was right, of course. She could have called when he went to the basement. She wanted to call. She almost did, but she forgave him. She did not know then what she knew now. Forgiveness did not mean that there would be no consequences or that she should not protect herself from another attack.

He interrupted her thoughts, "Look, I know Jacob and the guy is busy as heck. We tried to schedule our rescue dive lesson and it had to be scheduled a month out. So, I can't make out a report on the message because everyone gets mad and says things they don't mean. I can't make out a report on your thumb because it's an old injury and I can't be sure he did it. You *have* to call when it happens," he stressed.

"He says he is coming tonight to beat me up! I have proof he is capable. You can't do anything about that?" she squinted and looked to Betsy and Bob, who were respectfully listening carefully but saying nothing.

"If he comes tonight and breaks in the door, we can arrest him for that. If he does hurt you and you call us immediately, we can arrest him for that. Otherwise, we can't do a thing. He has not broken the law," he explained.

"He has broken the law. He has told me a thousand times that if he has to break down the door no one would be able to get to the house in time to stop him," she stressed, leaning forward uncomfortably, pain shooting through her tailbone down her left leg to remind her to stay in control of her emotions.

The officer raised his hand and let it drop. "But you have not called." He stood. "We will come by your house more often. Other than that, you have to call if he harms you or breaks something. Only then can we arrest him." He went to the back of his office.

Julia wanted to scream out of her frustration. She finally got the guts to do something legal about it and it was not enough. Evidently she has to be dead. She, of course, did not display this for her friends. She got up and headed out holding her anger back. Betsy and Bob walked her to her car. Julia hugged the woman and that was the end. Perhaps she was too unbelievable. Only until she got into her car and the couple had gone did she start shaking uncontrollably and tears began to fall. She needed a plan for tonight. She had no money to get a hotel and had to work in the morning. She needed to think.

After picking up the girls from the church and thanking Donna for teaching her class, she headed home. Suddenly Jan came to mind. She asked the girls if they wanted to stay the night with their cousins before school started. They were so excited and quickly packed. She gave Jan a call and as they pulled out of the drive, Brailey said there had been something on the front door and handed it over. Julia opened the envelope while they headed out of town.

Inside was a note along with a check from Sherry Nickels, a quiet, short, elderly woman who has led an early morning prayer time at the church since they moved to town in the 50's. She explained she was moved to give her some money and that her husband had already contacted several locksmiths who could come to their small town. Julia looked past the three numbers and read on. Sherry assured her that she did not know what was going on but felt that Julia should feel secure and have the locks changed. The check was for one hundred and fifty dollars!

Immediately, Julia wanted to use that money towards her car tag, but felt the conviction to do the right thing. If the Nickels felt led to have her locks changed at this moment in her life, she had to assume that God was preparing for something. It was an hour to Jan's house and she used that time to enjoy her girls, trying to calm her own nerves. On the way back, she would call for a locksmith.

Jan was not her usual, cheerful self and being a twin, Julia knew she wanted a few minutes to talk before she left. They went out for a walk around the block while Shannon and Jared played basketball and Brailey joined Mary to play with Barbies. Julia prepared herself to explain why she would call in the middle of the week for a sleepover. It certainly would not be easy since Jan never did like Jacob. She claimed he was not a nice person, and clearly she was right. Even in light of her blatant feelings towards him, she had been the most open of her three sisters for him to prove himself.

"I've been worried about you, Jules," Jan started out. "Something is going on with you and I don't mean just dropping off the girls tonight."

"I know. I don't really know where to start," Julia knew exactly where to start.

"Where is Jacob?" Jan asked.

"He and I separated a little over two months ago," Julia informed. "You were right about him, Jan. He is not a nice man. In fact, he is a dangerous man. I am so sorry I didn't listen to you." She stopped walking and looked at her sister. "You stood against me for my good and I didn't listen to you. Now I'm in a real mess," she confessed, feeling humiliated.

"Jules," Jan hugged her. "Don't. I'm just sorry for you. I wanted so much to be wrong about him. It's a good thing you separated. I'm proud of you." She stepped back. "Did he do this?" she lifted Julia's hand.

She nodded and pulled it away. "He isn't the man I fell in love with. I've tried everything. I did all that he wanted and it was never enough. I am in love with a man that is hardly around anymore. Yet, I keep telling myself he's in there. I have sacrificed everything, and now I don't have anything but my precious girls left. Just broken dreams and pain," she hung her head in shame.

"It's okay," Jan assured her. "I am here. Mom and dad are here. We will help you if you let us." Cautiously, her twin asked what everyone wants to know, "I have to ask, why didn't you call the police when he did this, Jules?" she motioned to her thumb.

"I've thought a lot about this, believe me," Julia sighed. "How do I explain so you can understand? To call the police is like starting my own house on fire. There would be no going back. By the time I wanted to call, he would become the man I love, repentant and kind. And well, we are taught to forgive."

"Then why didn't you leave? You could have come here."

"Jan, in a way it's like eating spicy food you know is going to be hard to digest. Why do you eat it? Why not stay away from it? You have the choice."

Jan laughed, "I ask myself that every time I have heartburn from the stuff. But it tastes so good!"

Julia smiled sadly knowing the conclusion of her small example. "Well, I love Jacob and he is great . . . most of the time. Sometimes he becomes indigestion. Everyone has their off days. It just becomes more frequent and severe over time. Unfortunately this isn't salsa; I married Jacob, bonded to him by a vow before God, and I felt like I didn't have a choice." She sighed, giving her a moment to reflect. "The truth is . . . to leave him has way more consequences than staying, as I am finding out. I have no income and I owe everyone, my house is a wreck, I have no friends, and I can't even begin to tell you how people react to all of this. And now Jacob is angry with me *all* the time. I feel like I have lost everything good in my life except for my girls. If I had appeased, he would be dealing with the debts, working on the house, and I would have time to figure out a better way for me and my girls. I kick myself for not being a better planner." Julia was trying to explain something she was only just beginning to understand herself.

Jan tried again, "But surely, now, you can go the police."

Julia nodded and started their walk again. "Jacob left a threatening message for me and I did go to the police but they said it wasn't enough to arrest him," she explained.

"Oh, Jules," Jan shook her head. "No wonder you don't want the girls there. You have to stay, too," she insisted. "I can't believe the police!"

"They are friends with him so they aren't going to go out of their way for me. Anyway, they can only do what the law allows. Look, I'm going back to change the locks. Plus, I have work tomorrow and I *need* the money," she declined Jan's offer. "Thank you for your help. Thank you for being a good sister to me." Julia draped an arm around her.

"Do you need anything else? I can give you money?" Jan asked.

She knew Jan and her parents had tried to help but she pushed them away in her stubborn belief that all were against Jacob. Even though Jan had taken extensive classes on abuse for her career and had tried to save her, Jan had learned to leave her in God's hands. Julia now knew that help had to be accepted by the victim first. Although she knew Jan desperately wanted her to stay, Julia felt the tug of responsibility for her financial strain and feelings of shame pulling her away. She began to doubt the validity of his threat making it seem more unlikely. She had only left the girls as a precaution.

"I'm going to be okay. I got a job and will be back on my feet in no time." Julia smiled. "I do find it strange that my phone has not been disconnected yet."

"That is weird. Did you call the phone company?" Jan questioned.

"No. I don't want to jinx it." Julia giggled.

After saying her good-byes to the kids, she thanked Jan again and headed home. The weight of the girls' safety was lifted, but now the finances took hold of her. How was she going to pay off a six hundred dollar cell phone bill? She had to make her car a priority since she was driving daily with illegal tags and no insurance. Yes, the first check had to go towards the car. She would have to take things according to priority, nibbling off the debt a little at a time.

Now, she needed to call a locksmith. Pulling onto the highway shoulder, she dialed one of the numbers. She did not get an answer. She dialed the next number on the list but, again, no answer. She sighed before trying to call the last number on the list. A man answered and could come out right away. She was in luck. The man knew who she was, thanks to the Nickels, and had been waiting to hear from her. What a blessing! Julia breathed thanks to God.

She knew it was time to call her parents as well. Her dad answered, which was unusual as he often was outside working on something. She was glad since he expressed more support than her mother. For some reason, her mother never accepted Jacob either and now her expressions showed disappointment. Perhaps it was for not listening to her and her twin sister. Perhaps it was because of the mess she was dragging them into.

Once, when they were alone, her mother advised that Julia hide her tax return money from Jacob. She remembered looking at her mother, a wonderful example of a Christian wife, and reminding her that the money was as much his as it was hers. Her mother said she was concerned for her and the girls and setting some money aside might be a wise thing to do. Julia remembered almost tearing up when she told her mother that she had vowed to love Jacob for better or worse. She had vowed that no matter the circumstance she would be the best example of a wife that she could be for her daughters.

She believed God would bless her, the marriage, and the family for her obedience.

Needless to say, she was glad to visit with her dad rather than her mother. "I have the totals on our debts now, Dad, and it isn't pretty," she chuckled a little to cover her embarrassment.

"Hold on, Jules," he called her mother over. "Okay, you're on speaker phone now. We're ready."

Julia sighed, she would be talking to her mother after all, and really, it was the right thing to do, just hard. "Well, as I said, I believe I have the total amount we owe, aside from the mortgage and what he might be hiding from the shop and personal loans." She felt herself tremble as she lifted the notebook into view. "It comes to $86,342.22 as of this week. Interest continues, of course." She held her breath for their response.

"Okay," her dad did not miss a beat, but she could hear her mother sigh her name. It was like a stab in the heart.

"I know it is a lot, shocked me, too," she tried to explain. "I honestly had no idea," her voice quivered.

"It's okay, Jules," her dad sounded matter of fact. "The important thing is to get the debts cleared up that are in your name."

"That amount is in my name, Dad," Julia answered somberly.

Now there was a pause. "Well," he started again, "What does he owe in his name?"

"From what came to the house, he owes $47,869 plus interest," she read the numbers and then added, "and I believe he owes back taxes. I do not know the amount but it must be substantial because he has bankruptcy lawyers trying to get a hold of him and one mentioned that if Jacob did not get back with him soon the IRS would be seizing his accounts."

Her mother sighed again and whispered that she was leaving.

"Okay, don't worry about what he owes. Let's take care of what is in your name. I want you to call the ones that are in collection and work on a pay-off amount. You can usually bargain down the amount since the company you owed has written it off and passed it on. I will get you a check tomorrow to pay them off. Okay?"

Julia wiped her brow but did not let on to her shame. "Okay, Dad. I'm so sorry. I will pay you back."

"It is not yours to pay back, Jules. Don't worry about the money. You have other things to be concerned about." He was a rock of comfort.

"Thank you again, Dad. Please thank Mom for me, too." Julia's mom did not handle disappointment well. When it came to fight or flight, she had the flight part down. When things were uncomfortable she would either change the subject to recipes, butterflies, or excuse herself and disappear. "I will . . ."

Her dad stopped her. "The money is the Lord's, Jules. We love you and it is here to help you and the girls. Jacob is the one at fault, okay?" he did not expect an answer. "Let's get this cleared up so you can concentrate on more important things like those granddaughters of ours."

She could tell he was smiling. "Okay, Dad. Thank you. Love you." They hung up. She felt like a loser and spent the trip home praying and giving thanks. It was relaxing to listen to the local Christian radio station. The words soaked into her like a dry sponge to a puddle of fresh spring water.

"You are my hiding place. You always fill my heart with songs of deliverance. Whenever I am afraid I will trust in you . . . I will trust in you . . . Let the weak say I am strong in the strength of the Lord. I will trust in you," the artist sang.

"I will trust in you," she whispered and a tear dropped. She did not have time to cry. She did not have time to feel. She had to meet with the locksmith and get through the night to make it to work the next day. She could not afford to lose any time from work. With God, all things are possible and no one, not even Jacob, can thwart His plans for her. God is in control and she would put her trust in Him. She wiped the solitary tear away and sang along.

From my experience, I realize that a lot of people have different views of what role they are willing to play in helping someone in an abusive relationship. Many times, the best help is being a friend. It is strange to me how one sentence from one person at just the right time stood out and caused me to rethink my "paved" thought patterns. I remember a family member, whom I was not very close to, said that I deserved better. That played in my head over and over, helping me to make the choice to go to the police. A wonderful couple offered to go to the police with me. Few understand the sacrifices-mentally, physically, socially, financially, and more powerfully the effects on our children's welfare-that leaving entails. I know . . . many of you have thrown your hands up in frustration. Trying to force steps did not bode well with me and staying away only alienated me farther from healthy relationships. I thank those of you who dared to be my friend during my time of chaos! I thank those of you who dare to be my friend during my healing! I thank you who cared!

Helping Someone Who Is Battered

Do you know someone who is abused?
- Do you see or hear about injuries that reportedly resulted from "accidents"?
- Is someone you know frequently berated or belittled in front of others?
- Does someone you know try to control a person's every move?
- Is someone often late or absent from work or quits their job because another person demands it?
- Is there a history of violence in the family?
- Have you noticed changes in her/his behavior or the child/ren's behavior or in appearance?

Steps for approaching someone you suspect is being abused:
- Let them know what you have observed—"I noticed the bruises you had last week and you look upset and worried today."
- Express concern that he/she might be abused—"I thought it was possible that you are being hurt by someone and I am concerned about you."
- Make a statement of support—"No one deserves to be hit by someone else."

Things to say to a friend who is afraid to leave:
- I am afraid for your safety and the safety of your child/ren
- It will only get worse
- I am here for you when you are ready to leave
- You don't deserve to be abused

"My, Lord! I hurt from his cruelness! Please, Lord, release me from this hurt. But I must be faithful even in darkness! My heart is broken! My finances in the black! O God! My life is in ruin for HIM! Heal me! I beg You, Lord, release me from this torment! Have I not put my face to the floor? It's just one thing after another! What will he do to me? I know You are in control. Praise Your name in all that I must endure. I will lean not on my understanding. I surrender again to Your will. I love You no matter what. I just hurt . . ."

Chapter Seven

The Battle

Donna was getting ready for bed. Her husband would not be home from work until after she was asleep. She did not mind, though. They had lived this way for twenty years and she was used to it. What she was not used to were her boys being gone. All four were in college now. She could not believe it. Stepping into the kitchen for a last drink, she felt a comfortable presence. Perhaps it was silence. She smiled.

As she walked back to her room, she thought about church tonight. It was strange that Julia did not come to class. She had seen her earlier walking towards the room and her daughters were in class. Something was amiss. Perhaps she should give her a call tomorrow. She turned off the light and crawled under a sheet, too hot for a blanket.

Her mind slowed and she could feel herself relaxing. She closed her eyes and allowed her mind to drift. It went to Julia again. She really did not know that much about her. They had worked on some church projects together and had gotten along. When the youth director asked if she would sit in on Julia's class, she did not have to guess the reason, having heard some complaints that Julia was not sticking to the Bible. After spending a number of weeks observing, Donna could only give a good report. She did not see anything of concern in Julia's teaching content and found herself looking forward to each lesson, feeling challenged in her own walk with the Lord.

She turned to her side. Although Donna was not in the loop for local rumors, she knew there must be a lot of talk about Julia around town. She was a lovely woman who spoke openly about Jesus and what He was doing in her life. Yet, she was separated from her second husband. Some have giggled at her pious attitude in light of her social decline. Donna had to hand it to the woman, though. She came to this little town as a single woman with two children and never missed Sunday school, church, or Wednesday night for years. She volunteered regularly and ministered in a variety of ways, more than could be said for those chuckling under their breath about her.

Donna turned to her back again recalling a time when they were riding together in a car, dropping off church kids at their homes. The kids had asked questions about how the world will end and Julia was explaining what the Bible had to say about it. In the middle of her explanation, Julia shifted gears and asked a girl, who only attended special church events, if she had accepted Jesus' gift of salvation. In a matter of a minute, she summarized a road map to salvation through the book of Romans. She started with chapter three explaining that everyone has done something wrong in his or her life and the consequence of that sin is death. However, she went to the last part of chapter six and stated that a person can accept Jesus' free gift of salvation from that punishment. Then, with words of delight, she ended with chapter ten verse thirteen where she explained that whoever wanted this free gift just had to ask for it. It sounded so simple and she was done just as they got to the girl's address.

Before the girl shut the door, she smiled and said she would think about it. Julia insisted that they all pray as they drove away from the girl's dilapidated trailer home. The next Wednesday, the girl was at church and shared that she had accepted Jesus' free gift of salvation. Julia was getting ready to help the girl's mother clean up their living situation and asked if anyone wanted to help. Donna remembered Julia's smile, a delight springing from deep inside. She just had to join Julia in the ministry and they spent an entire day cleaning together. She was now of the opinion that Julia was a remarkable woman with a love for people in need, be it physical or spiritual.

No, Julia was in a hard place in her life and here she was under the scrutiny of those that should be wrapping their arms around her. Donna did not know what was happening in Julia's life, but she did know that Julia really needed their prayers and kindness. With that thought, Donna went into prayer on Julia's behalf.

Upon arriving home, there was a white van parked along side the street in front of her house. Fear rising within her, Julia almost forgot that the locksmith was going to meet her there. His appearance when he stepped from the van did not help her insecurity, being a large man with long stringy dark hair, streaks of gray peppered throughout. He was the kind of man you would expect to crawl off of a Harley. Regardless, she had to gather her wits and greet him.

As it turned out, his manner was quite the opposite of his presentation. Her fear was gone in moments and they lapsed into conversation as he toured her home, counting the exterior doors. He did not ask her why she needed her locks changed nor did he ask any uneasy questions. He was full of stories and shared openly about his family. In fact, although it was after ten at night, she felt secure with him around.

Camael knew the signs. He had seen them before when Julia just entered high school. A group of seven boys bullied her to the point where she could not take it anymore. In a mental battle, she contemplated suicide, but Camael was able to bring to mind verses she had learned over the years, sweeping her internal library through her heart to salvage hope. Now, her mental stability was on edge again. She could only see the dark side of her church, the pastor, her family, and herself through the lens of her pain. If they lost today, she might lose hope and be open to making poor choices that would cause more suffering. The team would then have to rely on the children. That is, if she survived the night! Camael could not help but wish he had been successful in keeping Julia at her twin's house for the night.

Swooping overhead, Chayyliel pumped his massive wings once before landing solid in front of his leader and announced that the husband was parked down the block on a side street. Camael looked to where Chayyliel pointed and could see shadowy figures leaning against the vehicle. It was time to present Chayyliel as a bystander and motioned him to the roof. The powerful angel bolted to perch above the garage. When he exhaled the wind picked up and stirred even the dust on the street.

Camael shuttered, feeling the tension mounting. His team managed to block the other locksmiths' schedules so this one would be the only one available tonight. His appearance definitely had the fortitude to intimidate Jacob. He smirked. He would keep Julia engaged in conversation so she would not feel the tension around her home. With her occupied, he focused on Suriel.

This healing angel, who seemed to smile all the time, was small but had a significant gift. Her experience with healing was vast and her connection with the Spirit strong. Although she was older than he, she regarded him highly and requested to be part of his team when his Sealed entered crisis, which complimented Camael. She seemed to know his very thoughts and often did not need instructions to follow his orders. Camael was more than blessed to have her with him during these battles.

He went to the porch where Suriel joined him, lightly touching his arm. He looked down at her with a grin and her eyes twinkled back through a shadow of seriousness. He looked to the place where the husband parked. She stepped forward and vanished.

He was waiting for Ariel, who was again detained. He could not figure out why she was always late, but hoped for their sake this would not become a pattern. She was to rally support and from the looks of their robes, she was having a hard time. He sighed as he scanned the sky. Suddenly, he felt his spirits lifted and light begin to spray from the house. He looked down to see he was glowing and then checked Chayyliel, who was now standing on the roof like a beacon and loving it.

Rubbing his hands together, he was ready. He turned his sights to the house across the street and the vehicle a block down. In the light of their backing, he could see the Demonics and was taken back by their numbers. Overhead, he spotted Demonics circling. What was it about this couple that demanded so much attention? Clearly, the death of this marriage was necessary for their evil plans.

Jan sat on the floor next to all four kids. They had their heads bowed and hands folded. Each was looking beyond themselves and to that part of them that could reach beyond space. They were connected in the Spirit, drawing from a desire growing within. Together, on bended knees, they asked for protection for their loved one. Light sprayed from each chest dancing throughout the room in perfect harmony as communion with the Father united their hearts. The melody played within each mind the familiar words 'where two or three are gathered in my Name, there I will be also" (Mt 18:19).

Just before bed, it was customary for Jan to tell a story containing a Biblical principle or virtue. They knew she would have a few questions for them in the end to make sure the lesson was well understood so they listened carefully. This usually spurred on conversations until she had to force them to go to sleep. But, before she turned out the lights, they would pray together.

This time, in the middle of the story, Shannon interrupted and asked if they could pray right then. Mary jumped in excited for a commercial break. She loved TV commercials and lately was taking them seriously. So, for the past week Jan had been trying to teach about marketing techniques and that not everything on TV could be trusted. Mary was really hooked on one about giving to food drives and Jan could not argue against that one because she had taken a lot of time to explain why they were giving food to Aunt Julia.

Brailey jumped into position and insisted everyone kneel. Although Jan would normally try to keep them focused, she followed suit and allowed the disruption for the sake of the lesson, which was on the power of prayer. Each took their turn from youngest to oldest, as was the tradition. Afterwards, in an unusual twist, Brailey felt the need to take another turn and so Jan chalked it up as part of her free spirit. When Jared felt compelled, she began to take notice and decided to let the Spirit direct them. Soon, they were all on their second round of prayer for Julia. Jan smiled and silently thanked the Lord. *Jules certainly could use a little more prayer*, she thought, wishing her twin was in the safety of her home as well. It warmed her heart to see the children in earnest prayer. How could God refuse a prayer from these innocent little ones with such pure motives? She could see their faces glow with faith and remembered how Moses' face did the same from being in the presence of the Almighty. Looking up, she could feel the warmth of God's breath on her face as the third round of prayer began.

⟡

The locksmith excused himself to get more tools from the van after removing the doorknobs from the exterior doors. Julia sat in the house feeling a sudden flood of fear. Peeking out the front window, she looked down the street. The night felt heavy and extra dark. She began to tremble as she questioned her decision to return home. The shaking strengthened her fear and she thought to pray for peace. Not just for her peace of mind, but for Jacob as well. It would be wonderful if he could be busy or too tired to make good on his promise.

He usually did not follow through on his threats. The times he did hurt her were unplanned results of his temper. His frustration would build until he just exploded into uncontrolled, destructive behavior. Although she knew he was capable of anything and he liked to threaten, she believed it to be unlikely that he would follow through. However, he was behaving strangely, even for him. She peeked out the back door to the fence. Sometimes, he did do odd things. Irrational actions come from irrational thoughts.

Once, during a birthday party, he took her aside and told her that in the past he had worked for the mafia as a "strong arm" to collect money. He had added, "Once in the mafia, always in the mafia". She remembered being skeptical about the information and baffled as to why he would tell her this during a child's birthday party. Thinking over the information later, she determined he must have been in need of her attention. Now she wondered if it was true. Now she wondered if she ever really knew her husband at all.

As she stood by the back door, she warned herself not to underestimate him or his threats. It is time she gave his words the serious attention they deserved instead of dismissing them. Especially in light of the money sent to her for the locks. When they are changed, she would feel a bit better about her safety. Right now, she had a heightened sense of fear and was looking forward to when the brutish locksmith would return to the house.

~⚜~

Camael was standing next to Julia by the back door when three streaks of light catapulted towards him. In an instant, Ariel, along with Sablo and Zazriel, stood on the back lawn with a smile. "Welcome!" he greeted. "What are the girls' guardians doing here?" he asked Ariel.

"The guardians of the sister's family urged us to come," Zazriel explained expanding his muscular chest. "And since I trust Ansiel with my girl, I was more than willing. Plus, you may need a heavy lifter tonight."

"Very willing! And for the record, I trust all the guardians over there," Sablo pulled out his sword awkwardly. "Hey, with a little more practice I might get the hang of this doodad." He laughed with his golden curls bouncing.

"We will certainly need your help." Camael pointed to the Demonics circling above.

"Not just here," Zazriel lowered his head, "but they are moving back and forth from Wichita."

"It is true," Ariel walked to Camael. "There had to be . . . I don't know . . . legions of them." She looked worried.

Camael nodded. "The house is ours. They do not get into the house. I want the action near the husband. Zazriel and I will be the front line with Sablo as our rearguard. Ariel, you will fight tonight as our champion." He saw her gasp with wide eyes, but said nothing. "Do not fear, you will be in Wichita agitating Elma's husband," he grinned. "Tonight, we fight offensively with distraction."

"What of Chayyliel and Suriel?" Ariel glanced up at the favored champion sitting on the roof like an observer.

Camael noted the team's expressions of concern but dismissed them. "It is time."

He led them through the house to the front and stepped from the porch heading directly towards the SUV parked down the block,

96

ignoring the Demonics in the street. In a flash, he raised his sword and threw it like a javelin into the heart of the largest demonic by the vehicle. The demon fell and evaporated leaving a small red light that streaked across the sky away from view.

Camael had time enough to see Ariel take off like a rocket; so fast that none could keep up with her. He turned his attention to a demonic that was charging at him, sword drawn. Camael reached into his robe and pulled a dagger in time to run his blade down the demon's sword, moving it to the side enough to avoid damage and then plunging his knife into the heart of it. Again, it evaporated and Camael turned in time to reach back, grab his sword sticking out from the vehicle and push his dagger into a third demon while striking down another with the swing of his sword. As they evaporated, he glanced to see Zazriel punch a demon twice his size and then slice another in half with his gleaming sword, all the while singing "Onward Christian Soldiers".

Camael spun around to face the husband who was staring down the street with disgust. The angel then focused on Mastema, the demon of hostility.

Betsy tossed and turned in bed until her husband complained. So, she left his side and went to get a glass of warm milk. Sitting at the kitchen nook topped with a scattered assortment of magazines and papers, she decided to read for a while, but her spirit was still restless. She turned on the television. Flipping through the cable channels, she looked for something of interest.

Strangely, with over a hundred channels to watch, she could find nothing. Turning off the television set, she finished her milk and picked up the newspaper. As she looked over the sports page, her mind drifted to Julia's daughters. *Those girls are so precious.* She loved having them over for a day last summer. Betsy should have invited them again to her little farm. Brailey just loved the dogs and Shannon enjoyed working in the garden. It was a lot of fun to have young girls around again.

Her heart sank thinking of Julia. How happy she looked a couple of years back when she brought Jacob around. There were those that felt Julia should not see anyone because she was divorced. Since her first husband had died Julia didn't think it was an issue for her to remarry. Some people thought it was good for her to find someone, but getting married after only a year of dating was surprising. Most people in the community date for several years before making that big leap. Betsy thought, in light of her older age, perhaps years were not needed. But now, look where poor Julia was . . . and that poor house they are living in!

It was no coincidence that she ran to the church during her lunch break to fetch something from her Sunday school room just as Julia and the pastor met in the kitchen. She felt guilty eavesdropping, but was glad when she heard Julia's prayer after the pastor had left. She felt she was at the right place, at the right time, to do the right thing. It was a Divine Appointment set up by God Himself. She knew she could get Julia some help, even if the treasurer did not feel it was any of their business. Helping a single abused mother was what the Helping Hands Fund was set up for! She was determined to do more for Julia with that fund as well.

If that was not enough, the events of this evening were enough for the church family to step in and do all they could for Julia and her daughters. How the police could just ignore that message in a small town like this was beyond her comprehension. Bob could not stop talking about it all the way home! City council was certainly going to hear about this. It was rare for her husband to get so worked up, but when he did, things definitely changed. First things first, she needed to go to God. Tomorrow, she would call to make sure Julia was fine.

Her heart sensed the Savior call her name again more urgently this time. Realization crossed her face. "That's why I can't sleep," Betsy shook her head. After years of spending time with God, she should have known. "Well, next time just hit me over the head, Lord." Folding her hands, she went to prayer to talk with the Lord about Julia and what she could do to be an encouragement to her.

❦

The growing fear within her caused Julia to shrink back from the door and look to the phone. Perhaps she should have someone on the phone in case the locksmith was a wolf in sheep's clothing.

She grabbed her cell phone and flipped it open. It was just shy of midnight. Who could she seriously call at this time? Jan would need her sleep with all those kids. Betsy did say that she could call anytime, but after midnight? No, she was being silly.

Pushing the cell phone into her pocket, she went to the front door to wait for the locksmith to return. The van door was open and the light within illuminated him moving around. Glancing to the sky, the moon was covered by an eerie blackness in contrast to the glowing streetlight, casting its spell on her unsettling thoughts. Was Jacob really going to come? Was he watching her right now? She stepped out onto the porch and looked down the street just as the locksmith jumped from the van. A whisper of caution crossed her thoughts.

Suriel sat in the passenger seat of the red Expedition, invisible to both the eyes of the Sealed and the Demonics. She had been sitting among them for some time, getting them used to her presence before the battle started. Camael was a great strategist and when he shared with her his idea for her gifts, she was more than pleased to pull it off. Although it was always hard to watch such violence and do nothing, she had learned from experience that every battle has its moment of truth, where both sides realize that the outcome has already been written. The war was already won when Jesus rose from the dead and sat at the right hand of God.

She watched the husband, as his fingers tapped the steering wheel, no radio or distractions. He was quiet but restless with his anger apparent in his expression and sighs. When Camael's sword struck the demon, sticking into the vehicle, the husband shifted his weight sharply forward showing Suriel the bulge in his back waistband. The gun was present. She closed her eyes and asked the Lord that the gun would remain where it was. When she opened her eyes again, Camael was looking sternly through the window at her, though she knew he could not see her.

Ariel looked behind her to find a trail of demons trying to follow her. She would have enough time to strike the husband before they caught up. Thank the Lord that she was fast! Swooping down and dodging between the Garvey buildings, she bought herself a bit more time. Or so she thought. On the other side of Main Street there were three demons waiting for her.

Somersaulting, she was able to reverse direction and dodge into the backside of the Garvey building where an open food court waited dormant until the next workday. She jetted along the underground hall and shot out of the other side only for a moment before entering the second Garvey building. Rising up through the elevator shaft, she exited at the seventh floor and headed north to an old hotel turned apartment building. She raised another two floors before making it to her destination.

Spreading her wings, she stopped an inch from a man who had been pacing and now stood still looking out a large floor to ceiling window high above Wichita. She leaned close, carefully putting her lips next to his ear and breathed her words like hot vapors from a kettle. He winced as she bluntly declared that his wife was falling in love with her scuba instructor. She turned up the heat by asking him what he was going to do about it. His breathing quickened as he seethed with rage while she outlined the time Elma was spending with Jacob, texts and calls. Her truth was powerful and effective. She could see his jaw clench as he let out an angry growl signaling success. He had reached his boiling point. Ariel saw Azza through the window coming with sword drawn. Chayyliel was good to have warned her about him. She had just enough time to tell the man that he was a coward to say nothing about his wife's affair.

Suddenly, as if removing the kettle from the heat, she raised her wings and dropped five floors in seconds. Azza passed through Elma's husband and plunged after her. Ariel tucked in her wings and tilted to her side, shooting out of the building like a bowling ball toward pins. Demons tumbled away from the collision and others slashed their swords only hitting air.

Ariel glanced back in time to see Azza coming dangerously close. She drew her sword and held it down in front of her legs. As he struck, she pulled her wings in and tucked her knees to her chest, stabilizing the sword with her feet. The clash caused her to spin like a cannon ball out of control and Azza lost his grip on his sword, slowing him down to retrieve it.

No other demon wanted to get close to her as she spun with great force, lest they get harmed from her sword whipping around. Ariel did not know when she should open up, worried that the demons following her would strike as soon as she did. So, she shot over Wichita like a shooting star.

Jacob sat up and pounded the dashboard as he watched Julia step from the porch onto the sidewalk welcoming a man with a smile. It was well after bedtime. Pulling out a small pair of binoculars, he turned the dial in the middle while muttering some profane words. Suriel reached over and put her hand in front of the lenses distorting his view. Before he threw the binoculars down, she pulled back, enjoying Zazriel's tune outside.

Omias jumped up on the back of the seat, his toes curling around the headrest while he crouched over cocking his head this way and that trying to figure out if someone was there. He stuck his hand out through the space and passed right through Suriel, cocking his head another direction. Suriel cringed from the pain of his passing through her, but remained silent. She had to keep her eye on the husband, who was no longer in his seat.

She slid out unimpeded by the vehicle's boundaries and walked around Jacob to see clues as to what he might do next. The music stopped. Then Zazriel fell through her and landed at the husband's feet. She wanted to reach down and help him up, but stayed loyal to Camael's instructions. Sablo slid by and wiped out the three demons standing over Zazriel and pulled him up out of her view. Then, the moment she dreaded arrived. Jacob pulled out his gun and the silencer to put them together.

Suriel lowered her head and trained her eyes on the barrel of the gun, intently narrowing her concentration. Camael's outcry from Uzza's strike did not sway her. Omias and Mastema loomed over the husband's shoulder and muttered encouragement toward ending his pain, digging into his flesh with their sharp nails. Still, Suriel did not turn from her focal point. The gun raised and pointed directly in front of Suriel. She reached up and put her finger into the small hole on the end, her focus now on his eyes.

Omias screeched and Mastema dug his nails in deeper, light beginning to drift from the holes. Jacob narrowed his eye and closed the other. Taking a breath, Suriel came into view of the spirit world, her finger firmly stuck into the barrel of his firearm. She shouted in her high-pitched voice, "NO!"

Shocked by her sudden appearance, Mastema lost grip and fell off Jacob's head and onto the SUV. Omias stopped screeching, confused, darting his eyes from the Sealed to Suriel, like a crow taking in information and trying to process more than its small brain can handle. Zazriel had his back to her on one side and Camael on the other, both defending those trying to stop her interference. Sablo had backed up and was now between the vehicle and the house. Suriel noticed that Jacob's eye had widened and he was not as intent as before. So she pushed on the gun and shouted again, slapping the side of his pants where his cell phone was snug in its holster. The gun lowered slightly, pointing now directly into Suriel's face.

Omias began to screech yet again and Mastema flung himself back up on Jacob's head to regain control. The husband raised the gun, narrowing his eye to take aim. Gritting her teeth, Suriel touched his heart, but before any goodness could come of it, Omias hit her hand away still screeching. She made the effort with purpose, but the scrawny, angry thing would not allow it, hitting her. She eyed him and then looked at Camael for less than a second. Distraction was their offense in this battle, she reminded herself. So, she slapped the cell phone pouch again and it vibrated.

Climbing like a monkey around the husband's back to the pouch, Omias tried to get to the phone first, but Suriel flapped her wing over it. He opened his mouth and chomped down, ripping at her sensitive barrier. She did not cry out, but reached over with her free hand and touched its nose. Overcome by sneezing, Omias scampered to the ground and away from the battle, snot spraying everywhere.

The phone continued to vibrate. Suriel looked Jacob in the eye to speak to his heart, but a blow to her face sent her to the ground. With her finger removed from the gun and her wing no longer covering the phone, Jacob was open to their suggestions. She looked up to see Mastema coming for her and in an instant she vanished.

Before the demon could get back to the husband, he had lowered the gun and answered the phone.

⤨

Julia followed the man back into her house, but before she stepped through the door she thought she saw someone on a side street a block down. The locksmith distracted her with a question and she followed answering him.

⤨

"Elma? What's wrong?" Jacob answered as he slid into the SUV and closed the door quietly, laying the Glock on the console next to him.

As if someone had called a time out, the Demonics stepped back and turned their attention to the phone call. Camael took this moment as an advantage and silently sent orders to his team. He noticed Chayyliel stand up on the roof and pointing to Aboddon swooping down beside the white van. Camael took a couple of steps into the street to see what Aboddon would do next. He could see their leader taking in the clues as to what had been happening in his absence.

"Calm down, girl," Jacob continued his call, "it's going to be all right, I promise. He doesn't know anything because there is nothing to know. Don't worry about it. Look, I have a thing I have to do and then I'll meet you at my place." He rubbed his face and looked over to the house. "How long?" he glanced at his watch and sighed loud enough for Elma to hear his frustration. "Half an hour." He hung up and punched the car door, tossing the cell phone to the passenger seat.

Camael nodded to the gun and the safety lock seemingly engaged on its own. Mastema jumped down to the console and tried to take the lock off, but his nails would not cooperate, slipping when he thought he had the right amount of pressure. He did not notice the flickering image of Suriel next to the gun as she thwarted his efforts.

Camael threw his knife with lightning speed behind him. Zazriel caught it and with the flick of his wrist spun the knife like a skipping stone knocking three demons from their feet, whistling the tune of "O Be Careful, Little Eyes". Sablo leaped like a frog and took each of them out with his sword as Camael sprinted for Aboddon. Aboddon drew his sword and the Demonics went back into battle with full force.

As Aboddon struck Camael, Chayyliel snuck up from behind and grabbed him. He roared like Camael had never heard before and all the Demonics turned to see what had happened. Knocking the sword from the demon's hand, Camael took quick aim to rid himself of this enemy. However, before he could make the fatal blow, Aboddon shrunk and slipped out of Chayyliel's grasp. Uzza had come up rapidly to catch Chayyliel's attention and engaged him in battle. So, Camael chased the shrunken Aboddon around the van, but the dark foe had slipped underneath. Dropping to his knees, Camael fished for him with his sword before daring to peek at his whereabouts.

While glancing under the van, he saw the scrawny Omias scampering into the house. With heightened concern, he gave up on Aboddon and rushed after the annoying demon that had managed to penetrate their boundary. He entered the back room just in time to see the small demon laugh and leap at the locksmith only to fall flat onto its back. Camael watched as the idiot Demonic shook his head and tried again to enter the man. Again it fell back, this time rendering him unconscious. Camael chuckled and scooped up the demon with his sword, carrying him out the front door. With a loud voice he called for attention and then slung the sword into the tree in the front yard pinning the dangling demon to it.

For ten minutes, the husband had stared at the lit house waiting for the large man to leave. Suriel tapped his watch. With a groan of frustration, he pushed the gun back into his waistband and started the vehicle. Still unwilling to leave, he idled, keeping his eye on the house. Suriel tapped his watch more urgently. Then, with reluctance, he revved the engine and put it into gear, pealing away from the curb and racing right past the house to make it back in time to meet Elma.

Suriel was left behind where he had been parked during their battle. She allowed herself to be seen again by the spirit world and smiled at the remaining demons in her vicinity. The impact of her appearance and the husband's absence caused them all to retreat. She was tired and glad it was over. As she started toward Camael, she felt a sharp pain in her side. Camael, Zazriel, Sablo, and Chayyliel turned their eyes to her with shock and rushed to her aide, their swords striking any demon on the way.

Turning around, she faced Mastema, who was studying her. She looked down to see the puncture and the light flooding out of her. With her energy draining, she reached out and brushed his hand lightly before she crumpled to the ground. Suriel watched the demon whimper and screech as his hand started to shrivel. Holding it, he stumbled back and then staggered away.

Zazriel was the first to her side. He took her into his strong arms and shot into the sky towards Heaven, a mournful tune drifting down to the other angels below. Camael, Sablo, and Chayyliel did not follow, but the wounded angel could feel their offered prayers for her healing. As she pressed into Zazriel's hold, Suriel prayed for Julia. A single tear, a medicine of love, flowed from the corner of her eye and slid down her cheek before falling into the night.

The sound of tires squealing was just like Jacob. Julia hurried to the front door, her hand on her cell phone in her pocket. She looked out the door to see the taillights of an SUV turning off her neighborhood road. That could have been him. Shaking her head, she tried to decide if she should call the police and at least have them check it out. But, before she could make up her mind, the locksmith motioned he was ready to change the front door lock. With a sheepish smile, she stepped aside.

He apologized for taking so long and promised to be out of the way in no time. Feeling more at ease, she waved her hand in the air and told him to take his time, better to have it done right. This brought smiles to them both and he lapsed into another story. She listened and sat on the couch, feeling the long day begin to nag her for rest. Although she was thankful for his charisma, she was more thankful that he had been there most of the night.

When he finished, she wrote him a check and handed it to him with gratefulness. He nodded and did not even look at the amount as he slipped it into his top pocket that had a patch with "peace" stitched into it. She had not noticed it until now, just as he was leaving. With a twinkle in his eye, he laughed and bid her a good night's sleep, waving and still conversing with her until he was in the van.

Julia stepped out from under the porch and looked to the sky, wishing she could see God at work in her life. A drop of water splashed across her forehead and a tingling sensation washed through her as if she was being cleaned inside and out. Her left hand came to her forehead and rubbed the moisture between her taped thumb and finger. It had an unusual texture. The tingling continued down her thumb to the middle of her palm. Holding out her hand to the sky, she felt no other raindrops. The van roared to life and she slowly stepped back inside closing the door and turning the newly installed lock. Lightly praying her thankfulness, she went directly to her bed and fell fast asleep without even changing her clothes.

The white van drove down the block and when it turned the corner a flash of light disrupted the view of its course. Sophia flapped her wings gently as she approached the house, taking in the sight of Omias flapping about against the tree to get loose of Camael's sword. Smiling, she went inside to check on Julia. Stroking her head, she sang a song of peace and then went to find Camael.

The street was in a state of flux. Demons wanted their wounded and yet were leery about getting them with the angels still patrolling. Taking their time, the team came together on the front porch to assess the battle's success. Sophia watched as Camael called for his sword, it flew to him freeing the fitful demon. Omias dared to stick its tongue out at Camael, who pointed his sword at it with a threatening gesture. That was all it took for the rascal to take off.

Camael ruffled his feathers and then closed them in tight, telling the patient angels he was ready to address their concerns. Sophia looked over the group and noted that Suriel, Zazriel and Ariel were still missing. She glanced to the sky noticing a small light moving through the night, then turned her focus to her leader.

"The battle tonight was a success," Camael announced but raised his hand slightly. "But at a cost. Suriel was badly wounded and so Zazriel took her to the Father. She is in His hands. She will be fine," he announced confidently. There were audible sighs and heads dipped slightly. He continued, "We will have to be careful since we are now missing our healer. Still, we accomplished everything we set out to do."

A sharp thud turned all their attention to the street but Sophia could see nothing. Sablo stepped off the porch and looked up and then jumped back under the porch as another blur of light bounced on the lawn and back up into the night sky. Leaping to the air, Chayyliel chased after it leaving the rest in wonder. Sophia could not help but lean out from under the porch to see the ball of fire unfold and spread into a beautiful twirling angel of wings, hair, and flowing whiteness.

"It's Ariel," Chayyliel announced from above. "She's a bit dizzy, but she'll snap out of it." There was a hint of tittering in his voice.

"I cannot wait to hear about this," Sablo laughed as Chayyliel guided Ariel to the porch in less than a direct path.

"She looks so pretty with her hair all fanned out like that," Sophia pressed her smile trying not to offend by laughing as Sablo so easily allowed himself to do.

"Our Champion," Camael introduced as Chayyliel steadied her. "Glad to see you made it to our meeting." Even the leader could not keep from chuckling.

"Thank you," Ariel now giggled along. "I have to say, I've never been more effective in a battle than I was as a spinning ball."

Having enough of poor Ariel's disorientation, Sophia stepped up and with a quick pull sat Ariel on the ground level-headed. "Better?" she asked.

"Much!" Ariel stood up and gave her a heartfelt hug. Sophia was delighted in Ariel's openness and glad they could get everyone back to the meeting at hand. She greatly anticipated getting more information.

"As I was saying, our champion did a great job in distracting Julia's husband with Elma's needs. This not only divided his attention and diminished his anger, but also drove the demons back to Wichita and away from Julia. We saved her life," Camael nodded his thanks to them all. "Sophia," he smiled, "did a great job as a locksmith." He gestured to her and she took a slight bow. "We all can see why you have such presence with the Sealed," he joked and she had to smile. "We put the Demonics at ease with Chayyliel taking a roll of observer for this battle. Perhaps, if they feel he isn't a player, he will be unexpectedly more effective for the one that is coming."

Sophia straightened with the others when another battle was mentioned. This success seemed like a turning point. To all of their dismay, this was only a step closer and Sophia could expect to spend more time with Julia and this team. In a way, it saddened her. She was always hopeful for fast recoveries but when they persisted, her heart broke for the pain that the Sealed had to endure.

Camael continued, "As suspected, there are Demonic legions gathering in Wichita, seemingly spurred on by the break of this marriage. Aboddon is spearheading something much larger. Of course, Julia is *our* responsibility, but she is also the jewel in the midst of this chaos." Camael paused as his eyes filled. "Get ready. The Archangel is coming."

Blame is one of those words that still does not sit well with me. My abuser was wonderful at putting blame on me for everything and anything. In fact, I was good about putting the blame on me. It has taken a lot of counseling to get me to a point where I do not accept all the blame for things going on around me much less things that are happening to me that I do not have control over. Living in an abusive relationship is a journey of baby steps paved with acceptance and understanding. Although I am a college educated and well discerning woman, I found myself in an abusive relationship that was very difficult to leave. I was an excellent planner and organizer, but leaving required a great deal more than the resources I had at my disposal by the time I was ready. Blame only cripples the ability for a victim to make healthy problem solving choices.

Do Not Cast Blame

Do not ignore the situation. The problem will not work itself out. The violence will not end until *someone* takes action to stop it and will most likely increase with each incident. Domestic Violence is not just a family problem—**It is a crime.**

Your support and encouragement can be of tremendous value to a friend involved with an abusive partner. You can ease the isolation and loss of control she/he may feel by listening to her/him, providing her/him with more information on domestic violence, and helping her/him to explore options.

Do not blame the victim because she/he does not leave the abusive relationship. For most of us, the decision to end a relationship is not an easy one. A battered person's emotional ties to her/his partner may still be strong, supporting his/her hope that the violence will end. If she/he has been financially dependent on their partner and leaves with the child/ren, they will likely face severe economic hardship. She/he may not know about available resources or perhaps friends or family members have been unresponsive in the past. Religious, cultural, or family pressures may make her/him believe it's her/his duty to keep the marriage together at all costs. The partner may have used violence or threats of violence when she/he has tried to leave in the past. Many abusers use the child/ren to make their partner remain in the relationship by threatening to obtain sole custody.

Lend a sympathetic ear. Let your friend know that you care and are willing to listen. Don't force the issue. The average times a victim of domestic violence leaves an abusive relationship before breaking away for good is eight. Keep your mind open and try not to judge. The last thing a victim of domestic violence needs is to lose another friend—adding to their isolation. Focus on supporting your friend.

It cannot be overemphasized that **domestic violence is a crime** that can result in serious physical injury and even death. If you are a neighbor or otherwise know that a battering incident is occurring, CALL THE POLICE IMMEDIATELY. You can ask to remain anonymous.

"I surrender, Lord. I surrender to Your will. Though I feel weak and ground to the dirt, I will surrender. If You want me to take on more abuse, scoffers, accusers, and blame then I will do it. For Your will is good! You are my master and I am but a servant. Your will is my wish. Help me to be obedient, Lord! Help me to be strong enough to endure! I love You more than all others! Praise Your Name in suffering and in joy! Praise You forever and at all times!"

Chapter Eight

The Decision

Julia woke up late and had to skip a shower to make it to work on time. During stop lights, she put on makeup that Jan had slipped into her purse last night. As she put herself together she listened to the radio where Pastor Rogers spoke of the "dirty birds", which are demons, who snatch away the Word of God before it can settle into the hearts of men. She wondered if this was true for Jacob. He would often complain that reading Scripture did nothing for him. He had to see it or experience it to understand it. After a conflict, she sometimes would see him with the Bible open on his desk but his eyes focused on the ceiling. Perhaps the "dirty birds" were stealing the goodness from his soul.

She pulled into the lot and parked. With no time to hear the pastor's closing statements, she dashed into the back door and slipped her timecard through the slot. The clock beeped just when it turned eight o'clock. She smiled and made her way to her desk. Passing through the paint and photopolymer station, she got to see her work come to fruition. The Mexican-looking woman caught her eye but did not wave or smile. As Julia passed by, she nodded. Julia nodded back without missing a step, pleased with the gesture.

Ned was already at his desk and had a few files ready for her to work on. As she sat at her computer, Lloyd came by and asked how she liked the job. She was amused by his cowboy demeanor as he casually leaned on the desk. Her answer was positive and he tossed her a white envelope before moseying on. She opened it quickly hoping it was her paycheck. With a smile, she thanked God for His kindness. Yes, it was only four hundred dollars and, although she was used to making more, she was grateful. Today, after work, she would be legal on the road!

In spite of her lack of sleep, today was looking good. She opened her first file and started the hunt for the information she needed to layout fire escape signs for a Holiday Inn. Getting increasingly frustrated with their organization, minutes quickly ticked by as she continued her seemingly endless search. Minutes became an hour and a half. Her focus was loosing steam as fatigue set in. Julia sat back in her chair with a sigh and turned her eyes to the ceiling tiles.

"God, is it really going to be this difficult to find one file?" Julia questioned. "Could You give me a hint? And today had started out so good . . ."

"Hello, cutie," a chipper voice behind her interrupted.

Julia spun around to see a tall and rather good-looking black man dressed in the latest style of designer jeans and button down shirt tails un-tucked. He smiled back at her, the contrast with his skin made his teeth gleam along with the small gold chain peeking from the opening of his collar. "Hello, back," she returned the greeting.

"I'm Kealin," he stuck out his hand and shook hers. "So you're the newbie in the art department, eh?"

Julia could not help but smile. "Yes, and you are . . ." she motioned to the cart loaded behind him.

"I'm the mail man," he laughed and removed some tubes from his cart, putting them by one of the plotters, his snug sleeves showing off the muscles underneath. "I'm from shipping. It's pretty much a one-man department." He chuckled. "So, how do you like it here so far?"

"I like it very much. The work is good and the people are very friendly," she reported with sincerity.

"That's what I like, too. I've been here for seven years and have no plans of leaving. Well," he glanced to Ned and waved with a smile, "I better deliver. Have a good day." He pushed his cart, arms bulging again, to the sales department and she could hear him asking after their day as well.

This Kealin character was a breath of fresh air. She has known people like him before. They are always positive and bring a sense of fun to their environment. Of course, what goes up must come down in equal value. She waved back at him as he came through again, his cart much lighter.

Turning back to her search for the elusive electronic file, she spent another twenty minutes trying to find it, tapping into multiple hard drives connected to the system. Clearly they needed hard-drive maps. She pulled out her pen and made a note to bring up that option to Ned later. For the rest of her day, she worked on hundreds of maps and even got to help laminate some with Dali, a college student from India. Julia's thumb was so sore from the work, she could hardly keep up. But they managed to finish before she had to clean their area and clock out.

Her mind was so wrapped up in getting to the tag office that she almost did not notice Kealin waving at her from the side of the building as she slipped into her car. She smiled and waved back before shutting the door. Kealin was talking to another tall man who took a box before jumping into a supped-up black Explorer. Pulling out from the parking lot, she noticed a red SUV down the block by the curb. Her heart raced. Julia took a deep breath and gripped the steering wheel. Whispering a quick prayer, she drove the car towards him. She could see Jacob in his sunglasses staring at her. Julia held his gaze trying to decipher his mood while slowly passing. She jumped as her phone rang.

"You know, you *are* driving illegally, Jules," Jacob warned.

"I'm on my way to the tag office now," she openly shared.

"You better be careful or the police will stop you and then *you'll* be in a mess." He hung up.

Julia looked into her rear view mirror and saw him following close behind. Tucking her phone under her leg, she decided to take a different route to the tag office. Still he followed.

"God," she prayed out loud, "I'm afraid. Will he call the police on me? Does he know I went to the police on him? I know they are friends . . ." she let her mind race faster than she dared to drive, not wanting to draw attention. She made a quick turn onto a busy street so Jacob could not turn directly behind her. At the stoplight, she could see him three cars back. "Will I make it to the tag office?

Oh, Lord, please help me get to the tag office without a ticket," she pleaded.

The light turned and she made a right turn onto another main road, her heart pounding. After a couple of blocks, the red SUV was right behind her again. Her cell phone rang and she could see Jacob on the phone. Picking up her cell, she checked the number. It was her dad. She answered and made a left turn at the next light.

"Jules," her dad usually got right to the point, "the money should clear by Friday to your account. You let me know if you have any more surprises. Were you able to negotiate some of the figures?"

"Um, some," she looked to the mirror and did not see the red Explorer. Flipping her head, she checked her blind spot and saw nothing. Feeling the pressure to get to the tag office, she stayed on the main roads. "The credit card isn't in collection so they would not budge on the payments. Evidently, my wedding ring is in my name, too. So, they were not interested in negotiating that either. But guess what, I got my first paycheck," she tried to sound more positive, mimicking Kealin's attitude.

"That's great," her dad congratulated her. "As far as the debt, you did a good job in tracking and negotiating. I have heard that some companies will work with you. So, it is well worth the effort. Let me know how it goes," he was ready to go.

"Thanks, Dad," she felt the shame returning. "Thank mom, too." They hung up and she noticed a police car pull in behind her. Her chest pressed hard with the knowledge of her disobedience to the law. She knew she deserved a ticket for driving when she should not have. Almost ready to pull over without the lights whirling, she spoke aloud, "You are right. I should have worked harder to find another way without breaking the law, God. If I had not been so prideful, I could have called my sister or a friend or . . . someone," she confessed. "You are good, so good. I don't want to do things on my own, God. I need You and I need to hear You. Please, forgive me. And, if You would, show me a little mercy right now." She pulled into the tag parking lot with the police car following her. She exhaled and got out.

The officer approached her with his notebook in hand. "Ma'am, do you know why I'm here?" he asked.

"I'm told not to assume anything, but if I were to guess, it would have something to do with my tag." Julia could feel the rise of her emotions, wanting to cry to relieve the stress, but she kept control.

He nodded and flipped open his notebook. "Do you have a driver's license and proof of insurance?"

She searched her purse and pulled out her billfold. It was difficult to slide her driver's license from the snug plastic window. "I hurt my thumb so I'm having some trouble getting it out," she felt like she needed to explain.

"I can see that. Looks like your nail is about to fall off," he made his observation. "Hey, aren't you Jacob's wife?"

"Yes," she switched hands hoping to be coordinated enough with her right hand. Julia, diverted the recognition, glanced up. "Oh yes, you were on our dive trip to Table Rock." She smiled and finally handed her billfold to him. "Could you pull it out for me? The insurance card should be right behind it."

"That's right. How's the scuba shop going?" The officer continued the conversation while pulling out the license along with the stack of cards behind it.

"Um, I think really well. He has certified more than any shop in town and a lot of students are going on the dive trips to get their open water completed."

"How's he holding up under all that?" he looked at her.

"Well, I'm not sure. Jacob and I are . . ." She fished for the right words.

"You have a lot of older insurance cards here," he thumbed through them shaking his head, "and they're all expired." He looked up at her and watched her reaction.

"Oh. I'm getting that resolved today. I got my paycheck and headed right over here to get the tag fixed and then call the agent to get my insurance up to date." She showed him her envelop from work.

"Wait right here, Julia," he ordered and went back to his car to run a check. When he came back he said, "Ms. Anderson, you have a clean record and with all these older insurance cards I can see that you have maintained your insurance for years. Had you lied to me or justified your situation, I would not be as merciful as I am going to be. Go right into that tag office and get things straightened out. I got a hold of your agent and he is expecting your call." He nodded and returned to his car not mentioning Jacob or the scuba shop again.

She obediently went directly into the tag office. It was a long wait but well worth the peace of mind. Fortunately, she was able to call the agent while waiting in line and he worked with her to get her insurance updated at the same time.

"Thank you, God, for taking care of me. Thank You for showing me mercy. I know You had a hand in this because I am sure that officer would have given me a ticket otherwise. Knowing Jacob, he probably told the cop to scare me a bit," Julia guessed, "Thank You, thank You." Her chest filled with a warm glow and she sensed God's presence. She smiled and soaked in His peace as she sat in her legal car.

Her mind went to a memory of Jacob stopping a young boy in their small town convenience store and asking him if he was going to pay for what he had taken. She was so embarrassed since the boy was not even near the exit. Jacob had gotten a badge from one of his buddies to help with some drug busts in the Sedan area, which he never did. Looking for every opportunity to exercise his power, he created some situations. His fun was short lived; however, since he was asked to return the badge when they realized he had a felony for theft on his record from his high school years. She reminded herself to turn these memory flashbacks to something positive, as instructed by the online counselor. "Thank you, God, for getting that stupid badge back to where it really belonged." She grinned. Not exactly what the counselor meant, but she was okay with baby-steps.

She was just about home when Jan called to say they were about fifteen minutes away from dropping off the girls. The timing was perfect. They should arrive at the same time. With a smile, Julia was ready to switch on the radio for a sermon when she noticed a red Expedition coming up behind her fast. Her heart quickened as she kept her eye on it. At the last moment, it swerved into the other lane and sped past her. Cutting her off as it moved back into her lane, she had to apply the brakes to avoid a collision. She needed to focus, so the radio remained silent.

The Var filled with laughter, as the story got more and more ridiculous. Brailey had started it with a lovely young girl who was interested in getting ready for a dance. The story took an interesting turn as each person had a chance to add their ideas. By the time it was Jared's turn, the girl had mutated into a bad bunny bent on selling carrots to aliens, whose only interest was in shoes. Sablo held his midsection laughing along with the Sealed. Even the other guardians were chuckled at their creativity. The only one not laughing was Pashar, gifted with prophetic discernment. She enjoyed the entertainment with a pleasant smile but felt uneasy the moment they headed toward Wichita.

Pashar had many similarities to the one she cared for. Although Mary was stretching out to be taller than her classmates, she hadn't surpassed Pashar's height yet. The petite angel was glad for that. Mary had a darker, Hispanic complexion with very expressive features. At one moment Mary could have the sweetest face of an angel. At the next she could contort her brown eyes and bright smile to resemble a squirrel bent on revenge. Pashar liked to think she taught her such a gift as an infant by spurring on interactions with those cooing over her. Pashar's own expressive face would hover over the crib and entertain the child for hours. So she subtly bragged about Mary's skill at every opportunity.

But now, Pashar's face held an expression of concern. When they passed through the city, all the guardians were acutely aware of the heightened number of Demonics present, loitering around. While on the road to the little suburban town where Julia and her family lived, the feeling grew more intense. So, in spite of the fun around her, she could not let go of the thought that something terrible was about to happen.

Poking her head above the Var, she looked to the little town for clues as to what caused her anxiety. High in the clouds, she spotted the Demonics. One darted towards Wichita. Whatever was happening in that city, this town was going to play a part. She drew near to Mary, causing the little girl to lessen her giggles.

"You sense it, don't you," Zazriel quietly questioned Pashar. She nodded, staying silent. He looked at her suspiciously. "Do not fear," Zazriel slightly turned a smile while flexing his arms, "Mary will be safe."

Pashar raised her chin and opened her mouth, "Every word of God is flawless; He is a shield to those who take refuge in Him."

Zazriel recognized Proverbs 30:5 (NIV). "Sometimes He uses us to be His shield for the Sealed," he whispered into her ear.

Pashar tilted her head as understanding filled her, a glow came from her mouth. She whispered back, "Today, Mary is the shield." She did not divert her eyes from his.

Seeing the Holy Spirit flow through the petite angel to the little girl who was now calmly listening to the story as the others laughed, the gentle giant of an angel was curious as to what would happen next. Moving with amazing ease and flexibility so he could look into her dark eyes, he could see the strength built in Mary that was beyond her years. Pashar put her hand on the girl's shoulder and pressed down. Ever since Mary was old enough to understand the world she lived in, Pashar would press on her shoulder when she was needed. Most underestimate the power of ministry a child can have. She was lucky to have a parent that facilitated her child's gifts and was open to the leading of the Spirit.

Although strong in character, Mary was also quite sensitive. It was a wonderful combination. She could be bold without the consequences most of her kind would have to endure. Plus, the Creator blessed her with a sense of wit, allowing her to lighten the sting truth can have at times. This ability helped her keep friendships in spite of her brave words. Mary was a comedian and enjoyed making people laugh, her expressions added to her humor. The cousins often joined in on whatever accent she preferred for that day and even her mother would play along. Mary, like an actress on Broadway, played many parts. She was a leader, discerner, and confronter.

Today, Mary was going to be taking a step of faith and play the part of protector. If she passed the test, she could possibly save a life. Pashar knew the unsettled feeling within her was preparation for growth and with growth often comes pain. No guardian wants to see their Sealed suffer. Most will pray that their Sealed would be spared. Pashar was not like them. Pain was a wonderful tool to recognize that something was not right. Without pain, change could be more easily dismissed and lessons harder to learn. Hebrews Chapter 12 teaches that those who are trained by pain reap a harvest of peace and righteousness. This golden nugget of truth caused Pashar not to shy away from it for her Sealed.

As they pulled up to the curb in front of Julia's house, everyone inside grew quiet. Sablo wrapped his arms around Brailey and Zazriel pulled out his sword while lightly touching Shannon's top lip, shushing her. Pashar noticed the other two guardians doing similar movements, whereas she was mustered up her Sealed for action. Looking outside, she saw Aunt Julia talking to Uncle Jacob through the red SUV's window and looking upset.

Jan instructed the kids to go directly into the house as Shannon opened the side door. They did not run or make much of an effort to wave their welcome, but obediently filed into the house. Once inside, it was as if they were released to be themselves again. Jared made some joke about the bad bunny and they all began to talk over each other. Mary laughed and glanced out the front window, catching a glimpse of Julia on her tiptoes next to the idling vehicle. Then she noticed Shannon's glassy blue eyes staring out the window, too.

Pashar pointed as she spoke, "Mary, go get Julia. Mom needs her help." She pressed on her shoulder.

Mary sauntered to the door and looked out to see Aunt Julia gripping the side of the car door mirror. She could see something was not right and fear grew within her. Shannon came to her side, eyes dripping tears. Mary touched her shoulder as Pashar pressed again. Mary stepped out. Just then Zazriel came rushing to her, but Pashar motioned for them all to stay calm. She could see the soft glow coming from Mary's heart and knew she was not alone.

Mary walked up to her aunt, humming a little tune. Jacob let go of Julia's neck when he saw the young girl approach. Taking her aunt's hand, Mary said, "Mommy needs you, Aunt Jules. Hi, Uncle Jake." She waved at him with her free hand and flashed an innocent smile. Julia backed away from the SUV letting Mary lead her away. Inside the house, Mary let go and ran off to find Brailey, leaving Julia to rub her neck and take a couple of breaths before finding her sister. Zazriel wrapped his strong arms around Shannon, who quietly stepped into the bathroom.

Pashar was very proud of Mary and praised her by tickling her heart. Mary giggled, but Pashar was not at ease yet. So she joined the leader and his team by the front door to listen in.

"He isn't going to leave without his stuff," Chayyliel informed. "He has a demon of greed with him the size of Texas, Boss."

Looking stately with precisely trimmed dark hair, Camael nodded as he looked outside. He was the most careful angel Pashar ever knew. "Tell the demons they can have the garage temporarily."

"Really?" the young and athletic Ariel questioned. "He had her by the throat just a moment ago and now you are going to let him and the demons into the garage? I don't understand," releasing the words easily, she made her anger apparent.

With white feathery hair moving in the breeze, Sophia gently put her hand on the arm of the young questioning angel. "We must be peace keepers today." Her voice was soft, making Pashar want to know her better. "Camael is wise. Trust his judgment," she warned.

Camael waved his hand to the large angel, who went to open the garage for the husband and his entourage of demons. Then he turned to Pashar. "Thank you for your help," he nodded. She touched her heart and pointed to Heaven with a smile. She liked that this team had their own signal to give the credit to the Lord; they were just the means of His will. Camael grinned and ruffled his feathers.

Jared leaned forward on the couch and moaned, "I gotta eat." Pashar spied his guardian giving zerberts on the boy's tummy, the sound of the garage door opening in the background.

"Let's go to Big Jed's Pizza," Shannon announced Zazriel's choice as she came from the bathroom.

"No," Julia shook her head, but her eyes focused on the garage door to the house. "We can make something here," she went to make sure the door was locked.

"You know, pizza does sound good," Jan joined the kids, looking out the front window to see what Jacob was up to.

Sablo started chanting, "Pizza! Pizza!" and in turn so did Brailey. It caught on and soon all the children were chanting for pizza, including Pashar's Mary.

"Okay, pizza it is," Jan announced as her craving for Dr. Pepper danced on her tongue. "I'm buying." She grabbed her keys and the kids all marched out after her, making a run for it before Julia could change Jan's mind. Faith smiled her victory as she followed.

Pashar watched Jacob tossed the rest of the tools he didn't take the first time and more boxes into the back of his Expedition

without care of where they landed. Omias dodged each toss as it
frantically tried to escape. She knew the Father allowed the spirit
to continue because it caused more chaos in its own army than it
did anywhere else. She giggled at the thought. Although she was
concerned for the house, Pashar was glad they were leaving. Zazriel
patted her back and climbed into the Var. Sablo had the kids all
chanting for pizza again, while keeping his eye on the demons by the
garage. Camael, Chayyliel, and Ariel decided to stay by the home to
keep an eye on things and maintain boundaries.

At the pizza place, they had their pick of tables since the dining
room was nearly empty. While they waited, Jan decided to take them
on a virtual vacation. She told them to shut their eyes. Picturing
the descriptions, they each imagined how it must be to go to Paris,
France. She described their troubles in getting their luggage to fit
in the overhead compartment on the plane and even went as far
as to describe the man behind the desk at their hotel with his tiny
mustache. Everyone enjoyed their imaginary vacation all the way to
the top of the Eiffel Tower, and talked about the many wonderful
things they experienced as they ate their pizza. "I'll never look at Paris
the same again," Sablo teased.

Julia was in good spirits when they left Big Jed's Pizza. It felt
good to have a full tummy and to see the girls enjoying their cousins.
Life did not seem so bad until they rounded the bend and saw the
house from a distance. Trash lay all over the yard and down the
driveway with the garage door left open. The Var grew quiet as they
pulled up to the curb. Julia's mouth fell open and her heart seemed to
miss several beats, much like the aftermath before her.

In order to get the trailer out of the back yard, Jacob had decided
to rip out the wood fence. The gate lay on the ground and parts of
the fence were strewn beyond that, as if he just hitched it up and
busted through. Looking into the backyard, she could see the fence
destroyed there as well. He must have tried to go out the back way
first. Julia looked over the destruction without a word.

"What a mess!" Mary stated with an English accent.

"Indeed." Jan added flatly.

Without fear, Brailey opened the Var's slide door and headed for the front door of the house, skipping over some of the trash. The rest got out and followed, Shannon slowly made her way with trepidation.

Jared came up from behind Julia and draped an arm around her, "Mom says 'whoever makes the mess should clean it up'. Let *him* clean it up," He smiled and ushered her into the house. "If only . . ."she thought with a laugh.

Soon, they were all joking about how much more work it had to have been for Jacob to cause such a mess. Brailey started a scenario and then Mary added to it. Julia sat on the couch and listened as they warped the possibilities into ridiculous conclusions. Catching Jan's eye, she winked at her and they both snickered shaking their heads. Yes, it was entertaining to make fun of the situation, certainly lightened the mood. Still, deep inside, Julia knew Jacob would not be coming back to clean it up. She knew who was going to have to take care of the mess, as usual. She sighed.

Refusing to let Jan and the kids stay late to help clean up, they stood on the front lawn waving goodbye as the Var moved out of sight. Then, Julia sent the girls inside to do some chores as she went to the garage to survey the damage. It looked sparse at the back where the worktable was, but at least most of the materials for the house were left behind. Jacob had grabbed all the tools, ladders, and things he considered his, which her dad was now paying off. She wondered how she was going to finish the house.

"God, how can he do this to us? How does he expect me to finish this house? Does he even care that he has left me with no money, a gutted house, and now, no tools? I don't understand!" She wanted to yell her frustration but held it in.

The side door opened and Shannon poked her sandy blonde head out. "Mom, you had better come in," her clear blue eyes stark with apprehension.

She followed Shannon to the kitchen where the knife drawer was open. She pointed and Julia could see that Jacob had come into the house and taken all the knives, except for the dirty one in the sink. She went to check the lock, which was fine. Her mind raced about how he had gotten in. Then her eyes went to the sliding glass door. She could see it was off its track and leaning against the entrance.

Her heart sank. She would have to do something to make it secure tonight. She and the girls worked with it for at least half an hour to get it back into its track and closed properly. Unfortunately, the latch had been broken and would not lock anymore.

She considered calling the police. After all, they did say if he broke something then they could arrest him. Unfortunately, he left the garage door open allowing anyone access. She could never prove it was Jacob. *It must be nice to break the law whenever he likes and not have to pay the consequences,* she thought with sarcasm. A verse whispered in her head, "Do not deceive yourselves, no one makes a fool of God and man will reap exactly what he sows (Galatians 6:7-GNT)." She sighed and felt a little better.

Julia thanked the girls and let them go play in their rooms as she went to the end of the pool sidewalk and sat down, her new habit for thinking things over. For reasons unknown to Julia, this place seemed to draw her. It was quiet and felt safe. She could think clearly here. Perhaps, it was because of the open sky and warmth of the sun. Looking around at the debris from his exit, she could not help but feel overwhelmed beyond her limit. She could not cry. All she could do was sit and feel sorry for herself and her children. She sat for a long time, thinking, hurting.

"Who takes the knives?" she questioned the only one that could hear her, the only one that could understand what she was really going through. "God, what am I to do now? I feel like giving up." She thought about the knives again. "Were the knives a message?" she turned her eyes to the clear sky half expecting an answer. A gentle breeze swept past her cheek and left an idea.

With a burst of energy, she jumped up and ran back into the house. Going from room to room, she took anything that was his or reminded her of him and put it into a box. Three boxes later, she came into the unfinished basement bathroom to find a message scratched into the old mirror leaning against the wall over the vanity. The words 'watch your back', double lined with the reflection, stared back at her. Shaking, she moved back until she sat on the end of the bed.

How deceived she had been! Hooked into believing that her love and sacrifices would be rewarded with God's blessing of a lasting Christian marriage and a restored husband, she had believed in a mirage. She honestly thought that through support, fasting, prayer, and kindness she could win Jacob back to the charming, thoughtful man she had fallen in love with. "With you by my side, I can change," he had said. Now, staring her in the face, were the words of reality. He did not love her. He was not going to change. His words and flowers from before wilted in her memory.

Getting up, she remarkably felt nothing, emotionally drained. She grabbed the box with the last of his things and went to the garage to put it with the others. Then she noticed that he had left behind a rather important item high up on a shelf, a dive computer possibly worth a thousand dollars. No doubt, he would realize that he does not have it and he would want it. Her thoughts began to churn as she realized she could sell it and use the money to quiet the bill collectors. Holding the computer in her hands like a rare jewel, she felt conflicted.

The phone rang, postponing her decision. Grabbing a pen and notebook, she answered to find it was the IRS. *Not another stress*, she thought. The man was specific in needing to talk with Jacob directly, although she explained she was his wife. He, in turn, explained that Jacob needed to call him immediately to settle his past tax debts. When she asked the amount, the man would not disclose the information. She explained her situation and the inherited financial debt. The man carefully chose his words in saying that the amount was significant enough for her to get a lawyer.

Now was as good a time as any, she thought as she pulled out a phone book and opened it to the attorney section. There were so many listings that she did not even know how to decide. An ad stuck out that had free consultations, so she dialed and was surprised to get a live person so late in the evening. She asked about her obligation to pay her husband's IRS debt, sharing that they never did their taxes together or shared accounts. Thankfully, this put her in good standing of not being responsible for *his* past taxes. With conviction and legal understanding, the lawyer strongly suggested a divorce. She now was given three firm suggestions for divorce: the pastor, her parents, and oddly enough, the tax attorney. She turned her attention to divorce lawyer ads, looking at the pictures until she found a friendly face, a woman by the name of Patricia Swallow.

After making an appointment for August twenty-fifth with the answering service, she started to gather the records she would need to get things rolling. Was she really going to get a divorce? Did she have Biblical grounds? She did not know if he actually slept with Elma, but the relationship was clear, even by his own admission. He had also broken every vow he ever made to her. She needed to protect herself and her girls. As long as she was married to him, he could come into the house and the police could not do anything about it unless he broke something or hurt someone. Was she really going to wait for that to happen? It would be irresponsible to do so!

Either way, she needed legal advice. Somehow, she was going to have to get twelve hundred dollars together for the retainer fee. Julia looked at the dive computer. Could she sell it without retaliation? Christians are to be peacemakers. There had to be another way. She learned *that* from the car tag ordeal. Surely there was help for women like her. Taking out the phonebook again, she looked up anything that might resemble a crisis center. Armed with only three numbers, she started her quest for outside help.

Unfortunately, the search was cut short. It seems without a police report there was no aid available. She did not have a report since the police would not write one without immediate proof. She asked about counseling but the only opening was during her work hours on Thursday afternoons. So, she decided to take up their offer for a lawyer at a discounted price. After calling, she realized she was not going to be able to afford it since they billed per minute even with the discount. "*What discount?*" she muttered.

"Why is it, God, this has to be so hard for me? I tried to do the right thing. I loved and forgave him like a Christian wife should. I tried to give him a chance to change. Because I did, I can't press charges until he hurts me again? I have to put myself and my kids into harms way in order for the system to work? It doesn't seem right," she complained. "Do I have to go on Oprah for help?" she now whined.

She set the phone down and slumped into a chair. Ironically, she had called the YMCA's women's crisis hotline, which employed her abuser as an instructor of scuba diving. She had even worked with the YMCA on marketing scuba to the Wichita and El Dorado area. Shaking her head, she thought about how she was going to get the money to crawl out of this unending pit her own husband dug for her. She suddenly had a new appreciation for Joseph imprisoned in a dried well by his jealous brothers. At least she had some freedom. She smiled as a thought occurred to her.

Julia called the girls and told them they had to get out of the house and do something. She needed a break from the walls around them. Brailey mentioned a bike ride so they all hopped on their bikes and rode all over town until it got dark. It was a good game of follow-the-leader while working off some of the stress. By the time they got home, they were ready for some tomato soup and rest. After devotions, she tucked each of them in and sang the goodnight song before closing the doors.

Needing a little more time to unwind before bed, she downloaded a sermon from "Leading the Way" with Dr. Michael Youssef. Half way into the lesson, the phone rang. Since it was so late, it could only be her sister . . . or Jacob. It was the latter and he wanted his prized possession: the dive computer.

When Julia mentioned the mess he left behind, he yelled that she was the one who caused all of this to happen. Had she been the Christian wife she claimed to be, she would have submitted to his authority as the head of the house. Jacob quoted scripture defending his God given right to demand respect and obedience. Julia knew this lecture by heart for it was the only sermon he knew and he liked to preach it often. He continued to yell on. If she were not so controlling, he would not have had to defend himself all the time. He was tired of her !@?# and was ready to move on. She was too difficult to live with and maybe she needed someone to beat her to get some respect. She felt powerless as she sank into the pit of guilt and intimidation. Julia calmly replied that the dive computer would be in the mailbox and hung the phone up. Then she called the police and asked them to check on her before she took Jacob's computer and boxes out to the mailbox. Knowing him, he was probably just down the street.

> *Yes, I remember when I was my abuser's "light" and everything he said to me was kind and complimentary. Slowly, over time, he became more and more critical. I went from a professional woman who took care of herself, to a pitiful looking woman who worked at home unless my husband wanted me to accompany him for his work. In my constant appeasement and submission, I did not realize that I no longer got mail, answered phones, had access to money, or had friends or family in my life. Oddly enough, his spin on the situation was that I was a controlling woman who was too difficult to live with. He rallied his family, friends, and our church to his perspective and they supported him fully. I don't blame them. I fell for his persuasive tactics, too. I have learned since, those things that he accused me of doing were usually the things he had been doing. He needed reassurance I was not doing to him what he was doing to me. Ironically, reactions to abuse often manifest in controlling behavior towards things that victims can control, therefore, substantiating the abuser's case.*

Warning Signs

The abuser becomes more hostile, more often. Incidents of intimidation increase as well as demands. The victim's self esteem is driven down in preparation for the assault (physical or otherwise). The victim will think that it is about anger, when it is really about control. This gives the abuser an immediate advantage because the victim is trying to appease him/her.

The victim reacts normally to the irrational behavior of the abuser causing the cycle to continue. As the victim adjusts over more exposure, the reactions diminish causing the abuser to make stronger threats to get the initial reaction they need to reset. Thus, what started out as throwing something in anger develops into physical harm and sometimes death. Without professional help, this cycle will continue. It is not about the victim, it is about the abuser's need for control.

Physical Abuse

TWISTING ARMS

TRIPPING

BITING

PUSHING

SHOVING

HITTING

SLAPPING

CHOKING

PULLING HAIR

BEATING

THROWING HER DOWN

USING A WEAPON AGAINST HER

PUNCHING

KICKING

GRABBING

ISOLATION
Controlling what she does, who she sees and talks to, where she goes.

EMOTIONAL ABUSE
Puttin her down or making her feel bad about her self.

ECONOMIC ABUSE
Try to keep her from getting or keeping a job. Asking for money.

INTIMIDATION
Putting here in fear using looks, actions, gesture, destroying her things.

Power and Control

USING MALE PRIVELEGE
Treating her like a servant. Making all the big decisions

SEXUAL ABUSE
Making her do sexual things against her will. Physically attacking the sexual parts of her body.

THREATS
Making and/or carring out threats to do something to hurt her emotions. Threatens to take children.

USING CHILDREN
Making her feel guilty about the children using the children to give messages.

PHYSICAL ABUSE

"My life is Yours, Lord. I once had a dream that I would be a wife and mother. My husband and I would raise our family and be in ministry, building God's kingdom. I had no delusion about perfection in marriage or my husband. In fact, I embrace differences as a way of pushing me to try new ways of living life. But when did I accept abuse? You know I desire to share my life with someone forever, but, Lord, my dream is dead, even with this second chance. I hand You my dream, a dream You created in me as a child. By Your grace, give me a new one. Please give me a passion for something else!"

Chapter Nine

The Divorce

Riding shotgun for a dive trip with a bunch of Demonics was not Chayyliel's idea of a fun vacation. He knew the man was sealed, but that did not mean he had to like him or what he was doing to his family. He swung his fist over his shoulder and knocked Omias from his headrest. That creepy thing stank something foul. He could only hope it had enough brains to learn to stay away from him.

Looking at Jacob, he could see how the man could constantly deceive people. He was a good-looking man with blonde trimmed hair, light blue eyes and a stocky build like a football player. God created him to be strong and charming, gifted in gab. If only he would listen to the Holy Spirit and learn how to use that gift, he would be a rich man serving God with a guardian by his side. Instead he was in constant discipline, his pockets full of holes. The man could make money, but he used his gift for selfish gain, which only brought him trouble, chaos and never ending unrest.

At the gas station, Chayyliel got out of the truck with Jacob and the dive team to stretch. Even the Demonics felt cramped with all the passengers. Taking a stroll to the gas meter, he watched as Jacob prepared to swipe the Discover card to prepay for his gas. With quick reflexes, Mastema pushed his fingers into the slot as Jacob pulled the card through. The machine flashed an error message. Jacob swore and swiped it again. Mastema interfered again excited by the frustration he caused. Chayyliel shook his head knowing Jacob was going to have more money problems throughout this trip.

A large demon came around in time to see what was happening and pushed the angel's shoulder away from the meter. Chayyliel narrowed his eyes, ignoring Jacob's swearing as he swiped his card again. Standing straight, he stepped back, unaccustomed to being pushed by anything. The demon moved around Jacob to face Chayyliel almost as if to challenge him.

"Your name," Chayyliel ordered.

"Vapula," it answered low and slow, accentuating the consonants.

Chayyliel knew Vapula only by reputation. It was a demon of science and philosophy. It was constantly creating disorder with false logic and was a genius. This evil spirit was known all over the world as Evolution. Chayyliel watched as Vapula wiggled its hand through the hose, its eyes glowing red. Chayyliel studied it with interest until Vapula was finished. Then, with his fast reflexes, the great angel pushed the demon's shoulder knocking him through the meter. Mastema clung to Jacob in amusement. Vapula roared as it fell to the other side and snapped to its feet glaring at him, eyes dimmed to gray.

"Go away," Chayyliel ordered and watched it reluctantly back away to the other side of the vehicle. Jacob was finished filling up and ran into the store to grab a pop. With some joking around, he got everyone loaded back into the Expedition and pulled away heading south to Dallas, Texas where they would board a plane for San Juan, Puerto Rico, the cheapest route from Kansas.

Chayyliel opted to stay at the gas pump to see what Vapula had accomplished. The next car to fill up was a Honda. He settled down into the passenger seat, while another guardian reclined in the back, and prepared for the start up. It would be interesting to see how a small car takes the kind of gas Vapula had conjured up. A young Vietnamese girl got into the driver's seat and turned the key. She then turned it back off. The motor had purred so nicely that she could not tell it was running. She turned the key again and put it into gear. The Honda, with its new passenger, took off like a brand new luxury car and did not need to gas up again, though she drove until midnight before stopping at a hotel. There Chayyliel decided to leave the peaceful ride and get back to task.

⚜

At work the next day, Julia's mind was on her lack of money. Before bed she looked into their emergency Discover card and found it maxed out to the tune of four thousand dollars! *The Creep*, she sneered under her breath. The charges showed that Jacob was heading to Puerto Rico again. During her break she checked the scuba blog and it confirmed his trip. She sat back and wanted to scream. She takes phone call after phone call from debt collectors and he goes on a dive trip, which rarely made any money in the long run after paying for dinners and tipping generously to look successful.

Dipping her head for a prayer of forgiveness, she noticed Lloyd coming around with a clipboard taking down names. Overhearing that he was offering overtime to volunteers, she was quick to his side to see if she was eligible. He looked at her and asked if she was up for some messy jobs and she nodded emphatically. With a grin, he put her name down on the list. Five in the morning on Saturday, she was going to get some overtime. She was going to get a bigger paycheck!

The rest of the day was a breeze. She sat in her car during lunchtime so people would not ask why she was not eating. She used that time to crunch numbers and make arrangements to settle debt with the money her father had given. She had no idea why her phone stilled worked when Jacob's had been turned off, but she was not going to complain. Of course, she was going to pay some of the phone bill when she got her next check, but until then, she was biding her time and thanking the Lord.

By the end of the day, she had met a number of other employees that were going to be doing overtime tomorrow as well. She wondered if the Mexican lady would be there. She would like to get to know her. By the time she made it to the parking lot in the back most everyone had left, eager for the weekend. She did see Kealin, however, visiting with a fellow leaning on the black Explorer she had seen before. She waved and he walked over to her.

"Hey there, cutie," he flashed his smile and walked with her a bit. "Didn't see you all day. How'd it go?"

"Fine. I got on the list for overtime so I'm thrilled," she smiled and pulled her keys from her purse.

"Oh yeah?" he laughed, "I'll be there, too. Can't beat time and a half!" he lightly slapped her on the back.

"They pay more on weekends?" She did not know that the rate would be higher.

Kealin laughed harder, "It's the law, girl. I could tell the day I met you that you had never worked in manufacturing. You've never been paid hourly, have you? What did you do before coming here?" He stopped by her car.

She dipped her head and shrugged, "I was married and now I'm . . . well, you're right. I've never worked in manufacturing." She looked away at random cars.

"Hey, sorry to ask. Didn't mean to get into your personal business," he turned sincere and she felt a little stupid about opening up as much as she did. It was never a good idea to bring your personal life into work.

"No, Kealin, I'm sorry," she smiled. "I'm trying to get back on my feet now. I'm sure everyone has their sob story, so I don't want to bring my drama up," Julia explained.

"Look," Kealin took hold of her shoulders and looked her in the eye, "we are like a family here. You're part of that family now." He removed his hands. "So how many kids you got?"

Julia had to chuckle at how he managed to bring things to a light note without awkwardness. "You're all right, Kealin. I'll show you some pictures tomorrow, okay? Gotta get going." She unlocked her car and opened the driver's side door.

"Have a good one," Kealin waved already half way to the back door of the shop.

"You, too," she shouted back and carefully got in. Sitting for a moment before turning the key she thought about the extra money she would get for doing overtime. Quickly taking out her notepad, she jotted down some numbers and smiled. With the overtime, she might be able to pay the phone bill off.

The girls were in rare form when she got home. It was their last weekend before school started. She wished she would be able to take them to their first day, but she had to leave before they did to make it to work on time. So, she was determined to make their weekend together a fun one. Proclaiming that Saturday would be their lazy day, the girls cheered and were already making plans to watch *Anne of Green Gables* all day long as a movie marathon. Since they did not have cable, they only received three good channels. With little interest in broadcasted shows anyway, Julia had gotten into the habit of going to the library to check out movies for free. She smiled and motioned for a library run. Racing on their bikes to see who would get to the library first, she slowed down to let Brailey get the best of her.

Moments later, Julia stood by the door of the library talking with an acquaintance while the girls check out the movies. "I didn't know you did graphic design," Tabby exclaimed while letting her dog off the leash so Julia could pet her.

"Graduated with a graphic design degree but built a career in television animations for commercials over the past decade," Julia knelt to scratch the Dotson behind the ears, which made the little dog lean in for more.

Tabby thought aloud, "We've wanted to start some art classes with the recreation center. Would you be interested in teaching a few?"

Julia stood up with a big smile. "You bet. I'm in bad need of some income and this could be an answer to prayer, Tabby."

"All right, you could teach over at the middle school art room after school hours. Just write up a class summary and we'll get it in the paper," Tabby held out her hand and they shook on it.

"Guess what, girls," Julia gave the dog another pat before heading out, "I've got another job!" She whooped and pushed the door open. "And now I'm gonna beat you both home." She dashed to her bike and gave it a shove as she mounted. The two girls came barging out in hot pursuit.

Waking up at four in the morning was like starting up an old model A for the first time in twenty years. Julia rolled out of bed and stumbled to the shower. Still, she made good time, grateful for the much needed income. There was quite a group at work and they took no time in getting busy. From what she gathered, the big wigs were coming to town and Sign & Tech Graphics wanted to pass inspection with flying colors. The entire interior was going to get a fresh coat of paint and once they found out she was good with a brush, her job became cutting in around the trim.

Somewhere around eight in the morning, Lloyd came through to see how everything was going. He did not stay long and she could see the group shift to a more relaxed manner, visiting and taking smoke breaks whenever the need urged. She liked it. One by one, as she moved around, she got to know employees and something about their lives. Likewise, they felt free to ask her about her life. A bit unsure about sharing, she tried to skirt around anything too personal.

She met a black woman named Shanna, whose husband left her with four kids and was just now buying her first house. When they were alone, she warned Julia to be careful around Debbie, the decals and final assembly supervisor. But before she could say why, Debbie interrupted them. The supervisor was a petite woman with a spunky personality. Although loud and somewhat amusing, she had a definite leadership quality about her that Julia liked. As it turned out, her husband was the supervisor of the wood shop where her brother also worked.

Julia found it fascinating that a company would employ so many family members because most companies make it a policy to keep free of possible family issues. They allowed dating relationships as well. Everyone seemed open about these connections and even the issues between employees. Thus, a few asked about her status and she was quick to report that she was married.

Kealin was there and came to sit with her during the lunch break. She intended to continue working, but Debbie insisted that she go outside to get away from the fumes. She found it interesting that no one clocked out even though the break lasted well past the thirty minutes allotted. She knew it was not right to be paid for sitting and visiting with cute Kealin so, when the guilt overcame her, she went back to work.

Most people left five hours in, after taking the lunch break, of course. A few stayed and she was thrilled to be one of them. Just short of eight hours of work, an older woman showed Debbie some signs that had been done wrong. So, Julia offered to stay even longer to correct the problem, leaving just the three of them working in the building towards the end of the day.

The older woman teased Debbie by asking how many bruises she had this week. Debbie bragged she was accident-prone and could not help it. Julia also discovered the older woman, Gwin, was married to the police chief of Eastborough, a town swallowed by Wichita but unwilling to admit it. Julia could not help but think that he was the one that gave her husband a ticket once. She had warned Jacob to never speed through that area, but did he listen? Julia snickered to herself.

Finally, the signs were perfected and their small party was tired, calling it a day. Julia calculated her time as she went to her vehicle with a spring in her step. She had put in twelve hours of overtime and every dime she got was for her to spend the way she wanted. For years she could not spend anything or go anywhere without her husband's say. Now, although the money had to go to his debts, she got to say which one and when. It was a small victory, but one that gave her a great deal of satisfaction. She called the girls. There would be enough light in the day to go rollerblading yet.

Camael sat at the dining table with Sophia and Ariel. "She is worn out," he observed. "I am concerned about her and the church is not able to aid her as I had hoped."

Sophia fanned out her wings and then pulled them in. "Camael, God does not give more than they can handle. He stretches her for His good. The church is also under stress as they look for a Shepherd." She turned her eyes to Ariel. "So young and passionate you are," she spoke more for Camael's sake. "God has placed you here with us to grow. Soon, you will be stronger and wiser, ready for the Great War, the Tribulation."

Ariel perked up. "Truly?" she questioned with excitement. "I was not sure if I would be chosen for such a great honor!"

Camael pointed at the younger one, "You see?" he shook his head. "You are too eager and ignorant. That Great War will be full of sadness. *These* are the battles of wonder that turn hearts! The Tribulation is for the lost . . . few won, many lost." He stood and went to the antique French doors that barely stayed closed when latched. "The End will be different than what you see here. This woman is a saint suffering for the actions of another Sealed. I have been with her since God breathed life into her and she has always had a heart for our Lord."

"If the husband is Sealed, where is his guardian?" Ariel questioned, confused.

Sophia dipped her head. "The husband has stepped away from God."

Camael turned and went to the other side of the room to stand by the sliding glass door. "God is always calling His loved ones to Him, but they have free will. Some choose to ignore Him. Some choose to defy Him. He disciplines them so they will remember Him. When they close their hearts to Him, they cannot hear His Word, His guidance. They walk away from His protection by their own choosing," Camael looked to Ariel to emphasize his next words.

"At any moment, the Sealed can turn back to Him and He will reconcile with them instantly. It takes nothing but a repentant heart. Then, the protection returns, the guardian restored, the relationship growing fuller than before." He smiled and spread his wings. "It is a glorious moment."

Camael felt revived and ready to plan. "Let's talk about this church." He smirked. "I think I have an idea."

The alarm went off and Julia did not want to wake up. Still, she had to get going so the girls would not miss Sunday school. Just the thought of church made her groan anymore. Ever since she could remember, her family always went to church on Sundays and Wednesdays. Anytime someone was going through a rough time, the church pulled together and help them through. She wished she had that.

Singing the *Good Morning* song, she woke Brailey and Shannon to get ready. Julia swept her hair up into a clip and washed her face. Makeup was a luxury still, so she would not use it except for work. God would understand.

At church everyone was full of smiles and polite greetings. It all seemed so superficial to her with exception of Betsy and Donna, who made sure they came by and asked after her and the girls. The pastor seemingly avoided her, which she preferred. Then there was Abigail, whom everyone called Abby. Seeing Julia, she made a beeline to talk with her. Julia looked for an alternate route, but it was too late.

"Julia," Abby reached out and squeezed her arm. "How are you? I just heard about your . . . troubles," she put on an expression of concern.

Julia pasted on a pressed smile and appeased, "Yes, well, we are relying on the Lord." She made a movement towards the table in the classroom to set down her Bible and purse down.

"I am so sorry," she kept hold of her arm and then moved in closer. "What ever happened? You two seemed so happy," she almost whispered.

"Well," Julia searched for the right words, "we all have things we need to work on. I do thank you for your concern." She tried to keep her smile though it was wavering.

"You can count on us. If you need anything, I mean anything at all, someone to listen, I'm here for you," Abby stressed and then hugged her long in front of the whole class. Julia felt embarrassed and very uncomfortable. She hardly knew this woman and considered her the "busy body" of the church. She would not trust this woman with the intimate details of her life for anything. Everyone in town would be well versed on her troubles, with Abby's complimentary commentary included.

"Thank you, Abby. I appreciate that," Julia nodded and sat down hoping the woman would not sit next to her.

Abby patted her hand and placing her things right next to Julia's, took the chair to her left. And so, Abby patted her hand from time to time giving her a knowing look so others could be suspicious of what has happening. It was humiliating and Julia could not wait to get out of Sunday school and sit with her kids during the service. However, even throughout the worship time, she felt Abby's eyes on her, along with a few others that found this sudden friendship interesting.

Like a racehorse, Julia grabbed her daughters' hands and bolted out of the church for home as soon as the last prayer ended. The walk in the warm sunshine did her good and cooled her temper. Brailey and Shannon shared what they had learned about the Beatitudes and she began to lose speed feeling ashamed of how she treated Abby. It was possible that she had good motives and was sincere about her invitation. Asking for forgiveness, Julia cleared her conscious and then asked that God would help her to see Abby in His perspective.

Shannon let go of Julia's hand and adjusted her Bible making an offhand comment, "Ms. Abby sure was friendly today." She sighed. "Oh, by the way, this was in our church box." She handed her a gift card for the local grocery store.

Ariel winked as she took off for Abigail again. The woman was stuck with the demon of gossip, causing her to be a source of folly for others. This cost her integrity of which her guardian angel was fully aware. Ariel felt sorry for the poor guardian that trailed the busy body constantly having to pick her battles. Strong and callused, the guardian angel was like a survivalist with true grit. Camael warned Ariel that it would be tricky to get past this guardian to do her work. Her mission was to nonchalantly intrigue the attached demon's curiosity in order to use Abby's temptation for gossip. If done correctly, Abby's persistence would push Julia to where she could get the help she really needed. Agitating the demon worked well and Ariel felt assured that she could get the job done.

Ariel had simply swooped down beside the guardian and asked her if she had noticed that Julia's husband had not been around, more for the demon's sake than the guardian's. The demons ears tingled for the information while the guardian signaled Ariel to remain silent. Ariel played on her youthful innocence and continued to ask questions. Realizing this was going to be a lost cause, the tough guardian gritted her teeth and folded her rough arms refusing to answer. Ah, but the demon reacted beautifully. Ready for another round, Ariel made her way to the woman's home to find her guardian ready to fight even a fellow angel for her Sealed, which was commendable. Ariel was coy and asked different questions to ensure the wanted action until the guardian dismissed her with force.

Delighted that her first assignment with Abby was successful, she moved onto her second with Betsy, who was in need of a vacation. The poor dear had a CEO husband that had flown all over the world and yet she had not even been out of the country. Their girls were grown and out of the house, so there were no more excuses. Ariel would make sure of that. A soft glow illuminated from the woman's heart as the Holy Spirit whispered "Spain". Ariel smiled wide, planted her feet in the woman's kitchen not budging until Betsy could think of nothing else. Ariel was beginning to understand that God never forces people, they have free choice. However, He did allow her to persuade and with Betsy so determined to help Julia, even if it meant forcing a revival on the reluctant church, God had a different plan.

⁓≈⁓

The lawyer's office was posh and the people working there were dressed to the teeth, literally. Julia snickered, as the fashion today was to have bright white teeth only achievable through cosmetic treatment. She wondered what Patricia Swallow would look like.

She shifted her thoughts to the divorce. It should be simple since they were broke and most everything was worthless. He would not want the house because he could not afford to fix it up. He would likely walk away from it anyway, like most things he committed to. In fact, the news was saying it was this kind of attitude that had caused the economy to teeter on a deep depression. Julia related.

A receptionist, labeled as "executive of first impressions", called Julia's name and showed her to a conference room where Julia put her folder on the long shiny table and sat back in a padded leather chair. She knew her parents would not mind if she used their money for the retainer fee. Eventually, someday, she would pay them back. For now, for the sake of her and her kids, she had to protect herself from Jacob's poor decisions.

Patricia came in with a limp and shook her hand. Although she had the same look of success as the rest of her colleagues in the office, she had a genuine trueness to her manner. Julia instantly knew she had found the right person to represent her. In fact, as fearful as she was about sharing her story, it came out without much reluctance. Patricia listened with true concern and then gave her advice: emergency divorce.

"Isn't there some sort of legal separation that can protect me and my girls and yet keep me right with the Word of God?" Julia wondered out loud without asking if Ms. Swallow even knew the Bible.

"Julia," Patricia looked her square, "God made marriage as a sacred union to be a testimony of the relationship Christ has with the church, a forever bond of lasting love. He never intended marriage to be what you have experienced. God hates divorce, true. He hates reoccurring and unrepentant sin as well. The wages of sin is death. That is why God allowed Moses to set up guidelines for such marriages, because of the hardening of hearts. Even Jesus gives the exception of marital unfaithfulness. Jesus is a perfect groom, but Jacob has broken his vows to you and abandoned you. He has chosen another woman over you and refuses to give her up. He intends to harm you. He is not repentant, which is proven in his consistent behavior. Jacob's heart is hard and he will not change without treatment and," she leaned forward and touched Julia's hand, "certainly not without turning to God."

"He is Christian man. He is a good man," Julia's eyes welled up as she defended her husband, "He just . . ." Then she realized what she was doing. She had heard it from others in her group meetings and now she was doing it. She was defending a man for who he could be not for who he had chosen to be.

"Listen to me," Patricia removed her hand, "He is not a good man." She let that sink in before continuing. "He may be a Christian, but his actions are not those of Christ's. He treats others better than you and you are his wife, the one he vowed before the Almighty to love . . . and protect." Then she pointed to Julia's thumb, the nail gone and the new skin pink with sensitivity. "This is not love, Julia. Good men do not hurt their wives." She tilted her head. "You have done all you can. You have tried to reconcile, but he has free will. Although you have done nothing to deserve this, you need to get a restraining order at the very least. The best you can do is to get an emergency divorce or you will continue to suffer the consequences of his choices. This is what I advise as your counsel."

Julia nodded as she looked at her thumb. She had studied the subject of abuse long and hard and knew what Ms. Swallow was saying was true. "We can't say anything about the abuse though. I don't want him getting any more upset than he is already. And he needs to keep the business going so he can pay off his debts."

"Okay," Patricia pulled out her pen, "let's go a different route then. I will need to get a listing of all the debts . . ." Julia pushed a list to her. "Great. And your assets?" Julia pushed that list to her. "Looks like you were on your way to that divorce after all." Patricia glanced at her. "Have you been to the doctor for that thumb?"

"No. We don't have health insurance and he left me with no money," Julia's eyes were full of tears but not one drop escaped.

"You better get it looked at. Have you seen any medical professional at all?" Patricia glanced up again.

"Well, I went to a chiropractor after . . . when I hurt my back." Julia fiddled with her thumb testing the tenderness.

Patricia held her pen to her chin. "Was it because of some accident related to Jacob? Perhaps something that the chiropractor could attest to that you needed medical care for but you did not return for more treatment?"

"I suppose," Julia now looked at her curiously.

"Do you think you could get a signed statement to that fact?" Patricia asked.

"I think so. I told him the truth as to how it happened because he knew that my excuse was bogus. He could attest to that but I don't want to upset Jacob. I don't want him to come and . . . do anything," Julia slowed to a whisper.

"I understand. What I'm trying to find out is if we can say he withheld treatment from you. If we can establish that, we can get the restraining order and the emergency divorce without mentioning the abuse," she explained.

Julia was relieved when she left the law office. Patricia was a Christian woman who had a way of comforting her. It was a big step that Julia did not want to take, but she felt God was telling her to let him go. God always gives her three powerful and irrefutable confirmations when He wants her to do something big. Yes, God is in control.

⁓≈⁓

Sophia walked through the door labeled "Conference Room" glowing with a grin and a twinkle in her eye. "There is proof that not all lawyers are spawn from the Devil," she giggled as she pointed to the light escaping from under the door. "It was amazing! Her guardian need only whisper and she responds. I wish all the Sealed would have such a close relationship with their Creator."

All eyes turned to see two women emerge from the room. The professional woman gave one last encouragement to her client before concluding their meeting. As Julia headed to the exit, the elegant lawyer limped to her personal office followed by an ancient guardian who pleasantly nodded with a smile as he passed the team. Light spraying from Patricia's heart as she closed the mahogany office door gave proof she was already lifting their Sealed up to the Father in prayer. One by one each angel began to shine brighter and brighter feeling the support given.

"I wish she knew she had Biblical grounds for a divorce since Jacob has been unfaithful. It is done anyway. She will call the chiropractor for the statement," Sophia concluded her report as she had started, with a giggle.

Camael nodded with a slight smile in sadness. "I suppose I had better get over there then," he said with a sigh. "I am glad for the support for I understand he is a difficult man."

"Yes, he has a number of demons he struggles with so be careful of those that hide within," she advised.

"I will," he assured. "You be careful, too, Sophia. I'd hate for something to happen to you. In the absence of Suriel, you are much needed."

"Do not fear, Camael, I can be anyone or anything," she smiled. "I will camouflage myself and penetrate their headquarters to get the information. Perhaps I will be back to the house before you, the Father willing." She turned to the window and flew away.

"I will expect you," he added wondering what form she would take to disguise herself so the Demonics would not recognize her. He hated to fly through Wichita now that the Demonic traffic was so thick.

The meeting was set with Dr. Mueller for the end of his day. This gave Julia just enough time to get home and see how the girls' first day of school went. She believed in supporting local businesses;

therefore, when she did not improve after she fell over some paint cans months ago, she went to see the local chiropractor. He knew right away that her excuse did not coincide with her injury and so she confessed. In a way, Julia had hoped he would call the police for her so she would not be to blame. In a weird twist of fate, since it was small town, he said he would keep her confidence and he did.

He charged less since she did not have insurance and she paid in cash. Even with the payment reduced, one visit was all she could afford. In that time, she understood why he was known as a good 'ol boy. He acted as if he was a professional but his manners and humor were definitely crude. Either way, he was going to be her aid to an emergency divorce. For that he would get her business in the future should she or her kids be in need.

When she entered, they locked the doors but sat right in front of the street side window. *Nothing like being in a private meeting in full view of the public!* She tried to calm her discomfort and explained her situation while he had his wife write out a dictation. After working together on the wording, he referred Julia to his wife for payment and left the room. Not expecting to pay, Julia sat for a moment as she slowly pulled out her checkbook and lined the numbers. This was going to be a set back to her budget. She walked out with a signed statement which she practically wrote. No, she would not be going back there again.

The next day at work she made copies of the statement and faxed it to her lawyer. By the end of the day, she got an e-mail stating that the restraining order was filed and the emergency divorce sent. There would be a thirty-day waiting period before it was final unless Jacob signed off on it to make it effective immediately. Otherwise he could appeal it and drag it out to September twenty-fifth. Right now, he could do nothing since he was enjoying himself in Puerto Rico!

Camael paced as he tried not to worry about Sophia. It was already the next day and she was still gone. In fact, his team was down to four. Chayyliel was with the husband in Puerto Rico. Suriel was with the Father. Sophia was missing in action. If only he knew she was still concealed he could be more patient. He looked to Heaven hoping for revelation. Nothing.

The flapping of wings spun him to the bay window. The sound was too powerful for it to be Sophia. Chayyliel swooped down and came in strong, as always. Breathing heavily, his large frame passed through the house exterior wall as he stepped in. Folding his wings, which never really pressed tight to his back, he nodded to Camael ready to report.

"The husband is with a group of four business men, who are going for fun, and some policemen, who want to be certified rescue divers. He has no more money, the card he carried no longer works, and now he owes one of the men a pretty heavy debt, which I believe, was by evil design. The number of Demonics with his party is great, a legion."

This surprised Camael. "A legion?" he wished he had Sophia's information to make a good analysis.

Nodding, Chayyliel added to his information, "One of the business men proposed a way for him to pay back the money by running drugs. If Jacob can get the shipment into the United States without getting caught, he will forgive the debt and will offer a great deal of money to continue working for him."

"Drugs?" Ariel leaned on the bay window folding her arms. "Can we sway him?"

"No. Our orders are clear," Camael answered flatly. "This is what Aboddon has been working on. This is what Sophia was to discover. Chayyliel, you must go back and see what he decides. Ariel and I will go find Sophia. The guardians must stay with the girls." He was visibly shaken. "We need Suriel. Father, will you allow it?" he looked to the heavens in earnest prayer.

> *I have to say I was pretty ignorant about the law in regards to Domestic Violence. Most often my abuser "only" verbally threatened me and then there were some "minor" physical assaults. The truth is verbal threats and minor assaults are illegal too! Had I taken a strong stand from the get go, I would not have had to suffer as I did and my abuser would have had accountability and possibly professional help. It wasn't until I was finally ready to seek a legal separation that I was encouraged to get an order of protection and go through the process of an emergency divorce. Honestly, I was surprised at how much security it gave me knowing that if I did have to call the police, I wouldn't need to explain a thing!*

Protection from Abuse Orders

Orders of Protection—Any injunction issued for the purpose of preventing violence or threatening acts against another person.

Before you can get a protection from abuse order you and the other person you want protection from must meet **one** of the following requirements:
- You are in a dating relationship (a social relationship of a romantic nature);
- You have been in a dating relationship in the past;
- You are living together;
- You have lived together in the past; or
- You have had a child in common
- AND
- Abuse must have occurred. This means that one of the following has occurred:
- The person physically hurt you or a minor child on purpose.
- The person tried to physically hurt you or a minor child.
- The person recently threatened to physically hurt you or a minor child.
- The person engaged in sexual conduct with a minor child under 16 years of age.

The order prohibits the defendant from abusing, threatening to abuse, or disturbing the peace of the plaintiff. The defendant is also prohibited from being on or near the property where the plaintiff lives.

You CAN get help without an Order of Protection or a police report from many organizations!

"Thank You, Lord, for Your loving mercy! I know I do not deserve so much. I thank You for the job. I thank You for the funds. I thank You for Your help. Now, help me to make You my all. Only there will I be happy. Help me to be content with only You then. Broken hearts are too hard to survive. Forgive me for being weak . . . for wanting . . . for hoping for something You clearly don't want for me. I want to choose You. I want to be what You want me to be. Help me to desire that. Help me to become that. Amen."

Chapter Ten

Desperation

Finding Sophia was going to be more complicated than Camael expected. First, he had no idea where she was and would not be able to see her if she was in camouflage mode. It was certainly going to be a hit or miss mission. Not impossible, for with God all things are possible. Nevertheless, since her whereabouts had not been revealed to him, he would do as ordered to the best of his ability. "There is always a reason." he reminded himself.

With Ariel as his rearguard, they flew over Wichita drawing little attention from the Demonics. For now, he needed to get a scope of where they were settling. For the most part, they were in clumps as lookouts at the four corners of the city. Looking down from an even higher perspective, he could see the concentrated effort in the middle of the city one block west of Washington Street over a distributing company's warehouse. Interestingly, Julia's workplace was one block east of there. More than likely, the warehouse was where he would find the Demonic's headquarters. If he were Sophia he would start there.

Motioning to Ariel, they dove for the presumed heart of the Demonic's Wichita headquarters. The closer they got to the warehouse the more demons flew with them. In swarms of evil, they landed on the roof. Neither Camael or Ariel pulled their swords. They walked the length of the building studying of what they saw, demons

145

moving around them. At the end of the roof were larger demons waiting to confront them.

Camael looked them over, standing to one side of them and then moving to the other side. Then, as if he dismissed them, he stepped off the roof and spread his wings to drift down to the ground, Ariel now dropped back with watchful caution. He stood before the front doors where another set of large demons stood guard. Camael did the same with them as he did above, looking them over before skirting around them and into the building.

This time the guards roared out a warning and more demons came to usher the angels through the interior of the building. Camael allowed them to hover, but did not always go where they directed. Twice he veered off to peek into offices, thumbing through papers and looking over the rooms' contents. Ariel, on the other hand, became more and more wary, her hand resting on the handle of her sword with her eyes trained on demons' actions.

Soon, they walked right into the office where powerful demons lined the walls and two beautiful angels sat waiting for them. Camael gave the demons little notice but the two angels had his complete attention. This was more than he had expected and although he did not show his sadness, the sight of his own kind in such a place weakened his heart.

"To what do we owe this honor, Camael?" Amon asked in a pure tone while pulling a white feather from his wing.

Camael knew of Amon, one of the infamous fallen angels, but had never been in his presence. He was known for entrapping his unaware prey by catering to their desires. Seduction and manipulation was his game. Rumor had it that he was now a commander of over forty legions of demons. Most of the fallen angels that were not bound had high-ranking positions due to their superiority. Camael knew he did not have to answer him and considered remaining silent to keep from engaging the conversation, but he also needed to know if they had found Sophia.

"Curiosity," he replied and began to glow, keeping his eyes on Amon's every movement.

Amon turned to the other fallen angel and said, "And something more, I think." He chuckled sending an irresistible urge to follow their example from the very sound of his voice. A rippling chuckle flowed from the weak-minded guards in response. "Are you drawn to sin, Camael? Do you wish to join with us?" He tilted his head; his shoulder length blond hair seemed to sway in slow motion. In fact, his every movement seemed as if in a dream, flowing rhythmically to the sound of the soft and soothing musical voice. So enticing was the dance that few, without the Holy Spirit's help, were able to resist.

"No," Camael remained short. He was certainly feeling the seductive tug on his own mind, reminding him not to underestimate this opponent. Quickly, he prayed for strength and his glow brightened.

"I see," Amon stood stretching his wings to the width of the room not caring if he infringed on the demons' space. The wings were worn and tattered but still held their awesome beauty. "Perhaps your Sealed is coming this way?" he chuckled and nudged his companion angel on a strong shoulder. An echoed chuckle followed around the room.

Camael walked to one side of the room and ran his fingers down the edge of the battle worn wing. His eyes slowly shifted to the inviting eyes of Amon, who immediately pulled his wings in close sending a whiff of air about the room, the stink of the demons stirred along with a familiar smell. "How do you stand the stench?" Camael asked.

Amon lowered his head, his locks catching up, but kept his eyes level, "we smell the same." His eyes began to show a hint of red.

"No," Camael rested his hand on the handle of his sword. "We do not." Now he knew they had Sophia. Her smell had hinted to her presence. "You know why I am here," Camael was ready.

"Yes," Amon pulled a dagger and the demons all pulled out their weapons, getting restless. "I thought you might be smart enough to at least bring an army with you." The other fallen angel now stood up stretching taller than them all.

"I did," Camael smirked. Ariel came close to his side and began to glow, too.

Amon signaled a demon to look above for others. He narrowed his probing eyes as he waited to hear the report. When the demon returned, he shook his head having seen only his kind in the area. "Where?" Amon asked with a fluid gesture.

Camael pointed upward but did not take his eyes off of the leader. He watched Amon glide through the desk he had been sitting behind to stand face-to-face. The Fallen was looking to see a lie, but there was no sign of sin in Camael.

"Where!" he demanded as his eyes glowed bright red and his dingy blond hair went limp.

"Give her to me and we will leave in peace," Camael offered, tilting his head as he watched the transformation of the angel's beauty begin to fade.

"I am in control here. This is my domain. You do not come here and tell me what to do!" Amon stabbed the dagger into the desktop. His anger was not righteous so darkness surrounded his eyes and washed over his features from his now russet hair all the way down to his robe's tattered hem.

"I will not be patient much longer, Amon," Camael warned, leveling his gaze. Ariel pushed closer to his side feeling the tension, her fear apparent as she witnessed the results of sin on a fallen angel of the Lord.

Shifting his demeanor, Amon smirked and replied, "Seems your rearguard is inexperienced and beginning to show her fear." He looked pleased with his effect on the younger angel, softening his features slightly. He flashed a tantalizing smile at the new candidate for conversion.

Fear was weakness and made an easy target. "Concentrate," Camael drew Amon's attention immediately, diverting the Fallen's draw on Ariel.

"Your angel is here," he relented and the darkness lightened a shade. "We have her cornered but we do not have her imprisoned. She can leave whenever she wishes," he smirked and the darkness deepened again.

"You are a liar and it shows," Camael slowly hunched his shoulders mustering within him a righteous anger from the Lord. He quoted to the room's entertainment, "'For the word of God is quick, and powerful, and sharper than any two-edged sword, piercing even to the dividing asunder of soul and spirit, and of the joints and morrow, and is a discerner of the thoughts and intents of the heart.'" Then faster than a snake, Camael's tongue struck out as he spun it completely around the room. Every demon fell away leaving only their glowing red spirits to gather together in a corner. But the two large angels were quick to duck, saving their lives. Camael tilted his head and spoke, "I am the Lord's and you are the Cursed. This is your last warning." His voice was calm.

"You have scared her," Attempting to nurture her fear and gain ground, Amon tipped his sword to Ariel who blocked it lightly. The fallen angel chuckled and stepped back as chuckling ensued around him from demons replacing those vanquished. "But she is still of good mind." He lowered his sword and his features brightened. "As I said, your angel has concealed herself. We have an errand to do tonight and if she wishes, she can leave then without fear." He slightly bowed his head, his blond locks swishing forward and then bouncing back.

Camael stared at him for a moment and then shot upward into the air with Ariel at his side higher than the demons keeping watch. Then he slowed and hovered in wait. "Who can trust a liar?" he asked rhetorically, but loud enough for them all to hear.

Ariel waited a moment and then asked the burning question on her mind, "Where is the army?"

Camael pointed up and as she looked at the cloud cover, her eyes adjusted and then, as if seeing the trick of an illusion, she realized it was not a cloud but a host of angels compacted together whipping the elements of the air with the power of their wings. Ariel's mouth opened in awe of the shear number represented.

Night fell and a great number of demons followed the two fallen angels like a gray fog. Camael dropped down through the roof to find Sophia. He moved slowly through the building, sword drawn. Pointing to the end of a shelving unit, he sent Ariel to investigate. A shrill clash and spark jolted Camael to a halt. Then he bolted to where he last saw Ariel.

A sword swooped towards him and he ducked just in time. He caught a glimpse of Ariel's light streaking down another aisle before he had to elude another strike. Spinning through a hole in the shelves to another lane, he was able to engage in the ambush against him. The large fallen angel that had been with Amon was before him, eyes red and sword extended, appearance grotesque. Camael slashed his sword knocking the angel off balance and then kicked him to the ground. Camael's glow brightened as he felt the presence of the Holy Spirit.

The sound of a trumpet alerted him that the army was coming. The tainted angel was up in a flash thrusting his sword with great force towards him. Camael managed to save his neck but lost the use of one of his wings, sliding back through the hole he had come through before. Twisting over the shelving unit, he came at the taller angel from behind and struck his side. The damage was minimal and did not affect his next attack. The entire shelf unit came crashing down over Camael, who stood up with an expression of nonchalance as everything just passed through him. The fallen angel looked up with a grin only to see the Lord's army charging from above. As if to salute his opponent, the grotesque angel held his sword out and then vanished from sight.

Camael kept his sword up as he closed his eyes and sniffed. The smell of oil from the smashed containers covered the stench of the Cursed. He needed Suriel! Only she could clue him in now as to Sophia's whereabouts, but she was still with the Father.

The army was engaged in combat throughout the building while Camael went to the room where he had first met the Fallen. Was she still in the room? She would have left a clue for him. Searching through the papers, he noticed a handwritten note addressed to the boss. It simply said that shipments were coming into Wichita. Ariel walked in with two other angels. He held up the paper for her to see and noticed an addition to the note: an exclamation mark. The paper was Sophia! Camael raised his sword, fearful that the Fallen may be hiding near them. He turned to the others.

One of the angels ran out and then returned with another that was gifted in revelation. As the gifted one spoke, the image of the fallen angel began to appear, lying in wait for Sophia to reveal herself. Camael motioned for the angel to continue and soon the Fallen was in full view. Camael sheathed his sword and, with the help of the others, bound him.

Ariel watched as the disfigured angel returned to his former beauty.

The paper with the note drifted up off the desk and began to glow. In a flash of light, Sophia transformed back into her beautiful angelic form and sat down worn out. "I thought you would never get here," she put her face into her hands.

Ariel wrapped her arms around Sophia and Camael ordered the army to throw the Cursed into the holding place of darkness. He came to Sophia, one wing dragging on the ground, and knelt before her touching her head lightly with care. He and Ariel prayed over her and for the army. If only they had Suriel present. The Demonics knew they did not have their healer so they were bold and overconfident. He pleaded with the Father for Suriel again.

It had been a peaceful but difficult week. Peaceful because Jacob was away and she did not worry about him following her. She did not worry about him calling her or breaking into the house to harm her. She felt she had been to boot camp and this was her first week off since she started the divorce process. Yes, it had been peaceful to her soul and she could even say restful.

On the other hand, it had been difficult, too. They had depleted the groceries that were so kindly given them from her family, and the gift card had bought enough to make peanut butter and jelly sandwiches for the girls' lunches as well as more rice for evening meals. The money her father had given her paid all the debts that she had knowledge of with exception of two: the emergency Discover card and her wedding ring bill. They continued to watch every penny to make it stretch as far as possible. She began to consider the free lunch program at the school and going to the food pantry. What kept her back from pursuing these was the lack of discretion in receiving such support in a small community . . . and her pride no doubt. She wondered how the girls would take more rumors.

Although she felt better about the girls being in school while she was at work, she did feel bad that they had to get themselves to school on time, come rain or sunshine. On Tuesdays and Thursdays she did not see them much at all since she was now teaching art classes for the Recreation Commission. It did not pay much, but it did pay. She would get home in time to tuck them in for bed and talk about their day. For two weekends in a row now, she had managed to receive overtime. So, she was gone on Saturdays as well. It was hard to see them practically taking care of themselves, but she was proud of them for being responsible and resilient. If they were younger, she would have had to find a charitable babysitter. She was grateful to be spared that humiliation.

Their clothes were certainly something she was going to have to give attention to soon. For several years now, she had managed with garage sales. Now they had outgrown their jeans. Brailey started folding the bottoms into Capri's, which caused a fashion trend in her grade. Also, when her socks started getting holes in them, Brailey started wearing miss-matched pairs and soon that became the rage. In spite of her creative solutions, her shoes were still in need of replacement. Shannon had taken to wearing Julia's shoes though a bit big for her.

Today she was anxious to get to work because it was payday, and she was excited to see the check in her hands. It was more than she had expected and could not wait for lunch so she could tally her bills. Just before noon, word spread throughout the building that they were having a meeting. From the looks on their faces, she could see the employees were uneasy. Finishing her layout, she was one of the last to head upstairs to the conference room.

On her way up, she noticed Shanna going through her purse, late as well. Julia smiled and gave a sort of wave. "Remember me?" Julia came to her. "How did the house closing go?" she asked.

Shanna smiled big as she put the purse in the cubby under the worktable. "Of course, I remember you," she guided Julia towards the stairs. "The house closing was put off for this Friday. Man, I can't wait."

When they reached the room it was full and the two stragglers had to sit along the wall. The CEO addressed them solemnly reporting that the owners, who had come and inspected their business, were well pleased with their efforts. Then he talked about the economy and the devastating toll it had taken on many businesses across the nation. On the board behind him were the numbers showing what they had profited the year before in comparison to this year, and it was a considerable reduction. He announced that there would be layoffs on Friday, twenty-five percent. He regretted having to do it, but they had no choice. The employees filed out quietly and half clocked out for their lunchtime.

Julia's heart pounded within her chest as she pondered what this would mean for her and her girls. She was so new that she surely would be laid off. For the next hour, she prayed about God's plan for her. How was she going to make the money she needed to pay her bills? She looked at the paycheck in her purse realizing how much more significant it was after the news they were given.

It was time for her to take her break for lunch and, as she clocked out, she was surprised to see that the other shift was still having lunch due to the meeting. With a smile, she went to see Kealin, passing Debbie's husband who was carrying a vase of flowers. Kealin was sitting on a low table in the shipping area eating some pretzels sporting some new shoes. When she came into sight, he waved for her to come on over. She hopped onto the table next to him, catching sight of Debbie receiving her flowers but lacking a happy expression.

"How about that news, cutie?" he offered her the bag of pretzels.

Turning away from the curious scene, she delightfully took a handful of pretzels and focused on the conversation with her friend. She wanted more of the snack but her manners kept it to a minimum. "Well, I can't say it was a surprise. I'm not thrilled to be out of a job so fast. Nice shoes, by the way." She nudged him as she munched slowly and then motioned for him to look over at Debbie. "What's the deal?"

"Maybe he's in the doghouse or it's her birthday." He shrugged. Then, impulsively he yelled, "Is it your birthday, Debbie?" She yelled back that it was and to shut up about it. He laughed while shaking his head and looked back to Julia. "Hey, you don't have anything to worry about," he referred to the layoffs. "It's those that don't volunteer and come in late that have to worry." He pulled out some carrots and offered the bag as well.

She grabbed a few of them and tucked the pretzels into her pocket. "I hope you're right." She pulled out her cell phone. "I promised to show you my girls." She punched through the menu until she had a picture on the screen with Brailey's face right next to Shannon's.

Kealin scooted close to her making her feel warm and looked at the pictures holding her cell the right angle, his hand over hers.

"Beautiful! Just like their mother." He smiled those bright teeth again. "How old?" He released her hand and phone.

"Twelve and Thirteen now," she had to let that soak in, barely believing it.

"Good ages. Mine is eleven." He turned his smart phone to show her a picture of a girl with the same eyes and smile as his.

"Ah, I see you in her. She is a darling," Julia complimented and eyed the carrot bag wishing she could have another one.

"Here," he offered as if he read her thoughts. "Don't you ever bring a lunch?" She shook her head and stuck a carrot into her mouth avoiding an explanation. "Well, you're welcome to have some of mine whenever you like. I bring enough to feed me and then some." He laughed. "I'm too skinny so I have to eat all the time to get any bulk on me." He showed off a bicep and then glanced at the clock. "Woops, gotta clock in. You can hang here if you like for the rest of your lunch break." He jumped off the table and Debbie came by snapping her fingers for everyone to get back to work.

"I better get out of your way. I have something I need to do anyway. Thanks for the carrots and pretzels." She went out the side door to her car in the back. There she calculated what she could pay and prayed about keeping her job. Maybe Kealin was right. Maybe she would be spared.

Before first shift let out, Julia pushed the trashcan out to the dumpster. Her job required quite a bit more than just computer work. She did not mind except that her thumb was not very helpful and still painful with pressure. As she heaved the overfilled bag into the bin, she noticed Shanna marching to her car and driving off in a huff.

Curious, she asked Debbie if Shanna was all right and Debbie explained that she had to fire her for theft. A flashback of Shanna going through a purse made her cringe. Debbie advised that Julia keep a close watch over her purse as it happened often enough. Sometimes Julia felt so naïve. Taking the vase of flowers off of her desk, Debbie threw it into the trashcan and marched off. Julia bit her tongue and pushed the trashcan back to her area.

After work, she ran right into Kealin at the exit. Dropping his box, he immediately grabbed hold of her and danced her away from the door, singing a song from the musical "The King and I" in a nice melodic voice. She giggled and allowed him to lead her past signs and work stations until he could not remember anymore of the words. Laughing, he went back to retrieve his box as if this was a perfectly normal thing to do. Julia shrugged with a giggle and followed him. Helping him scoop the bundles back into the box, she found his humor gone. He took the box to his table and put it on the scale.

"Anything wrong?" she tossed him a bundle he had forgotten.

An awkward smile flickered as he caught it and dropped it back into the box. "Naw, you're just a fun girl, that's all. I'm sorry you have to go through whatever it is your going through. Your husband doesn't know what he has. If you weren't married, I'd scoop you up and never let you go." He was back to his flattering self and she pressed her back to the door.

"Well, I may not be married much longer," she winked. "Have a good night, Kealin. Thanks for the dance," she waved and left. She liked having friends again. She liked being treated special.

As soon as she got home, she would go through the mail. It was a privilege she had not had for several years. Now, she felt a sense of control and a bit of power in opening the mailbox. Although she did not like all the mail she got, she at least had knowledge of it. Turning to go back into the house, she noticed a man walking by that looked very familiar.

"Travis?" she blurted out as she looked at his face more intently.

"Julia," he came to her with hand extended. "You live here?"

"I do," she shook his hand. "And you?"

"Decades," he answered, his beautiful white hair dancing in the summer wind. "How long have you lived here?"

She had to laugh. "Years now. How funny is that? I probably moved here right after I stopped going to Central Community Church. I wanted a smaller town experience for my girls. Do you still go there?"

"Naw. Strange that I've never seen you around town." He laughed too. "So how have you been?"

"Um, well, got married and now going through a divorce," she summed it up and waved her hand, dismissing any feeling that threatened to surface. "It's a mess. Are you still running a fence business? If so, I could use a bit of help, as you can see." She pointed to the torn up wood fence. At least the yard looked better, clean of debris.

"I can see that. Noticed it on my walks around town. No, I closed that business a while back, but I would certainly be happy to help you. I still have a lot of my tools . . ." he walked over to get a better look. "Boy, you are going to have to put in a few new posts which mean drilling some holes, lady."

"I don't have the funds right now, but I'll give you a call when I do. How about that?" she had a lot more things to attend to and, although a mended fence would give her a better sense of security, it was low on her priorities.

"I tell you what, I think I have a friend that has some posts just laying in his yard. Let me give him a call and maybe I can come out on the weekend and get this back into shape. Don't worry about the money. It seems like you have a lot on your plate. I'd be happy to help you out." He smiled with a shrug.

"Wow, God works in mysterious ways, eh?" She was so happy that she threw her arms around him. "Thank you so much!"

He pushed her back and sheepishly said, "You better watch how you thank people in this town. Others will get the wrong idea. With your situation and all and me being a bachelor . . ." Raising a brow he stepped back and nodded. "But, I'd have to say that was the best thank you I've had in a long time." He chuckled.

Julia blushed with embarrassment as he stepped back again to continue his walk. At least he was willing to help without payment. They made a plan to put her fence in order the coming weekend. God was being so good to her. Surely He had a plan for this job of hers too. Stepping into the house, she looked around to see all the work yet to do. Yes, the fence was a small thing, but it was something. She pulled the girls into the kitchen and they worked together to make a list of the things that still needed to be done throughout the house and prayed over it. That night, she sanded sheetrock seams in the stairwell. She was determined to get a little done each night.

❦

Chayyliel had to hand it to Jacob; he was one cool cat. In spite of the short notice and the stress to pay back his wealthy customers, Jacob calmly strolled through Puerto Rico's international airport visiting casually as if this was like any other return from a dive trip. Within his dive bag, stuffed into the inflatable pouches of his buoyancy control device (BC), were two kilos of cocaine. It had been wrapped in plastic and bagged so dogs would not detect it, or so he was told.

Loitering around him was his entourage of demons and the dive team. Vapula stayed close dipping his hand into the bag every so often, wiggling his scientific fingers. They walked past an officer with a dog by his side and neither took notice. Vapula was good. That is all Chayyliel had to say about that. He moved to the counter where they were to check in their bags. He had to witness how this would go.

The line moved along with little wait until the divers stepped up. Jacob smiled and poured on the charm to the lady checking their bags. She took to it like bee to honey. He tried his Spanish with her and she giggled some more. Even the four men with him were being entertained; whereas, the man behind the lady looked irritated by the Americans. Taking the bags, he put them on the conveyer behind him in hopes to get this group through faster. When all was done and stamped, Jacob and his group moved on laughing. Chayyliel stayed to see how the bags would fare. Just as they moved to the back room, Omias wiggled out of the luggage handler and vibrated to its original shape as he hurried to the rest of the Demonics.

Rolling his eyes, Chayyliel could see that the thing had its purpose. It would be doubtful for Jacob to have gotten through security with drugs without the Demonic's help. As he tagged along, he wished Jacob would get caught and spend some time in the Puerto Rican prison system. Maybe then he would realize God's place in his life.

Passing through the walls and security without notice, he meandered to the luggage department, looking around at the various jobs. The dive bag caught his eye and he changed course to follow.

A heavyset man, with an even heavier demon of greed, grabbed the bag and tossed it onto an empty cart. On its way to the plane, another train of carts stopped along side and the man of greed moved ten suitcases to the cart with the dive bag. He then tagged each suitcase and sent the cart to the plane. Chayyliel jumped onto the cart and checked one of the suitcase tags. It had Jacob's name on it. All ten had the same tag addressed to Jacob. The demon of greed glared with eyes glowing red, trying to decide what to do about the nosy angel.

Chayyliel made it easy on the demon and jumped from the cart into the belly of the plane effortlessly. All around him were red glowing eyes. This was not good. Chayyliel opted for more comfortable accommodations among the passengers above. There would be no fear of the suitcases missing this flight.

Work on Friday was painful. People were quiet and diligent, working hard and doing their best to stand out as good assets to the company and Julia was no different. She went about her duties noticing the eyes that watched the upper management's every move. Opting to work through her lunch to keep physically busy cutting and peeling laminated signs, her mind whirled with plans for when they would make decisions for her department.

As Kealin made his rounds dropping off packages and keeping people informed as to who was called into the office, he encouraged everyone he thought would make it through. As he passed by, he winked and set a little box on her desk. Before leaving her area he whispered that Debbie's husband quit yesterday. They looked at each other and she raised her brows remembering the flowers in the trashcan. Kealin shook his head and moved on. She opened the box to find a bag of carrots and a hand written note saying that she was safe. Munching on a sweet carrot, she pondered how he knew. Just then, the boss walked through and called Dali to his office.

The visit was short and Dali came by to get his things. He did not say anything other than that he would see them later. Shortly after that, the CEO came through and said that the layoffs were through. Julia glanced at the note in her box as worry left her. She wondered if Kealin had seen the list when he dropped off a package. He was proving to be a valuable friend.

Lloyd came by with a smile on his face. Taking her aside, he asked if she wanted to get a little more overtime. He had caught on to her eagerness for extra hours and was going out of his way to make sure she got the option. Knowing that her daughters would understand, she added her name to his list. It felt good to deposit her check and pay the house bills in full. She would not need to fear dropped cell phone service and was even able to change her plan to a more reasonable rate, since she did not use very many minutes.

Yes, God had been good to her this week. She looked in on her girls as they slept and prayed over each one. God had given them the money to keep a home that, although in process of remodeling, provided all they really needed. God had fed them manna and she would not complain. She had faith that God would also take care of their clothes and shoes, too. He had promised to look after His own and never, not once, has He ever failed to keep His promises.

After checking Daily Strength, she screwed in sheet rock and mudded seams in the basement while listening to a sermon on temptations and how to avoid them. Right now, she was too busy and poor to even think about pitfalls. She set a large piece of sheetrock on two chairs with books stacked to the level she needed remembering how easily Jacob could hold a piece like this to the studs with one hand and drill the screw in with the other in a matter of a minute. She sighed. Maybe it was time to get some rest.

Camael was healing steadily but still very sore. Never had it taken so long for him to be back to strength. He wondered if this is what it felt like to be one of the Fallen. He remembered the looks of Amon's wings, scarred and worn. Without God's touch, their healing relied on the great angel, Lucifer, who now preferred to be called Satan.

Camael will never refer to him by that name, though. He favored the name God had given. Lucifer chose to defy God and mocks Him through his pursuits. His power is great, Camael would admit that, but he cannot come close to the Father's. In everything Lucifer does, he tried to become more like God. After all, he was made to reflect His glory. Camael saw Lucifer once and he was everything the stories claimed. He glowed brighter than any angel he knew. His beauty, perfect with jewels on his chest, gleamed in the light. His authority clear and his words so close to truth, so twisted within goodness, he could sway even the Lord's angels, as he did so long ago, sealing their fate.

Camael slowly raised his wings and ruffled his feathers. Yes, he lacked that snapping sound of strength, but he did not need it to be a strong leader. His team joined him by the front door with exception of Chayyliel. One member he had not expected also joined them, Suriel! Their healer was back and ready. Camael was grateful beyond words.

With her glowing touch, Camael's wing raised and straightened. He even let out a whoop of joy as he tested it and snapped his feathers. She giggled and touched each of them, quickening their healing and bringing the team back to their former strength. They greeted her with praises and Ariel flung herself into Suriel's arms for a heartfelt hug, nearly knocking the tiny woman off her feet.

"Welcome back, Suriel!" Camael greeted, "Thank you, God, for sending her back to us!" He smiled as he pointed to the heavens. "Praise God for bringing Sophia back to us as well," he nodded to the white haired angel as she pointed to Heaven. "We pray that Chayyliel is well and will be with us soon. Now, for the news from Sophia," he brought the meeting to order.

"The increase of Demonics in Wichita is due to a change in drug smuggling routes. Cocaine is coming into Wichita and then distributed all over the state. The Drug Enforcement Administration (DEA) has been investigating an operation out of Miami and Puerto Rico since 1999 and is now trying to get enough evidence to bring it down. From what the Fallen said while I was among them, one of the drug ring leaders has been heading up this new venture, compliments of Aboddon. Julia's husband, soon to be ex-husband, is being recruited as we speak," she let her voice drop low in volume.

Camael pondered the information before sharing his part of the puzzle. "Julia will be affected by this decision, should Jacob join their ring. We will know his decision when Chayyliel gets back. Our job is to make sure she is safe and ready. She is stronger than she thinks. Let's help her realize that," he rallied.

It was only eleven thirty when Debbie called overtime to a close. Julia clocked out and gathered her stuff. As she left the building, she waved to Debbie, who was smoking while waiting for her ride.

Julia jumped into her car feeling her tailbone whine from the force, reminding her to be careful. As she started her car, she looked over to Debbie again and a thought occurred to her.

Pulling along side of the woman, she offered her a ride home and she accepted. Julia put on some Christian tunes and noticed another bruise on Debbie's arm. "What was that one from?" she pointed.

"I ran into my desk at work. I should watch where I'm going," she waved her hand in the air with a sigh.

Julia chuckled as a memory whispered through her mind. She recognized the signs and felt compelled to share. "That's interesting. When my husband would loose his temper and get physical with me, I would explain my bruises just like that. I acted like it was no big deal so no one would ask more questions." She chuckled again. "I was so stupid," she added, feeling a warm peace come over her.

"No you weren't. You were just protecting yourself and your marriage," Debbie offered understanding, the kind of response she would expect from her group on Daily Strength. "It's no one's business anyway, right?" She glanced at Julia.

"Well, I thought I was protecting my marriage and helping him, but I was really making a safe place for him to continue to hurt me. If only I had called the police just once. He might have been forced to get the help he needed." Julia took a moment to let the truth soak in. "I know now He can't change on his own. We tried that for years and the abuse just got worse. Now he is free to hurt another unsuspecting person and I'm realizing that I can't get some help from organizations for abused women in this area because I never made a report. When I finally had enough and gained the courage to go to the police, it was too late. Now, I'm divorcing him and it's really been hard, Debbie. I wish I had called the police when he hurt me." Julia continued to share how she felt stronger and more secure as she learned more about abuse. "Healing starts with one decision. I just keep reminding myself to take baby steps," Julia paused as she noticed the warm sense of peace was gone. Debbie remained quiet except to give directions to her house. As she got out of the car, she thanked Julia for the ride, lit up a cigarette and shuffled towards her front door.

Julia prayed for Debbie on her way home. Working overtime and then rushing home to help mend the fence used up every ounce of energy she had left. Travis was a blessing and she really enjoyed his company. She could not have done it without him and she did feel more secure with the fence intact.

The next morning, she found herself pushing the snooze button, not wanting to get up for church. This time, Brailey got everyone moving to make it on time for Sunday school. Walking into the church, she spotted Abby coming straight for her. With a sigh, she made the effort to smile.

"Julia," Abby pulled her aside into the church office to speak with her. "I have a book for you that really helped me when my husband and I went through the *same* thing. You and I have strong personalities so it is difficult for us to learn how to be the submissive wife God intended for us to be. It took some time for me to learn but it made such a difference in my marriage." She over exaggerated her nodding as she handed over the book with bold red letters across the front that implied how to be a submissive wife.

Julia was confused. "I don't think you understand my circumstance . . ."

"Oh, I know how things are, Julia. But you read the book and we will talk later. I know God wants me to help you and mentor you. I know God will make your marriage whole again if you allow me to teach you." She pushed the book into Julia's hands.

Glancing through the open office door at those curiously watching, Julia gathered her wits and thanked her. If last week was not embarrassing enough, this week certainly did the job. Then Abby ushered her out, taking her arm like she was feeble and presented her to a chair nearby. Swallowing hard, Julia mashed the book into her purse the best she could, a third of it still waving its rear end of information for all to see. She stuffed it under her chair and crossed her feet around it hoping to conceal the bold red lettering.

Trying to look pleasant, Julia turned to visit with an older woman next to her and overheard Abby say all too loudly that she could not come and sit with her usual group because she was consoling a friend much in need. Julia closed her eyes tight and suppressed the urge to unload on the meddling woman. This busy body had no idea what was going on in her life and had taken it upon herself to diagnose the problem and set to mending it publicly. Julia made up her mind to set the woman straight as soon as possible in a private manner.

First, a victim of abuse and now she had to endure being a victim of humiliation. She would not take much more of this!

Before worship, she took the book to the church library and left it there. Perhaps someone else could benefit from Abby's kindness. As she walked towards the sanctuary where her daughters were waiting for her, the pastor stopped her and asked how her girls were doing. She gave her usual response and he moved on happily. With a sigh, she continued her course only to be stopped by one of her prayer team members, Sherry. While handing her a bulletin, she mentioned she was sorry she had not called but that she was still praying. This weighed on Julia's mind as she sat between her girls. She had set up a team of prayer warriors soon after the separation in hopes of establishing a circle of care. She had counted on their spiritual support and trusted that they would be faithful. Although she could not be certain they were not praying for her, they obviously were not following up on what to pray specifically. "Ask," came the familiar whisper.

In front of her was Tina, another prayer team member. Julia tapped her on a toned shoulder and asked if she had been praying. She admitted she had not been faithfully praying but that Julia could count on her from now on. Beginning to wonder if anyone had been praying for her, she then turned and whispered the same question to Donna, who smiled and nodded. During greeting time, she went directly to Betsy and asked her, who also affirmed she had been praying. Julia thanked her kindly and sat through the sermon wondering why these women of prayer had not called to find out how she had been doing and what her needs were. The Holy Spirit reminded her of some phone calls but she dismissed those calls since they had other reasons for contacting her.

In her heart, frustration built up as the pastor talked about love being a sacrificial action, again. He called the church to step out of their comfort zones and take the time to find out ways they could help one another in the church. Now, more frustrated than she had ever been at the church, she hoofed it out of the building as soon as the closing prayer was over, ignoring Abby's attempts to get her attention.

By the time she got home, her anger subsided and she felt like taking the rest of the day to relax. Following her lead, the girls watched *The Ten Commandments* and spent the rest of the evening doing nothing. After tucking in the girls, she went to plug in her cell phone only to see she had seven missed calls. She had forgotten to turn up the ringer after church. Her heart dropped as she scrolled through each call. They were all from Jacob. He only left one message saying that he was not going to sign the emergency divorce! *Typical rebellion. Like he wants the marriage,* she thought. To rid herself of more frustration, she went and pounded some brackets into the cut headers in the stairwell. She was thankful that her kids could sleep through anything!

Since the battle at the warehouse, Sophia could see a change in the number of Demonics in the little town. She flew up high to look down over the ranch style house they protected. The information from the Fallen had caused her to think through their position again. Camael was right. As long as Jacob was married to Julia, his choices were going to affect her and her girls. Such is the tie of marriage. The emergency divorce might be in effect in time.

She lowered to the back yard looking at the mended fence. She remembered watching the poor woman struggle to fix that fence herself! It had to have been over one hundred degrees that day. Julia had discovered an electric drill and hammer left behind in the basement and tried to screw a wood board back into the place from which it had been ripped. She worked to the point of great aggravation. Drenched in sweat, Julia set the drill on the ground, yet to have even one screw in place. After wailing a prayer, she tried again. Camael was impressed with her perseverance but in this instance it was a detriment. She needed to stop and investigate. Finally, she listened as he whispered, "Check the drill." Only then did she realize the drill was backing the screw out instead of driving it in.

Sophia chuckled out loud as she played the vision in her head of Julia running inside to tell the girls she got one screw in. They laughed and ran all over the house, thrilled about her achievement. Oh, but it was too much for her body! Praise the Lord for Suriel. For without her touch, that thumb would never have worked again, broken in two places! Plus her tailbone was fractured. No wonder she hobbled after only putting up a few boards. Now the fence was repaired and even if Travis was of help, she could have done without him.

She turned her eyes to the broken pool and sighed. Passing through the outside wall, Sophia looked over the house in its nakedness. It was time indeed. This woman would not get help from a church in transition, but she would get help from one that had much to offer. She caught Sablo by the arm and with a smirk, she reminded him of a tiny church in Viola that caught Brailey's attention when driving to a swim meet in Conway Springs.

Camael was right. Julia deserved more than help. She deserved friendship. She deserved healing. So it goes with abusive relationships. The abuser separates the victim and so they have few, if any, friends. Often times, they are even distanced from family. So far, Chayyliel was doing a stupendous job keeping Jacob at a distance. The man frustrated easily so Chayyliel only had to discourage him a few times before he gave up on stalking Julia. When Sophia heard he was tired of Elma and her complaining already, she went with Chayyliel for an afternoon and encouraged some of his scuba buddies to keep him diverted instead of bothering Julia. Although she was thinking more along the lines of recreational sports, they had the bar scene in mind. Still, there was nothing like infatuation to divide a man's heart and ambition. She grieved at how far he had wandered from the Father.

Sophia moved to the front porch to see Travis come up the drive, with a demon of lust trying to keep up and an anti-guardian of counterfeit light by his side. She recognized this anti-guardian from past experiences, full of beauty and long flowing hair to her feet. She was like a dream, wispy and soothing, but her heart was evil to the core. She could cause lifelong damage without even a weapon. She carried a vial of intoxicating desire and she smelled of allurement. Hanging from her belt bottles of disease and ailments jingled a soft melody of deceiving comfort. Sophia closed her eyes tight and pushed the door shut on that devil. This was one man Julia did *not* need in her life. The Demonics were shifting to a new plan, but she was on to them and was not going to allow them to trick this family into seeing green grass where there was none!

> *It is interesting to me how much I played this game of assessment. I would have to say that my thoughts ranged from empty-temper-talk to questioning myself if my abuser really did mean what he was threatening. If I tell one experience without stringing consistency, I often get a related story in response. For example, I shared that my husband had pushed me in his anger because I was not being as helpful in laying a wood floor. My friend shared that her husband had pushed her once when they were working on their garden. What I omitted was that my husband had also threatened to make me disappear so no one would ever find me and that pushing was a regular reaction from him. I recall I pondered his true intensions day and night.*

Risk Assessment of Abuser

Ten risk factors that help determine if the abuser will kill the victim:

1. Threats by the abuser to kill the victim, children, or self
2. Fantasies of homicide or suicide
3. Accessibility to weapons
4. A high familiarity with or use of guns
5. Fundamental belief by the abuser that the victim is owned by the abuser
6. Separation (greatly increases risk)
7. Abuser is obsessive over victim / family; can't live without them
8. Mental disorders, depression disorders; a sense of no hope without homicide and/or suicide
9. Repeated calls to the police and an increase in violence
10. Takes the victim and/ or family hostage

"O God, You alone are mighty! You alone are Holy! Without You, what can come about? Everyone and everything bends to Your will. You have deemed this for me. You have allowed me down this path. Help me be a good steward of what You have given me charge over. Help me to be a good mother. Help me to be a good homeowner. Help me to be a good worker, help me . . ."

Chapter Eleven

Letting Go

Glad to be called away from Jacob and his demon groupies, Chayyliel sucked in the fresh air, stretching in every way possible before turning towards his destination. He decided gathering information was not as interesting as it first seemed. He missed feeling the strength of his wings and arms in the heat of battle. There was little risk of Jacob getting caught after they left Puerto Rico since they would not be going through customs to enter the United States. Each man picked up two extra suitcases and simply put it into the SUV's trailer and started their drive home. No one was the wiser.

On the way home, they dropped off four suitcases in Texas, four in Oklahoma, and the last two in Kansas. In all, they distributed three hundred and thirty-three kilos of Cocaine. They made seven million nine hundred and sixty-eight thousand dollars. Of course, their split was more like three hundred thousand each. With that kind of money on board, Jacob wanted in and as cool as he had played it at the airport, the men believed they could use him especially with his dive background. Excited by the prospect of wealth, Jacob immediately went to the scuba shop to make plans.

The men met again at a very large home built on twenty acres outside of town to discuss the possibilities now that Jacob was involved. They agreed on various options and were still celebrating the new recruit when Chayyliel left them, seeing disaster in their future. The DEA will eventually catch up. The demons always mess it up. And this time, the angels are not going to allow Wichita to become a hub to the drug cartel. Watching the demons' influence the new plans for drug distribution, Chayyliel could see them entering homeless shelters, businesses, homes, schools, and even religious organizations. The word would be out soon and the battle for Wichita would be imminent.

On his way to meet with the team, the powerful angel was confronted twice by troops of demons. It seemed everything evil was glowing red these days. Being stronger than most, he overcame them with little effort. For the fun of it, he played with one of the demons like a cat does with a mouse when it's already had a meal. Then he remembered the information he carried and finished it off so he could be on his way.

As bold as the Demonics were becoming, the team was going to need the healer. Without one, every demon would be out to prove their worth in order to improve their status among their ranks. Chayyliel shook his head. They were so deceived. Angels always win in the end and they knew that to harm an angel would most certainly shorten their freedom. Only the protected commanders, the Fallen, were strong enough to engage in battle with little risk. These beings were powerful and beautiful, as the Creator had made them. Although scarred by battle, sin did not seem to change their appearance permanently as it did the weaker Demonics.

Swooping down to where Camael was standing on the front lawn, he made his entrance with his usual strength. Noticing Camael had his arms crossed and his eyes trained on the neighbor man, Chayyliel landed to his side not wanting to interrupt what might be going on. Camael smiled and welcomed him but kept his eyes focused across the street.

"I am trying to see if Omias is in him again," Camael explained.

"No worries, he was with me this past week," Chayyliel slapped him on the back. "And, Boss, I have a bit of news for you."

Camael turned his focus with a grin. "Good. I have some for you, too! Our healer is back!"

Julia had gotten a call from a wealthy couple that attended her church who wanted to come by and talk with her. She stood on the driveway waiting for them in wonder. When they arrived in style, she felt underdressed in her hand-me-down sweat pants and T-shirt. They were all business stating their willingness to help her get the house ready to sell as they discussed the state of her home.

This came as a surprise to Julia. Stunned, she showed them around the house sharing the plan they had had for each area. She continued the tour while trying to process the idea of selling. Where would she go? Her credit was so bad that she would not be able to buy even a smaller home. Rent was high in this area, being a suburb of Wichita and credited with a good school district. She had told the pastor that the low-income housing in town might eventually become her only recourse. Perhaps he was behind this visit.

Back outside, as the couple crawled up into their Hummer, they clearly laid out their option concerning the house. Although she had a good deal of materials, it would take a lot of hard work and people with expertise to finish. The couple offered to help with the drywall, but the electrical and flooring would have to be done by a professional. With the housing market in a depressed economically, she would probably barely get what she owed on it. "Beggars can't be choosers. Selling really is the only viable option" was their conclusion. "Once it's fixed up, we would be glad to make an offer," they tagged on before leaving.

Julia numbly went through the house to the back yard where she sat on the sidewalk in her usual spot. The warmth embraced her and welcomed her to stay awhile. She closed her eyes and tilted her head to the sky. The sun's rays caressed her face as a gentle breeze played with her hair. She savored each breath as if it were a kiss from God. For a moment her mind was at rest. Slowly the memories seeped into her sanctuary. There were so many dreams and ideas wrapped into this home. At this moment, it symbolized her life. On the outside it looked fine with a little bit of aged character. On the inside it had been gutted and left for ruin. Upon closer study, all that this house had gone through was for a better future. It used to be an older, ranch style house with a layout that was chopped up and out of date. Moving walls to modernize the floor plan were opportunities to make the house a good investment. The granite countertops and hardwood floors would boost the house's value higher than the other homes on their block. The open floor plan was desirable for a modern lifestyle.

In this economy, it would sell for a higher price because of these changes. That had been the plan. That was the dream they dreamed together for this house. She needed to let the dream go. She needed to let go of Jacob as well.

She looked to the sky and talked to her Lord. She wanted to see the house become all that it could be. Although Jacob would not longer be part of it, she wanted to make it their home, but these were things *she* wanted. She asked Him what *He* wanted. If He wanted the house, then she would give Him the house. After all, home was wherever she and the girls were. The up side of selling would be freedom from mortgage payments. She would not have to work so hard and would be able to spend more time with her kids. She shut her eyes once more and waited for a miraculous sign from God. The sun warmed her and she tingled from head to toe. She loved sitting in the sunshine. If only she could stay, but there was so much to do. With a sigh she got up and headed into the house.

Shannon met her at the door with a smile. "Guess what, mom," she built up Julia's curiosity. "Our old apartment is open for rent again." She smiled.

"God is sneaky, huh," Brailey wrinkled her nose and giggled. "It would be like going home." She hugged Julia and Shannon, making it a group hug.

"Well, girls," she warned, "I was just praying for God's will and sometimes what looks like the perfect plan isn't God's plan. Let's pray about it and see where He leads." She saw their faces lose their excitement. "It *is* pretty cool though," Julia giggled and they all hugged again.

While Ariel went to round up support and Suriel went to visit Jan's guardian, Camael looked to the already grinning Chayyliel, who appeared as an uninvolved witness. And so he was, for Camael needed him to keep an eye on Jacob since no demon would bother an army angel. Jacob would be gaining a crew of demons soon. He was no longer stalking Julia, which meant his dependence either transferred to someone else or was building up pressure deep inside him. If the latter, it would only be a matter of time before he exploded with unpredictable violence.

⁓⁂⁓

On her way to work, she decided to swing by the scuba shop to see how it looked. Preparing herself, she slowed down. She was shocked to see that it was closed down. Pulling into the next turn, she drove back to read the note posted on the door. Still containing some of the racks and display cases inside, the note read that Jacob Anderson had been evicted for not paying rent. She stood back and noticed the beautiful mural she had done was painted over with white. All their work was undone. She went to the back door to peer through the little window and found a note posted there as well. It read that any customers still wanting gear should call the number or visit the address posted. She jotted down the information and hopped back into her car.

Throughout the day at work she could not get out of her mind how fast the dive shop had closed. She could not understand how Jacob had certified more divers than any other shop in Wichita, of which he was extremely proud, and yet was unable to make a profit. He also had a contract with the YMCA, which guaranteed a certain amount of income. Also, there was the Puerto Rico trip this past week as well, though low profit. Since she was paying his debts, he should be coming out ahead. Something was not adding up. That shop had to be making money and yet, all his checks bounced this past week. She tried to convince herself that she needed to let it go. It was no longer her concern.

As she was leaving work, Kealin asked her if she was okay. Overwhelmed, she told him her story. Although she did not go into any details, she did share what was plaguing her mind, the mystery of the closed scuba shop.

"That's easy, baby," he draped an arm over her shoulders. "He doesn't want you to have any dibs on it. Debbie is going through the same thing. Who knew her man was a wife beater, too! If your husband owes back taxes then maybe he's dodging the IRS. Just look up the new address and see if he started a new business under a different name." Kealin turned to his computer and tapped out the address as her mind pondered what he said about Debbie. So that was why she has been gone for the past few days.

A map appeared causing Julia to step back, her hand to her mouth. It was one street east from where she now stood. She thanked Kealin for his help, and for listening, before running to her car. No wonder he was in the area to follow her! Looking around as she started the car, that old mix of fear and paranoia crept up the back of her neck. Her mind tried to control the panic she felt as she left the parking lot. Her heart was pounding in her ears and yet she heard a whisper say "Home".

Feeling a sense of urgency, she pushed the speed limits, careful not to go so fast as to attract an officer's attention. She just needed to be with her girls. At the last minute, she swung by her old apartment building to pick up an application. That would certainly cheer the girls up. When she got home, she started dinner early and waited to hear the garage door open for their return.

Right away she could hear an argument between them before they even stepped into the garage. With a sigh, she knew the peace and laughter they often brought her was not going to be the atmosphere for tonight. Brailey came stomping in and dropped her book bag on the floor by the door. Shannon stormed past her and tromped to her room, slamming the door shut. Without a greeting, Brailey laid out the problem before her mother, getting her side out before her sister could have a chance. Julia's heart sank as she began to understand what was going on. She hugged her daughter and then headed to Shannon's room.

Shannon sat on the edge of her bed with a book in her hand. As Julia knocked and invited herself in, Brailey trailed in behind her. "I know today was hard for the both of you," she stroked the back of Shannon's head and felt Brailey lean against her. "People are going to say a lot of things about me because of our circumstance, but we know the truth. Right?" Shannon nodded but did not look away from her book. Brailey said nothing, which was unusual. "People don't know what is going on so they make up their own explanations. Travis is an old friend and he helped us with our fence. From now on, we will leave the front door open anytime a man is here. That should help." Julia tried to comfort them with a plan.

"Maybe you shouldn't hug them either," Shannon added timidly.

"I won't hug them either," Julia patted her leg. "I have dinner started. Brailey, you better pick up your stuff and take it to your room." She turned toward the kitchen to tend to the soup as the girls slowly cleaned up.

Over the steaming soup, she silently wept to God. "Why? Why this, too? Why must my children have to defend their mother? Why do people have to be so cruel? Other people do worse and don't mind who knows!" Her reputation had always been pure. Even when her high school classmates were loosing their virginity, she stayed true and waited for marriage. Now, it was not enough for her second husband to abuse her, but the community had to label her as a tramp as well. What would be next? She looked to the refrigerator where she had stuck some verses. God is sovereign. She had to let go of her reputation, too.

Jan lay peacefully in bed as her guardian watched over her. Faith was very particular about Jan especially during the night. Since she was a little girl, Faith would visit her dreams. Over the years, dreams had become their special way of connecting. Even though she had developed a lot of different ways to influence Jan, her dreams made significant strides in her ministries. Jan placed high importance on them and paid attention to even the details. Tonight, Faith would give her a special dream.

After a visit with Sophia, Faith agreed to move Jan towards spending more time with her sister. In fact, it was Faith who convinced Sophia that having the children along would be most effective. She knew their strengths and, as a family, they would be a force of protection that would be unexpected. Sophia watched as Faith looked to Heaven and in an instant stepped into Jan's dream world.

All around her were children playing in a park. She could see Mary going down a slide and Jared waiting at the bottom to catch her. Faith had to smile at the memory of when they were so young. But she needed to complete her mission. She walked to where Jan was laying in the sun soaking in its warm rays. These times in her life were what Jan called "perfect moments" filling her with peace and contentment. This was her comfort zone and Faith was glad to have shared it with her.

"Jan," she called softly as she stood before her, wings slightly out so they would block the sun from Jan's eyes. "Do not fear," she smiled from the warmth of her heart. Jan had sat up, her eyes on the angel. "God has called you to visit your sister. You are to go and join her paper mache class." Instantly they were in the art room where Julia taught. Faith smiled and walked to the center table. "Jared loves to be in the center of things." Suddenly, Jared appeared with his sister and cousins, all laughing and making a mess.

"I won't be able to get my kids home by bed time. They have school the next day . . ." Jan reasoned while watching the kids laugh.

"Look," Faith directed, "the battle will be here." Immediately, the room was filled with ghostly images of demons and angels engaged in battle. Faith looked Jan in the eyes. "Where do you want to be?"

Jan looked around and then looked back to the angel before her and answered, "In the center of God's will." A beeping sound shocked her out of the dream.

Faith fell to the ground, visible again to Sophia. Helping her up, they both studied Jan to see how effective Faith had been. They followed her to each of the kid's rooms as she woke them up. Mary called her over and she stroked the young girl's thick dark hair.

"Mom, are you ok?" she asked as her eyes slowly showed consciousness.

"I'm ok," she smiled. "I just had a dream and you were in it."

"What was I doing?" she sat up rubbing her eyes.

"You were in Aunt Julia's paper mache class and making a mess," Jan stroked the girl's hair releasing the static with each pull.

"We had the same dream," Mary giggled, "I was making a pony out of paper and had stacks of canned goods all around me." She giggled a little. "I have to go to the bathroom." She wiggled out of bed and shuffled down the hall.

Faith began to smile as Jan thought over the dreams. "Coincidences are God's anonymous miracles," she murmured as she pulled the covers over the bed. Pashar stretched and sent the other angels a wink before shuffling down the hall as well.

Jan got up and slowly pinched her bottom lip, a habit when thinking, before leaving the room announcing, "Guys, we're going to enroll in Aunt Jules paper mache class!"

⚜

Chayyliel sat with his square chin propped up on his hand, bored. He had never been so inactive. Maybe God wanted him to learn patience and gain understanding of those who do surveillance. If so, he was definitely more appreciative. Glancing over his shoulder he rolled his eyes. Jacob was a twerp.

This was not Jacob's first time here nor did it look like it was going to be his last. The bar had captured his interest and tickled his fantasy. His heart was reaching out to fill the void Julia and the girls once occupied and the drink they served in this place not only warped his sense of reality, but also numbed the most sensitive part of his soul. Chayyliel hated being at a bar, watching all the people dancing, drinking, laughing, flirting, and hurting. It was not the laughing and dancing he hated but the combination leading to bad choices. A place like this tempted the inhabitants with all kinds of evil.

At present, Jacob was flirting with a woman of beauty and youth. She was clearly ten years younger than he and displayed interest. Chayyliel swatted Omias from his perch, sending him to the rafters, as he moved close to the woman to look her in the eye. She was Sealed. He looked around and did not see her guardian. Sitting back, he draped his muscular arm over the chair next to him where Vapula sat sticking its manipulative fingers into people's drinks. He looked at the large demon in disgust. Vapula grinned with a rotting set of teeth. Chayyliel sat up abruptly and glared at it. Taking in the aggressive move, Vapula slowly moved one chair over. Chayyliel relaxed again, bored.

His attention went back to Jacob, who was now playing with the ends of the woman's fingernails. Chayyliel's brows dipped. Was he to just sit by while sealed saints fall into sin? In a flash, he slapped their hands in one snap. Jacob jerked back as did the woman, holding her hand and looking at Jacob with offense. She grabbed her purse and

175

nudged her friend to leave. As they walked away, Jacob looked at his friends nervously shaking his head in confusion. Then he raised his glass, they did the same, and they drank down their poison, laughing loudly. Chayyliel rested his chin back into his hand.

*I never got to the arrest part. Once I actually decided to make
a call for help, but even then I didn't dial 911. I called my dad.
Still, I didn't get to ask for help since my abuser ended the call and
watched over me after that. I think at times that if I had dialed 911
perhaps he would have gotten worse. Of course, he was going to get
worse anyway. Perhaps that call would have kept others safe from his
temper. I was already in an insecure place. I believe not calling for
help and pressing charges is my greatest regret in how I handled my
abuser. Although, I thought I was protecting him, his reputation, and
myself for the sake of our future (fixed) relationship, I perpetuated
my abuse and did not gain him the help he really needed!*

The Arrest

When a person is arrested on a misdemeanor domestic violence charge the
abuser is taken to jail. In all cases of Domestic Violence, a police officer will be
the complaining witness. Since the charges are "police laid" the victim is unable
to drop charges or request the case be dismissed.

If the arrested person is booked on a misdemeanor charge they will be
allowed to bond out of jail, if they are able to post bail. If they cannot post bail
then he/she will be released after 10 to 18 hours on their own recognizance.

The arrested person will be required to sign a copy of a No Contact Order
and will be given a date and time to return to court to be arraigned on the
charges. Most arraignments are held the following business day.

During the arraignment the judge reads the charge to the defendant. The
defendant is advised to seek legal counsel and given a date to return to court to
enter a plea.

A second court date, the First Appearance, will be set if the defendant
pleads not guilty. The first appearance will be approximately two weeks after
the arraignment. The defendant will be expected to find a lawyer, apply for
a court appointed attorney, or decide to represent themselves (Pro Se) and
present that information to the judge. The trial date will be set at that time and
is usually a month away.

If the defendant pleads guilty the judge will set a sentencing date and the
defendant will come back on that date to meet with the judge and receive their
sentence.

* This is a general rule of how most states handle an arrest for domestic violence.

"Lord, where do I go from here? What is Your plan? I have so much on my mind, so much to do, so many worries and all I can do is wait. I can't interview for another job because I have to work. I can't do anything on the house because I'm either missing something to complete the project or I don't have the tools or skills. Please share with me what You see. Please help my girls cope . . ."

Chapter Twelve

New Beginnings

Looking over the schedule, Julia saw ink on every day. The girls were in volleyball and she had yet to make it to one game due to teaching art classes. She remembered back to when she made it to all their games and cheered for them as they smiled at their success. She felt bad now. Her girls deserved better, but what could she do? She had to pay the bills. She pulled the apartment application in front of her. It was all filled out but she had not mailed it. Brailey wanted to do it a number of times, but Julia was still waiting for God to say yes; three confirmations.

The apartment would certainly be a relief in reducing her bills significantly. But, until God gave her an answer, she just could not bring herself to send it. She did not want to be anywhere but in the middle of God's plan. She needed His protection and was not going to risk setting off on her own. "Trust in the Lord with all you're heart, lean not on your own understanding. In all your ways, acknowledge Him and He will make your path straight," she sang the Bible verse that played in her heart.

Julia's mind shifted to work. With the layoffs, she had been moved to another area to clean parts before they were painted, Lloyd being her direct supervisor now. Once as he moseyed by to check her work, he informed her that the company was not allowing overtime anymore. Even with that as the new policy, the end of the quarter was coming up and he said that they always had to stay over in order to get everything out. With a smile and a nod, he moved on to the next workstation, scuffing the heels of his boots to add a spring in his step. Her new position had moved her to the real first shift requiring her to be out the door at six in the morning. At least she was able to see the girls as they woke up. She also had the same lunchtime as Kealin.

Since she was not going to be working overtime, she needed to find another way to make money on the weekends. She had overheard someone talking about helping construction crews for extra money. Although she had no experience with construction; she was very experienced at cleaning up the mess it left behind. She noticed a few new houses going up in the wealthier side of town and forced herself to make inquiries.

The burly man looked her up and down and declined her offer mentioning that she would only be a distraction. Having been around aggressive journalists in the news business, she made her case that she could do the clean up after the crews left. Giving it some thought, he decided to give her a chance. She now had a job for next Saturday. With a smile, she thanked God.

While studying her calendar, Julia's eyes moved over to the Sunday block and her heart sank. Church was becoming a chore. She found it hard to be motivated to get up in time and even harder to step through the doors. Although Abby was a real deterrent, she knew it was more than that. It was inside of her. *She* had a negative attitude about her own home church, people she had been ministering to for years and loved! If she had to be honest, she would say it was because she did not feel like anyone cared about her or what she was going through. The truth was it was *her* attitude that was the problem. She loved them dearly but her hurt was causing her to be angry at them, which was unfair. Tapping her pen on the date, she considered taking a break and going to another church.

A knock on the front door interrupted her thoughts. Part of her was depressed enough to leave it be and sit in her stupor. But she just was not raised that way. Pulling open the door, she was surprised to see Travis.

"No, no, no!" Sophia let out her irritation. She did not want to see that man or his anti-guardian in the house, much less walking anywhere near it. She fumed as Julia left the front door open and showed him around sharing the things she had accomplished in spite of what needed to be done.

Chuckling, Camael followed along watching Sophia more than his Sealed, virtually ignoring the beautiful anti-guardian. "What has you so bothered?" he finally asked.

"Green grass," Sophia answered, folding her arms snug against her bosom. "You do not see?" She looked at him. "Camael, the word is out. Julia is on the market. Just look who he has as an anti-guardian, poor thing!" The beautiful spirit overheard and dreamily smiled at them as they went down the staircase. Travis stopped abruptly catching Julia off guard, bumping into him. The demon swept around them, her hands bringing them together. Travis steadied her with a grin and she laughed nervously. Then he checked the floor joist brackets. "You see now?" Sophia pointed stiffly.

"Julia is not going to be interested in this man. He is not what tickles her heart," Camael defended even though he was becoming concerned with the spirit's influence.

She raised a brow. "This is not about the heart, Camael." Then she reached out and slapped Travis' hand as he almost slipped it around Julia to resume their decent. The lovely anti-guardian swayed back, surprised, and Travis pulled his hand back without Julia's notice. Camael understood then and kept a closer eye on this Travis character, threatening the graceful devil with his dagger, until they left.

The phone rang cutting their farewell short and Julia dashed to catch it. Sophia jumped to action and tossed the cordless phone to the couch while Camael made sure the door was shut tightly. Julia frantically looked for the phone, listening for a clue each time it rang. Just as she answered, the person on the other end hung up. She quickly checked the caller ID.

Camael recognized the number from the note on the scuba shop. Jacob had called. "How did you know?" he asked Sophia.

She pointed to Heaven and replied, "Not to worry, tomorrow will change everything."

Brailey came running into Julia's room, waking her up with worry. "We're late! Wake up, mom, we're late!" She then ran out shouting to her sister.

Julia fell back again with a groan. She was not interested in getting out of bed. She was not interested in going to church. She just wanted to hibernate, but Brailey came through again and jumped onto the bed with more enthusiasm.

"Mom," she pulled the covers from Julia's head, "Shannon said that her BFF wants to go to church with us. She hasn't been to church in, like, forever! Can she go?" Brailey's eyes were wide with the chance to have someone new along. "Shannon is in ministry!" Brailey's eyes danced with excitement.

Sitting up, Julia nodded and pulled herself from bed. "Thanks," she directed her eyes to Heaven, "I needed that." She staggered to the restroom and found the toilet clogged again. With a sigh, she plunged, cleaned the plunger, and then finally started the shower. Julia noticed the bathroom seemed brighter than usual as she slipped into the warm water. She was a whole new Julia when she emerged from the restroom, dashing to the basement.

"Mom," Shannon called after her, "I can't believe you took a shower. We are too late to go to church!" She wailed and sat on the top step. "And I was going to take my best friend. Her family hasn't been to church since she was little," she pouted.

"Not to worry," Julia stood at the bottom of the steps pulling on a shirt, "we will still go to church . . . just not our church. It'll be an adventure."

"We're not going to our church?" Brailey stepped out from her room. "Better be careful, Shannon, your butt will get a splinter in it. Remember my foot?" She pointed to the rough steps and then shoved her foot into Shannon's face. "See that red dot?"

Shannon swatted the foot away with one hand. "Yes, I see it." She asked her mother, "So, should I text her back and tell her we are still going to pick her up?" Shannon carefully stood up and checked her pants for splinters. Brailey promptly stuck her face near her sister's bottom for a closer inspection, being the helpful sister that she was.

Julia tried not to laugh at the scene as she came back upstairs. "Sure. Where does she live?"

They had to drive almost fifteen minutes out of town to get the friend and it was already ten forty-five. She thought about going to Wichita to one of the big churches so the girls could experience something really different, but then Brailey started talking about the little church in Viola. Since they were close to it, she decided to check it out. Not exactly the "wow" experience she wanted them to enjoy, but as late as they were, perhaps they could make it in time for a small country church service.

The outdoor sign said they were just in time. It was a little brick building with large stain glass windows on each side instead of rows of small windows, giving it a unique look. The old wood floors creaked as they entered and only the sunlight brightened the small sanctuary. Up front was a stage with a hand painted mural behind the baptistery. It was quaint and she liked the special feel of it very much.

An old gentleman with shaky hands greeted her and each of the girls. He asked a few questions and Brailey took over the conversation, their voices filling the room mingling with a few others. A woman, old enough to be Julia's mother, invited them to sit with her and handed her a photocopied paper with the outline of the service on it. Looking around, there might have been a total of twelve people in attendance. Regardless, they were the friendliest church she had attended in a long time.

They sang, they prayed, and the sermon was biblically sound. The place seemed to radiate love and joy as the old hymns echoed in the hearts of the worshipers. She watched the sincere faces as the word of God was spoken and she felt at peace. Julia was greatly thankful for a Sunday with no stress. She visited with the woman that was next to her and found out that she was the pastor's wife, Evelyn Heart. Surprisingly, they discovered they were distantly related through Julia's aunt. She met the pastor, John, and thanked him for a good lesson on the unity of the body of Christ. Even the girls enjoyed their time and asked if they could come back and visit again sometime. Shannon's best friend was compelled to make church a weekly event in her life, provided she could find a ride and Shannon jumped at the opportunity to offer that service.

Evelyn pulled the roast from her hot oven and set it on the stove while listening to her favorite CD of gospel songs. She called over her shoulder that dinner was about ready and it did not take long for the men to sit at the dinning room table. She liked that they used the formal dinning room on Sunday's. It made the day feel special. She only wished that there were more family members to fill the rest of the seats.

She put the china platter with the roast, surrounded by steamed vegetables, in the center of the table. John smiled at her and held out his hands to give thanks for the food. She held one hand and her son held the other. With so many people unemployed and hurting financially, she truly felt thankful for what God provided for them.

"You gave a very nice sermon today, John," Evelyn complimented as he served her some meat, vegetables falling off the sides of his serving fork.

"Well, we did have guests this time," he winked. "Is that enough?" he asked the only other person at the table.

"A little more wouldn't hurt," Dan winked at his father.

It warmed her heart to see him each week. Many parents go weeks and even months between visits from their children. Silently she offered thanks to God for this blessing. Then she added a small request for grandchildren and smiled to herself.

"What are you grinning at, mom?" Dan forked a slice of bread from the basket sitting a little out of his reach.

"I know," John smirked, "She was thinking of the pretty thing that came to church today. Probably found out she was single."

"She didn't have a ring," Evelyn passed the mixed fruit to her husband. She knew he did not like most fruits, but he did have a thing for cherries and usually there would be two or three in a can.

"She's not his type. A mother of three teenage girls isn't quite what he has in mind, Honey," John dropped the bomb too early as he picked through the fruit bowl for a spot of red. "And she's related to us," he chuckled.

"Oh, John," Evelyn swished her hand through the air. "Her aunt is my cousin and the blond girl was a friend of her daughter's." She explained. "That does bring me to wonder if we should help her in some way since we are family." Both men looked up from their food. "She didn't say anything, but at the family reunion last week I was talking to my cousin who is the aunt to this woman. She mentioned she had a niece in our area that was going through a rough time. Seems her husband left her with a house halfway remodeled and financially broke. Poor thing."

"How 'half way'?" Dan interrupted, curiously eyeing his mother.

"Well, the demolition part is done," she hinted. "There was some talk of him being abusive, too."

Dan, a lean but sturdy middle aged man, sat back with his fork still in hand. His green eyes focused on nothing and his strong features tensed as he went into deep thought over the matter. Evelyn looked to her husband with expectation. They had learned long ago the signs of the Holy Spirit moving in their son. He had always been ready to help anyone in need. Through the years, he grew in service and learned to think things through before jumping into someone else's project. With tact and experience, he had become a man gifted in service without stepping on toes or hurting someone's pride. Evelyn loved to watch for Dan's special facial expression when the Holy Spirit gave him a challenge and he worked it to fruition. It was a beautiful thing to watch her child walk with the Lord. His face slowly relaxed and her heart warmed with anticipation. She watched for his jaw to clinch.

Of course, all ministries are not without sacrifice or temptation. The last thing Satan wants is a Christian undoing all his ruination. She took a bite and chewed. Yup, there is was. The muscle pulsed near his ear as he clinched his jaw. He was going to tackle the job. She smiled. *Dan will need extra prayer to help him through.* She got up and pulled a journal from her desk drawer quickly jotting down the prayer need. In her old age she needed all the help she could get to make sure she was on target with her prayers. Her forgetter was working better and better. *That's one thing that improves as one gets older.* She giggled at the thought.

"People today just do not understand how effective prayer can be", she mumbled to herself as she replaced the journal. *That's another thing that improves the older one gets.*

When she returned, John and Dan were already discussing how they could help the related niece of a cousin. Evelyn listened as they tried to figure out how to get in touch with the woman when an idea came to her. "We could check the guest registry." She felt warm with excitement as she always did when she was joining God in a project.

"They didn't sign it," John sighed. "I was going to introduce them, but . . ."

Evelyn interrupted, "Check! What about her check? I was impressed that she gave an offering."

John went to retrieve the offering bag and brought it out with a smile. "It's a good thing I married you, Ev. Here it is, address and all!"

The phone rang and Julia went through her routine in preparation for answering it. A familiar voice greeted her and Julia's heart sank.

"Hello, Julia. It's *Abby* from *church*. I was *worried* about you when you *didn't* come Sunday. Are you okay?" the voice dripped with concern, overemphasizing the essential words.

When she asked God for someone to care, it just had to be Abby! That is what she got for not being specific. Julia sighed and tried to have a Christian attitude toward the woman. After all, God *was* answering a prayer. "Yes, we are doing fine. We just visited a quaint little church in the country. Brailey saw it once and wanted to visit. I think it's nice to show the girls how different churches worship and yet be a part of the body of Christ wherever you are. Don't you?" She tried to divert the conversation.

"Well, I suppose. But, you are part of *our* body and I am here to *help you* through this tough time in your marriage. I have been praying and God told me to teach you how to be the submissive wife He longs for you to be. I know what you are thinking, because I was once like you. Let me tell you, your marriage can become amazing if you listen to me. Julia, you aren't doing yourself any favors with some of your decisions as of late. This town will only tolerate so much and then you will be shunned. You need me. Have you read the book I gave you?" Abby pushed the subject beyond Julia's limits.

Julia prayed a quick prayer for God to direct her words. "Abby, I want to thank you for your prayers and your willingness to help. The problem is, I don't think you understand what I am going through. I would appreciate your continued prayers though." She could only hope this would be the end of it.

Abby was persistent, "Oh, I *do* know *exactly* what you are going through. Trust me when I say I *know*. And I am not going to let you fall between the cracks. God has brought me into your life to save your marriage and I am going to do all I can to do just that. I can be very persistent, you know." She giggled to lighten the conversation.

Julia could tell the woman was not going to give in so she appeased to conclude the conversation. "Thank you, again. I need to get ready for the girls. They should be home any minute. Oh, and thank you again for your prayers." She could hear the woman say she would be praying as she hung up the phone. Julia felt terrible about hanging up on her but her counselor said she should discontinue any conversation she did not feel comfortable having. She certainly did not feel comfortable talking with Abby. In fact, she came to a new decision that that would be the last conversation she was going to tolerate from the busy body. From now on, she would ignore that phone number and any other way of communicating the woman tried. She asked God to forgive her but it was for her own sanity. She had enough on her plate. She just could not stomach one more thing.

After another meeting to announce more layoffs, Julia found herself in yet another position, taping parts for the Mexican woman! She would mask the lower regions of the part so that Carlita could run a squeegee over a screen and paint the top region of the part, thus making room number a different color than the background of the sign. She did not mind the work, although standing the whole time was uncomfortable for her back.

For some reason, Debbie kept coming by and joking around with the man that ran the photopolymer machine. Seemed childish to her, but that was Debbie's way. Perhaps it was the freedom given by her emergency divorce. She even came over and talked with Julia about some nonsense before heading back to her own department. Julia thought she heard Carlita sigh.

After another enjoyable lunch with Kealin, Carlita leaned over to Julia and said, "You know Debbie married." Her accent was thick and her English limited.

"No, she's not married," Julia kept her hands moving with the tape. "No married," she reiterated.

Carlita put her hand on Julia's and stopped her work. "*Is* married," she emphasized. Then she withdrew and continued her work.

Julia pulled more tape, her mind in a fog. Just then police officers came through with one of the guys from the woodshop in handcuffs. Everyone kept working, but already she could see the information spreading through the grape vine. He was a good friend of Kealin's so she knew he would be on top of what happened.

During the next break, she wanted to rush over and talk with him, but Carlita pulled her to the worktable and showed her a book. "Do you know Christ?" she worked at her annunciation to be clear.

"Yes," Julia's mind focused directly on Carlita. "Are you a Christian?" she asked.

"*Si*," she nodded with as smile, "I know Christ. I love Jesus," she stressed. "You love Jesus?" she pointed to the book and now Julia could see it was a devotional in Spanish.

"Yes, I mean '*Si*'," her heart pounded and she could not help but embrace the woman. How she prayed that she would have a Christian friend at work. She felt so alone sometimes and here she was. It had been no coincidence that Julia was moved into this department, working next to a woman who loved Jesus and made a point to share her faith with her! Julia said a quick *thank You* to God for the answered prayer.

Carlita's smile faded and she got serious with her. "You no see truth," she searched her English for words to tell her what the Spirit was trying to convey. "Debbie yes married, but no ring," she pointed to her ring finger naked of the same commitment. Julia looked skeptical. Carlita sighed and tried again, "She live with him now but still married, no keep promise," she pointed to the guy by the photopolymer machine. "Marriage is holy, *si*? You know now. "She stated it as a fact.

"Yes, I understand," she nodded and stepped back to her workplace to get started since their breaks were decreased to only ten minutes now. Debbie must be under the same thirty day waiting period for her divorce to be final as Julia was enduring, but had found someone to fill her void in the meantime, much like many of those in her Daily Strength group. Or perhaps Debbie's husband did sign the emergency divorce and Carlita was unaware.

"You," Carlita eyed her and then glanced to Kealin's station, "be careful, too." She tapped her hand on the table and began to sing; "This is the day . . ." she waited.

Julia smiled and sang the follow up. "That the Lord has made . . ." They sang on and turned back to their work. When it was time to leave, she patted her arm and said she would be praying.

Julia followed her to clock out, but before she exited, Kealin called her over.

"Girl, did you see what they did to my friend?" he was putting together a box for shipment as he filled her in on the gossip. "Man, just as his probation was up, they have to take him in. That's just wrong."

"What was he on probation for?" she leaned on the desk and ripped off a piece of bubble filler. She had watched him enough to know how to pack the boxes and have them ready to check the shipment papers before sealing the box.

"Drugs," he printed out the shipping label. "He's been good, keeping clean of that stuff for his baby and on his last day, they keep him on the hook. If he was gonna give 'em any information he'd done it already. Right?" The question was rhetorical. "Anyway, how you doin, doll?" he flashed her a smile.

"I'm fine. They've moved me to another area," she pushed the filler into the top of the box and motioned for him to put the shipping slip in.

"I noticed that," he slipped the pink copy on top of the filler and took the other to Debbie's desk. "You like it?"

She noticed another paper had accidentally slipped inside the box. She pulled it out, tossing it to the table and heaved the box to the cart for UPS to pick up in a little while. "It's a job."

"You know it," he laughed and leaned on the cart looking attractive. "Don't you teach art tonight?"

"Yup, starting a new class, paper mache," she pulled out her cell to check the time. "My girls are going to join in this time. You know, you ought to bring your daughter. I bet she would really love it." She noticed a text from her lawyer stating Jacob had come by to sign the divorce papers, but they still needed her to sign something yet. This was an unexpected surprise. "I can't believe it. He actually signed the divorce papers today when it's final anyway." Laughing, she grabbed a pen and wrote her lawyer's address on a folded sheet of paper lying on the table as a reminder of where the office was located.

"What a dork! Still, congratulations, Jules, his loss!" He came over close to her. "I tell you what, give me the info for the class and I'll see what we have planned for tonight," he winked, rubbing his shoulder to hers. "Now that you're free game . . ." he laughed at his overacted flirtation.

She loved how he made her laugh. She tore off the bottom of her scrap paper and wrote down the place and time. "Don't worry about the fee. Consider it a gift." She handed it to him.

"Naw, I got money," he put the paper next to his lunch container. "Maybe our kids will get along." He grinned.

She smiled back. "If she's anything like you, I'm sure they will," she was already half way to the door. "Later," she waved and pushed the door open.

It was a battle for a paper, which was like fighting tooth and nail for a feather that keeps slipping away at the last minute! Camael guarded the paper until Uzza came at him. Ariel slipped through and caught hold of it only to have it moved to another spot by Kealin. Sophia did not realize that Omias was inside the human giving directions until she thought the man's humor was not quite right. When Ariel looked into his eyes, a sword came piercing through. Even as fast as she was, half her face was cut, light pouring out and she called out for Suriel.

The healer was trying to help Camael, who was being held down by Semyaza, a very heavy demon. Uzza saw the opportunity and moved quickly toward the pinned angel with his sword raised. Suriel vanished as Ariel flew over and bit Semyaza's hand. When she sank her teeth deeper, he yanked his arm back enough for Camael to escape his grasp and just in time to avoid Uzza's strike. Suriel appeared and touched Ariel's cheek with a flash of light. Suddenly, Semyaza yanked the small angel back and smashed her down under his weight as he wickedly huffed at his triumph to show off. Capturing the healer caught all the evil spirits' attention since it was a rare thing to accomplish. Even Uzza stopped long enough to be impressed allowing Camael to rush to Suriel's aid. But Uzza recovered quickly and tackled Camael just short of his destination.

Ariel spoke, "The Lord is my strength!" and heaved Semyaza into the air giving Suriel's smaller frame time to roll away. In a flash, Suriel vanished as she bolted away to get a fresh run at the battle. Sophia could see that Suriel was going to be their best hope in getting the paper into Julia's possession.

Thankfully, Sophia was able to raise concern within Carlita earlier. Her guardian was overly protective, but cooperative. Once he was in cahoots, Carlita reacted like clock work. When her guardian said move, she moved. When he said touch, she touched. When he talked to her heart, the woman spoke and when the Holy Spirit moved, he stepped back. It was one of the best examples of a guardian and Sealed relationship she had ever witnessed personally. It must have been like that with Elijah, the great prophet.

Naturally, when Camael shared with the team that the archangel himself asked his team to retrieve an important document that would bring down the Demonics' plan like dominos, she understood the important role Julia was in position to play. Camael motioned their moment to move when Kealin's pal was arrested. The DEA was starting at the bottom of the chain.

Sophia sent Julia a text, as her lawyer with precision timing. Suriel was able to move the document into the ideal spot for Julia to jot down the information. And although Camael and Chayyliel got the brunt of the physical fight, playing linebackers, Ariel really had the raw end of the deal, being pinned in a corner for most of the skirmish, watching the action.

In the end, when they could focus beyond themselves, not one had a thing to complain about when they saw the army of hosts fighting above after Julia left the building. The amount of demons bombarding the area looked like the Persians attacking the Spartans. At least half of the angels in that battle were taken to the Father for His miraculous care. The rest of them were battered and torn, requiring Suriel and other gifted healers to take part in restoring them back to their glory.

Camael did not stay, wanting to protect his Sealed until she was clear of danger. Sablo and Zazriel were protecting the girls, thus were absent from the battle as well. However, the rest of the team, including Sophia, stayed back to watch the unfolding of events with Kealin. In fact, even the demons still within view were on edge to see what Kealin would do when he found his document missing from the box.

Ariel's curiosity got the best of her and she slipped next to the box for a peek inside to see what was so important. She noticed Sophia motion to Chayyliel, who reactively pulled her away. Omias snapped his head from Kealin's body and stared at her with flaming red eyes. Chayyliel took action and swatted Omias across the room, but Kealin was already alerted and went to the box to check it over. All stopped and watched. He became frantic, pulling the bundles out until he came up with nothing. He froze, thinking it through.

The army of hosts was not yet ready for the onslaught of a second wave attack. Demons dove into the building searching for the document, touching everything and threatening anyone who was in their way. Ariel darted from wall to wall, having no time to pull her sword. Chayyliel could not keep up with her and then was caught up in a sword fight with Uzza, slicing an area of hair clean from the ugly demon body. Everywhere Ariel turned, there were red glowing eyes looking upon her as if she was a feast after a long famine. Sophia tried to keep up with her, but the ancient angel was no match. Inexperienced, Ariel dropped to the ground, putting herself at more risk, wondering what to do, where to go.

Then a loud voice like a trumpet said, "God is our refuge and strength, an ever present help in trouble!"

A bright light burst through like an explosion without noise and blinded all but the angels of the Lord. Sophia was able to grab Ariel before a great wind swept through and carried her up and away. Trembling, Ariel clung to Sophia not aware of who really saved her. The wind died down and the light dimmed leaving the army of hosts and part of Camael's team high above the city. All this happened between the ticks of a second hand on a clock.

"I was surrounded by evil and then a message from Psalm forty-six blasted in my ears and . . ." Ariel exclaimed bewildered.

" . . . and God rescued us." Sophia hugged her tight. Timidly, Ariel pulled back and began to look around her fearfully at the many angels she had put into harms way because of her curiosity to look into the box. "Fear not, Ariel," Sophia soothed, "they are not thinking of you. They are concerned for Kealin, worried for him and for Julia."

With that, Ariel's expression softened and she realized the army had been dazed as well. They were now gathering to regroup for another front. Their massive army angel, Chayyliel, came by to see if they were all right. By then Suriel had joined them and they decided to meet up with Camael and his Sealed. Sophia stayed close to Chayyliel as he went back down far enough to see Kealin handing the box to the man in the black Explorer.

Abby checked over her grocery list to make sure she had everything. Then she looked around to see if she recognized anyone. The grocery store was her favorite place, other than church, for socializing and catching up on news. Scanning over the produce area, she recognized Donna. Casually, she rolled her cart in that direction.

"Well, how are you doing, Donna?" Abby smiled as she came up next to her. "Looks like you must be having Spaghetti tonight."

Donna smiled back. "Actually, that is for the food bank. What you donating?" She enjoyed motivating a positive action.

Abby quickly deflected the subject like a pro, "Oh, I usually donate to the food bank, but this time I thought I would donate some groceries to poor Julia and her girls. They are going through a tough time right now with the separation and all." She waited for Donna to join in and add a morsel of information.

"How wonderful of you to think of them, I am sure they'll appreciate it," Donna avoided the trap.

"They are such dear people. I hurt for the girls having to go through this at such a tender age. And this being the second time for them, too. I pray Julia will read the book I gave her on becoming a submissive wife." Abby wore a face of concern.

Donna's immediate frustration allowed words to escape unchecked. "Abby, for heaven's sake, she had an emergency divorce!" Donna stopped herself too late.

Abby was completely taken back by this new information and realized she was just standing there with an expression of shock but could not force herself from it.

Taking a breath to calm down, Donna regrouped and reasoned, "Listen, Abby, you and I have known each other all our lives. This is one time where you do not have all the information. You are doing more harm than good. Her situation is . . . well . . . obviously not what you think it is. Trust me on this." Donna paused awaiting some reaction from the busy body, but Abby stood speechless. Donna was not going to pass up the opportunity to tell her something she had wanted to for a very long time. Donna took a deep breath and continued, "Sometimes, a good friend doesn't need to know what's in a heavy load to help carry it. The Bible says we are to listen more and speak less. I guess we need to listen before we speak and I need to learn that just as much as anyone. I'm sorry for snapping at you. Please forgive me." She apologized from a sincere heart.

Suddenly Abby felt a flood of warmth come over her and realization permeated her mind. A fresh perspective whispered, "What if you are wrong?" Instantly she became tearful as the Lord opened her heart to the rebuke and she flung her arms around Donna pleading for forgiveness as well. "I only wanted to help. But to think I made things worse . . . I was so sure I knew what was going on." She sobbed as Donna patted her back.

As the two women parted, Abby vowed to make a change and learn to discipline her tongue, submitting to the Lord who provides help. She could have sworn she saw a glow next to her in the salad bar glass reflection. Deciding it was a sign from God and that all was forgiven, she knew her decision empowered the Spirit to do His will in her life. She loved coming to the grocery store.

⁓⋇⁓

Checking the address on the scratch paper, Julia swung by her lawyer's office to sign the last of the divorce papers. The receptionist, or rather "executive of first impressions", mentioned that Jacob was quite glad to be getting it over with and then she took the papers while offering her a good day. Although she knew she should not let it bother her, those words tumbled in her mind most of the drive home. Her thoughts were interrupted as the radio weirdly blitzed and turned on. It was not a sermon, but a call into a lawyer type of show. They were talking about legalizing marijuana and calling churches to sign a petition against this action.

Reaching to turn the station, she had to pull back to avoid a skunk in the road. With a sigh, she allowed the show to play since she was almost home and needed to watch the road. Just as she was going to turn off the engine, the man announced that he was concerned for Wichita, Kansas and the amount of drugs showing up around that area. If anyone had any information they should call 911 or the police to help rid Kansas of this corruptible evil that spurs on additional crime. He asked that the churches get in involved, sign the petition, and pray.

Julia sat back and pondered what he said. She was never around or used drugs. However, their lives could be affected by someone else who was trapped by the drugs' influence even if their school system did have a wonderful DARE program and her girls never got involved with drugs. After all, she never thought abuse would have been part of her life. She could be a part of the fight against drugs by praying. If all the churches of Wichita and the surrounding areas would pray about this problem, she could imagine the power that would affect those that are determined to undermine the law. She switched off the engine and prayed, not long, but it was a start.

She did not have a lot of time to prepare before her art class. Running inside the house, she quickly made some peanut butter and jelly sandwiches and dropped them into a plastic grocery sack hanging on her arm. At least the girls would have something to eat between school and class, which would not be over until late. Grabbing a stack of old telephone books, she balanced them as she struggled to get the door open.

The door swung back and there stood a tall, handsome man with black hair that slightly curled out from under a white ball cap. Hunched from the weight of the phonebooks, Julia stared from the entrance of her own home. She did not even notice the older man standing off to the side until she recovered from the shock. Before

194

she could say anything, the handsome man easily took the stack from her and smiled.

She was instantly drawn to his green eyes. Shaking her head from her trance, she managed to say, "Um . . . thanks."

He smiled again. "Where would you like these?" He raised the stack up a bit, the muscles in his arms grabbing more of her attention than the books.

"Oh," she took action and went for her car, "In the trunk would be fine."

He set them down with no trouble and looked to the sack on her arm. "Does that go in, too?"

"No," she felt her face flush. Only then did she notice that the other man looked very familiar to her. "Um, can I help you?" her brain trying to remember the face.

The younger man smiled and stuck out his hand, "I'm Dan." She shook it and turned to the other. "This is my father, John Heart." They shook hands and she waited. "You don't know me, but you know my father. He's the pastor of the little church in Viola," he gestured.

"Oh, oh, of course. You looked familiar to me but I couldn't recall where I had met you." she smiled as recognition flowed over her expression.

The older man explained why they were there. "This may sound silly to you, but we, the church, want to help you . . . with your house. My wife heard there was some construction going on in there and you could use some help." The pastor glanced back at the open front door.

"Um," she looked at it, too. "You could say that." She marched to the open door and held her arm out for them to enter.

They stepped in and stood in the entry area both putting their hands on their belt as they surveyed what they could see. There were definitely the same genes swimming in those boys. She had to put her hand over her mouth to keep from chuckling.

"Yup. It could use some attention," Pastor John swayed up on his toes as his son mimicked the movement in perfect synchronization.

Unable to help herself, she began to giggle. Trying to calm down just made it worse and soon the men figured it out and chuckled along with her. Almost recovered, she was about to say more about the house when the two men reached up to scratch their head, lifting their hats in the same way. She instantly fell into the giggles again, motioning for them to go back outside.

"Yeah," Dan chuckled and purposefully rocked to his toes again, "We'll have to get back with you if you're open to some help and get a game plan."

She shook her head. "I'm so sorry. It's been a while since I've laughed so hard. You two remind me of my dad and his father. They would stand the same way and had the same mannerisms when they were visiting."

"Don't be sorry. Laughter is good medicine. I'd rather you be laughing than crying," the pastor patted his son on the back. "We've been snickered at more than once."

"Well, I thank you for coming to visit me," she headed to her car, "I would appreciate whatever help the Lord leads my way. If your church is led to take on the challenge, then I welcome you." She shook each of their hands. "I hate to leave you and run, but I've got a class I have to teach and I'm late," she explained.

"Okay," Dan pulled her door open, "We came by a number of times but your car was never in the drive. At least we got to see some of what we're up against. When would be a good time to meet and go over a plan?"

Julia pulled from her purse the torn scrap paper and quickly jotted down her phone number. "I have a hectic schedule and my calendar is in the house. Why don't you call me later tonight around nine and we can settle on a date." She blushed as she tore off her number and handed it to him.

This time he chuckled at her but decided best to keep his mouth shut on that one. He took the number and waited for her to get in before shutting her door. He quickly hopped into his vehicle with his dad to move out of her driveway.

Julia could not believe her luck! She tossed the bag of sandwiches to the passenger seat and stuffed the torn paper into her purse. Remarkably, this day was an answer to prayer. First, she survived another round of layoffs and was moved to work with a woman who loves the Lord and sings praises with her while they work! Second, she randomly found a wonderful church that offered to fix her home. And third, her divorce was finalized. She was ready to throw away the apartment application and make a new life for herself and the girls. She was learning that sometimes what looked like the best plan may not be His plan. "Grow where you are planted," a voice seemed to whisper in her ear. She smiled. "I just might do that!" she said out loud.

She parked the car in the school parking lot and thought about all the blessings of the day. Was it not interesting that her life would begin to turn around when she was no longer connected to Jacob? Did his sin really have that much power over their lives? Her mind was flooded with bad memories, but she put a stop to it. It was over. Finally. She was making a new start. There was much to recover from and much to fix, but she could see now how God was with her from the beginning. He knew her pain and He protected her and her girls! She had been in His loving hands the whole time and she felt a warmth of security in that alone. Filled with a sense of peace and love, a momentum of worship grew within her soul. Overwhelmed by the intensity of her emotions, she could hold back no longer for it was bigger than she was.

"Praise God from whom all blessings flow!" she began to sing with her whole being.

Camael ruffled his feathers as he watched the soft glow of communion flow out of Julia's car, engulfing the parking lot. He touched his heart and then pointed to Heaven and the Father allowed him to listen to his Sealed one sing praises. This touched his heart, growing his love for this precious child of God. The Father's glory cascaded down from Heaven upon Camael and flooded him with wisdom and power. He stretched his wings out as wide as they would go and extended his arms to the Almighty soaking in all that was offered. He delighted in the sweetness of His presence. The light dimmed as his team joined him in the middle school art room. Camael turned from the window empowered and focused. It had been a long time since he had all seven of his teammates in attendance. Along with them, he had Jan's family guardians as well. With a smile, he rubbed his hands together with excitement. This was it. After all the pushing, pulling, and strategizing, the moment had come to decide the outcome. Their actions in this room would make the difference for Julia and countless others in Wichita and the surrounding areas. This would determine the fall of the drug hub campaign in Kansas.

He looked at his team and with enthusiasm as he addressed them. "Everyone is in place. We know what to do. Now is the time to show the skill of the Lord!" He watched with joy as they flapped their wings with anticipation. "There will be pain, for pain comes with anything of value. There will be errors, for sin does abound here on Earth. There will be death, for demons that deserve it," he raised his brow. "There will be victory, for no one can thwart the Lord's plans!" His voice ended with a shout and those within his circle whooped and hollered with him pointing to Heaven.

"Team, I am honored to work and fight along side you. I have thanked the Father for His kindness in giving each of you for my Sealed. I would not trade any of you for another. You are perfectly skilled for our task. Praise the Father for His knowledge! Praise the Father for His mercy! Praise the Father for this victory!" They flapped their wings again.

"Now," Camael looked to Sophia and Faith, getting to business, "You will draw your swords today, but do not forget your main goal. Jan and Julia must come to knowledge. Create a fear in them." He turned to Suriel, her sweet smile encouraging him. "Suriel, I cannot have you in battle. There will be much need for healing. The Demonics believe we have lost you and so this will be our advantage. Remain invisible and keep us strong. Pashar will be your rearguard so you will have to keep her apprized of where you are so she can protect you."

He rubbed his hands together again as he turned his attention to the warriors of this battle. Although he did not know Ansiel well, he knew the angel by reputation. He was skilled with the Word of God. Through speaking, Ansiel turned an entire army away from Israel, causing them to think they were being attacked. They not only fled, but also fought against each other on the way. Because of that event, the hosts referred to him as "the Constrainer", for he was able to force, restrain, compel, and oblige using the Word. He was also a master of speed. Angels had boasted that his speed was so great that it appeared he instantly jumped through space. A while back, he requested to be a guardian of a special boy named Jared and the Father granted his request. Although missed by the hosts, he seemed pleased and full of joy with his change in position. Lucky for Camael, Jared was Jan's son!

Camael's smile spread as he addressed him, "Ansiel, we are honored to have the opportunity to see you in action. I am sure you have heard of the document that we must protect and get into the right hands. I am counting on you to make sure it does. Ariel will be your rearguard; she is the fastest we have on our team. I think she might be up for the challenge." She nodded emphatically and went to stand next to Ansiel. "As for Chayyliel and Zazriel, you are the brute force and I am not holding you back this time. Show them what they are against." He gave them a nod. "Sablo will be our protector. This is it, team! God has already handed this victory to us. Now we just have to do our part."

Suddenly, they began to glow bright and each felt the strength of the Lord fill them. Looking up, Camael laughed as he saw an army of the Lord descend. He pointed up and then to his heart. The rest of his team did the same, honoring their Lord!

Julia felt refreshed and by the time she got out of her car, Brailey and Shannon were done with practice and ready to help her haul phone books into the art room. Quickly pulling out the sandwiches, she offered them to the girls and started preparing the room for class. When the girls were finished eating, she instructed them to start shredding the phone books into paper strips and piling them on a large table in front of the class. Brailey wanted a demonstration so Julia grabbed a scrap paper from her purse and tore it into strips and placed it where she wanted the pile. They set to work until they heard the familiar voices of their cousins.

"What a surprise!" Julia hugged her sister and managed to grab two fleeting hugs from her niece and nephew. "They are growing up. I'm not as popular as I use to be."

"I hear you," Jan reached over and forced Brailey and Shannon into a group hug. They giggled and showed the others their task of tearing paper, making a game of it.

"When I invited you to take a class sometime, I did not think you would take me up on it until summer," Julia filled bowls with her paste concoction.

"You know, what can I say? Mary had a dream of making a pony out of paper. So, here we are," she explained while helping distribute the bowls of paste to each table. Julia looked out the window. "Here come the students," pointing to a number of parents guiding their children towards the room.

"I better greet them," Julia rinsed her hands and Jan declared she would chaperone their kids. As she welcomed each student into the room, she recognized the handsome black man coming down the hall with his daughter. Kealin had come after all!

The entire team was ready and in position around the art room. Before Kealin had even arrived, there had been a number of fights over that document with large brutish demons.

Chayyliel called over his shoulder, "I think these devils are getting bigger and stronger!" Camael laughed and pulled up his sword, the gleam shimmering down its blade.

Sablo replied with his quick wit, "Maybe you are getting smaller. How long has it been since you've used those muscles of yours?"

Chayyliel put his massive muscular arms on display with his wings flared to their fullest extent in response and intimidated all the demons in the area. However, it was true that the demons were getting larger and more powerful. It was clear that this war had high stakes and Aboddon was making a more concentrated effort with each step towards establishing the drug hub.

Uzza barged into the art room and about had the document under his control when Sophia stopped him with a threat to have it ripped up. He hesitated as Sophia motioned to Brailey ripping paper. Calling her bluff, Uzza charged toward the purse thought to contain the paper. Quickly, Sablo poked Brailey as Sophia guided Julia's hand to the document. Camael and Chayyliel jumped in killing two demons on their way to the table where Julia had deposited the shredded document. Uzza fumed, focusing on Julia with red eyes swollen in anger. He huffed and stepped back, but not far. There, the angels stood guard as they waited for the Demonic battle cry.

Camael could not connect Kealin as a major player in the scheme of things, so he was a little baffled as to why Julia was so important to bringing an end to this drug campaign. Nevertheless, angels only know what the all-knowing God discerns they need to know and that was good enough for him. His main goal was to protect Julia.

Ansiel proclaimed, "But as for me, I am filled with power, with the Spirit of the Lord, and with justice and might. Micah 3:8." All the demons in the room, including Uzza, fell to the ground. As they jumped back up, Ansiel seemingly disappeared, but popped up next to the pile of torn paper. Moving at a speed so fast his hands were a blur, he sifted through the pile of paper in search of the strips containing the information.

A deep sound filled the air as the Demonic's sounded their charge.

⚜

"Did you have any trouble finding us?" Julia asked Kealin, her special guest.

"Nope, plugged the information you gave me into the GPS and it guided us right to you," Kealin smiled looking more handsome than ever. "Hey, I was looking at this paper you wrote on and noticed it was an important document. You must have grabbed it from my worktable by mistake. Would you have the other half?"

"Oh," she put her hand to her forehead, "I am so sorry," she cringed. "I don't know . . . today has been so hectic."

"Remember, you got a call and wrote something down, maybe about the divorce?" he pushed her memory.

"Right," she grabbed her purse and was about to look in it when she remembered taking the paper out. "You know, Kealin, I ripped another part off to give a number to some fellows that want to help me with my house. Can you believe today? I was leaving my house when . . ."

"Think, Julia, I need that paper. I don't mean to offend you, but I have to have it," he pushed harder.

"Oh, sorry, okay," she looked over her desk and then spied the table of strips from the phone book. A memory was beginning to form when Mary interrupted her thoughts. "Aunt Julia, can you show me where the rags are?" The niece pointed to her mother. Jan was busy dealing with spilled paste. With a sigh, she excused herself and rushed off with Mary to the other side of the room to gather rags.

When she returned, Kealin reminded her of his situation. Shaking her head, she could not remember. A mixture of embarrassment and guilt rushed through her veins, knowing she inadvertently caused difficulty for someone else. Jacob had said she did this so often it must be in her blood. Shaking the memory from her, she racked her mind for a solution. "Is there any way to get that information . . . ?"

"Hey, no problem," he scooted around the desk and put an arm around her seeing the emotion begin to tear her eyes. "Don't get too upset. The more you think about it the more flustered you will become. It'll come to you by the end of this class. Remember when Lloyd lost eighty some signs? Before shutting down, he recalled where they were and we got them sent off just in time." He gave her a squeeze and motioned for his daughter to come over. "Hey, baby doll, this is the lady I was telling you about from work. She's going to teach us about paper mache."

"Hi, I'm Julia." She shook her hand lightly, trying to give the girl her full attention. "Are you excited to make something out of paper?" The girl nodded shyly and she led them to a table close to her desk. "We better get started. I will introduce you to my kids later, okay?" She turned to address the class, "Alright everyone, let's get into our seats so I can demonstrate the first step to making paper mache." Julia moved to the front of the class, winking at her clan at the center table.

꧁꧂

The fight was on. Demonics stormed into the building, some able to pass through the walls and a few forced to find other ways in. Aboddon was like a prized Spanish bull as he pierced and knocked anything as he made his way towards the table, Azza as his rearguard. Uzza set his sight on Julia and Semyaza turned towards Jan. Glowing red eyes darted everywhere and the stench descended onto the entire town.

Amidst the dust of evil, the Heavenly Hosts sparkled like diamonds shinning through silt. They were organized, working together against the Demonics. Like a shield, they surrounded the roof of the room, side-by-side, and pressed out the attack from the air. Each held a bubble that they could stretch to whatever size they needed. The bubble looked so clear it was difficult to see it at times and although easily manipulated, it was so strong the Demonics could not penetrate it.

In the room, the angels fought like paired warriors, one as the striker and the other as a rearguard. Chayyliel and Camael fought together against Uzza and any other choosing to come against Julia. Camael blocked as Chayyliel struck, alternating as needed. Uzza was well protected by his hairy thick skin. They could strike him hundreds of times and never cause any life-threatening damage.

Sablo stood behind them and took out any demon that managed to break through. A small demon had crawled through the battle past the angels. As Sablo drew back to slice the little demon in two, he struck a larger demon on the head that was coming up from behind. He then finished off the small one and twirled his blade behind him in the same swing taking out the large one recovering from the thump on the head. He whooped to Chayyliel that he was getting the hang of the thing. From then on, Sablo kept an eye on what was going on behind him as well.

Within minutes, they must have vanquished a hundred demons with little injury to show for it. Camael had a large gash on his forearm. Suriel became visible enough to touch it and then vanished again. Pashar blocked a strike from above and then jumped back to keep up with the healer.

Five demons surrounded Aboddon with twirling blades, causing angels and demons alike to retreat from him. Barging through the angels protecting the table, he stabbed his sword towards Ansiel, who grabbed it with his quick reflexes and diverted it away. In doing so, the sword nicked his side releasing light. Feeling Suriel's touch, his strength returned and he rushed to the center of the Sealed table taking Ariel with him. From the table, they could see Aboddon pick up the pieces of the document with a wicked grin.

"For I will give you words and wisdom that none of your adversaries will be able to resist or contradict. Luke 21:15!" Ansiel shouted.

Sophia was instantly filled with a power surge and looked into a small girl's eyes saying, "You need paper." Omias jumped towards the girl and Sophia pulled her knife stabbing him in the leg, pinning him to the floor where he wiggled to get loose. The girl jumped up and went to the table grabbing the strips of paper seemingly blown into the air. She trotted back to her seat and pushed them into the bowl of glue, leaving behind Aboddon seething.

The class was in full swing blowing up balloons for the structure and gathering paper strips to start the outer skin. With eight kids and four adults, plus her family, the total number in the class was seventeen. She went from table to table to help and answer questions, tickled by the excitement from her students. Even Kealin was having fun while working with his daughter to build a long wiener dog.

While they worked, they talked about many things. But at Jan's table, they were playing a guessing game of Bible knowledge. Julia loved that game since she could tell how much the devotionals helped Brailey and Shannon in their relationship with God. She tried to take every opportunity to teach. She would even stop a movie to explain how the decisions of the characters affected the storyline. Julia passed by and entered the game by guessing the answer to Jared's question. Then she asked what woman sold purple cloth. Leaving them to ponder, she checked on the youngest student, four years of age.

The little girl was so cute with her blond curls and sweet voice, but she was not skilled enough to really press the strips to her balloon. Her mother worked with her and they were having a good time. Julia smeared more glue on the outside of the papers and complimented her. Before moving on, she reminded them to have fun and not to worry about perfection.

Ansiel spoke, filling Pashar with an energy surge, and then turned to Mary. Lahash interfered by smacking Pashar in the face causing her to fall towards Brailey. She looked the Sealed in the eye whispering to her just before Lahash kicked her to the floor. Then the skinny demon stepped into a fat boy and moved him to stand behind Brailey's chair acting interested in the girls' art projects. Pashar bit the boy's ankle and he bent down to see what had caused him pain. With all her might, Pashar scooted Brailey's chair back, knocking the boy over. He got mad and was going to yell at the girls, but Ansiel bent down and told Jared to pay attention.

Jared turned to see the boy on the floor and said, "Dude, that was the best fall I've ever seen. You're like a natural stunt man." He reached down and pulled the guy up as Lahash stepped out, eyes turning gray.

The boy shook his head and smiled, "You really think so?"

Jared nodded. "O yeah! You could be in movies and stuff some day!"

Lahash pulled his sword up over his head with a growl and aimed for Pashar. Before he could strike, Ariel threw her sword penetrating the demons chest. The skinny demon looked down to see himself evaporate. The red stardust left behind darted to the fat boy again. But Ansiel snatched it just before it could pass into the body and sent him to his prison of darkness as Brailey left the table obediently.

"Hi, mom," Brailey stood next to Julia with her hands full of white goop. "I guessed Lydia, did you hear me?" she followed behind her.

"No I didn't, but you are right. Now it's your turn." She stroked her hair and warned her to be careful not to drip the glue on the floor a little too late.

Time slipped by fast and soon she was giving a ten minute warning for clean up. Everyone hustled to put on last strips of paper and find a good spot on the counter for their paper mache to dry. Not paying too much attention to details, they washed their hands and wiped up their tables and chairs before making quick exits. Julia tried to make sure she gave each kid a chance to show her what they had accomplished in their two hours as well as say their goodbyes.

The only ones left, other than family, were Kealin and his daughter were trying to finish one more strip of paper. Kealin beamed his bright smile as he pointed at the different strips of paper on her dog. He certainly seemed like a good father. She came over and joined in on the inspection.

"That looks great, Neesha," she patted her back and then pointed to the dog's feet. "He has some great feet. I think he will stand perfectly." She winked at Kealin.

"It's a girl dog," Neesha corrected.

"Oh, I'm sorry. *She* will be perfect," she gave the girl's shoulder a squeeze.

"So, who are these rambunctious kids?" Kealin turned his attention to her family still cleaning their table up.

⤙☙⤚

The fighting was grueling with the constant onslaught of the demon legions. Uzza's hair stood on end and his drool flung with each swing of his sword. He was determined to have Julia. Even with Jan in the room, he did not turn from his focus. Camael could not overcome him nor could Chayyliel with all the intrusions of the other demons. Between blows, Camael ordered Sophia to create silence. It was time to use the kids to distance Julia.

He could hear the guardians sending the message to their Sealed. Focused on them, he did not notice Uzza's change in attack and received a blow to his face, light spraying out of his eye to his ear. The pain caused him to drop his sword and fall back where Sablo stepped up and plunged his sword into Uzza's heart, steam bellowing out. Roaring and thrashing, Uzza fell over Camael and then evaporated leaving his stardust to hover.

While Chayyliel and Sablo continued to battle for Julia's safety, Pashar fought to get Suriel to Camael. A large demon blocked the way. Camael focused on the fight and opened his mouth. In one flick of his tongue, the demon was split in two. The top half fell over before it evaporated, making way for Suriel. She appeared with her kind eyes looking down on him. A tear fell and his vision returned,

206

his insides washed clean and his strength better than he had ever known it. He jumped up and stabbed a demon coming over Suriel. She winked and vanished.

Julia stepped to her children and turned the older of her girls towards Kealin. "Ah, these?" she frazzled Shannon's hair as she tried to pull away. "This one is Shannon and over there," she pointed to the sink, "is Brailey." They both turned and smiled but did not say a word of greeting, which was unusual.

"Nice to meet you, Shannon," Kealin put out his fist and she knew to bump his knuckles. Still she said nothing. "What grade are you in?" he continued as if he did not notice the silence.

"Seventh," she answered quietly.

Julia chuckled and guided her to the table, "You better finish up cleaning." She tried to cover the rudeness. Shaking her head she almost apologized but Kealin, true to his nature, did not skip a beat.

"We had a great time. I am looking forward to coming next week. How about you, baby doll?" he draped his arm around his daughter's shoulder and she nodded emphatically.

"Well, I'm glad you both got to come. I look forward to seeing what you name your dog." Julia patted Kealin's muscular arm and stepped back hoping to get home before it got too late. She turned to rinse out a rag and start wiping down the tables again. Seeing Kealin and his daughter heading for the door, she waved goodbye and hurried to finish.

Faith, with sword drawn and dingy from the battle, backed up against her Sealed. She was breathing heavy from her exertion, protecting Jan and the kids. Glancing to the sister, she could hardly believe the team was still standing with so many determined to harm Julia. Semyaza, a demon with a large mouth full of sharp teeth, struck again and she kept him at bay while searching out the leader. Semyaza was determined to get to Jan, not leaving this fight, eliminating all intrusions even if they were of his own kind.

Aboddon was the biggest, scariest demon Faith had ever seen up close. She had heard he was skilled and had a gift of motivation. Glancing to the sky, the motivation was certainly apparent. The sky looked dark with legions of demons still coming at the hosts. She was done with swordplay and changed her attack. She kicked Semyaza in the knee, butted him in the head with the handle of her sword, and then pushed her dagger into his ear until the tip showed through the other. Her eyes moved to Aboddon who was right behind Kealin.

She spun around, catching three other demons, but only killing two. Faith looked Jan in the eye. "He is bad," she informed. The demon that had escaped death now had her in a choke hold. Unable to breath, unable to move, she pushed out her wings enough to jab her dagger back, through her feathers and into the demons belly. The evil spirit fell but was replaced by another.

She spied Sophia instructing Brailey and motioned to her. Sophia flew over and vanquished four demons on her way. The large demon that had a hold on Faith turned and fought Sophia while holding his captive with its enormous arm. Sophia finally stepped back and lowered her sword. It nodded and turned its back to finish off Faith but fell back instead and evaporated. Faith raised her brows to see Suriel, with her sweet face, holding the other dagger from Faith's belt.

The healer took her arm, sending her medicine through Faith's body, and asked, "Are you alright, dear?" Her eyes were angelic with a trace of cleverness.

"Much better," Faith breathed easy and shot Sophia a broad smile. "Clever little thing, isn't she?" Sophia raised her brows and twirled her sword in time to vanquish another demon determined to make its mark in the world.

Faith gave a nod and slipped her sword back into its sheath. In an instant she and her Sealed were surrounded by demons seizing an opportunity. Suddenly, Faith grew pale and her eyes glazed, as if shooting from her fingertips, she threw her hands out wide, and an unseen disease attacked her enemies. The demons all shrunk back from the mysterious angel, wide-eyed, waiting to see what would happen to them. Faith returned to her natural color and glanced at Jan to make sure she had heard her. No, the demons did not die . . . yet. Then the disease began its work. They all began to flail about, itching and wailing for relief, until disintegrating into puffs of stardust.

⤜✣⤛

Julia was going to ask the girls for their help, but they were having such a good time with their cousins looking over the other projects that she opted to let them enjoy. Jan was standing at the end of the counter watching something. So, Julia followed her gaze and was surprised to see Kealin still lingering with his daughter looking at the middle school art on the other side of the room.

Julia moved to another table and her attention went to Brailey, who had called Shannon over to look at the youngest girl's piece. Sensing he was missing out, Jared joined them with Mary tagging along. They were all really looking closely at the pathetic paper mache the girl had attempted to create. Thinking that they might be making fun of it, Julia went over and put her hand on the back of Brailey's neck.

"What are you kids doing? I hope that you are *looking* at this girl's art as art," she warned thinking they should know better since they lived around constant creativity that did not always work out. "Remember, never make fun of someone's artistic style."

"No, we wouldn't do that," Brailey hugged her mom knocking her back almost as if on purpose. Raising a brow, she looked down at her daughter. Something was up and she noticed Jan making her way towards them seeing the signs as well.

"We're just reading the paper on this one," Jared explained with his face still close to the piece.

Shannon's eyes were wide and Julia knew that face. Now Jan came in to take a look, asking Jared to point at what was so interesting. Julia rolled her eyes and went back to wiping down the tables, leaving Jan to deal with it so she could finish up.

Jan guided the kids away and picked up a rag to help with the tables. She worked her way to the same table Julia was at. By then, Neesha had pulled Kealin back to the paper mache to look at what was of interest to the other kids. Jan eyed Julia and being twins she knew what she was telling her to do.

Grabbing both rags and tossing them into the dirty laundry bin, she dismissed the rest of the clean up. "It's time to go everyone. It's getting late," she pushed in a chair and started to gather her purse and some other things.

⁓⁂⁓

Camael felt like they had triumphed until that little girl pulled her father to the document strips on the art piece. He could not leave Julia as Azza had taken Uzza's place, which left Aboddon without a rear guard. It was time for Chayyliel to shine. He nodded and Chayyliel left his side while Sablo stepped in.

Watching Chayyliel was like watching World Wide Wrestling. He had such a charisma about his style of fighting that it was actually entertaining. Yes, that angel loved what God made him to be. He barreled towards Aboddon, picking up demons on the way and hurling them at the targeted evil spirit who dodged and sometimes vanquished.

Without backup, Aboddon was tackled by Chayyliel knocking him back and sending his feet to the air. Camael cringed thinking how that blow would affect the great Aboddon's reputation, should he make it through the night. Ducking a swipe of a sword, Camael vanquished the demon in front of him to restore his view, as Chayyliel had snatched up his annoying emissary, Omias, from where the knife pinned him to the floor and was beating Aboddon with him.

Demon after demon pounced on Chayyliel to rescue their leader. Some evaporated as they landed and others evaporated under the pile causing a drop of those above. Camael could not see Chayyliel anymore, but he figured as long as there were demons dissolving, he must be okay. Then, with an explosion of demons flying all over the room and landing everywhere, Aboddon stood with his arms out wide. Although cut up from head to toe, he had proven his ability to overcome.

Then a hand reached up out of the pile of moaning demons and yanked down on Aboddon's belt. He went down again. It certainly was not a flattering fight for the great evil spirit. Camael could not see what was happening, but before he had to turn his attention back to his own fight, he did see Omias stumbling out of the pile dazed and wobbling around.

⚜

Just then, Neesha exclaimed, "Daddy, your name is here!" She pointed to the art that interested everyone.

He bent down and brought up the piece to look at it closer. "So it is!" he smiled. "Julia, I found that paper I was looking for." He laughed out loud.

She came to his side and peered at the piece, but he lowered it too quickly for her to see anything. "I guess I won't have to send for another copy after all."

"Kealin, you can't just take that little girl's project. How would your daughter feel if someone took hers?" she gently took it from his hands and replaced it on the counter. "You better just send for a copy. This one is destroyed and will be painted over next week. Nothing can be done about it now." She motioned for him to head for the door.

He hesitated, "You know, it is still wet enough. We could pull the strips that I need and replace them with fresh ones, improving her piece. She'll think she did better than she really did, boosting her confidence," he smiled and gave her a wink. "Come on."

Julia shook her head. "You don't know kids very well then, Kealin. They always know their work," she chuckled. "Trust me; you don't want to deal with the parent of an upset kid." She nodded at her girls to get them going. "Plus, it's getting late and Neesha looks tired." The girl yawned.

"You're right, of course, babe," he started for the door a second time. "We'll see you tomorrow at work." He waved like usual.

"Okie dokie," Julia waved back and went to turn off the lights.

⚜

The demons retreated almost as fast as they came. Although the lights went out, the angels' presence produced enough glow to keep the closer demons still visible. Camael watched Sablo drop to his knees to catch his breath, not used to so much fighting. Suriel would revive him when she could get to him. Instead, Faith stepped up and reached out to touch him but he leaned away.

"No way, I saw what you did to all those demons. No thank you!" he shook his head.

She flashed a mischievous smile, "Oh that was nothing. Wait until you feel this." Before he could move away, she patted him on the head.

"Wow!" Sablo jumped as his muscles puffed up. He felt taller, stronger, and full of energy.

"It won't last, so enjoy it while you can," she smirked.

With a wink at Faith, he grabbed Aboddon off of their team member and body slammed him to the floor as the great angel shook the pile of demons off. Chayyliel eyed Sablo who flexed into a body builder pose. Stunned, the massive angel suddenly realized who he was. Sablo jumped into the air and brought down an elbow on the recovering demonic leader, smashing him to the ground again. He reached up and slapped Chayyliel's hand as to tag him like in a wrestling match. The army angel took action and grabbed Aboddon by the feet as Sablo rolled off the roaring demon, and whirled him around knocking Omias to the wall on the other side of the room. All the demons slinked to the dark corners as they watched their leader being flung straight up into the air. Sablo came from nowhere, planting both feet to Aboddon's midsection. The evil demon let out a wail that scared most of the demons to retreat to the sky. Chayyliel watched Aboddon twirling through the sky out of control. The wrestling tag team angels doubled over in laughter. Sablo managed to say, "Not bad, Chayyliel, but I gotta say, I really think you are getting smaller." He gave Faith two thumbs up as Chayyliel furrowed his brows and flexed every muscle in his body. Sablo mirrored him and Chayyliel compared their physiques.

Camael, however, had no time to lose. He went to Julia and looked her in the eye, telling her to get the piece of art.

She stood for a moment by the counter and then started for the door without the object. She was so stubborn sometimes about rules. Sophia and Ariel stood by the door shaking their heads. After all they had been through; they hoped she would submit just this once. Julia was about to leave but turned again to retrieve the art that caused so much concern.

His smile faded as he looked down to see a blade sticking out of his body. The blade was pulled back and light sprayed from him. In a daze, he turned to see the room full of another legion of demons and in front of him stood Aboddon himself. As Camael fell to his knees, he looked past the Demonic leader. Like a linebacker, Chayyliel came from behind charging full speed but before he could cause Aboddon any harm, Amon's Fallen angel appeared and struck him down with his sword. Light sprayed from him as he plunged to the feet of the disfigured angel shadowed with evil.

The demonic victors turned towards Julia. Camael struggled against the pain to get up, holding his midsection. He had to protect her! He saw his sword back in its sheath. He should have never let his guard down in such a battle. With every bit of energy left, he called the sword to him and hurled it towards the Fallen angel. It began to fall short so Ariel took aim and threw her sword, deflecting it back on course striking the Fallen in the back, slicing both wings from his body. He arched backward and roared, causing Aboddon to turn in time to see Sablo pounce on him; and Chayyliel's sword pierce him through. The great demon had an expression of disbelief while fading to star dust.

The Fallen vanished from sight with a flash, dropping his sword to the floor. Demons converged on that point and Camael lost the strength to see if it could be recovered. He could hear his lungs trying to breath. He could feel his heart slowing. The pain was subsiding. The light coming from him dimmed. He could hear Sophia ask Suriel if she could heal him.

A soft, familiar voice called to him. He opened his eyes, though they were heavy. The voice called him again. All he could see was light. Blinking, he tried to focus. In the midst of the light, there was an even purer light. He strained to look deeper. Within the pure light was movement that began to take shape. The outline sharpened and the details began to fill in. His lips spread and his heart quickened. He knew who it was. It was his Lord!

Out in the parking lot, Kealin was just getting Neesha buckled into his white Land Rover, even at the age of eleven, making sure she was safe. Julia had to nominate that man for Father of the Year. She waved one last time and joined her sister by her Var. "Let's go, girls. It's gonna be really late by the time your cousins get to bed. They have a long drive ahead of them." She leaned to give Jan a hug.

"Did you read what was on that piece of paper?" Jan whispered.

"Not yet," Julia let her go and slightly adjusted the sack she had packed the sandwiches in. "But I intend to." She patted the sack and gave her twin a look. "Was that weird or what?" she scrunched her nose.

Jan helped Mary after all the other kids had oddly climbed into the Var in silence, no joking or giggling. "I think we should all leave here together." She shut the side door. "Smile and get into the passenger seat."

Julia did as ordered and only when she had her door shut and the interior light went off did she look out to see that Kealin was still in the parking lot. "How would you like some ice cream?" Julia offered the kids in the back sensing from her twin that they would not be going home.

No one cheered but Shannon spoke up softly, "Maybe we should go to the police instead."

Julia turned to look at her and Jared spoke, "'Because he loves me,' says the Lord, 'I will rescue him; I will protect him, for he acknowledges my name. He will call upon me, and I will answer him; I will be with him in trouble, I will deliver him and honor him.' Psalm 91:14,15." He boldly quoted a Bible verse he had memorized. He was known as the Champion of Bible Memory at Wednesday night church. Motivated by prizes, he conquered the list given to the kids so quickly that he was given a special list of extra verses to memorize.

"That's it," Jan turned her key and pulled her vehicle out of the parking lot. "When Jared starts quoting Bible verses, best to listen." She pasted on a smile and waved at Kealin's Land Rover as they passed by, Julia mimicked the action.

Now Mary had something to say, "Do you have your cell phones on?"

Jan and Julia both looked at each other and quickly checked to make sure. Then Julia looked at Brailey, "Do you have anything to say?" she raised a brow for the children were exhibiting their spiritual gifts at the same time. But she shook her head silently, looking fearful. "Don't worry, kids. God is our protection just like Jared said."

"Let's pray," Mary's voice was back to a happy tone.

Jan wasted no time and jumped right into prayers while driving to the police station downtown. Before pulling up, Julia had an uneasy feeling. A whisper filled her heart urging her to leave. "Not here," she immediately told her twin.

Continuing down the street, Jan turned right onto the angled road that led out of town towards Wichita. On the way, Jan spotted the white Land Rover coming up behind her. She looked at Julia who knew in an instant to look behind. Then all the kids turned to see what was going on. Julia slowly turned back and looked at the bag in her hand. "Investigate," ordered the whisper in her heart. So, she pulled the sticky ball from the sack and Shannon turned on the overhead light.

No one said a word at first, but then Jared could not help himself. "It's a lot of money."

"No duh," Brailey bounced in. "It's for drugs. During our DARE program we learned about Kilos and stuff."

"He's a drug dealer, mom! He is a very bad man," Mary blurted.

Jan calmly answered. "We are going to take it to the police and let them take care of it." She turned to Julia for confirmation.

Julia sat shaking her head as she looked over the different strips with addresses, billing, and amounts of cocaine for distribution. "It all makes sense now," she looked up. "I mean, I kept seeing him take boxes to this guy in the parking lot after work. I'm the only one in my department that leaves at that time and parks in the back. But he didn't sweat it." She put her hand to her mouth, "Oh my, when he dropped a box, I actually tossed him a bundle that had fallen out! I might have even helped him pack some of it up! No wonder they never went on the UPS truck." She let the art fall into the plastic bag.

"Julia," Jan pressed, "Where should I go?"

"And I will lead the blind in a way that they do not know, in paths that they have not known I will guide them. I will turn the darkness before them into light. Isaiah 42:16." Jared quoted again and sat back with his arms crossed pleased with himself.

Julia's first thought was the police station at the edge of town, but then the inner voice whispered, "Gwin". She remembered her co-worker whose husband was police chief of Eastborough. "Let me make a call." She pulled out her cell and scrolled down the numbers for her contacts. Thank goodness she had entered the supervisor's number, just in case she did overtime in her department. A rough voice answered, it was definitely Gwin. She explained her need to come by and visit with her husband. Gwin swore, but relented under Julia's persistence.

❦

Chayyliel would have insisted on taking Camael to the Father, but he knew that Camael would have wanted him to stay with the battle for his Sealed. The teammates were stronger than ever now, especially Sablo. Suriel was good medicine and, unbeknown to them, Faith was a master of disease and body. Most of his team was in or around the Var, protecting it as demons bombarded them on the road to Wichita.

The great angel had to admit, he was more than concerned about them going to Wichita. The legions they had been fighting would not compare to the number they would meet in the city. Already the moon was blackened from those in the air. With the loss of two major leaders, the Demonics were thrown into chaos.

Learning from the surveillance he had been doing, Chayyliel understood the importance of knowing what they were going up against. With this in mind, he did not catch up with Julia's group but joined the hosts that stayed behind. Watching Kealin's next move revealed to all present that he was not the nice guy he was pretending to be. After breaking into the art room and not finding the art piece with his document, he drew a gun from his jacket and shot three times into the door as he left.

When he got into his vehicle, he ignored his daughter and made some calls, putting the gun on the console next to him in plain view of Neesha. Since she did not react to its presence, Chayyliel presumed that she was used to it.

Although he was among hundreds of army angels with skills like his own, they were no match for the number of demons surrounding Kealin's vehicle. The angels kept high above Jan's Var while analyzing what Julia's family were going to meet once they came into Wichita.

Without Camael, Chayyliel thought he better get with the team and see if they had a plan.

He dropped through the roof and in the middle of Shannon and Jared, who were sitting silently. "Why didn't they go to the town police?" he asked anyone that might have a clue.

Sophia turned from her position between the driver and passenger seats. "The police do not trust Julia since Jacob is a good friend." She huffed, disgusted.

"Amazing," he let his head drop back on the headrest. "He can take man's money, never pay it back, give some sob story, and they will give him more. If Jacob can do that with policemen, just imagine how easy it is with unsuspecting people," He sighed. "Certainly gives Satan credibility."

"She got rid of one deceptive man only to be caught up with another," Ariel tossed her thumb over her shoulder to the vehicle trailing them.

Zazriel spoke up. "We got rid of Jacob, now we need to get rid of Kealin. Have any information for us, Chayyliel?"

"Yup, the guy is not a sweetheart. He has a gun and he unloaded three bullets into the art room door when he discovered the art piece missing," Chayyliel sat forward.

Pashar looked to Ansiel and nodded. "We have a plan," Ansiel smirked.

Navigating for Jan, Julia followed Gwin's directions while keeping an eye on the Land Rover behind them. Finally, they were in front of Gwin's house, a modest home with a white picket fence. The Land Rover parked behind them and Kealin came to talk to her. Taking a deep breath, she held the cell phone to her ear and rolled down the window.

"Yes, we're here," she talked to her phone. Over his shoulder, she saw Gwin open the front door. "Kealin, what a surprise!" she exclaimed.

"Hi, Kealin," Mary snatched the bag off of Julia's lap and crawled up wrapping her arms around her aunt's neck. "Are you dropping off food, too?"

Kealin smiled and shook his head. "No, darlin'. But I did forget something back at the school. I've had a time trying to get you to pull over!" he raised his cell.

"Oh, I was talking to Gwin," she hung up and checked. To her surprise, he had called her six times. "Wow, even with modern convenience of cell phones . . ." she laughed nervously, noticing Gwin in her robe on the front step lighting up a cigarette, but not coming over to their vehicles.

I know," he looked over his shoulder to see her, too. "Whatchya doin here?" He turned back to her suspiciously.

"Food, remember?" Mary giggled and raised a can of fruit. "We're donating to the food bank for the police drive."

"Kind of late, don't you think?" Kealin looked to Julia again.

Mary jumped into the conversation again. "Hey, didn't you see us at the art class? We've been busy and today is the last day to drop it off . . ." her voice trailed as she retrieved the sack of canned goods from the back of the Var.

Julia shrugged and turned her attention to why he was at her window. "What did you forget? Maybe I could swing by on my way to work tomorrow and pick it up."

"My daughter's favorite hat," he shrugged and looked down the street. "You know how kids are. She wants it for school tomorrow."

"Sometimes we don't get what we want," Shannon stated as she leaned forward between the seats.

"Now Shannon," Julia scolded with a wink.

"It's true," Brailey added her part as she pushed Shannon back to make room for her. "Once, I wanted to wear my boots to school but my mom would not drive to grandma's house for nothing!" After that, the other kids added their stories with Kealin laughing along.

⌗

Demons were dropping all around the Var in piles and the angels were turning the night to red star dust on the block. Faith stepped out with a mission. The rest of the team surrounded her fighting off more Demonics. She centered her purpose and closed her eyes, reaching out to Jan.

Then with a feeling of substance, she opened her eyes and said, "End this."

Jan leaned forward still holding onto the steering wheel and blinked a couple of times as she seemingly looked right at Faith. Before fading back into the spirit world, Faith looked to Kealin and shook her head.

"Excuse me, Kealin," Jan jumped out of the Var and circled around with some bags of canned food, one containing the art piece. "We had planned to take the kids for ice cream afterwards but it is getting late. I'm afraid we may not even get to do that. I'm sure Neesha will understand. In fact, it looks like she's asleep already." She nodded to his vehicle under the light as she reached for Julia's car door, causing him to have to back away.

"I'm not worried about tonight. I'm worried about tomorrow morning. Anyway, sorry to disrupt your schedule, Julia. But, hey, if you are going back soon, I could wait and follow you since Neesha is sleeping," he bargained.

"Well," Julia hesitated.

"But you promised ice cream," whined Brailey.

"I scream, you scream. We all scream for ice cream!" Jared started the chant and the rest joined in.

"I did promise the kids ice cream and you know I have to keep my promises. I think we are going to be out a little longer than you will want to wait." Julia shrugged.

Sensing he was not going to win in this game, he backed off. "Ok. Then just bring it to work. It should be on the counter where the projects are." He slowly walked to his vehicle. "Hey, I wouldn't want to cause you any hassle, girl." He waved and opened the door. "Tomorrow."

Jan gave Julia a look of annoyance and all six of them filed into Gwin's house. It was a comfortable home but filled with smoke. The kids made themselves at home on the couch.

"What was so important you had to come by in the middle of the night?" Gwin's rough voice was a bark misrepresenting the woman's heart. There was one thing Julia could say about Gwin; she was loyal to the employees under her charge. Not one went to the office without her present and standing behind them. Gwin was harsh in vocabulary, but all mush inside.

Julia pulled the sloppy paper mache from her sack and handed it to Gwin's husband. "If you look closely to the part that is half sticking out, you will see a bunch of numbers . . ."

She did not need to say anything more. He held up his hand and moved to the kitchen table setting it down while putting on his glasses. "I will have to take this for evidence." He looked at the kids.

"Oh, it's not one of theirs. It belongs to a student of mine." Julia explained farther than she needed, "You see, I accidentally took a paper from Kealin's workstation and used it for scrap. When I got to my art class, I just added it to the strips of paper we were using for paper mache. Unfortunately, Kealin and his daughter also took that class and noticed it on this piece. You saw outside that he followed us here. We didn't know where else to go."

He nodded and grabbed his cell phone leaving the room. While he was making calls, Gwin pulled out some ice cream for everyone, which boosted their spirits and gave the kids a sugar high. *God reveals, protects, guides, and serves ice cream.* Julia giggled to herself and sent a prayer of thanksgiving. Jan gave Julia the twenty-minute warning look, which was usually how long it took for a sugar high to run its course and leave the kids complaining and crying.

"You did the right thing, girls," the police chief came into the living room in uniform. "Give my apologies to your student for taking her art." He raised it up and then put it back into the bag. "I talked with the DEA and believe it or not they have been investigating Sign & Tech Graphics. Someone has been distributing a large amount of cocaine this month all over Kansas. If this paper is true, Kealin is our guy."

Gwin agreed, "It makes sense. Nothin' out of the ordinary for a guy that runs the shipping department. I always thought he was a little weasel." She lit another cigarette.

"This list," he shook the bag, "is vital information listing everyone that is involved and the distribution of the drugs and money. According to what I read, he got sixty-six kilos of cocaine last month from a guy called Mr. Business. We now have their addresses and location of drop offs, which are happening tonight. So, I've got to get this over to the DEA right away." He grabbed his keys. "You did a good thing for your community." With that said, he was out the door.

Jan sighed and rounded up the kids. Mary made sure Gwin understood the bags of canned goods were for the police food drive. Just as Julia was stepping out, Gwin caught her sleeve. "You might want to stay in a hotel tonight."

⁓※⁓

Hitting the dash again and again, Kealin raged as he drove down the block. Suriel sat in the passenger seat of yet another hostile man and vehicle load of Demonics. She certainly had her fill of angry people. However, she had a gift of invisibility and that made her perfect for intervention. She was glad God gifted her with healing so she could also have moments of goodness as well. It was a nice balance that gave her a sense of purpose and satisfaction.

Right now, as the battle continued above, she was like Kealin, seemingly unaffected by the chaos. Yet, she knew it would not last. Chaos grows and would soon invade their space as well. Being invisible only works for a time. She looked to the gun and sighed. And that kind of protection rarely protects.

Kealin held his cell to his ear, waiting for an answer. "Hello? Mr. Business?" Suriel listened in on his side of the conversation. "No, I don't have it yet. I mean, I sent it on like normal, but I made a copy and am currently making sure it disappears." He gritted his teeth. "No problem, man," he faked a laugh in his normal positive manner and the demons chuckled, too. "No worries here, sir. It's all good. Just enjoy your trip back and we'll settle things when you get in," Kealin laughed about something and then ended the call, "Peace, out." As soon as the call was disconnected, he about threw it to the floor, but it began to play the popular song "Dangerous", so he answered it instead.

"Yo, babe," he glanced in the rear view mirror and adjusted it so he could see Neesha sleeping in the back. "We're on our way back right now. Love ya." He snapped it shut and then threw it to the floor with some choice words.

⁓❦⁓

In the Var, Julia looked to Jan questioningly. It was like trying to guess the reasoning behind Jacob's actions all over again. To her, Kealin was a kind soul who loved to laugh and look at the positive side of things. Now, it would seem he was deceitful and involved in some dangerous activity.

Jan drove them back home in silence, allowing the sugar crash to lull the kids to sleep. It was a long day and spiritually exhausting. Julia thought perhaps she was over thinking everything. Doubt slipped in and Julia decided Kealin would not do anything rash. After watching him with Neesha, she could not imagine him capable of hurting anyone. No, he would wait for tomorrow.

Jan dropped her off at the school to get Neesha's hat and take her car home. As she walked to the art room, Julia thought about Jan's offer to have them over for the night again. She felt she was making it worse than it really was, as usual. Upon turning on the light, Julia noticed that the fire escape door was ajar. A voice whispered for her to leave and she obeyed immediately, running to her car. In her haste, she left the light on in the school building.

Racing to her house, she called 911 and made it home before she could even explain her worry to the dispatcher on the other end. Before going into the house, she looked around for any suspicious activity. Jan was inside helping her girls to bed while leaving her own kids in the Var, still sleeping. With a cop on his way, she hung up and rushed in to tell Jan what had happened at the school.

"Maybe the girls should skip school tomorrow and all of you come to my house tonight," Jan tried to reason with her sister once again.

"I can't afford to miss work," Julia sighed. "Let's see what the police say and go from there." They agreed.

The cop came and said that it looked like the break in at the school happened over an hour ago. *Perhaps Kealin did that before leaving town, which would explain why he was behind them when they headed to Wichita,* Julia reasoned. The police did a sweep of the property and then left telling her to call if anything out of the ordinary happened.

222

Feeling assured, Julia decided to stay home and send Jan on her way. She had already inconvenienced her enough. Leery, Jan submitted and headed for home, praying the whole way.

Exhausted, Julia checked all the doors and just crawled into bed fully dressed. In minutes, she was asleep.

⚜

Stomping, Sophia circled the living room, muttering her frustration.

"Let's make her go," Ariel looked at the other angels, confused.

"Free will, girl," Sablo explained as he left for Brailey's room, now deflated to his normal size.

"I don't understand. We have been influencing her this whole time and now we can't do anything to make her go to her sister's house for the night?" Ariel let her hands dangle.

Zazriel tried to explain more thoroughly. "We can only suggest or advise, but Julia," he looked over at her, "is a stubborn woman. Only Camael and the Holy Spirit know how she works inside. She has made up her mind, so we must work within that." He sighed and leaned back to check on Shannon. "Guess I better get." He pulled out his trumpet and left.

Faith, Pashar and Ansiel came to the front door where the others were meeting. "We're off." Ansiel reported. "Wish we could stay and see how this all plays out, but the Father has spoken and we are to go with Jan." They prayed together and then the three joined their Sealed on their way back home in the glowing Var.

"Enough moping," Sophia placed her small fists on her padded hips. "We need a game plan." She looked to Chayyliel.

"Wow, God is stretching me on this assignment." He chuckled and tried to think.

"I know, Sophia can come as a police officer and tell them that they are in danger and need to get out," Ariel interjected with brows raised. "I like that plan," she nodded.

Sophia shook her head. "Becoming one of them is not as easy as it seems. A lot of forethought and planning has to come into play. That is why we had Camael or the Father to work out those complexities."

"Guess we are gonna have to fight it out," Chayyliel passed through the door enough to check the sky and then popped back. "It's not looking good," he reported.

"No, it is not looking good at all," a voice came from above.

They all gasped to see Camael descend to their level. With jubilation, they greeted him, which brought Sablo and Zazriel out of the bedrooms to investigate.

"You're looking new, Boss. We haven't got a lot of time, so . . ." Chayyliel pushed.

"Right, my stubborn Julia . . ." Camael began to grin as an idea came to mind.

Sophia nodded to Ariel, "You see? The Father has gifted each of us with the right tools at the right time."

They leaned in as Camael let them in on plan *A* and plan *B*. They listened intently. Plan *A* was to implement their emergency protocol. At least then the girls would be out of the house and probably cause Julia to call for the police. However, after spending twenty minutes shouting and singing "Bo Bo" the girls did not stir. They were just too exhausted to hear a thing!

With a nod, Zazriel dashed to Shannon's room. There was a thud. Sablo smirked and went to Brailey's room. Plan *B* was underway. Camael had a special plan for Julia.

A noise awakened her and Julia looked at the clock. It was three in the morning. She listened and waited. Hearing nothing, she lay back down and closed her eyes, but could not drift back to sleep. A creek from the house caused her to flinch. After searching the house with the only remaining knife she owned in hand and looking out the windows to find nothing disturbing, she slowed her breathing and relaxed. *All this drama for nothing*, she shook her head. Then she remembered a woman she admired as a prayer warrior sharing that sometimes she would wake up in the middle of the night, wide awake, for no reason. As her relationship matured with the Lord, she realized that God was waking her up for prayer, time to spend with Him, uninterrupted by the bustle of the world. The other women in the study affirmed her, sharing the same experience.

Perhaps she was experiencing the same thing right now. Glad to be mature enough to recognize the opportunity, she knelt by her bed for prayer, sliding the knife a ways away from her. Her heart filled with warmth drawing her closer to her Lord; she soon put her forehead to the floor, communing with Him in earnest gratefulness. Thanking Him with all her heart, she spread herself out on the floor, face down, and humbled herself to His will . . . where she fell asleep.

⚜

"Well?" Camael glowed bright as he looked to Zazriel.

"On the floor under the bed," his smirk illuminated light. "Fast asleep."

"Brailey?" Camael asked Sablo.

"Not quite on the floor, but definitely concealed," he chuckled.

"Ok, we have a small window of opportunity here." He nodded to each one. "Julia is on the floor asleep, but I'm unsure for how long." With a signal, they all fled the house to join Chayyliel on the roof, where he stood guard.

From above, they watched over the Sealed by poking their heads through the roof between fighting off any attacks. Then they spotted Kealin and his entourage of demons. He had left his vehicle a block away and was now feeling confident enough to go into the home. All around him were demons of great strength, checking every direction. Kealin's bright teeth gleamed in the night when he saw how easy it was to break in through the glass sliding door. Armed with a flashlight in one hand and a gun in the other, he began his search.

One demon remained outside keeping watch of the angels on the roof. After the battle at the school, he did not like how easy this was going. He made a motion and roughly fifteen demons came down close from the night sky. Camael knew it was a tactic just to keep them busy.

Sophia, who was peeking through the ceiling, watched Kealin head straight across from where he entered to the French doors of the bedroom. Seeing no one in the bed he moved on. Sophia popped up long enough to report to the team and then poked her head down again to see him make his way through the kitchen and the living room finding a couple of full plastic sacks. Emptying out trash onto the floor he sighed with disgust.

Suddenly, Sophia was pulled from the roof by a demon. Although startled, she quickly joined the fight, reducing the demons to nine. Ariel took her place, spying on Kealin as he passed the bathroom and checked the children's bedrooms. He put his hand on each bed curious by the absent family. Taking it as opportunity, he went through the rooms quickly until he entered the spare room again and saw a knife on the floor just beyond the tips of Julia's fingers, which were peaking out from under the bed. Ariel chuckled while sharing that Kealin was on his way out, not even checking the basement, his imagination obviously getting the best of him, thinking someone had gotten to her before him. With that news, the four remaining demons retreated. Sablo had to hold in a laugh with his hand. Although elated by the results of Camael's quick strategy, no angel let down their guard until Kealin was out of town and Suriel was back by their side.

"The battle here is won," Chayyliel announced and looked to Wichita where they could see one side of the sky begin to glow bright and the other side red.

"Go," Camael told him.

Chayyliel looked to his boss for a moment and then, with an appreciative nod, he pumped his massive wings taking off to lend help there. Camael chuckled. He did not have to say anything twice to that army angel. That's when he noticed Ariel looking at him with hope in her eyes.

"You can go, too," he swished the air with his hand. "Better take Suriel with you." He did not even see her spread her wings as she sped away. Suriel would catch up to them when they reached the edge of the city.

"Are you going to watch from here?" Sophia sat next to Camael on the roof.

"I am not leaving this house without my Sealed," he replied with the passion of his heart. "If you would like to go, you have my blessing."

"I've been in enough battles over the centuries," she put her arm around him.

Soon Zazriel and Sablo joined them on the roof. They sat in silence, as a mighty battle was getting ready to commence.

⚜

Ariel had never seen so many angels gathered together except before the throne of the Lord to worship! Of course, then they were angels of peace. Here, they are angels of action, lighting up the sky in contrast to the other end of the city.

Chayyliel flew straight to the mightiest, strongest, revered, and honored angel, Michael! Ariel felt star struck in the presence of the Archangel. Still, the awe that swept over her dictated her to do something, so she smiled and clasped her heart, weak in the wings.

"We come from Camael's team. We would like to join," Chayyliel announced.

"You are welcome, Chayyliel." He pointed to the army hosts. Being so close to the Archangel, Ariel thought Chayyliel looked dwarfed as he smiled from ear to ear. The army angel saluted and shot to the line. Michael then turned to Suriel. "I am glad you are restored. We can use more healers." She nodded and then pointed to Heaven. "You would do well with the chariots."

Ariel's eyes grew wide as she saw Suriel enter one of the center chariots. The entire first three lines were made of gold chariots, each being pulled by two large white stallion horses. The powerful animals stomped their feet as though they were on ground and puffed air from the nostrils. In each chariot a large army angel dressed in armor from head to toe held a spear in one hand and the reins in the other. It was impressive indeed, even from a modern world perspective.

"You," Michael bent down to look at Ariel as he rubbed his chin, "can stand by me as one of my rearguards." With a grin, he turned behind him and pointed to a group of twenty-five elite angels. Each one wore armor specifically designed for their group and had two swords and two daggers.

"Thank you, O great Michael!" she clasped her heart again.

"No," he took her hand and softened his expression. "Dear one, I am only a servant like you." He turned his eyes upward. "He is the one you clasp your heart for. He is the Great One! Only He is deserving of all honor! He is the one that stripped all His power and glory to enter into the body of man, to endure the harshness of the world, to suffer blamelessly, and die a painful death for their sake! To Him give your all, Ariel." He was glowing so bright Ariel's mouth hung open in awe of the Father's glory shinning through the great Archangel.

A trumpet blasted into the peace of the night and lightning streaked across the sky. As Ariel joined the elite rearguards, thunder rippled over Wichita with each stamping of the horses, vibrating through her body. She peeked from behind an army angel to see the preparation for the charge. The hosts were at attention and the chariots burst into flames as another streak of lightning marked the night with sparks of light. Thunder clashed and the hosts straightened even taller as the horses reared up.

Michael held up his sword, the size of the Eiffel Tower, and shouted, "He, the Almighty, reveals deep and hidden things; He, the Almighty, knows what lies in darkness, and light dwells with Him!" The host of angels praised the Lord in unison.

Ariel looked to the sword. She could see that it had been sharpened by the Word of God, an ever-moving sheen gleaming over it. The lightning grew fiercer and for once Ariel could see the legions of demons opposing them. Countless heads in the darkness with laser red eyes staring across the sky of turmoil at them, at her.

The enemy had their own form of chariots that looked like modern tanks with cannons pointed directly at them. Behind the tanks were lines of demons with helmets and armor that shone only when the lightning flashed its light across the city. It was terrifying to Ariel. She could see they carried swords like hers only dark and tarnished from wear. She could also see they carried weapons she did not recognize, large and frightening. Her eyes were drawn to a great figure much like the archangel, Michael. It commanded attention with its decorative armor and large demon bodyguards. She knew it had to be Baal, the ancient Fallen that demanded to be called a god and to be worshiped like the Most High.

Many humans have died for Baal over the centuries. Countless souls just handed over to him for the sake of his title. Women tossed their babies as sacrifices. Men raped women as offerings. Priests tossed their wealth to him with no return. He was a monster now. His foretold beauty had long since died. His sin was like a disease leaving him with a withered rotting appearance. As ugly as his heart had turned him, he desired more, his greed a never-ending hunger. Ariel was glad it was not Satan! She did not think she could stand in the presence of *his* evil!

The weather turned frighteningly fierce causing weather sirens to sound throughout the city. With a clash of thunder and a network of lightning, Ariel nearly lost her legs when she saw the most gigantic angel she had ever seen in her existence. He was large enough to put one foot on one side of Wichita and another foot on the other side. With hands on his hips, the flash of light revealed him blowing the wind that roared through the ranks of the evil army. The next flash showed him clapping his hands and the thunder echoed through their hearts. It was a massive show of the Father's greatness!

In all this, the Demonics did not back down nor did they show fear. In fact, Baal raised his enormous sword and shouted his rebellion over the thunder. The Demonics shouted in response and Ariel felt like the sky moved. She could see evil had power and she knew that Satan wanted to be like the Father. It was known that even the Archangel respected Satan's power. Although the Fallen were still gifted as the Father created them, sin was warping the strength and potency of those gifts. The more twisted their hearts became, the more chaos their gifts brought. Ariel might be young and inexperienced, but even the smallest of angels knew that truth.

Suddenly, the wind died, the lightning ceased, and the thunder became quiet. The sky still did not show its stars, but the giant angel was gone. The Demonics considered this a success, though they did nothing to cause it. With both Michael and Baal holding their swords high, Ariel expected the battle charge to be signaled at any moment. The anticipation grew in her body and her senses were heightened as she watched for that gleaming sword to fall. All eyes were fixated on their leaders.

Ariel noticed the sword's shine diminish. The moving gleam ran down the blade and did not return. Slowly, Michael lowered his hand, keeping the sword straight up. Baal laughed thunderously and his army joined in. Michael looked up and the hosts did the same. A loud voice broke through Heaven, "Be still and know that I am God."

The Demonics quieted as an immense hand descended.

Ariel fell to her knees, cowering behind an angel as she trembled watching the gargantuan hand, glowing from glory, lowered over them all. The army angel she was holding onto knelt, too. She pulled her eyes from the hand and saw all the hosts going to their knees, including Michael, who was then lowering himself even farther.

She wondered how the army of Baal was responding and saw they, too, were compelled to bow. Baal tried to keep his sword high, but as the great hand turned palm down, he was forced to lower it. The feeling of wonderment filled the air and Ariel wanted to stay forever in the moment. It was the presence of the Father!

Baal's eyes grew hot and red. They began to be like a laser, a red beam scoping over the scene as he looked around him. With strength Ariel had never seen in the presence of God, he stood and raised his sword in defiance! With a roaring shout, he struck his sword down and the evil ranks of his army jumped with a start. Her ears were filled with the roar of the army as it rushed forward and fired their mighty weapons upon the still kneeling hosts.

Swiftly the hand of God swept over the darkened part of the sky and like fireworks the Demonic army popped, exploded, and burst as they disintegrated leaving a great cloud of red dust to hover and fade away. Ariel could only think of the verse from Exodus 14:14, "The LORD will fight for you; you need only to be still." When the Father pulled His hand back to Heaven, there was no battle to fight. He had given them victory without the fall of one of their blades, for Michael still held his sword, gleaming again, upright.

After sharing all this, I have to say that I was not your typical closet victim. I did share my situation with my chiropractor, my abuser's mother, the pastor, as well as the police. Seemingly, no one was concerned. I could spend a lot of time with statistics, but the main point would be to share that you probably know someone "secretly" being abused right now. We have laws to protect, but they cannot work without taking some involvement, even anonymously. Taking even a small step towards change helps not just the victim, but the abuser and future victims. Unbeknown to me, my sister and mother were working with professionals to find a way to help me. Thank you for caring! Their church provided professional counseling for me and acceptance. Thank you for loving me!

Signs of Abuse

Does someone you know:
- Insult you, call you derogatory names or belittle you?
- Turn minor incidents into major arguments?
- Have sudden outbursts of anger or rage?
- Prevent you from going where you want, when you want?
- Prevent you from working, attending school or seeing family or friends?
- Destroy your personal property?
- Humiliate you?
- Use intimidation or manipulation to control you or your children?
- Threaten to hurt you, your children, friends, or family members?
- Expect you to have sex on demand or force you to engage in sexual acts that you don't want to do?
- Control all the finances, force you to account for what you spend, or take your money?

If you answered yes to any of these questions you *may* be a victim of domestic violence.

Remember.
You are not alone.
You are not to blame.
You can get help.

IvaChoice.net

"How great Thou art, my awesome God! You are my all. You alone know me. I Praise You always and in all I do. You are unlike anything or anyone. Who can compare to You and Your goodness? I am ever in awe of You. You have cared for my girls and me. You have watched over us. You have protected us and have had mercy on us. How grateful I am! Thank You, my Lord! Thank You, my Savior! Thank You, my God!"

Chapter Thirteen

Healing Begins

She woke up with a jolt, feeling as if she overslept. In fact, she had forgotten to turn on her alarm and was dangerously close to getting to work late. Knowing that she could be put on the layoff list for being tardy, she did not even look into the mirror before bolting out the door, stumbling over some trash on the floor, wearing the same clothes from the day before. On her way, she called the house from her cell phone while checking her appearance in the rear view mirror.

After three calls and her heart racing from worry, a sleepy Brailey answered the phone. She apologized for not getting there sooner, explaining that she woke up trapped between her bed and the wall and had quite a time getting out. Julia knew the scene, for she had seen Brailey do that over the years. Brailey assured her mother that she was going to wake her sister so they could make it to school on time. She also said she would call if they had any trouble and they went over the "Bo-Bo" protocol.

Julia parked in the first space available and dashed into the building, clocking in exactly on time. Carlita grinned already in full swing with her work, but looking rather tired for just starting out her day. Julia dropped her purse under the worktable and set to taping. Carlita tapped on the table and turned to pull the squeegee. With a quizzical look, she read the piece of tape with writing on it: "In God, whose word I praise, in God I trust; I will not be afraid. What can mortal man do to me? Psalm 56:4". Julia pondered on the verse as she worked.

Then Carlita turned again and said, "This is you, last night." She looked at her with droopy eyes and then scooped up more parts to be painted and went back to tipping.

Julia's mind went to the events of last night. How could Carlita have known what had happened? Maybe Kealin spoke to her already or Gwin. Oh, she forgot Neesha's hat! She felt conflicted about returning it in light of last night. Was he really a bad man? Was she just paranoid from all the hype? Carlita tapped her shoulder interrupting her thoughts and pointed to the paint thinner. "Need more," was all she said and went back to her work. Grabbing the container, Julia headed for the supply area, which would take her past final assembly. Looking around she found that both Kealin and his pal, who worked in the woodshop, were not present. As she filled her container, she prayed for them, for her family's safety, and thanked God for Carlita's insight. Clearly, the Holy Spirit had made Carlita privy to her need for safety last night.

On her return, she passed by Gwin, who spoke quietly. "Did you catch the news this morning?" Then she backed into the paint booth and set to work again. Julia's curiosity kept her thoughts busy for the morning. She couldn't wait to get the scoop and it was killing her to wait.

During break, she spoke with Carlita about the verse, who asked if she had ever been to a *Vagilia*. Julia shook her head and Carlita explained it was when her whole church, young and old, stayed up all night in prayer, a vigil. They sacrifice sleep for the sake of the prayers they wished to bring to the Lord.

"Last night, we do this and I pray for *you*," she shared. "God tell me *you* are this verse. No man can hurt you for you trust God. *He* protect you." She pointed her finger to Julia's chest. "He protect *you*." She said it again.

Julia smiled and nodded her understanding. Tears filled her eyes and warmth washed over her heart in realization that God not only protected her last night but had someone who really cared for her praying over her. "Can I come to one of your prayer meetings sometime?" She wanted to witness a *Vagilia*.

"Is all in Spanish," she shrugged.

"Is prayer in a language He cannot understand?" Julia grinned.

"True. You come. I help you know what to pray and we all pray together." She laughed. "I hold you to come now. I invite. You come, okay?"

Julia agreed. Their break was over and she knew she would have to wait to discover the news Gwin hinted at. They sang and worked together while learning little phrases in Spanish and then in English, laughing at their attempts. Although Carlita invited her to have lunch together, Julia set her mind to looking up the news for the day on a nearby computer. She typed in the local news station website she used to manage and read the top headline: Wichita Police Make Record Cocaine Bust. She read that local DEA and federal law enforcement announced this morning that they made the biggest drug bust in city history with the help of local police. Scrolling down she read that a number of men were arrested and more arrests were expected in the next few days.

She felt a tap on her back and she spun around to see Gwin. "Not bad for a newbie," her raspy voice cackled a laugh. "My hubby got a raise."

"Kealin?" she asked.

"Ain't in that story, but he got busted. Hubby says he's cooperating so he don't have to serve too much time, that's how it goes." She walked away towards the snack room, change jingling in her hand. "Guess he ain't gonna be worrying about layoffs no more." Julia could hear her laughing even after turning the corner.

She continued to read the rest of the article. It said that through DEA and FBI surveillance, they were able to follow a trail of drug deals across the state. There was no mention of the Eastborough chief of police or her contribution and she was glad. She just wanted to get back on her feet and find some sense of normalcy.

She started to call her sister, but an incoming call interrupted. She answered without fear that it would be some debt collector or Jacob ready to yell at her. The man on the other end was the kind pastor from Viola wanting to see if this weekend would be available for laying a countertop for her. Other than her clean up at a construction site, the calendar was empty for that day and her heart was filled with gratitude. Then she dialed her twin and told her all that had happened. Jan asked if she and mom could bring lunch for everyone on Saturday and they agreed on sandwiches. Healing was beginning.

Singing praises through the rest of her work day seemed to rejuvenate her soul and filled her to the brim with joy. She was having a good day! With a sigh, she tried to remember the last time she had such a day. There were no fears nagging at the back of her neck or worries occupying her mind. She was completely present with her Lord, earning a pay check, and working with a friend. She smiled. She had a Christian friend.

It was Friday and Julia was looking forward to a restful evening with her girls. A movie night was long over due. She calculated how much money she had and decided they could splurge for beef and cheese chip dip. Tomorrow she would get up early and get to the construction site to start her third job, the extra cash a blessing. In the afternoon, the church group planned to start work on the house, another blessing from above. It was going to be a glorious weekend!

"Just call me Mr. Business," the man slapped Jacob on the back as they entered the airport rolling their scuba bags behind them accompanied by some of Jacob's dive students.

Jacob laughed while nodding to a policeman, "*Hola*, Carlos. How's Narco?" he knew not to touch the drug sniffing dog beside him.

"*Bien*, Jacob," Carlos answered and waved him and his group on.

A few of the men with Jacob shook their heads and laughed again. Jacob had made many friends this trip. That was clear to Chayyliel. He nudged Camael and pointed to the man called Mr. Business. "Here it goes. It's kinda nice not having to fight demons and getting to see the show."

They watched as the wealthy man took a cell phone call off to the side of his group, four monster demons hanging around him. It lasted only a moment and when he returned, he asked Jacob to watch his bags as he went to the bathroom. Jacob made some lewd joke Mastema had whispered into his ear and the man left them shaking his head from the jeers. The demon of hostility snickered at his easy influence on Jacob. Clinging to his back with only one hand, he continued to whisper crude comments entertaining while offending the group. He felt at ease with this assignment since the beginning. Although infuriated with the angel that withered his other hand during battle, he remained amused with the conflict he caused. Over time, the small dive group made their way to the counter. One of the men from the group, with three large demons, decided to check on what was taking Mr. Business so long. Jacob made another raunchy joke and the rest of the group snickered.

By the time he stood at the check-in desk, Jacob was looking concerned for the two missing men. He asked about Dora who usually manned the desk, but the new woman would not share that information. He finally explained that he was missing two men from his group that needed to check in as well. She tilted her glasses and looked over the top at him.

Chayyliel nudged Camael again. "Isn't she good, Boss?" he bragged. "You would never know she was our little ol' Sophia, would you?"

Camael shushed him, "Common, this is the best part."

One of the dive students behind Jacob looked to the desk attendant and held up a badge pointing at the dive instructor. The undercover cop had a tough, stout guardian who was twice his size. His wings rose with every breath as the great angel flexed his back muscles. Standing with a wide stance and arms folded, he was the perfect body guard for the cop. His bald head and furrowed brow completed the intimidating demeanor. Even Chayyliel was impressed. He clearly had been an army angel prior to this assignment. He gave a slight acknowledging nod to Chayyliel as Sophia raised her eyebrows and calmly wiggled her finger for Jacob to lean in close. Mastema pulled on Jacob as he realized things were changing but was not as persuasive with only one good hand. The demon became more frantic as the policeman with the dog walked toward them and tugged harder to alert his pawn. But Jacob obeyed the woman and grinned as he leaned forward.

She spoke softly, "Mr. Anderson, *por favor*, go with Carlos. He will help you with your *amigos*, friends, *si*?" she leaned back and called for the next person in line.

Carlos directed him away from the line and asked, "Jacob, you're missing some of your students?" He escorted him to a side door with his dog right beside him.

"Oh, they aren't students, just along for the dive," Jacob was feeling uneasy as Mastema repeatedly whipped him to run. Jacob came to a stop and looked back at his group. "I've got it under control." Jacob flashed a smile and patted Carlos on the back.

"We will find them. No problem. Come," Carlos motioned for him to follow.

"What's this about?" Jacob didn't budge.

"This is about your *amigos*," he smiled and Narco walked through the door. "You see? Narco no afraid." Carlos laughed.

Jacob held the door. "Hey, Carlos, they went to the restroom. I'll go and check there, okay? No need for camera hunts or whatever." He let go of the door and thanked him as he started for the restrooms, Mastema now on his back jumping up and down to get him moving faster like a jockey on a slow horse.

"Jacob, no make this hard, eh?" Carlos put his hand on his gun holster. "You come with me and things will go lots smoother."

Jacob's eyes went wide with realization. Suddenly he took off running, the demon wildly whipping and screaming.

"Common," Chayyliel pushed off from their vantage point to follow the chase.

Camael pushed off too, winking at Sophia. They flew through the airport, which was suddenly sparse of Demonics. Jacob was quick for a stocky man, running the length of the long hall, other police joining in on the chase. Jacob searched franticly for an exit as he sprinted around travelers. Up ahead, he could see the red lit sign but before he could reach it a dog came barging out the door leaping for an attack. Jacob went down wailing. Narco bit down hard and shook his arm causing it to bleed.

The undercover cop came running with gun in hand to make the arrest. He was fit and able to read Jacob his rights while Carlos called Narco to his side. Jacob swore and the cop shook his head stating that wasn't very Christian of him. Mastema had made his escape by jumping from traveler to traveler. Hidden in the empty vessels, the angels had to search by looking each human in the eye. The great body guard stood by watching carefully when suddenly he marched up to an old feeble woman sitting in the waiting area and reached in. His massive hands gripped Mastema by the neck and yanked him out. But Mastema, desperate to survive, clung to the woman's chest screaming causing the woman to cough uncontrollably. Chayyliel and Camael came to the great angel's side with swords up but stopped short when Mastema threatened the human's life. Seeing her face turning blue from continuous coughing, the people nearby came to her aid and yelled for someone to call 911. The bald angel furrowed his brows, tilted his head and drew his sword. Camael quickly informed the great angel, "I know this demon. He has the power to take a life. You must let go." Without hesitation, the angel cut both arms off of the demon releasing the woman to gasp for air. He then expertly swirled the sword over the stunned demon and vanquished Mastema before he could get away.

"Now that was awesome!" Chayyliel whooped and slapped the comrade on the back. The stoic angel grinned for only a moment and then gave a nod before following his Sealed. "An angel of few words," Chayyliel nodded back. "I like that." Camael laughed as they watched the paramedics come to check on the recovering old lady now laying on the floor with several travelers tending to her.

A group of cops now had Jacob cuffed and were escorting him to a side door away from the view of travelers. But Jacob wasn't going down that easily. He struggled against their hold on him jerking, kicking, and swearing.

"I'm an American! I want my lawyer! I didn't do anything wrong. You're going to pay for treating me this way!" Jacob threatened. "Look at what your @$#? dog did!" he showed his bloody arm. "Oh, I'm gonna sue! I want my phone. I have witnesses to this abuse!" He broke free and ran toward the travelers watching. "You see how they are treating me, don't you?" Carlos held Narco back as the undercover cop caught up with Jacob. Just before he could grab the bloody arm, the enraged prisoner fell face forward. The cop's guardian had nonchalantly shoved Jacob as he passed by. Chayyliel chuckled. He really liked this army angel. It took several policemen to get the writhing prisoner up, who was now bleeding from his nose and forehead. Chayyliel caught the fleeting grin on the otherwise stoic angel.

Carlos shook his head. "It is very bad to threaten police, Jacob." Before the door shut, Camael and Chayyliel witnessed Carlos punching the prisoner in the stomach.

"What a show! Now aren't you glad I brought you along?" Chayyliel put up his fist.

Camael eyed the fist and then formed one and bumped his knuckles, "Yes, Chayyliel, I have to say it satisfied me to know that he cannot hurt Julia anymore."

Sophia landed by them and bumped Chayyliel's fist, too. Camael gave her a look and she smiled. "It is good to keep up with the times. Bumping knuckles is cool and it will help you to relate to your Sealed better." She winked. "And since you are a strategist, you will like to hear how this all came about." She waved her hand to the airport. "The undercover police officer in the group over there took scuba classes from Jacob last summer. It seems he pulled Julia over for overdue tags not too long ago."

"I remember now," Camael's mind clicked in. "I tried to reason with his guardian but he was firm, allowing him to do his job. In the end, he was merciful. Praise the Lord."

"Well, when he saw that she was hurt, had an amazing history of insurance, remained truthful, and shared about the success of the scuba business in spite of a separation, he became suspicious. His guardian, Vizek, wouldn't let him dismiss it, being a discerner. He reminded his Sealed how his mother would cover for his father's abuse. The clues were obvious to the cop not only from his training but from his childhood of domestic violence. He wanted to help her, but she had not made a report. So he prayed for her and asked God to show him how he could help her. When his brother talked about the investigation his DEA unit was involved in, he urged him to look into the scuba business as a possible cover for drug smuggling.

Jacob's credit report came back as recovering, but his wife's credit was horrible. Upon a closer look, everything she owed had to do with dive trips and scuba gear. He knew from his trip to Table Rock that she did not even dive and had witnessed Jacob's controlling behavior towards her, as well as his hot temper. His training said to follow the money, but there was no trail to follow when it came to Jacob or the shop, which was certainly fishy. When he discovered that Jacob was going on dive trips to Puerto Rico in spite of the shop's closing, his guardian led him to the passenger lists which led him right to Mr. Business. So, he contacted Jacob and went undercover."

"Wow, now that's investigating!" Chayyliel laughed. "I had no idea! The whole time I was hanging with his dive students, his guardian didn't say a word!"

He looked to Camael, who was still taking in the information and pulling it together. "What of Mr. Business and his partner?"

"Well, Mr. Business and all his partners are about to meet with *Mr.* Vizek very shortly." Sophia grinned and added, "Jacob will give them all up. He is a selfish man. After all, he owed everyone, including the IRS, and yet threw around money like he grew it on trees." She shook her head as her smile faded. "Poor Julia and those children . . ."

Now Camael perked. "Not poor." He had a twinkle in his eye.

When she got home, Shannon and Brailey stood in the kitchen side by side with big smiles across their faces. Julia did not expect to see them for another hour, so something was amiss.

"Mom," Shannon began as Brailey twisted back and forth with giddiness. "Today was an in-service day for the teachers." Julia raised a brow now very concerned as to what the girls had been up to for the whole day. "So, we cleaned the house and made you supper." They parted and held out their arms in display.

They expressed delight as she looked over the wonderful meal of rice and meat with corn. Then she let them lead her around the house to share what they had accomplished. She complimented them on each thing and enjoyed her homecoming very much. It was a precious gift for a single mother.

After they ate an early supper, she proposed they go for a bike ride, since it had been a while and the weather was becoming cooler. But the girls had something different in mind. They changed their clothes and pulled on work gloves.

"We are going to help earn money for our family. Let's go get that construction site all spick and span." Brailey pushed her sleeves up as she announced their decision.

Shannon beamed as she added, "It's not all up to you, mom. We can help if you let us and we are very good at cleaning." She gave her mom a hug. Julia's cup was overflowing with pride. Her children surprised her in more ways than even they were aware of.

Julia was not going to stand in their way. She was going to encourage this as long as it would last. Once they arrived at the site, they worked together on the outside and then moved to the interior. They visited about all the things going on at school and sports. They sang praise songs and popular Christian songs from the radio. When it was too dark to see, Julia had to put a stop to their determination so they could get to bed on time. They would need to be ready in the morning, since pastor Heart's church was coming to work on their house in the afternoon.

The girls smiled and pulled off their gloves to look over the work they had accomplished. Julia had to admit, it was a rewarding job. Work well done tickles the heart with pride and a sense of accomplishment. It just feels good. They praised each other over the different tasks they completed. Feeling successful, they headed home. After tucking in her exhausted girls and thanking them for their help, she took a long hot shower and spent time in prayer. The house glowed in the night from the glory of God and the angels brightened with strength because the prayer of the righteous is powerful and effective. As she finished her devotional in First John, she slipped down in her bed and made a mental plan to wake up early to finish the cleaning job at the site.

"I have one last thing to do," Sophia touched Camael's shoulder and leisurely flapped her wings to do an errand she would greatly enjoy.

Not too far from where Julia lived was a small farmhouse in the country near Conway Springs. It was dilapidated and no longer a working farm, but it suited the owner just fine. She took her time getting there, enjoying the landscape and the openness Kansas offered now clear of the Demonics. The sunsets were beautiful, for the sky was a clear canvas, no hills or mountains to obstruct the view.

Julia's life was like that right now. The chaos of sin was no longer obstructing her future.

Dipping down, Sophia lightly let her toes touch the ground. It was a pleasing place. She could feel the memories of good times resting over it. As she entered the house, passing through the living room window box, she spied the one she had come to visit. He was doing what many do when finishing a long hard day's work.

Greeting his guardian with a smile, she came before him and looked him in the eye. Yes, he was ready. It was time. She softly bowed her head and offered a prayer on his behalf to the Lord. His guardian joined her, taking her hand. When she finished, she patted the hand and her eyes conveyed her love for this home, this man, and the angel watching over him.

"I am glad you have come, Sophia. I have missed you," the guardian smiled.

"It has been a while," she looked at the man. "He is lonely." She saw into his heart as he stared at the television set soaking in the empty entertainment, passing the time before bed. She leaned in and touched his heart. "It is time," she whispered to him. "Do you hear me?" she pushed and his eyes welled up with tears. "You have mourned long enough." She continued. "The Lord has brought someone to fill the void. She is not perfect and you will both need time. Become her friend, Dan. You and Julia can heal together. Remember Romans 8:28, 'We know that all things work together for good for those who love God, who are called according to His purpose.'" She paused and then pulled away.

It felt good to come back. She had enjoyed her time as a guardian to his beloved. But, like all things, time had moved on and she had many other wonderful experiences. It was the Father's gift to give her a chance to see Dan again, his gracious and ever supporting guardian, and to know the one that would fill his heart again. She smiled as she lifted her feet from the ground and praised the kindness of the Father.

※

It was a beautiful morning, the birds were singing and the sun was shining brightly. She had learned to get up at five in the morning for her new position at work, so getting up at six felt like sleeping in. Grabbing a couple of crackers to hold her over, she left the girls a note and headed out. She cleaned cheerfully in the solitude until some men came to finish painting. The burly man who hired her motioned her to join him in the front doorway.

He uncrossed his arms and stepped to the porch. "Seems someone was here working yesterday evening," he chuckled.

"Yes, sir," she felt she needed to explain. "I decided to get a good start yesterday . . ."

He held up his hand and pulled out a paper from his clipboard. "The boss and I came by last night."

Bewildered, she asked, "You're not the boss?"

"Naw, I work for the Hearts." He pointed to the logo on his truck. "Heart Construction."

"Heart Construction?" she wondered if the pastor was related to the owner. "Should I speak with the owner?"

"He's working at a different place today. What I was gonna say is that he was very impressed with your quality of work and wants to offer you our other sites, if you want them." He held out a paper with five other addresses.

Surprised, Julia took the paper and looked at each address. "Yes. Of course! Thank you. Um . . . when I finish up here and . . ."

He took off his hat. "You ain't finished?" He handed her a check.

Taking the check, she smiled, picked up her bucket of cleaning supplies, and stepped back with a wave. "See you at the other sites." Then she ran home with jittery flutters of excitement throughout her body. When she arrived at her house, she found a line of trucks down her street and people moving about her home with purpose. The girls exclaimed she was not to be back yet, but it was too late. The surprise was spoiled in their eyes, but just as effective in hers. Dan came from the garage and pulled off one work glove to shake her hand.

"Ms. Anderson," he smiled sheepishly, "seems we couldn't pull this off." He chuckled as his father came up behind him. "We got a hold of your daughters and they thought you would be gone all morning. They wanted to surprise you when you came back in the afternoon."

"Well, I'm sorry I spoiled your surprise." She smiled and shook her head. "It is still a wonderful surprise and I'm very happy, thankful." She nodded. "What can I do?"

Dan grabbed her hand and towed her to the kitchen. "We're going to need some decisions made. These ladies from the church can't decide on anything." He let go of her hand and kissed his mother's cheek. "Have at it ladies, we're ready to get some countertops in." He marched to the garage and ordered the other men to stack the materials so he could see what was available. She could see he was a man who got things done so she was confident that her house was in good hands. The women enveloped her and her daughters for the next two hours as they picked out Formica countertops, factory finished hardwood floors from a liquidation warehouse—which turned out cheaper than laminate—and tiles. She enjoyed watching the girls be a part of the new dream for their house. She enjoyed the feeling of friendship and belonging. It felt humbling and yet comforting to have others taking care of her, asking about her, and loving her. In a sense, she felt more at home than she had in years.

By lunch, her mother and sister showed up excited by the number of workers finishing drywall, doing electrical, and preparing for flooring and tiles. Her dad came walking through the door carrying a tool belt and gave her a light hug. "Do you think you could use another hand?" He smiled as Julia nodded and introduced him to the pastor. She showed off the new countertops and the cousins did their own walk-through tour. Or rather run through. Jan winked, pointed to heaven, and then announced they had set up a picnic at the park for all.

Everyone left the house for the city park, only blocks away. Julia took a moment to look over the work that had started and ran her fingers over the new countertop. It was smooth and perfect, adding a sense of luxury in the midst of chaos. Her lips flicked a grin. Perhaps God sees her like this. Among all the chaos in her life, He sees one of His own, a jewel, she and her girls. She went to the door and looked one last time before pulling it shut; her heart full of thankfulness.

Camael knew Julia was now on a good path. She is, and always has been, in His hands!

Ruffling his feathers, he called his team together by the front door. Looking them over, he nodded praise to each one. In turn, they all pointed to Heaven and then to their heart. He was thankful for their sacrifices and the giving of their gifts. "I believe we shall now return to some normalcy," he winked and they all laughed. Was there ever normalcy for a family bent on ministry?

"This is where I leave you, Boss," Chayyliel stood straight in honor of Camael's leadership. "Ever need an army angel, I'm your guy."

Camael chuckled heartily. "Come by and see how we are doing sometime. I'm going to pray we will not need an army again." Chayyliel said his goodbye to the other teammates and in one pull of his large wings, he rocketed away.

Suriel offered a soft hug to each one and as a last gift she touched their heart filling them with a precious piece of God's strength. She was a sweet thin angel with some mighty gifts. Ever smiling and positive, she said little and yet managed to say so much. With a slight grin, she pointed to Heaven and then as she pointed to her heart she faded away, no longer visible to them.

Camael turned to Sophia and wished she could stay. There was so much for Julia to heal from yet. She seemed to understand his thoughts, for she looked to Heaven and asked to stay a little while longer. She smiled at the answer, her eyes showing joy for the extended visit.

"I shall see you at the picnic." She chuckled and took Sablo on one arm and Zazriel on the other. "You two need much instruction if you are going to get your young girls to mind you as they grow up." Zazriel looked a little worried and then splashed a big smile. He scooped Sophia up into his arms and took off for the sky singing "When we all get to Heaven". Sablo was already laughing with golden curls bouncing as he followed. Those two were like the children they cared for. Camael shook his head.

"And now you, Ariel," he placed a hand on her shoulder. "Where are you to go?"

"I am to train with Ansiel, so I shall be seeing you from time to time," she laughed. "You cannot be rid of us all."

Camael gave her a nod. "Well, shall we go to a picnic?" He passed through the door just as the phone rang.

Poking his head back into the house, he saw Ariel watching the phone. It rang again. He shook his head at her. Ariel looked at Camael and then back at the phone again. Curiosity was getting the better of her once again. She just had to know. By the third ring, the old answering machine kicked in.

"You have reached Julia, Shannon, and Brailey. We are unable to come to the phone right now so leave us a message and we'll get back to you." There was some giggling in the background and the message ended for the caller to record their message.

"Jules," it was Jacob's voice. "Jules, if you are there pick up the phone. Please?" Ariel tilted her head as she listened in. Now Camael passed back through the door with interest. "Look, Jules, I don't have my lawyer's number memorized and I only get one call so this is important. I am in a prison in Puerto Rico. I need you to call Dave and have him get me out. Tell him I can pay whatever it costs. I didn't do what they said I've done. It is a total set up deal down here . . . yeah, I'm almost done, @$#? idiot . . . Look, Jules, if you ever loved me at all, call Dave." He sighed. "I know you're a forgiving person, a true Christian woman. I need your help . . . look, I'm using the phone right now. You said I had five minutes so get off my . . ." the connection was cut.

The machine went quiet leaving a blinking light to indicate an unheard message. Ariel looked to Camael. Then she looked to the blinking light. She looked at Camael again. Camael raised a brow. Ariel smirked and as quick as a flash she pushed the delete button.

"Oops," Ariel snickered.

Iva Choice

About the Author

"In His Hands" is a work of fiction based on the author's true life experience. As a graduate of Wichita State University with over a decade of experience in news graphics and production, Iva Choice has become a passionate advocate for victims of abuse. In sharing this story, she hopes not only to empower readers and show God's loving interest in the details of our lives, but through the sales of this book financially support safe houses throughout the nation. Iva Choice resides in a small Kansas town surrounded by her family.